Color of Law

Color of Law

a novel by David Milofsky

For Lyn, with best wishes

David Milofsky.

⬤ university press of colorado

Copyright © 2000 by the University Press of Colorado
International Standard Book Number 0-87081-581-4

Published by the University Press of Colorado
5589 Arapahoe Avenue, Suite 206C
Boulder, Colorado 80303

The University Press of Colorado is a cooperative publishing enterprise supported, in part, by Adams State College, Colorado State University, Fort Lewis College, Mesa State College, Metropolitan State College of Denver, University of Colorado, University of Northern Colorado, University of Southern Colorado, and Western State College of Colorado.

The paper used in this publication meets the minimum requirements of the American National Standard for Information Sciences—Permanence of Paper for Printed Library Materials. ANSI Z39.48-1984

Library of Congress Cataloging-in-Publication Data

Milofsky, David.
    Color of law: a novel / by David Milofsky
       p. cm.
ISBN 0-87081-581-4 (alk. paper)
       1. Mayors—Election—Fiction. 2. Milwaukee (Wis.)—Fiction. 3. Police corruption—Fiction. 4. Race relations—Fiction. 5. Civil rights—Fiction. 6. Journalists—Fiction. I. Title.

PS3563.I444 C65 2000
813'.54—dc21
                                                            00-044723

Design by Laura Furney

09 08 07 06 05 04 03 02 01 00   10 9 8 7 6 5 4 3 2 1

To Jean and Jennie, and also to Elizabeth and George

Acknowledgments

Color of Law is a work of the imagination, and while it does draw on real places, any resemblance between characters in the novel and people, either alive or dead, is purely coincidental. Nevertheless, a book this long and complex does not come out of a vacuum. Over the years I was working on this novel, many friends and colleagues gave generously of their time and knowledge, and I wish to acknowledge them here. David C. Rice, of the Attorney General's office of the State of Wisconsin, Woody Garnsey, and Rebecca Givins have all shared shared with me their extensive knowledge of trial law and procedures. Mr. Garnsey also allowed me free use of his firm's law library, something that was immensely useful in researching cases relevant to my novel. *Color of Law* would not have been written, however, were it not for the contribution of my friend Curry First, who read several versions of the novel and whose patient explanations of civil rights law stretched long into several nights and weekends. His commitment to human freedom has been an ongoing inspiration to me. I am also grateful to Judge Henry Reynolds for allowing me to observe cases in his courtroom for several weeks in 1990. Timothy Hoelter, Vice-President for International Trade and Regulatory Affairs at the Harley Davidson Motor Company graciously provided details regarding the unusual history of police motorcycle patrols in Milwaukee and put me in touch with the police liaison unit that his company maintains with the Milwaukee Police Department. Lois Blinkhorn, formerly managing editor of the *Milwaukee Journal,* provided many useful services and introduced me to Dick Leonard, formerly the editor of that excellent newspaper. Mr. Leonard patiently explained newsgathering methods in practice at the *Journal* during his tenure and took an interest in the project that it may not have merited at that time. Jo Reitman, librarian of the *Journal,* once again generously provided both clippings and microfiche records of civil rights activities in Wisconsin and was unfailingly helpful during my research.

I would know nothing about the civil rights movement in Wisconsin or anywhere else had it not been for the inspiring example set by my late mother, Ruth Dorsey Milofsky, whose Paint Box Art Center was among the first Title One projects funded in Wisconsin. Similarly, the Reverend Lucious Walker, formerly executive director of Northcott Neighborhood House, was both my friend and a shining example of courage and principle in defense of civil liberties. Lewis T. Mittness, Harout Sanasarian, Dennis Conta, Harold Ickes, Jr., Joseph Czerwinski, and Mary Louise Munts, provided grass-roots political experiences that enabled me to imagine the political sections of this book. I am grateful to all of them.

During the writing of this novel, I received support from the National Endowment for the Arts in the form of a creative writing fellowship, from the graduate school of Colorado State University, and twice, at crucial times, from the MacDowell Colony, the best place in the world for a writer to work.

I am grateful to the reference librarians of the Milwaukee Public Library for guiding me through the library's extensive local history collection and to my friends and colleagues, Clint McCown, Bruce Ronda, Rosemary Whitaker, Leslee Becker, and Pattie Cowell for their friendship and support. Loren Crabtree, Provost of Colorado State University, and Robert Hoffert, Dean of the College of Liberal Arts, have been unfailingly supportive in providing me with travel grants necessary to the research and writing of this book. The faith shown in me by my publisher, Luther Wilson, has given new life to my work. I appreciate the help given me by him and his capable staff, especially Laura Furney and Darrin Pratt. Teresa Harbaugh and Stephanie G'Schwind have both provided crucial support and the kind of cheerful encouragement that makes hard things seem possible. Joyce Meskis, of the Tattered Cover Book Store, and Patti Thorn, Books Editor of *the Denver Rocky Mountain News,* have both encouraged me professionally and given me their friendship. Finally, my family has both tolerated my mental and physical absences and been the most profound center of support for this and all my other creative activities. I am grateful.

These rules shall be construed to secure fairness in administration, elimination of unjustifiable expense and delay, and promotion of growth and development of the law of evidence to the end that the truth may be ascertained and proceedings justly determined.

—*Federal Rules of Evidence for U.S. Courts and Magistrates*

1959

One

Tommy Paley was driving west on Wright Street, trying to stay warm, when Rogan waved him over. It was so dark that Tommy didn't like to get off his motorcycle unless there was a damned good reason, especially in the Core. Milwaukee had changed since Tommy was a kid, but it was still more a collection of small towns than a real city. The Third Ward belonged to the wops, and the Germans lived in the big mansions on the lake. The Jews had filled the center until they started making money and moving to the West Side or maybe the northern suburbs. The South Side was for the Polacks, except for a handful of Yugoslavs, but to Tommy they were all the same, and as far as that went, they were all OK with him. He was Irish himself, but he never had problems with Polacks. They worked hard and kept their noses clean. If there were problems, they tended to take care of them without anyone else's help.

The north side was a different story. Before 1950, Milwaukee had been basically an all-white town. Then, all of a sudden, there were 100,000 niggers living in a few square miles of the inner city. Some people said they came for the welfare, but Tommy knew they did the work no one else wanted. The bus stops were crowded with nigger women in the morning going out to clean the big houses on the lake and every busboy in town had black skin. But change made everyone nervous, and it was up to the police to keep the ghetto quiet and contained. If things were going right you never saw a black face east of Holton or north of Capital Drive. And any nigger who went on the south side would be taking his life in his hands. Tommy wasn't sure he liked the arrangement, but no one was asking him. Those were the rules and generally they worked. Which brought him back to Rogan.

They had been together in the Academy, and Tommy remembered John before that, from high school, when they both played basketball in the city league. But Tommy had never liked Rogan, and the fact that he had no good reason didn't change anything. He thought he'd be getting away from the problem when he wrote applying for the cycle corps, but Rogan was waiting as soon as he got in, and Tommy started to feel like he was cursed with the sonofabitch for life. When John took him for a beer after work and tried to introduce him around, it only made things worse. Tommy felt bad resenting a fellow officer who was trying to be his friend, but he couldn't help it. There was just something about John Rogan that made him wary, the way he walked, hands cupped out to the side and his cocky habit of leaning back on his heels and looking at you out of the bottom of his eyes.

Rogan always needed to be different. Even in his dress. He wore the uniform because you had to, but here in the middle of winter when it was about a hundred below and all the other guys were wearing their Big Bennies and the gauntlet gloves that ran all the way up your arms and still you froze your ass, Rogan had on his light jacket and plain leather gloves. The guy was something, but if you saw a bikeman down you were supposed to go over and see what was going on. It was the code and Tommy was trying to be a team player. It was important to him. Besides, his ears were ringing from the bike's engine, so any excuse to get off was welcome.

Tommy parked and Rogan offered him a butt. "Take a load off your feet," he said.

Tommy looked around, but there was no place to sit. The street was empty of cars or pedestrians, which made sense to him. It was too goddamned cold to go for a walk, especially down here. There were few lights on in the dingy houses that lined the streets, and the overhead lamps cast a yellow glow in the mist. He shrugged and accepted a light. Rogan was a man of medium height, which meant he was short for a bikeman, most of whom were over six feet. You had to be at least 5'9" to get in and Rogan might have made it by an inch but no more. This was mildly surprising since Tommy remembered him playing bigger for Tech. John was a forward with arms on him and he wasn't afraid to mix it up down low with the big guys. Now he lounged against his Harley as if it was eighty degrees and they were over by the lake looking for women. Tommy wondered why Rogan had waved him over.

"You war-horsing?" the other man asked. "This ain't your regular beat."
Tommy shook his head. "Walker's on vacation, so I pulled his line. But
I haven't been on my beat for weeks." Strictly speaking, the bikemen didn't
have beats. They all patrolled the whole city, shaping up every morning for
whatever assignments the sergeant felt like giving them. It was what they all
liked about it, the independence, not being attached to a district. They tended
to be where there was the most action, if there was a big accident or some
crowd control problem, which kept things interesting. The chief took particular pride in the bikemen, considered them an elite group, which was why
they had the special uniforms and also why they were on the streets twelve
months a year, unlike any other police force Tommy had ever heard of. Still,
most of the guys had preferences, beats they'd rather ride, and if the old
man wasn't on you for something, he'd keep that in mind. If you were
lucky you could ride the same line for years, running from one end to the
other every eight-hour shift. At least you got to know the people and what
to look out for that way. But Tommy wasn't lucky. No one had ever accused him of that.

"Pissed the sarge off?" Rogan asked sympathetically.

Tommy nodded. "I was late for roll call because I was half in the bag
and the sonofabitch hasn't let me forget it." He shivered. Even in the big
leather coat, he was cold when the wind blew. But it was only two hours to
the end of his shift, and he was already thinking about what he was going to
drink on the way home. He was in no hurry to get back these days, and he
always made sure he had a good buzz on by the time he made it. Sometimes Lucy's light would still be on when he rolled in, and then he'd just sit
outside on the steps and smoke until he was sure she had gone to sleep. That
or he'd make sure he was so loaded he didn't care what she said.

Rogan threw his butt in the street and stretched. "Think I'll check these
houses and get some niggers," he said.

Tommy looked at the battered fronts. He thought he saw a dim glow
deep within the one on the corner, but he couldn't imagine going in there
looking for trouble. Rogan was just running his mouth, as usual. "You're on
your own there, Buddy," he said. But Rogan just smiled.

A car rolled past, going east. "Busted taillight," Rogan said. "Come on."

Tommy hadn't seen anything; it was just a passing car and he wasn't
paying attention. But Rogan was gone, and by the time Tommy got on his
bike and down the block, John had the guy spread-eagled on his fender.
Tommy got down and approached carefully, from behind, his right hand
on his gun. The street was still empty and snow blew around in the gutters.

It was cold as a sonofabitch, but when Tommy saw the driver was just a teenaged kid, he relaxed. As he approached, Tommy thought he noticed the kid looking at him, but Rogan snapped the boy's head back in a hurry. To Tommy's surprise, he was going through the whole drill, ordering the kid to put his right-hand palm up on his head, then the left, then frisking him up and down. Amazing. Rogan was getting ready to cuff this kid, maybe take him downtown and book him, all for a broken taillight. Tommy wondered what the desk sergeant would think of that.

The kid was wearing a light raincoat with a small gray hat pulled down over his eyes. He looked as if he was about to say something, but Tommy heard nothing. Then, just as Rogan was about to put the handcuffs on, the kid took off, running like a bat out of hell toward Sixth. "Shit," Rogan said and started after him.

Tommy didn't understand what was going on. Let the kid run; they had his car, his registration. Unless the car was stolen, which he had to admit was a strong possibility. But it still made no sense. Why were they running down this kid on a cold winter night for a traffic violation? But Rogan was already down the block and Tommy had no choice but to back him up.

By the time he made the corner, Tommy was puffing and the kid was pulling away. He stepped into the street and looked for a car. Then he heard a shot, though he couldn't say where it came from. A Chevy turned onto Wright and Tommy waved it down. "Police emergency," he told the driver. "I need your car." The guy looked tired, probably on his way home from work and he didn't need this. Tommy felt for him, but he couldn't run anymore. "Hit it," he said.

They caught up with Rogan in half a block and Tommy swung open the door. "Cocksucker can run," John said, out of breath. Tommy noticed his gun was out.

"What's going on?" the driver asked.

"Escaped burglar," Rogan said. Tommy looked at him. "Sure," John said. "It was on the bulletin, that grocery over on Brown."

Tommy remembered a holdup. The proprietor of the store had been shot. He hadn't gotten a good look at this kid, but he was doubtful. "I thought that guy was bigger. Didn't they say six feet, two hundred pounds?" But Rogan didn't respond.

They came abreast of the kid now. He was running easily, legs high, arms pumping, the tails of his coat spread out behind him on the wind like a sail. He looked so graceful that Tommy hated to interrupt. "Here we go," Rogan said and jumped out of the car, which was still moving.

"Get the sonofabitch," Tommy shouted, surprising himself with his vehemence. And he was out of the car with his gun pulled too.

The boy darted to his left when he saw them, like he was going to try to run behind a little white house that, like all the others on the street, was dark, though it was only eight-thirty. But thanks to the ride, Tommy and Rogan were fresh now and gaining.

Rogan ran up the snowbank, practically on top of the kid, who was heading down the service walk at the side of the house. If he jumped, Tommy figured he'd have him. Then he heard a shot, and even before he saw what had happened, he knew this one wasn't in the air.

Tommy slipped, trying to stop in the icy street, and by the time he righted himself and got up to the house, the kid was stretched out on the ground. It was very quiet now and smoke was everywhere. Rogan was putting his gun back, still panting from his run. "The fuck happened?" Tommy said. "Why'd you shoot him?"

Rogan didn't seem upset, just out of breath. "You saw it," he said finally. "I had no choice; he was coming at me." His voice was soft, matter-of-fact. But Tommy hadn't seen anything. One minute the kid was running, the next he was down. That was all he knew. But Rogan's manner unnerved him, made him doubt himself. If he had shot someone he'd be on the fucking roof, but John was calm, so maybe he was telling the truth. It beat the hell out of Tommy what was going on.

Meanwhile, the kid wasn't moving. Tommy bent down and put his hand on the boy's neck, searching for the jugular vein. He didn't really know what he was doing, didn't know first aid, but he figured he should do something. There was no pulse he could find, but it surprised him how warm the body was against his cold hands. The kid was burning up. "I think he's dead," he said.

This got Rogan's attention. He grabbed the kid's wrist roughly and held it for a moment. Then he shook his head as if he was finally beginning to understand. "Goddamn," he said. Because shooting someone was serious business, even for a hotshot like Rogan, and even if the person he killed was a nigger kid no one cared about. Every killing was investigated by the higher-ups, and the officer was suspended while the investigation was going on. Everyone knew that. Tommy had been on the force for five years and had never had his gun out of the holster until tonight, but he knew this was trouble, even if they decided Rogan had been right.

Now a man wearing an overcoat over his pajamas approached. A white man, which surprised Tommy. He didn't know there were any whites left in this neighborhood. "I live across the street," he said. "I heard a shot. What happened?" Tommy saw a teenaged boy standing behind his father at the curb. Great, he thought. Now we got the whole family out here. The man looked down at the dead boy on the sidewalk. The kid wasn't much older than his son. "Did he do something wrong, officer?"

Tommy started to answer, but then a terrible weariness came over him. The question was basic, but there was nothing to say, nothing he could say that would satisfy anyone. The man had a point. It seemed like you ought to do something wrong in order to get your ass killed, but all this kid had done was run away. He had been scared, that was about it. Mostly, however, Tommy was tired and overwhelmed by the situation. One minute he had been driving down the street worrying about nothing but staying warm and the next he was involved in a murder with witnesses. The white house and the whiteness of the snow blurred his vision, and he wondered if he was crying or just cold. The kid was the only black thing around. Then he shook himself awake. They had to get organized, or at least look that way. They were cops, for Christ's sake. He had to report the shooting, get some backup out here and an ambulance. There was a chance the kid might still make it. "I'm going to have to use your phone, if you have one," he said. "Can you show me where it is?"

The man nodded dumbly and retreated, still staring at the boy on the ground. Then Tommy walked over to the Chevy, which was still waiting at the curb where they'd left it. "Thanks," he said to the driver. "Sorry we had to inconvenience you tonight." The man nodded and placed the car in gear. Tommy thought about telling him to forget what he'd seen, but he had the feeling that wasn't necessary.

When he got back from calling in their location, Rogan was kneeling next to the body, and when he stood up, he motioned to Tommy. "Check that out," he said.

There was a four-inch switchblade curled in the dead boy's fingers. Tommy hadn't seen it before, but he wasn't looking at the kid's hands then. "I didn't see any knife before," he said.

"I told you," Rogan said. "Fucking kid was coming at me. Look at the size of that thing. I'd have a hole in me the size of the Grand Canyon if I hadn't put him down, I'll tell you that right now."

Tommy shook his head. He remembered a sergeant at the Academy telling them to carry throwaways in case they ever had to do a nigger, but he had figured it was just talk and didn't take it seriously. Now he wondered about Rogan. He could see it, could imagine what Rogan would be thinking. Why ruin my service record over some nigger kid? Despite his dislike of the other man, Tommy couldn't really blame him. What was done was done and there was nothing to change it. "I just didn't see it, John," he repeated. "But I was behind you, coming up, and I slipped in the street."

"Goddamned right," Rogan said. "It happened fast. One minute I was up behind him, the next thing I knew there's this fucking machete coming at my ribs."

Now Tommy thought the kid's skin looked gray, as if it had started to fade in death. If they stayed there long enough he might actually turn white, just like them. There was a small dark hole at the base of the boy's skull, and it looked so delicate that it was hard to believe the shot could have done any real damage. But Tommy knew the truth was otherwise. Every cop carried the same gun, a .357, but their ammunition was special, designed not to exit the body as an ordinary bullet might, but to mushroom once it was inside and blow up. The coppers called it a "hot load" and it did incredible damage when it hit. Tommy imagined the bullet ricocheting around inside the boy's body, but the thought sickened him and he turned away. It was important to stay calm, to figure out what to do and figure it out fast.

Rogan's eyes were soft, almost as if he knew what Tommy was thinking. "Look," he said. "It wasn't like I wanted to kill the kid. Why would I chase him for two blocks if I just wanted to grease him? But why did he run, why'd he leave his car behind, and where does a kid like that get money to buy a car in the first place? Then when he pulled that blade I had no choice, you can see that, can't you, Tommy? We got to get together on this because once we get downtown that's what they're going to want. You know anytime a cop's involved in a killing all hell breaks loose. So we got to agree on our story about what happened."

Tommy didn't know how it had become his problem all of a sudden. He hadn't shot anyone. But he knew Rogan was right; he was there, and if he didn't back up his partner, they'd both look bad. Tommy shrugged. "We got the knife," he said.

Rogan nodded thoughtfully. "Yeah, and probably he was that burglar, like I said before. Chances are he was. Maybe somebody will ID him." Rogan seemed hopeful all of a sudden, as if he thought he'd get a medal out of this.

But talking helped and Tommy's exhaustion was lessening now. It was a problem, that was all. Something they had to work out, but they were partners, they were going to do it together. "OK," Rogan said. "How's this.

He jumps out of the car and yells, 'You won't catch me, I'm a hold-up man!' and he's waving the knife around?"

Tommy hadn't heard the kid say boo, but he had been back up the block when Rogan pulled his car over and then he'd started running. "I thought you didn't see the knife until later," he said.

"Yeah, that's right," Rogan said. "OK, so I had him there against the car, you saw that, and then he started running and we chased him and then it all happened just like I said before, just like you saw it."

Tommy didn't know what to say. He couldn't argue with Rogan because he didn't know for sure what had happened himself, even though he had been there the whole time. That was the confusing thing; he didn't know what had been going on right in front of him. But how could he tell anyone that? "If you say so, John," he muttered.

"Right," Rogan said. He seemed pleased with himself, gaining confidence now. "That's good. He fits some of them bulletins to a T. How do we know he ain't a fucking hold-up man anyway? Swear to God, that's the first thing went through my mind."

The guy was amazing. He was rolling now, working on his story, refining it, as if he was writing a goddamned TV show or something. One minute Rogan had been talking about going through vacant houses looking for niggers and the next he stops a car for a broken taillight and shoots the driver. But now, to hear John tell it, the whole thing had been planned and he'd been crime-stoppers all along, responding to the bulletin about the Brown Street robber. Tommy shook his head. The way Rogan was going on was making him nervous. "That's it, then?" he said, anxious to be through with this.

Rogan nodded. "That's what we'll tell them. You got it now, Partner?"

There was a siren in the distance coming closer. A bar on the corner had its doors open and people had begun to gather across the street, though no one had the nerve to advance toward the two bikemen. Tommy wondered where they had all been before and whether anyone besides the guy in the pj's had seen anything. Now the siren was louder, and for no reason, Tommy looked at his watch. It was almost nine, time to call in for his hourly mark, to let them know where he was. He wished he had pulled the hook in that call box he had seen a few blocks back. In the middle of all the confusion, police procedure offered him some comfort. But he had screwed up again. He hadn't made his mark and now he was stuck in this situation with Rogan. The two things seemed connected in his mind.

"What about it?" Rogan said, his voice sharper now. "You with me on this, Partner? You got it all?"

The two men were close enough to touch, and though they hardly knew each other, Tommy felt joined together with the other man. What had happened made it that way and that's how it would stay. He had never felt comfortable with other cops, never been included in their bull sessions about hunting and women. The only place he fit in was in the bar, and then he was usually too loaded to know if he was fitting in or not. But he knew about cops hanging together and not crapping out on your partner. That's what was happening now. "I've got it," he said.

"OK," Rogan said, and patted his shoulder. "That's good then. That's all right."

Charlie Moran, a detective sergeant, and two uniforms were in the first car. Tommy knew Moran from the neighborhood, and he respected him. Moran was probably ten years older than he was, old enough that he had seemed like a grown-up when Tommy was still just a kid playing ball in the streets. He remembered Charlie as a tall, skinny pitcher on the St. Pete's baseball team and then later the general approbation among the parents when he had joined the force after high school and service in Korea. In fact, Charlie Moran was part of the reason Tommy had decided to become a copper, though he had known from the beginning he wanted to be a bikeman, and this hadn't changed when Moran was promoted to detective and got to wear plainclothes to work. Any asshole could ride in a car, Tommy figured, but you had to apply to be a bikeman and they didn't take everyone who wanted in.

After a year riding in a squad, Tommy had written for the motorcycle corps and he had been admitted, though at first they made him ride a checkerbike and handle traffic patrol, helping old ladies across the street. Finally, he got a solo and he had been patrolling on his own ever since. Now, he had trouble meeting Charlie Moran's eyes, though the other man seemed calm enough.

"What happened, Tommy?" Moran asked and looked at the kid's body.

"Sarge, we shot a guy," Tommy said.

"Both of you."

"I did it," Rogan said.

Moran looked first at one, then the other. "Go sit in my car," he said quietly to Tommy.

The uniforms outlined the body in the snow, and then a crew from the ambulance put the kid on a stretcher and took him away. No one was hurrying; there wasn't much point in it now. Tommy sat in Moran's car and waited, listening to the radio. It was warm and there was a pipe and tobacco pouch on the dashboard, which gave the car a homey atmosphere. More squads were arriving all the time. Two uniforms made a diagram of the scene. Then they fanned out, looking for witnesses, Tommy thought. He wondered where the guy in the bathrobe had gone. Moran stood talking to Rogan, his hip cocked, one hand in a pocket, relaxed, as if nothing unusual were going on, which reassured Tommy. Probably Charlie had seen a lot of this.

Finally, Moran returned to the car. He was a big man with a deep crease between his eyes that made Tommy think of his father, though the old man had been dead for ten years. Now Moran took off his hat and let out his breath. It was warm and Tommy felt sleepy and secure.

"OK," Moran said. "I want to know the truth. I want to know what the hell you're doing with Rogan and why you're not patrolling on your bike. I called headquarters and they said you didn't pull your nine o'clock mark. So what were you guys doing out there and why's that kid down on the ground?"

In the dark car, Tommy felt like confessing his own confusion about the shooting, his own doubts. Moran was just a guy from the Third Ward, almost a friend. He could trust him. But something held him back, some loyalty to Rogan he didn't fully understand. Anyway, even if Rogan had pulled the trigger, Tommy had been there. He was in it too. There was no getting around that. So Tommy told Moran he was war-horsing because the sergeant had pulled him off his regular beat, but he left out the part about being late to roll call. He was driving alone when he saw Rogan on the ground and pulled over, like he was supposed to when another officer was down. That much was true—Moran couldn't say anything about that. But then Tommy repeated the story he and John had agreed on about the knife, and he could tell the detective wasn't buying it.

Moran just sat quietly for a long time, looking straight ahead, saying nothing. Finally, he turned to Tommy. "I'm just telling you this because you're a kid from the neighborhood and I feel a responsibility for what happens to you," he said. "This whole thing is nothing to me. Rogan, even the dead kid, I could give a shit about them. But once we go downtown and you file your report, it's out of my hands. And you want to watch out with this, for your own self, I mean. Rogan's a bad ass, a real shit head. You don't know how bad he is, so take my word for it because I do. You think you're standing behind a fellow officer, backing him up, and I understand that, but you're seriously wrong, Tommy. We got a dead kid out there, and it doesn't matter that he's a nigger or what he is. You don't want to be in this with Rogan unless you have to be."

Moran was scaring him, and though Tommy knew he was trying to, that this was part of the game, that they tried to separate you and break you down, he couldn't shake off a growing feeling of dread. Still, what could he do? He'd already told the story, the same one Rogan had. He couldn't back away now; they'd agreed on it. "What do you mean?" he asked.

Moran wiped his face with his hands as if they were a towel. "He's got complaints all over the goddamned place," he said wearily. "People coming into the precinct saying he responds to calls then beats the shit out of everyone in the place, women, kids, doesn't matter." He turned in his seat to face Tommy. "Look," he said. "I know you bikemen, how you all think you're tough motherfuckers and the rest of us are pussies, but this guy's something else, take my word. I checked your record and so far you're in the clear. You don't want to screw things up for yourself by fronting for a loser like Rogan."

Tommy didn't know what to say. He had the feeling Moran was telling the truth, that he was looking out for his best interests, but he couldn't be sure. He hadn't shot the kid, but it would be his word against the other man's if he changed his story now. And what would the other guys think if he ratted out on Rogan? He wouldn't be able to show his face at roll call. Besides, if they stuck together, this would all blow over in a few weeks. "I don't know, Sarge," he said.

Moran nodded. "So you're sticking with this then," he said, tapping his notebook.

"That's it," Tommy said. He could hear himself breathing shallowly and felt an enormous pressure in the middle of his chest.

"OK," the detective said. "We got nothing more to talk about then. Let's go." They got out of the car and walked slowly over to where one of the uniforms was talking to Rogan.

"How far away were when you shot him?" Magnusen asked.

"Not that far," Rogan said, indicating the street.

"Show me," Magnusen said, and Rogan stepped off about twenty-five feet.

"Hell of a shot," Moran muttered. "In the dark too. Ought to put him up for a marksman's medal."

"Maybe it was a little closer," Tommy offered. Rogan had been on top of the kid, for Christ's sake.

Magnusen looked at Tommy, then he spoke again to Rogan. "This about right, John?"

Rogan didn't look at Tommy. They were on their own now. He nodded. "Looks like it to me," he said.

Magnusen put a piece of ice on the ground to mark the spot, then he paced it off and measured with a tape he took out of his pocket. "Twenty-three feet nine inches," he said to no one in particular. He wrote this down in his notebook.

"You agree on that, Tommy?" Moran asked. The others were moving away.

"I don't know. I'd say it was a little closer. Maybe ten or fifteen feet. But I was in back of them, running. I didn't really see how far away Rogan was."

Moran nodded and made a note of this. Then he turned and looked at the crowd of silent blacks lining the curb. Considering how many people were watching, it was amazingly quiet. Only the noises of the ambulance and the coppers moving back and forth interfered with their conversation. But there was a strong impression of menace in the air. Tommy remembered the acrid smell of cordite and smoke right after Rogan shot and imagined he smelled it still. Maybe it was just death he was smelling. He looked around and wondered if it was possible that no one had seen what had happened here, that there were no witnesses in the growing crowd of people. Still, even if that were true, he doubted that anyone on the street believed John Rogan had been acting in self-defense against a crazed burglar when he shot that boy down.

Moran might have been thinking the same thing. He looked at Tommy with what seemed to be a mixture of compassion and disgust. Then he looked around the crime scene and gestured toward the car. "Let's go downtown," he said. "You boys sure fucked up my night."

Two

The Safety Building was on State Street, next to the courthouse, and both newspapers had reporters stationed inside listening to the police radio. By the time Tommy and Moran got there, the writers were in the hall waiting for them. Moran held Tommy lightly by the elbow as they walked in and just said, "Later," when the press came at them. Then he put Tommy in a room with a pad of paper. "Write what you told me," he said and closed the door.

Tommy looked around. There was nothing but a chair and a table. The walls were bare, but he knew there was a two-way mirror in one of them. It was an interrogation room, like he'd done something wrong, like he was a criminal. He wondered where Rogan was. Moran had separated the two of them at the scene, and Tommy figured they had him in another room by himself and were waiting to see how their stories matched up.

It was cold in the room, but Tommy felt sweat dripping from his armpits. Then as the reality of his situation began to sink in, Tommy's hands started trembling and he dropped the pencil on the floor. This was a big thing, a shooting, even if the copper was right. Tommy had never been involved in one before, but he knew the drill. Rogan would be suspended during the investigation, and he might be too, even though he hadn't done anything. That much was normal procedure, but thanks to Moran, Tommy was beginning to get the whole picture now. Rogan wasn't just any copper; he had a file full of misconduct notices, which meant this wasn't going to be a routine investigation. And he was involved up to his ass. The worst thing was Moran had tried to warn him, tried to help him out, but Tommy hadn't wanted to listen.

He sat at the table and ran his hands through his brown hair. It was starting to go in the front already; if he wasn't careful he'd be bald as a goddamned egg by the time he hit thirty. Twenty-six years old, he thought, and the worst thing that had ever happened to him before this was getting his ass chewed out by the priest for goosing Judy Jurawski in CCD. Now he realized that his fists were clenched. Got to relax, Tommy thought, got to figure this out. He took a deep breath, then another, and slowly he began to feel better.

Tommy was easy-going; he liked to have a few drinks, some laughs. He'd gotten into bar fights once or twice, but you could expect that. He didn't know what to think about murder, how to think about it. Cops got used to carrying guns because it was part of the job. You had to have a weapon on you twenty-four hours a day, even though Tommy had never fired his except on the range. To him, the gun was a piece of clothing, like wearing shoes, and Tommy didn't think much about it. In fact, his first reaction when he'd heard Rogan shooting had been surprise. The rest came after. Out on the street, when he and Rogan agreed on their story, it had seemed easy enough, and now Tommy wondered if it was because he was still in shock. He didn't like niggers, who did? But Rogan had shot the kid, not him, and he was just making things worse for himself by writing a report saying what Rogan had done was OK when he hadn't really seen it.

It didn't even make sense the way Rogan wanted to tell it. How could the kid have come at him if he was twenty-three feet away? But Tommy didn't have to get into that. All he had to say was he didn't know, which was the truth. He didn't know if the kid came at Rogan and he didn't know why Rogan had shot him. Let them think he was stupid; maybe he was. But that was better than lying to save John Rogan's ass.

Sitting in the cold room, it all came back, the kid's mouth opening and closing like a fish, as if he was going to say something. Then Rogan's gun going off, that big Ruger pounding the air and smoke everywhere burning Tommy's eyes. He remembered that the kid was wearing these fancy striped pants and silk socks, or maybe they were nylon, real thin for winter anyway, and black Stacies with long pointed toes and heel cleats. How the hell could he run in the snow with shoes like that? Tommy wondered. And where did he get the money to pay for them? But the kid was faster than hell; they never would have caught him if Tommy hadn't stopped that car. He wished he hadn't now; he wished that he'd just let the fucking kid run.

He remembered what Rogan had said about searching the houses and getting some niggers before the kid came along. But Tommy wasn't sure he hadn't just been blowing smoke. What was he going to do, kick the doors in? Someone would have called the cops. Except they were the cops. The thought made Tommy smile and then he didn't feel so bad. How did he know Rogan wasn't right anyway, that the kid wasn't the burglar who'd been holding up grocery stores on the north side? And if he was, then they'd done everyone a favor. The word was that guy was a slasher and there was a copper in the hospital with his face held together by thread to prove it. But Tommy's heart sank when he remembered Moran calling Rogan a bad ass. For a detective to say that about another officer wasn't a good sign, not good at all. Tommy tried again to reassure himself. Maybe the whole thing would blow over after they sweated them for a while; yet the more he went over it in his mind, the more confused and hopeless he felt.

Tommy thought of the man who had picked them up, the guy in the Chevy. He remembered thinking the driver would forget about what had happened. Fat chance now. Once he knew he could get his name in the paper, he'd be posing for every photographer in town. Then there was the neighbor in the bathrobe, the one they'd told to get lost. He'd be back. And who knew what other witnesses would show up and say that Rogan had just shot the kid and that was it. It was hard to believe there was no one in that bar looking out the window when it all went down. And then it was their word against the others, but given Rogan's rep, it would be Tommy's word that would matter, which put him right back in the middle of things.

Tommy felt the pressure in the center of his chest again, as if someone had parked a truck on top of him. He opened the door and yelled for the cop on duty. "I got to talk to the Sarge," he said.

Moran was out of breath when he arrived. He still had his coat on and his hat brim had left a bright red crease in his forehead. "What's the matter?" Tommy asked.

"All hell's breaking loose out there. It got on the ten o'clock news and now the office is filled with niggers who say they're related. Goddamn kid must have fifty brothers and sisters."

Tommy felt his stomach go hollow. "I been thinking," he said. "I got to tell you that what I said out there, I'm not really sure anymore."

"Not sure?" Moran looked at his watch impatiently.

Tommy nodded. "I ain't saying Rogan's lying, but from where I was, I mean, I'm not sure anymore about the knife."

"What is it exactly you're not sure *about?*" Moran drew out his words as if he were speaking to a child.

Tommy plunged on, determined to get this out. "From where I was, in back of them in the street, I'm just not sure about that knife."

"Are you unsure about whether there was a knife or just whether or not the kid came at Rogan with it?"

Tommy felt miserable, under suspicion. He had thought he could talk honestly to Moran, but this wasn't going the way he'd hoped. "Just the whole thing, Sarge." he said. "I didn't even see John shoot the kid; I heard it."

Charlie Moran looked at him and shook his head. Then he pulled a handkerchief out of his pocket and rubbed his forehead. Finally, he sat down next to Tommy and let out a big sigh like he was being real patient, but Tommy could tell he was seriously pissed off. Moran smiled, his lips but not his eyes, as if Tommy were some kind of idiot. "The fuck you talking about, Tommy? Out in the car I said to tell me exactly what happened, am I right? And I told you to make it the truth. I even told you what an asshole Rogan was, how I'd looked in his wrapper downtown before I came out to the scene, didn't I?"

Tommy nodded dumbly. There was nothing to say.

"And then you told me how you two chased this kid," Moran looked at his notes, "Jimmy Norman, and he had a knife and yelled he was a holdup man. Am I doing all right so far?"

"Yeah," Tommy said. "That's what I told you."

"And then the kid slashed at Rogan and called you sonsabitches, so you had to shoot him, isn't that right?"

"That's what I told you, but it ain't right, Sarge. It's not the truth."

"Shut up," Moran said. "So you told me your story and I came down here and told the captain and he told the chief and he told the TV guys and it's on the news and we got half of Africa out there plus every reporter in town. That's where we are right now. Then you call me in here to say you're not sure what you said before is right and you want to change your story. Is that what you're telling me, Tommy? I just want to be sure I'm following you."

Tommy could see Moran's point. His ass was on the line too, not to mention the chief's, and the whole damned department when you got right down to it. It wasn't a good situation. "So you're saying you don't want to know what really happened?" he said slowly.

Moran sighed heavily. "Sure, I want to know. Because I'm naturally curious and a seeker after the truth. But the thing is, I already know, because you told me all about it in the car." He paused and looked sympathetically at Tommy. "Look," Moran said. "I got a wife and two kids at home. You got a wife too, if I remember. So, for everybody's sake, figure out what you want to say and then write it down in your report. But don't start telling me something different from what you said before because I'm not listening." He stood to leave, then turned back to Tommy. "One other thing," he said. "If you go in and tell the captain this conversation ever happened, I'm going to look real surprised and deny it, OK?"

Tommy felt helpless in the face of Moran's sudden anger. It was hard to believe he was involved in an in-house investigation of a homicide and he didn't seem to be able to avoid getting in deeper. "Rogan didn't mean to do it," Tommy said, trying again but realizing immediately how stupid that sounded. The gun didn't fire itself. Moran looked unconvinced and, worse, uninterested. "I think he was just going to hit the kid in the head," Tommy added, his voice trailing off in the empty room. It sounded lame even to him.

"Just write your report, Tommy," Moran said. "I've got to go."

Despite his failure to impress Moran, Tommy felt more at ease after he left. He had tried to tell the truth—no one could say he hadn't. He had tried, but they didn't want to know. And what he had said about Rogan was true, whatever Moran might think. John wasn't that bad a guy; what happened could have happened to anyone. For some reason Tommy thought about Norman's shoes again. Where would some kid from the ghetto get enough money to buy patent leather Stacies? They had to be thirty dollars easy. But this wasn't his problem either. He wasn't a fucking clothier.

Like Moran said, all he had to do was finish his report. Concentrate on that and forget the rest. He hadn't done anything wrong. As far as he was concerned, it was regulation all the way. He'd responded to another officer's call, then backed up his partner. When it was over and the kid was down, he had called for backup and now he was cooperating with the investigation. He squared his shoulders and began to write.

When Tommy was done, he went upstairs and handed Moran the report. Rogan was sitting in the office, but the detective didn't say anything to either of them. Instead, he went out in the hall to talk to the reporters. Then they all went down the hall to a conference room, but still no one said anything to the two patrolmen.

Motorcycle cops spent most of their time on the street, so Tommy hadn't had much contact with the press. From talking to the other guys, he knew reporters rarely visited a crime scene, preferring to hang out in the press room, getting whatever they could from the brass, which made a kind of sense when you thought about it. Crime scenes were confusing and everything had to come downtown sooner or later. Unless it involved someone important, in which case the press would be all over the place. But that was unusual. A dead nigger kid wouldn't be worth their going out in the cold.

But Tommy was curious about the press and wondered what they made of the coppers. Occasionally, he'd walk past the pressroom and see them talking on the phone or reading the papers. It seemed like a pretty soft life, but he never went inside and they paid no attention to him. The only one he knew at all was Bob Joseph, a young kid from the *Times* with peach fuzz for a beard and clothes that hung on him. Joseph had interviewed Tommy about a traffic case a year ago and seemed OK. At least, he hadn't misquoted Tommy. Most of the coppers distrusted reporters, figuring they were just looking for a story and didn't give a shit if they shafted anybody. But the word was that Joseph was different, that he actually worked at his job.

Now the door opened and Walter Martin, the chief of police, walked in, looking rumpled and unhappy. Tommy knew the chief didn't just show up for the hell of it. Even the reporters seemed impressed that he had made an appearance. The chief stood there for a moment waiting for the room to quiet down, then he said, "I have a statement. After that, I'll take questions." Joseph and the others got out their notebooks and Martin began to read.

"As some of you know, a man was shot tonight by one of our motorcycle officers, Patrolman John Rogan. The victim's name was Jimmy Norman, and he has now been pronounced dead at County Hospital. The family has been informed."

Tommy figured everybody knew this already, but hearing Martin say it made it seem official. The chief's voice was flat, but he didn't seem upset by what he was saying. This had a subtle effect on the room, and gradually the reporters seemed to relax a little, though the tension was still there. Tommy looked across the room, but Rogan wouldn't meet his eyes. He was staring at the floor, shoulders hunched, a cigarette cupped in his right hand.

"All of our officers are outstanding public servants," Martin continued. "But our motorcycle patrolmen are an elite corps. Assignment is competitive and they are carefully selected. Their training is exhaustive and continues beyond the Academy. All our officers are required to qualify with firearms twice a year, and it is worth noting that the bikemen routinely have the

highest averages in the department. They are our frontline and face danger
on the streets every day. Taking a human life is a very serious thing, and all
of our officers are instructed not to fire unless they have no choice. They
are taught to warn suspects, to apprehend, even to disable them, but not to
fire unless it is absolutely necessary. They are told not to kill."

"So how'd this kid get dead?" someone called out from the back.

Martin ignored this, and Tommy was impressed with the chief's
self-possession. It made him feel better about himself. "I believe that officers Rogan and Paley conducted themselves in a professional manner," the
chief said now. "I believe they had no reasonable alternative to the choice
they made, regrettable as that choice was. Now let me tell you a little bit
about the individual who was killed tonight." He paused and looked down
at some notes.

"Mr. Norman was twenty-two years of age, but in his short life he had
been arrested nine times and was released from the House of Correction
ten days ago. He was illiterate and couldn't pass a driver's license examination, and he had drifted from job to job since moving here from Alabama."

The reporters were writing madly, and Tommy admired the way the
chief was handling the whole thing. It surprised him that the kid was
twenty-two because he looked younger, but he liked what the chief was
saying. Norman was no Boy Scout was the point. He couldn't even read,
for Christ's sake, and he was from out of state anyway, like half the niggers
they arrested every day. Tommy supposed where he came from shouldn't
really matter. This wasn't Russia; they had an open border with Illinois. But
no one asked the niggers to come here, and it seemed like half of them
were in some kind of trouble a week after they got off the Greyhound bus.

Now Joseph asked, "What were the priors, Chief?"

This seemed to please Martin. "The last six were traffic offenses," he
said. "But four years ago Mr. Norman was arrested for carrying a concealed weapon and the year before that for abuse and carnal knowledge of
a child. He was on probation when he was killed."

"So Rogan shot him for a broken taillight?" It was the same guy who
had spoken before.

This would have pissed Tommy off. He would probably have clocked
the guy. But Martin was cool as a cucumber. It seemed like nothing could
bother the chief. "Officer Rogan stopped Mr. Norman's car because it had
a broken taillight, which you're aware is against the law," he said. "But that is
not why he used his service revolver. After apprehending the suspect, the

officer attempted to subdue him. As he was about to secure Mr. Norman
with handcuffs, the suspect broke away and both officers gave chase. During their pursuit, the officers fired warning shots in an attempt to halt the
suspect. Finally, Mr. Norman threatened Officer Rogan with a knife.
Officer Rogan responded as he did because his life was in danger."

The problem with this as far as Tommy was concerned was that most
coppers would have figured hell with it when Norman took off. It just
wasn't worth freezing your ass and running halfway across town to give
some kid a traffic ticket. The fact that Rogan not only went after the kid but
actually shot him made sense only if you knew Rogan was a hothead who
liked to hurt people. But the reporters seemed untroubled by Martin's explanation.

"You said Norman was a suspect," Joseph said. "Were you referring to
the Ike's Grocery holdup?"

Tommy knew Ike's was the store on Brown that had come across on
the bulletin, but he was surprised the way all this was coming together. It
was almost like Joseph was part of the team. It didn't even seem to matter
so much now that the whole thing was bullshit. The way the chief told it,
the story they had cooked up made more sense than what had really happened. It was that convincing, that real. Tommy found himself nodding his
head in silent agreement, though no one had said a thing to him so far.

"He's a suspect," the chief said slowly, "one of several." Tommy thought
it was good that he was careful, that he didn't just blame the robbery on the
kid. Let them wonder about it for a while, that was better. "We're going to
bring witnesses to the morgue and attempt to get a positive ID," the chief
added. "Any more questions?"

The press conference broke up in a clatter of metal chairs. After the
reporters left, Tommy expected the chief to be friendly. Not that he thought
they'd get a commendation, but considering the way he had backed them
up, he figured Martin believed that it was really Norman's life against theirs
and that they had done the right thing. But Martin's eyes were hard and cold.
There was no small talk; it was almost as if they were the criminals. The
chief's gaze rested on each of them for a few moments, then Martin turned
to Moran. "OK, bring in the family. Rogan and Paley, stay until we're through,
then you're back bright and early and you don't talk to anyone about this."

Moran went out and came back with a woman and two men. They
remained standing, though there were plenty of empty chairs. The woman
was tall and thin. She wore a black raincoat and had a blue kerchief tied
around her head. Even though they were in a room in the Safety Building

surrounded by cops, she didn't seem intimidated. Her expression was proud and angry, as if she was willing to take on the whole damned department. The men were different. They hung back, shoulders slouched, and looked more the way Tommy expected niggers to look when you got them downtown. It was hard to say what their relationship to each other might be, but the woman seemed to be in charge. And while he wasn't scared exactly, the woman's anger was impressive. Tommy was glad he didn't have to go up against her.

Moran made a gesture of introduction. "This is Mrs. Brown, the victim's sister . . ." But the woman brushed him aside impatiently and honed right in on the chief.

She pointed her finger at him and said, "I don't know why I got to hear my baby brother's been shot on the teevee. I don't why nobody got to us before that anyhow." Her voice was harsh in the small room and deeper than Tommy would have expected. It surprised him that her main concern seemed to be timing. He would have expected tears, but Mrs. Brown was dry-eyed.

"We're sorry for your loss, ma'am," the chief said. "An officer was on his way to your house, but he was delayed."

"You got that right," the woman said. "When they say Jimmy got killed? Eight-thirty? And ten o'clock and the police still can't make it ten blocks away? Maybe he stopped for coffee."

The chief looked to Moran for an explanation, but Moran just shook his head. "That ain't all," the woman continued. "That boy lived in my house for five years and he never raised his voice. You can't tell me he's no burglar, can't tell me he threatened no one with a knife. It just wasn't in him."

The men were quiet. One nodded his head and said, "That's right," but otherwise they just watched, their large hands dangling below their waists.

Now Moran held out the knife with its blade extended. "He threatened the officer, ma'am."

"No, he did not." The woman shook her head vigorously. "Because that ain't even his knife. I got his knife right here." And she pulled a small butterfly out of her purse and held it up.

"Could I have that please, ma'am?" Moran asked politely.

Mrs. Brown shook her head angrily. "No, I am not going to give you this knife," she said. "Because if I did, you'd switch them and say this was the one Jimmy tried to kill these two men with." She looked contemptuously at Tommy and Rogan. "These two big motorcycle policemen with all their guns and fancy training so scared of my little brother Jimmy who's getting slapped around by the girls in our neighborhood and couldn't beat on anyone if his life depended on it, which I guess it did." Her voice was rich with irony. Tommy was ashamed to be there, ashamed of what had happened, but that wasn't going to help anything. He looked away, avoiding Olivia Brown's eyes.

"Besides," she continued. "Why would my brother have a knife in his right hand when he was left-handed, can you tell me that? And if he had this big knife and he was slashing away with it, why wouldn't the policeman have shot him right then?" She accompanied this with a slashing motion that made the chief stiffen and slip back in his chair. "Why'd they chase Jimmy for four blocks if he was so dangerous and so fearful to them?" she asked, and now her voice had a plaintive note in it. "Why'd they chase him all that way and *then* shoot him down? Can you tell me that?"

She dragged out "fearful" as if she were singing a gospel hymn, and the feeling of well-being and security that Tommy had built up during the press conference began to fade. Chief Martin seemed ill at ease, and this bothered Tommy because the woman's questions were exactly the ones he would have asked had he been in her place. Olivia Brown was tough and smart, and this surprised and worried Tommy, whose experience had been limited to blacks who had been beaten into subservience by life or the police or both.

But the chief had had enough and moved to regain control of the meeting. He hadn't risen to his present position by letting Negroes push him around in his own building. Martin stood abruptly and said, "That's all. We've tried to express our sympathy and concern, but I don't think you people want to hear what we've got to tell you."

Now one of the men spoke. "What you mean is we don't want to just sit back and watch while you hunt our young men down and kill them like rabbits. How'd you like it if we went out shooting cops?"

This was the wrong thing to say. The chief looked hard at the man, as if he was memorizing his face. "Don't you even think about that, my friend," he said. His voice was soft but menacing in the small room. "I'm feeling generous now, and I am sorry for your loss, whatever you might think. So I won't count what you said as a threat. But you make anything that I think even looks like a move on my men and I'll own your ass. Do you understand?" The man matched his stare for a moment, then turned away. The chief held his position for a long moment, then said, "OK, Charlie, this meeting is over. Get them out of here."

Moran started moving the group toward the door, but the woman shook his arm loose. "I got one more thing to tell you," she said. "And that's that we got a lawyer. You ain't heard the last of this. You can't shoot my brother down like a dog and we just forget about it. You better trust me on that." She stood, hands on hips, staring at the chief, then Tommy and Rogan in turn. Finally, she allowed herself to be pushed out of the room.

When they were gone, Martin looked at Rogan and said in a surprisingly mild voice, "What I don't see is how you could shoot at a man from that far away and hit anything. You must be a hell of a marksman, Rogan." Tommy remembered Magnusen had measured twenty-three feet from the block of ice in the street to Norman's body. He was glad he had told Moran that Rogan was closer than that.

"No," Rogan said, sounding glad to be able to speak. "It wasn't like that. We were fighting. He was as close as you to me."

Martin shook his head. "That's not what your report says." He looked at some papers in his hand. "The kid was running away, it says here. And Magnusen says you showed him right where you were when you fired your gun and that he marked the spot."

For the first time, Rogan looked at Tommy, but Tommy wasn't going to get in deeper than he already was. "What's going to happen to me?" Rogan said helplessly.

"I don't know," Martin said. "Maybe nothing. But I can tell you the D.A.'s not going to be happy with what we've got here. I can tell you that right now. The reports contradict each other, we've got a dead kid, the family's mad as hell, and the papers are all over us. Maybe an inquest, but we're not building much of a case. I'm always going to back up an officer, but you can't just kill someone for a traffic violation, Rogan. You know that."

Martin's voice was stern, but Rogan looked so miserable that the chief's expression softened. "OK, everyone's tired. Go home and get some sleep. Maybe we can straighten all this out in the morning. It'll look different anyway. And we might get lucky. Maybe the kid actually held up those grocery stores after all. You never know." He stood and nodded, as if he was considering what he had said, as if he was reassured by it. Then he left the room. Tommy felt sympathetic and considered inviting the other man out for a beer. But the air in the room seemed dismal, hopeless, and there didn't seem to be anything more to say. They'd have to wait and see what happened. So he just said, "Take it easy, John," and followed the chief out the door.

The bikemen hung out at a bar called Braun's on the corner of North and Humboldt, and Tommy stopped there on the way home, just to cushion himself a little. He was nursing a brandy when the bartender called out, "I seen you on the news, Tommy. They had your picture and everything."

George must have thought he'd be pleased, and another time he might have been. Yet Tommy couldn't escape the feeling of gloom. It seemed to have taken him around the throat and even the brandy couldn't entirely erase the bad taste in his mouth. But George didn't know this and there was no point in being unfriendly, so Tommy nodded and lifted his glass. Now George came over and leaned familiarly against the bar. "Don't let it get you down," he said. "The TV said he held up that grocery store in the Core and, dark as it is down there, no one can see anything anyway."

George had been a bikeman himself before he retired and opened the tavern. He meant well, but nothing was going to reassure Tommy tonight. He wondered what they had said on the news, but the papers would have it in the morning. He could wait. "I could see OK," he said now. "But thanks."

George slapped the bar rhythmically with a cloth. The few people in the room were far away and couldn't hear the conversation. Tommy wondered if his wife had seen it too, if he'd have to go through the whole thing again with her when he got home. He finished his drink and rose to go.

"I'll have one with you," the bartender said, trying to hold him. Tommy appreciated the gesture, but it was beginning to feel close in the small room. "I'd better get home," he said.

"Up to you," George said. "But just remember one thing, Tommy. From one old copper to another. Don't ever think they wouldn't do it to you, anytime, anywhere. It's you against them out there and everybody knows it, everybody who matters, anyway. Don't kid yourself about that."

Tommy nodded, but in his mind he was back, standing over Jimmy Norman in his fancy striped pants and pointed shoes. He saw Jimmy lying on the freezing service walk outside the little white house in the snow, his skin slowly going gray. George might be right, probably he was. Maybe the kid would have done Rogan if they'd given him the chance. Tommy didn't know about that. But it didn't matter now. The point was he had no chance, not from the get-go. The kid hadn't done anything but run because he was scared and now he was lying dead in the morgue and Tommy was lying about it to save John Rogan's ass and he didn't know why. That was the fact and that was what was important, not what somebody else might have done at some other time, in some other place.

Three

When Tommy came to work the next morning, he had things under control. He'd read the Post at Webb's while he ate breakfast and everything sounded OK. Say what you wanted to, Jimmy Norman wasn't the first nigger who ever got shot running from a crime scene. The way the paper played it, listing all his priors and saying he just got out of jail, you got the feeling he deserved what he got. If he wasn't guilty, why did he run?

Sitting at the bright yellow counter surrounded by ordinary people who weren't even thinking about the murder gave Tommy some perspective. An old lady smiled and the guy on the next stool moved his papers around to show respect. They felt safer because he was there. It was crazy to let the whole thing get to him. What he needed to do was get past it and move on.

But as soon as he hit the Safety Building, Tommy got a funny feeling in the pit of his stomach. Usually, the guys would get there early for coffee and a smoke before roll call. It was a good time of day, one of the things Tommy liked about being a bikeman because everyone was relaxed and friendly. But while the other guys didn't exactly avoid him this morning, he had the sense he'd interrupted a conversation. One about him. Rogan wasn't even there. Finally, the sergeant told him he wasn't riding today, that he was supposed to report down to the Detective Bureau. The sergeant was OK and didn't broadcast it. But everyone knew. Tommy had the feeling that they were all watching as he took his gear and walked out the door.

Moran was waiting when Tommy got to the office, which made him feel a little better. Even with what had happened, he still thought of Charlie as a friend. He'd never met Inspector Halloran or Captain Tanner, and neither Chief Martin nor Rogan were there. Magnusen was sitting in the corner. Halloran gestured Tommy to a chair as the others moved around in the small room. Halloran was maybe fifty, balding with a gut on him, and Tommy had heard he was OK, that he'd even show up and buy a round at Braun's every so often. He didn't know anything about Tanner.

Halloran had a bunch of papers on the desk in front of him, and Tommy figured they were the reports everyone had written the night before. "OK," the inspector said. "I've been reading these reports for two hours now and I got to take them to the D.A. in a minute, but before I do I'd like to know what the hell really happened last night. Just for my own curiosity. I got one report says Rogan was twenty-five feet away when he shot the Norman kid; another one says ten feet. One says the kid tried to slash Rogan with a knife; the others don't say anything about slashing. We got a report that the kid said he was a holdup man and called Rogan and Paley sonsabitches. Another one says yeah on the holdup but doesn't say nothing about the sonsabitches. And the other one doesn't have anything about holdups or sonsabitches. Rogan's not here on purpose in case you guys got something to say." He looked at Moran and Magnusen and Tommy. But no one offered anything, so Halloran said, "OK, fuck it. Let's go see Lathrop."

Rogan was waiting when they came out, and they walked up to the district attorney's office together. Rogan's expression was anxious, and Tommy could tell he wondered what had gone on in the room. He didn't blame him. If he had been Rogan, he would have just assumed that everyone was going to sell him down the river. There was no chance to reassure the other man, but Tommy felt sympathetic. Rogan's face was pinched and red, and it looked like he hadn't gotten any sleep. Tommy had given up staring at the ceiling at five and left home without speaking to his wife. One thing he didn't need right now was Lu asking him a lot of questions he couldn't answer, even though it made him feel like a shit not to tell her what was going on.

"You OK?" he asked Rogan as they climbed the stairs.

The other man shrugged. "I've been better. I talked to the chief for an hour last night after you left. Now the D.A.'s going to chew out my ass."

Tommy nodded, but before he could say anything Moran interrupted. "In here," he said, and they all filed into Lathrop's office. Tommy had never seen the district attorney before, but no one bothered to introduce them. Lathrop was short and trim with neatly combed hair and deep-set eyes that made Tommy feel like he was looking right through him. He took a seat to the side of the district attorney's desk, out of the line of fire.

Lathrop nodded to the room, then got right into it. "Inspector Halloran tells me we've got some problems," he said. Then, without anything more, he dropped his eyes to the desk and started reading. He took his time, going back to examine some pages and making notes along the way, before he finally gathered the reports in a neat pile and looked at the men before him. "Which one of you is Patrolman Rogan?" Lathrop asked.

Rogan raised his hand like he was back in school, and Lathrop said, "Let's start with you. You say this young man," he looked at the papers, "Jimmy Norman. You say Mr. Norman had a knife and that he threatened you so that you were forced to shoot him from a distance of twenty-three feet nine inches. Is that correct?"

"It was actually a little closer," Rogan said, but Lathrop cut him off.

"For the moment, let's just stick with your report," he said. "Is that correct, according to your report, Patrolman?"

Rogan shrugged and agreed. "Yes, sir."

Lathrop nodded. "OK. Detective Magnusen, your report states that Rogan told you he was twenty-three feet nine inches from Norman when he shot. Is that correct?"

"He didn't tell me that," Magnusen said. "He showed me where he stood. I marked it with a block of ice and measured from there to the body."

"And you measured twenty-three feet nine inches?"

"Yes, sir."

Lathrop looked at Rogan quizzically, but he didn't say anything. Instead, he turned to Tommy. "You're Paley?" Tommy nodded. Though the room was cold, he had started to sweat. "Well, Patrolman Paley, your report differs from the other two. You say Rogan was just ten or fifteen feet away when he shot Mr. Norman." Lathrop looked at Tommy with a slight smile on his face. For some reason he didn't understand, Tommy wanted to please Lathrop. It went beyond the natural desire for approval from a superior; Lathrop seemed different than the rest. At the same time, his natural skepticism told him to be careful, that no one in this room was on his side.

Tommy cleared his throat. "It looked about that far to me, sir."

"But you didn't measure it? I mean, you weren't involved in the block of ice?" The way he said this made Tommy think Lathrop didn't have much respect for Magnusen's investigative methods.

"No, sir. I don't know exactly how far away he was."

"Thank you," Lathrop said dryly. He turned back to Magnusen. "Your report doesn't mention the victim lunging at Rogan with a knife."

"He didn't say anything about that to me," Magnusen said. "I only wrote down what he said."

Rogan might not be a prize, but Magnusen was beginning to get on Tommy's nerves, sitting there like a goddamned choirboy. You'd think they'd give Rogan a break on something, maybe understand he was a little confused, that anyone would be under the circumstances. It was hard to believe Magnusen didn't know about the knife. The kid had it in his hand when he was lying on the ground, for Christ's sake. Even if Rogan had somehow forgotten to say anything about it, Magnusen must have seen the damned thing.

Lathrop looked thoughtful. "It's difficult to see how Mr. Norman could lunge twenty-four feet to threaten Rogan with a knife, isn't it, Detective?"

"I don't know, sir," Magnusen said. "What Rogan told me is in my report, though."

Lathrop nodded again, then just sat there, letting the significance of what he was saying settle in the room. The others shifted uncomfortably in their chairs. It was pretty obvious Rogan didn't mean the kid threatened him from across the street, but that was the impression Lathrop was giving, that the whole thing was ridiculous. But Tommy kept quiet. He wasn't going to talk unless someone asked him a direct question.

Moran took a deep breath and let it out. Tommy wished Lathrop would just let them have it if he was going to and cut the tension. This wasn't helping. But tension was probably exactly what the district attorney was after. Make them all sweat until he got what he wanted. If they didn't like it, too bad. What they wanted was nothing to him

Now Lathrop turned to Tanner for the first time, and when he spoke there was a bite in his voice. "Captain, these reports have to be consistent. I'd look like a damned fool going before a jury with this."

No one had mentioned a jury before, and Tommy had the sudden image of doors closing in front of his eyes. Tanner turned to Magnusen and said, "Maggie, you'd better get with Rogan and write a new report."

Magnusen shook his head stubbornly. "I already wrote my report. I measured the distance last night and I put down the truth as good as I know it. Somebody else wants to change something, that's up to them. Not me." Magnusen sounded like a child trying to get out of a household chore.

Lathrop's voice came between them. "I can't listen to this," he said. "I'm an officer of the court and I'm not asking that anyone falsify anything.

What I'm saying is that this is a mess no one could make sense of." He held up the sheaf of papers and shook them in Tanner's face. "This isn't much of an investigation, Captain. A man has been murdered and you can't even agree on the basic details of what happened. Now, what I want is for you to bring me one story and I want it to be the truth as you understand it. Is that clear?"

Tanner nodded. Tommy could tell he didn't like being talked to this way in front of his men, but there was nothing he could do about it. Instead, he glared at the detectives. Magnusen's face was red, but he looked right back at Tanner, like he didn't give a shit what the captain thought.

"There's one other thing," Lathrop said. "We never heard from the driver of the car Paley stopped, but the Normans' lawyer called. He claims he's got a witness who didn't see a knife. They haven't produced this guy yet, but if they do, I'm going to have to order a coroner's inquest. In the meantime, we'll try to put up a good front. Anything else, Inspector?"

Halloran cleared his throat. "We're still trying to tie Norman to these robberies. Turns out he's three inches smaller than the guy on the daily bulletin, but those things aren't that accurate." He handed Tanner a slip of paper. "You'd better have someone take this witness to the morgue to see if she can ID Norman."

Tanner looked at the paper. "Name's Em," he said. "Maggie, maybe you could buy Em a few drinks on your way?"

"Damned if I'm going to buy anyone drinks to save Rogan's ass."

Tommy wondered what Magnusen had against Rogan. Maybe he was embarrassed because he hadn't pressed him harder in the first place, but that wasn't Rogan's fault. Yet in a way, Tommy admired Magnusen for standing his ground. Tommy was amazed that no one did anything about it. It had never occurred to him that you could embarrass a captain in public and not suffer for it, but Magnusen seemed to be blessed.

Halloran took it all in and looked at Tanner, who just shrugged. Then he said, "Is that all, sir?"

Lathrop looked bemused. "Just get me those reports by this afternoon." Then he said, "The press is coming in, and I think Rogan and Paley should stay here. I don't want it to look like we're hiding you boys."

Tommy wished they were being hidden, wished he could just go away somewhere until the damned thing blew over. Because it would; sooner or later it would go away, and he was getting tired of all the moralizing. The kid was dead and that was too bad, more than too bad; it was a shitty deal for him and for his family. But Tommy didn't believe Lathrop or Tanner or

Martin really gave a damn about the truth. If the stories didn't match, then they looked bad, which was all they cared about. It was all some kind of game he didn't understand very well, except he knew he wasn't really a player. He and Rogan didn't matter. They were being put through the ringer to save the D.A.'s ass, which as far as Tommy was concerned didn't really need saving. Guys like Lathrop with their MacNeil and Moore suits and fancy briefcases would always do all right. But Rogan had nowhere to go if he got kicked off the force, and neither did Tommy. If they weren't coppers, they weren't anything. What's more, no one ever talked about what was really going on, which when you got down to it was simple. You had one dead nigger kid and two white cops. That was how most people would see it. Black against white, and Milwaukee was the whitest city Tommy had ever seen. You didn't have to know much to know that.

The next day both papers carried stories based on the new version of the murder Tommy, Rogan, and Moran had come up with. Now Rogan had been six feet away when he shot after Jimmy Norman lunged at him. The Times even had an artist's drawing of the knife and quoted Lathrop saying, "Patrolmen Rogan and Paley were in imminent danger due to the knife slashing of that man. Under the circumstances, I see no reason at present for a coroner's inquest. In my opinion, the officer had a right to shoot."

Which should have been the end of it, but Tommy didn't have a chance to relax because the same day, the Normans' lawyer produced signed depositions from his witnesses saying none of them had seen a knife. It didn't really matter who the witnesses were. They had been there and they contradicted the official version of the killing, which they were now calling voluntary manslaughter. The district attorney was doing his best, implying that Norman had been guilty of various crimes before Rogan shot him, but Tommy didn't like the sound of manslaughter. He didn't like that at all.

The county decided to do an autopsy on Jimmy Norman, which seemed pretty stupid since everyone knew what had killed the kid. But the family was screaming louder than ever and they had to do something. Mrs. Brown was quoted in the paper saying that Jimmy wouldn't have harmed a fly and the only reason he ran was that he didn't have a valid driver's license. Tommy didn't see how anyone could know what Jimmy was thinking that night, even his sister, but it didn't take a genius to see that things didn't look good.

No one seemed to care that this was a convicted felon, and none of the papers checked with the parents of the little girl Jimmy Norman had jumped, but bringing this up now would be like pissing into a hurricane. What they had to do was keep their heads down and wait.

Which wasn't easy. The papers were falling over themselves trying to find new angles for every edition. No one called Tommy, but the Times ran an interview with Norman's pastor, who said Jimmy sang in the choir and was active in the Thanksgiving food drive. There was talk about some ministers organizing a protest march, which would be a first and might just bring the whole thing to an end. Tommy figured a few hundred niggers marching down State Street would probably start a riot once the Polacks heard about it. But when Tanner told him to take a vacation, he was relieved. He hadn't been on his bike since the night of the murder, and he was getting tired of sitting around.

"Disappear for a week," Tanner said. "Spend some time with your wife, maybe get out of town, but don't go too far. We might need you."

Tommy agreed, but staying home just gave him more time to go over the whole thing. He couldn't see what was so special about this kid. Not that Norman deserved to die, but the press wouldn't drop the story. When they couldn't get anyone to ID Norman as the Ike's Grocery robber, things got worse. The Times ran an article with Norman's sister saying her brother only used his knife for cleaning fish he caught off the McKinley pier. In a box next to the story, they ran a picture of Norman in a confirmation gown.

"What's going to happen?" he asked when Moran called.

"Nobody knows, but it doesn't look good for your buddy."

"He's not my buddy," Tommy said. He was getting tired of this routine. "I hardly knew the guy, I told you that. I was just driving down the street and he waved me over. I hadn't said ten words to him before that."

"Sure," Moran said. "Anyway, we can't just walk away now. Every day the sister's got some new picture of Norman to show the papers. This kid's going to be more famous than Henry Aaron by the time she's through. What's more, there's probably going to be an inquest."

Tommy didn't know what that meant, but the word made him feel hollow. He imagined himself standing before an enormous altar with priests in robes asking him questions. "Maybe I should just tell the truth," he said.

"You already did," Moran said. "It's in your report. We got the inspector, the chief, and the D.A. on record supporting you. Rogan goes down now, it ain't just him—it's the department. They even met with the mayor."

"The mayor?" Tommy was impressed. "What did he say?"

"How the fuck should I know?" Moran said. "But no one's real happy, I can tell you that."

"I thought everyone always believed the cops," Tommy said.

"Usually, we don't shoot ourselves in the foot," Moran replied.

Moran was right about that. They'd fucked up badly. The only thing Tommy didn't understand was why they couldn't just put their heads down and push right through it. No matter how bad it was, there must be an end somewhere. But he trusted Charlie's judgment. And he knew enough about the department to know that if you got orders from the top, you followed them and didn't ask a lot of questions. "So when's this inquest going to be?"

"We're not there yet," Moran said, his voice softening, as if he could sense Tommy's fear. Tommy tried to think of some way to hold Charlie in the conversation, but Moran just said, "Hang in there, kid." And the phone went dead.

Tommy hadn't had this much time on his hands since high school, and he didn't know what to do all day. Usually he got up early with Lu and they ate breakfast together, which was OK, though there was still some tension there. He hadn't told her much about what had happened, but on the other hand, she didn't ask. He began to think she really didn't care, which was fine with him. He was happier just keeping quiet and letting it go.

When he got up, Lu would have the coffee going and sometimes there'd be rolls fresh from the bakery. They'd eat and read the paper. They had never talked much about their jobs and they didn't now. Lu wasn't worried like a lot of cop's wives about whether he'd come back. Her father and uncle had been bikemen, and what she had learned from her mother was never to think about what Tommy was doing once he was out the door. There'd be plenty of time to think if something happened. He could have been driving a bus for all the concern she had shown for his safety. But down deep Tommy thought she cared about him, even if she was reluctant to show it. He wasn't the most affectionate husband either, so he really couldn't blame her.

Around seven she'd jump up as if someone had shocked her. "I'm going to miss my bus," she'd say. Then she'd get frantic and start running around the apartment gathering her things, which was kind of a joke between them because for Lu late was being a half hour early. Tommy would play along, saying, "You'd better hurry." And this just made her crazier, so when she'd come out she'd have her coat half on and her slip would be showing, but he could tell she kind of liked it. It was their way of flirting with each other. Then she'd peck him on the forehead and race out, slamming the door behind her.

After Lu left, the house got real quiet. The other tenants in the duplex were elderly and didn't make much noise and the phone never rang. Tommy would pour himself more coffee and finish reading the paper. On a good day, he wouldn't be in it.

After breakfast, Tommy would get cleaned up and go out. Cops were supposed to pass physicals every two years, but Tommy had gotten out of shape since joining the force. Too many donuts, he thought. He had a spare tire around his middle and his wind was lousy. It was a goddamned disgrace for a young guy, especially an ex-athlete. But it wasn't going to go away just thinking about it and the inactivity was killing him, so he started walking.

It was cold as hell in February, and the gray sky just seemed to sit on the chimneys as Tommy walked past the empty houses, but it was better than being cooped up indoors. Tommy tried to make a game out of it by buying a stopwatch and keeping track of how long he walked. He remembered in high school the coaches would make guys wear rubber suits when they wanted them to lose weight, so he loaded himself down with the Big Bennie and his motorcycle gloves and boots. The clothes were heavy as hell, and after four blocks in that outfit, he thought he'd have a heart attack, but it made him feel better to sweat.

He remembered the day he bought the leather coat. You couldn't just go anywhere. They had designated stores, and so he had driven down to Meyer Krome's on the south side and the old man himself had outfitted him. Tommy was so proud that he wore the big coat around the neighborhood until Lu told him he looked like a storm trooper. Now it felt good to wear it on his walks, especially when his wind started improving and he lost a little weight.

Most days, Tommy would head north, up Humboldt and around the bend, where the homes got bigger. He'd walk over the Capitol Drive bridge and into Shorewood for coffee and a sandwich at the Pig 'N Whistle. When he tired of that, he'd go back the other way to Locust, then east over the viaduct past the high school, and up to Plotkin's on Oakland. No one recognized him in the restaurant, which was filled with old Jews playing cards. Tommy thought about showing his shield for a free lunch but decided it might not be a great idea to draw attention to himself right now.

By the time he got home, the Times would be out. So Tommy would read the same stories the Post had run in the morning to see if the world had changed since then, which it never had. Later, he'd drive down to Braun's and shoot the shit with the guys coming off the first shift until dinner. That was his routine, and as long as he stuck to it he did all right.

The only thing that was surprising was that no one seemed that interested in him. Tommy hadn't expected guys to treat him like a hero, but he'd thought they'd take him aside and try to get the real story out of him. It never happened, and now he realized it was because they didn't want to know.

It was the same with Lu. Tommy had figured she was giving him time to get over it, but after a week he brought it up himself. She listened patiently for a while and even asked a few questions. But then she cut him off because there was a movie on television she wanted to watch. Tommy thought maybe she was worried about him, but she said that wasn't it.

At night, Tommy would lie in bed, unable to sleep, looking out the window at the power lines bent under the snow. Sometimes he'd rub up against Lu's big ass and she'd hike up her nightgown and let him do what he wanted, though even sex didn't satisfy him for long and they still didn't talk. He felt he didn't know her anymore, that she didn't care what was going on with him and, increasingly, even that didn't matter. He remembered his mother talking about people "growing apart." Tommy hadn't known what she meant, but now he wondered if that was what was happening with him and Lu.

They had been high school sweethearts. She was a cheerleader and he lettered in two sports, so no one was surprised when they got married after he got back from the service. It was a big wedding at St. Pete's, and half the east side was invited between the two families. They got their pictures in the East Side Chronicle, and it seemed like something that was meant to be. But the trouble between them started early because Lu didn't want him to be a cop. At first Tommy couldn't believe it, didn't take it seriously. It was true that he hadn't discussed his career with her, but he didn't think he had to. Who ever heard of a man asking his wife's permission to take a job? Besides, half her family was on the force. But Lu said that was why. She said she didn't want to spend her life alone, the way her mother had.

That was the last thing she had said about it. Once he was out of the Academy and riding a bike, they never discussed the job, so Tommy figured she had worked it around in her mind and gotten used to the idea. Back then, his uncle could have gotten him an apprenticeship at Maynard Steel. But Tommy had always looked up to coppers in the neighborhood. Still, no one ever got shot carrying a lunch pail or punching a clock. It occurred to him now that this might explain the silent treatment his wife was giving him.

After their marriage, Lu had found work as a candy-dipper at Gimbels, which was supposed to be temporary, but as the years went by it got to look pretty permanent. She had always wanted to be a nurse, but they figured they'd have children, so there was no sense in her starting school if she was just going to quit. Later on, she could go back when the kids were older. They took the floor-through on Fratney and started putting away money for a house. On weekends, they'd go out with friends from high school or even take in a movie downtown on Wisconsin Avenue.

But things got tense again when Lu had trouble getting pregnant. The doctor made Tommy jack off into a jar, which wasn't that easy in the cold examining room. Then he poked around inside Lu and said there was nothing wrong, that they both checked out. The doctor had his office at St. Mary's and Tommy noticed a couple of blue babies in bottles behind him on the shelf, but the doctor never said anything about them and Tommy didn't either.

The doctor told them to relax, that nature had a way of taking care of these things. They were young; they had time. But it wasn't all that relaxing with Lu taking her temperature all the time and touching herself down below to see if everything was the way it ought to be. If things were really OK, she ought to be pregnant, Tommy figured, and he began to feel he was under the gun, like everyone really thought there was something the matter with him. His mother-in-law didn't make things easier when she told him he should wear boxers and take warm baths twice a week.

"Where'd she get her degree?" Tommy grumbled, but he had to admit changing his underwear couldn't do any harm, so he went down to Penney's and bought a dozen pair. A year went by and nothing happened, then another year. Now it was five, and Tommy couldn't remember the last time either of them had mentioned having a family. They'd stopped setting money aside because there didn't seem to be much point in it, and now they lived from paycheck to paycheck.

Even if they didn't talk, Tommy knew the whole thing bothered Lu and his heart went out to her, though it was hard for him to show it. When he saw her sitting hunched over her crochet at night, he would remember that she had only taken the classes in the first place so she could make booties for her babies. He would put his hand on her shoulder, or stroke her neck, but this seemed to make her uncomfortable. And then they didn't touch each other at all. And he didn't know what had happened or how to stop it.

Yet when he asked her outright, Lu said she was fine, that it was Tommy who was upset, and she was right about that. The waiting was killing him, especially since he didn't really know what he was waiting for. No one had said whether there'd be any action against him, though if Rogan was charged with murder, he'd be an accessory. But he was still on the force, even if they hadn't told him when he could get back on his bike. He got paid every two weeks like all the other guys, but he didn't do anything and this made him feel as if he didn't really exist, except on paper.

One night the phone rang late and Tommy went for it fast, not wanting to wake Lu. At first he just heard raspy breathing, then John Rogan's voice was in his ear. "How you doing there, Partner?" Rogan said.

"Hanging in," Tommy replied. "How about you?"

There was a long pause. "There are people in this town who'd like my sorry ass," Rogan said. "You ain't going to help them get it, are you?"

Tommy felt his chest tighten involuntarily. He didn't even like this guy calling him Partner. They'd had a fucking cigarette together and then Rogan had killed a kid. That was it. He didn't want the other man depending on him. "Why'd you have to shoot the goddamned kid, John?" he asked at last, knowing there was no point to the question.

Rogan sighed. "I had no choice, you know that. You were there. It's not like I'm popping kids all the time or anything. I ain't had my gun out of my holster five times since I've been on the force."

Tommy knew this wasn't true. Rogan was a hothead. Like a lot of the little guys on the force, he had to show how tough he was all the time by pushing someone else around. When he wasn't using his gun, he was doing it by fucking someone else's wife. But knowing this didn't change the fact that Tommy still felt sympathy for the other man. When he thought back to that night, he remembered the aching cold and the smell of smoke in the air, but that was all. He had no clear picture of Rogan before the shooting. No matter how much of an asshole Rogan was, Tommy couldn't say with any certainty that he was lying. The department higher-ups wanted everyone to think Rogan was just a bad apple, out of control, but the truth was more disturbing than that. It could have happened to a lot of guys on the force, maybe even Tommy. Rogan had pulled the trigger, but there was no point in pretending he was some kind of animal. He was just farther out than the rest of them.

"Why don't you just say you were holding the gun wrong, that you had your finger on the trigger instead of wrapped around the butt, and when you went to hit the kid it went off."

"Who'd believe me now?" Rogan asked. He sounded amused.

"Why not?" Tommy said, getting excited. "Maybe you'd get off with a suspension like that guy a few years back. What'd he do, shoot into a crowd in a bar? That's worse, a lot worse."

"You don't get it, do you?" Rogan said. "That just isn't possible. It's too late. No one cares about the truth anymore. Lathrop's on me like a rash. The chief too. They're trying to figure a way to fix the inquest, you know, get a good panel, one that'll believe us. So that's the point. As long as you stick to the story, we're OK. You're the only one really saw what happened out there, and they'll always take the word of a cop over a bunch of niggers." He hesitated. "So that's why I'm asking if you're with me, Partner."

Tommy heard Rogan breathing again, a slight wheeze in his voice, as if he were an old man. Outside a snowplow went by on the deserted street, leaving a delicate path in its wake. Tommy began to shiver, but he didn't know why. Why should this little shit scare him? It didn't make sense. But Rogan had something Tommy didn't, and Tommy had seen it in the street that night with Jimmy Norman lying dead on the ground between them. Rogan didn't give a shit. He'd do what he had to do to protect himself and he wouldn't look back. "If it was him or me, I'd give it to him in a minute," he'd say. And while he was doing it, Tommy would be thinking things over. That was the problem and that was what scared him now.

"Are you with me?" Rogan repeated, and this time Tommy heard menace in his voice. But it wasn't just Rogan that scared him—it was all of them, Moran and Martin and Lathrop and the Norman family, the whole damned situation. Then he felt anger rising inside him. Why should Rogan be calling him in the middle of the night putting him up against it? What the hell had he ever done? But anger was hard for Tommy and always had been. He remembered being a head taller than anyone else in the neighborhood and his mother telling him to go easy because he was so much bigger. His size was a responsibility, she had said, something God had given him, and he had to be careful with it. And so he had always held back, even when the other kids taunted him or threw things.

Now when he spoke, his voice was low, resigned. "Sure, I'm with you," he said. "Where else would I be? I'm in it too."

Four

The autopsy report was released on February 13. After examining the powder burns on Jimmy Norman's coat and neck, the county medical examiner said Rogan's gun had been only a few inches away when he fired, perhaps as close as one inch. The inquest was scheduled to start the next day, Valentine's Day.

"Do I need a lawyer?" Tommy asked Moran.

"What for?" the detective replied. "You didn't shoot anyone. Might not be a bad idea for Rogan, though."

But as it turned out, the inquest was anticlimactic. Although the mayor had announced that the case would be tried by a "blue ribbon jury" of civic leaders, the jury turned out to be a bunch of ward-heelers and downtown businessmen friendly to the administration. And Lathrop managed to discredit the testimony of anyone hostile to the department. Sitting in the hearing room, Tommy had the same strange feeling he had experienced listening to Chief Martin talk to the press—that what he had seen hadn't really happened, and that this version simply made more sense and therefore must be true.

Tommy knew even as the judge was giving the jury instructions that Rogan was in the clear. They were out for only half an hour, and when they announced that Norman's death was a justifiable homicide, there was some grumbling from the back of the room, where the family was seated, but less than Tommy expected. The police department was like a large boulder rolling down a mountain and it was impossible to stand in its way without being crushed. Apparently, the Normans realized that, but Tommy was surprised at the ease of the whole thing, especially considering the way Norman's sister had come on with the press.

As he left the room Tommy felt the tension in his shoulders and shrugged to relieve it. It had been a tough couple of weeks. He had begun to think his whole life would be ruined because he stopped to have a cigarette one night with a head case, but now it was over and he could forget all about Rogan and Jimmy Norman. He even thought he had learned what was really important in life. He was going to go home and try to work things out with Lu and then move on as if none of this had ever happened.

Only it wasn't over. Later, Tommy would think of the inquest as being only the beginning, the shooting itself having no reality at all, being part of his imagination, his dreams, his nightmares. Two days after Rogan was exonerated by the coroner's jury, Norman's minister called a prayer meeting at the New Zion A.M.E. church and five hundred people showed up to protest, including an assemblyman who was running for district attorney. Something called the Meeting for Social Advancement pulled in four hundred more, and a minister at another church was planning a march on MacArthur Square to demand that Rogan be fired.

The march got the chief's attention, but surprisingly, Martin seemed to be all for it, as if he didn't understand that he was the one being attacked. Though he didn't criticize Rogan, the papers had the chief down there planning parade routes with the ministers and promising police protection. Tommy figured they'd need it once the Polacks heard what was going on, but the only people who came out against the march were a few ministers who wanted everyone to stay home and pray. Tommy knew praying wasn't likely to satisfy anyone, but he figured it didn't have much to do with him until he went down to the station to pull his shift and they told him to go home. When he asked what was going on, Moran came out to calm him down.

"I'm calm enough," he told the detective. "I just want to know what's happening."

"The chief thinks you should stay away until all this dies down, " Moran said. "Don't forget, Lathrop has to get re-elected, and so does the mayor."

"It'd die down a lot quicker if the chief wasn't going to all these goddamned prayer meetings," Tommy said. "Anyway, what's that got to do with me? I did what I was told."

Moran put his arm around Tommy. "I know you did," he said. "The chief and Lathrop know it too. They just figure the whole damned city could go up if a couple thousand niggers start marching to MacArthur Square."

"Martin's leading the way," Tommy protested. "I read in the paper he's planning the fucking parade route, for Christ's sake."

Moran shook his head patiently, as if Tommy were a child. "What's he supposed to do? He can't stop a parade. Take my word, this'll blow over just like the inquest. Give it some time, but meanwhile stay away, for your own sake."

Moran's tone made Tommy nervous. "What are you talking about, Charlie?" he asked plaintively. "I've been a team player on this; I did everything you told me to. I stayed with Rogan's story because you said it was too late to change anything. I went along with you and the chief and the D.A. So what's this 'my own sake' shit? Are you threatening me?"

"Relax," Moran said and wrapped a long arm around Tommy's shoulder. "All I'm saying is go home and stay there until you get a call."

"When's this call going to come?"

"You expect me to predict the future? It'll come. Just do what I'm telling you to do."

In the end, Tommy agreed to stay away from the station because he had no choice, but he couldn't relax. There was too much going on. There were prayer meetings twice a week now, and Norman's old man had come up from Louisiana to sue the city for wrongful death, saying the coppers had covered up Jimmy's murder.

With nothing else to do, Tommy started walking again, but after the coverage the inquest had received in the papers and on television, everyone in Plotkin's knew who he was and he no longer enjoyed anonymity in the neighborhood.

February turned to March and he still hadn't been called back. It was harder being inactive now that it was warmer. Tommy would stand at the window watching the wind blow the trees around and think it was what life was doing to him. At night he was so restless that Lu began sleeping on the couch, and when he'd wake up she'd already be gone without having said good-bye.

One night she told him she was going to move in with her sister, that she thought it'd be better for a while. Tommy remembered how after the inquest he had promised himself to work things out with her; somehow he had never found the right time to say whatever it was he was going to say and now he didn't know what had happened. Whatever it was, it seemed to be all over his life. Without meaning to, he had fucked up again. He wanted to do something dramatic, hold on to her knees and beg her to stay. He wanted to plead with her, ask her to give him another chance, to believe in him. He even had the feeling she wanted him to do this, but something got in his way, as it always did. In the end, he stood proud and silent, next to the refrigerator with his hand grasping the door so Lu wouldn't see his fingers shaking. "Up to you," he said.

"You haven't said anything in a week," she said, giving him an opening.

Tommy looked at her standing there in her pink pedal pushers and felt his heart do something. He wished she could see in his eyes what he wasn't able to tell her. "Kind of hard to talk to yourself," he muttered.

Lu dropped her eyes to the linoleum and was silent. "Well, you know where I'll be then," she said at last.

"Don't go unless you're not coming back," Tommy said, not knowing why he'd said it because it wasn't in him to talk tough like that, especially to a woman, especially to Lu.

"Have it your way," Lu said, her voice sharp in the small, drab room. And that was it. Even though Tommy tried to call later and apologize, the damage was done. She wouldn't come to the phone, and after a few days her sister said it would probably be better if he stopped calling for a while.

What made it all worse was that the headaches and dreams returned with a greater intensity than before. Jimmy Norman would be standing there, his mouth open and his right hand extended, like he wanted to shake. Then he'd be on the ground with blood all over the place and these gigantic shoes on his feet. Tommy wanted to yell "Stop!"—that it wasn't that way at all, but in the dream he couldn't talk and Rogan wasn't around. Up at three in the morning covered with sweat, Tommy was afraid to close his eyes again for fear the dream would return.

And because he didn't sleep well, Tommy was too exhausted to continue walking. Instead, he started going to Braun's earlier in the day. Sometimes he'd arrive right after breakfast and help George open. Now his gut was twice as big as before, and without the routine of the shift to keep him straight everything seemed to run together. One night he awoke at four to find he'd passed out behind the bar and George had just left him lying there.

The only good thing was that the ministers were so busy fighting over who was in charge that they almost forgot about the march. The day that had been announced came and went and Tommy figured that was just what Martin had planned. Then Norman's father passed out on the witness stand, which got him a six-month delay. Time was working against the family because no matter what had happened people tended to forget after a while. The papers were hinting that the old man was a psycho and the latest Meeting for Social Advancement had only drawn fifteen people.

Tommy finally got called back the third week of March, and though he was put on a checkerbike and couldn't ride solo, even traffic patrol was better than sitting at home. The other guys kept their distance at roll call, but this didn't bother him. You couldn't really blame them for not knowing what to make of it all; he didn't know himself. But a month went by and nothing changed. At Braun's everything would just stop when he walked in and there'd be heavy traffic at the pinball machines. After a while, Tommy stopped going to the bar. He had a bottle at home; he didn't need other people around to get pissed up. He told himself it wasn't his problem, but the fact was he was lonely.

One afternoon when he couldn't remember having slept or awakened, Tommy decided to go to church. He'd never been big on mass and had only gone because Lu insisted. But St. Mary's was just down the block, and even though it was a Polack church he walked over thinking he'd just sit and try to collect his thoughts. Without knowing exactly how it happened, he found himself in the confessional spilling everything to the priest. It went on fifteen minutes before he started thinking he was wasting the father's time, even though that's what the priests were there for.

"Are you truly sorry for all you've done?' the priest asked when Tommy stopped talking.

"Yes, Father," Tommy said. And it was true, he was. He said his Our Fathers and Hail Marys and left the church feeling a little lighter. But the dreams came back and now Tommy felt desperate, out of control. He even thought about seeing a headshrinker the Department had brought in, but Tommy doubted that would do him any good. He knew what was wrong, and he couldn't do a damned thing about it.

In April, Lu's lawyer had Tommy served at work in front of everyone, and he decided to move out of the flat. They'd only gotten it because they were going to have kids, but now the place seemed too big; walking from room to room following the dust devils just made Tommy lonelier. He took an efficiency above a dry cleaner on Holton and waited for the other shoe to drop.

It didn't take long. He was sitting in a tavern on Concordia minding his own business when some drunk asked him if he'd killed any niggers lately. Tommy tried to laugh it off. It was kind of funny when you thought about it. If the guy was really sympathetic with the Normans he wouldn't call them niggers. And if he wasn't, why should he be on Tommy's back? "Let me buy you a beer," Tommy said.

But the guy wouldn't back off, and Tommy finally got him in a head-lock, nothing violent, just thinking he'd turn the guy around and push him away. The next thing Tommy knew he was under a pile and women were screaming. Then the place was full of cops and Tommy had teeth marks on his fist, even though he couldn't remember hitting anyone.

It turned out the teeth belonged to one of the coppers and Tommy had put him on the floor. When they backed him up against the wall, they found the Smith and Wesson Airweight clipped to the back of his belt. "I'm a cop," Tommy said. "I've got to carry. Anyway, I never pulled the damned gun."

They booked him for resisting arrest, which was crazy because the cops had probably saved Tommy's life, coming when they had. But he couldn't make bail so they put him in the drunk tank overnight, which was where Moran found him in the morning.

"Do I look like I'm in shape to take on five cops?" Tommy palmed his gut. "Get serious, Charlie. It was a setup."

"Someone hold a gun to your head and make you go to that bar?" Moran's voice was quiet, reflective. He sounded kind of like the priest. "You're embarrassing the Department, Tommy."

"I told you, I was just sitting there and this guy started in on me about killing niggers," Tommy said.

Moran nodded. "OK, tell me if I've got this right. These coppers who don't know you told this guy to go into the tavern and pick a fight with you so that they could come and book you for resisting? Is that it, Tommy? Am I right so far?"

It didn't sound too believable the way Moran said it, but Tommy was convinced of his own innocence. "I didn't do nothing," he said stubbornly.

Moran nodded. "It's always someone else, aina? You're the most inno-cent guy I've ever known to get into so much trouble."

No one was interested in prosecuting a cop and the charges were dis-missed, but a week later Tommy got a letter saying he was being dropped from the force for public drunkenness. He had the right to appeal, the letter said. Tommy thought this was kind of like kicking a priest out of the church for praying, but Moran wasn't sympathetic.

"You brought it on yourself," he said. "I told you to keep your nose clean."

Tommy was getting tired of the other man's moralizing when they were supposed to be friends from the neighborhood. "Come on," he said. "They wanted to get me. I'm practically killed in that bar and they book me for resisting. Now it's this."

"Sorry, kid," Moran said. "There's nothing I can do. Appeal, if you want to."

Tommy knew this would be a waste of time, and he'd had enough of hearings. It was even kind of a relief to have it over. The only thing that haunted him was the feeling that something of value was being taken away from him. He'd wanted to be a copper since he was a kid—and not just a patrolman but a bikeman. He'd made it and was doing all right and now it was all gone because of Rogan and his goddamned temper. Tommy thought he could have taken losing Lu if he still had the job, but seeing both of them disappear was too much. He felt hollow inside, as if he didn't know who he was anymore. He was afraid to look in the mirror, afraid of what he'd see there.

He moved again, this time up to the east side, and took a job as a security guard at a bank in Shorewood, where no one knew him. He had never imagined he'd end up as a rent-a-cop, but nothing was going according to plan. The job was easy and paid pretty well and that was all he asked. The divorce was final in August, and while the dreams hadn't stopped completely, Tommy at least had his drinking under control. This wasn't the life he had wanted, but things were better.

In November, a story in the Times said Rogan was going up on conduct unbecoming an officer. Quit or he was out, Tommy guessed. Rogan had been "associating" with a married woman. This was perfect, Tommy thought. They'd gotten him for drinking and Rogan for screwing. The next thing you knew Martin wold be making recruiting speeches to the Boy Scouts.

He called Rogan to commiserate, but to his surprise, the other man wasn't upset. "I'm getting the hell out of here," Rogan said. "After what happened, I got no future in Milwaukee. I'm lucky I stayed out of jail."

"Where are you headed?" For a moment, Tommy hoped Rogan would take him along. Any place would be better than here.

"I've got a friend in Colorado owns some trucks."

"You're going to be a truck driver?"

"Why not? Maybe I'll meet a better class of people."

Tommy laughed and wished Rogan luck. Rogan said he'd need it, then his voice got hoarse. "I'll never forget what you did for me back there,

Tom. You didn't even know me, not really. You could have let me hang and I wouldn't have blamed you. But you were a stand-up guy. You didn't deserve what happened."

It helped to hear someone else say it, and Tommy felt himself tear up with emotion. "No one deserves what happens," he said, surprising himself because he hadn't known that was how he really felt. But it was true. "Even that nigger kid. He didn't deserve to get wasted. He was just out there and we were too. The way I see it, we're all three down the toilet because of what happened. Moran and Martin and Lathrop and them were acting like they were behind us. But it wasn't about us at all. The whole goddamned thing was about covering their asses. Once that was done we just embarrassed them by still being around."

Rogan didn't say anything, and Tommy thought he heard a train whistle in the background. Then he said, "I'm not that deep a thinker, but I'll tell you something I haven't told anyone else. Every week, sometimes more often, I'll get an envelope with money in it. Sometimes it'll be just a few dollar bills, sometimes a five. Once I got a ten. No notes—they never write anything—but I know what they're saying. Swear to God, I feel like the whole goddamned city was there with us that night, helping me pull the trigger on that kid."

"Sonofabitch," Tommy said. "What do you do with it? The money, I mean?"

"Keep it," Rogan said. "What else? Goddamn right. I can use it where I'm going. Now you take care of yourself, Partner."

Discovery

Five

Bob Joseph sat reading his notes from the morning and drinking coffee. It was a Sunday in August, the sun was shining, and through the open window Bob thought he could smell the lake. It would be a good day for sailing. No one was in the Times newsroom who didn't have to be, but Bob wasn't as comfortable anywhere else. As a child, he had gone with his grandfather to the old Das Neue Licht office after church to get the first papers off the press. It was on Twentieth and Vliet above an office supplies store, and though it wasn't required of him, the old man had made it a ritual that, for unknown reasons, included his grandson. First, they'd stop at a German bakery to get kugel for the pressmen. Then Heinz Jozef would walk around the large dusty room, picking up papers and putting them down, chewing an unlit Garcia y Vega while he waited. After reading the new edition, he'd talk to the Linotype operators and then they'd all have a glass of schnapps.

From his desk, Bob counted three people moving slowly at the other end of the vast room and one copyeditor at his desk, fewer than used to be at the Neues Licht but there was less to do now, fewer mechanical tasks anyway. He remembered his grandfather saying a good newspaperman never stopped working. When you're riding the bus or just going for a walk, keep your eyes open and look around, he'd say. You'll notice things, and after a while, you never know quite how, they'll end up in a story and make it better.

Bob smiled at the memory, but his grandfather was from the old school. He'd arrived in Milwaukee in 1910, when competition was hot among the eight German papers in town, and even after World War I had sent most of them into oblivion, Heinz Jozef had hung on, writing his column, attacking Hitler, and even reviewing movies. The Kino was closed now too, and except for the occasional art film that made its way to the Downer, so was the thriving German culture that had characterized the city. You could still get Wiener schnitzel in Milwaukee, but that was all. And the only tangible reminder Bob had of his grandfather was a framed picture of the old man in an overcoat and hat proudly holding a paper headlined ALLIES LIBERATE DEATH CAMPS.

Bob missed his grandfather, and not just for personal reasons. He missed what he had represented. There was no one like him on the staff of the Times, including Bob. They had all become professional, which meant journalism was no longer a way of life, just part of it. A job, not a calling. They came and went on time and carried attaché cases. No one smoked and few of the younger reporters drank anything stronger than mineral water. Coming in on Sunday mornings was a way to stay connected not only to a happier time but to a different kind of journalism. Now he stretched and looked at the notes spread out on the desk like bits of colored cloth. He was covering the campaign of a good-looking young Pole named Andrew Hedig who was making a mayoral run and he had been working since eight o'clock trying to put a story together.

In a way it was a waste of time because no one believed Emil Mueller could be beaten. He'd been in office twenty years, longer than any sitting mayor in the country, and everyone except the most rabid liberals admitted he'd done a lot for the city. But in Milwaukee any Polish candidate was news, so Bob felt obliged to pay attention. Someone was going to replace Mueller eventually, and besides, Bob liked Hedig, liked the way he handled himself.

Still, there wasn't going to be much interest in the election in the middle of the summer, and Bob knew the city editor wouldn't give him much space. He went through Hedig's bio again anyway; maybe something would jump out at him, an angle he had missed before. The candidate's father was a machinist at Harnishfaeger, and the family lived in a bungalow in Bay View, where Hedig had grown up. After making all-state as a third baseman, Hedig had gotten a tryout with the Braves and spent a summer in the deep minors before graduating from Lawrence in Appleton, home of Joe McCarthy. Someone had said Hedig had trained for the priesthood too, but there was nothing in the file.

After Lawrence, Hedig went to Yale Law School, served in the Peace Corps, and worked on a congressional staff for a year before coming home to clerk for a federal judge. He had been offered a job by one of the downtown law firms that traditionally hired graduates of Ivy League law schools, but here Hedig's career path diverged from other young men in similar circumstances. He chose to enter politics, but not on the national level, passing up a run at a congressional seat. Instead, he ran for the State Senate, where he surprised everyone by working diligently and rising to become chairman of joint finance before he was thirty. The file was full of speculative stories about Hedig running for governor or Congress or accepting some big job in Washington, but he had never left Wisconsin.

This aroused general suspicion among the press, with the deep thinkers assuming Hedig had skeletons in his closet that wouldn't withstand national scrutiny, but nothing had turned up so far. Wisconsin, like other provincial areas, was hurt and disappointed when its native sons left to try their luck in the East. Yet those who stayed labored under the general assumption that they weren't good enough to succeed anywhere else. Accordingly, no one accepted at face value Andrew Hedig's claim that he wasn't ambitious and liked his life and hometown.

Yet Bob could see it. The life Andrew Hedig had made looked pretty attractive to him. A big house, money, a pretty wife. Many people would be satisfied with less. Still, it was hard to accept the idea that someone with so much talent would be satisfied with being a wheel in Madison, and now Hedig had given the skeptics satisfaction. At forty-six he was running for mayor, a little long in the tooth but still a kid compared to Mueller, who had gone to the executive cut when Hedig was still in high school.

And running hard. Even if no one gave him a chance, Hedig traveled with a full complement of reporters and television cameras. Tall and slim, with blond hair that drooped attractively over his forehead, Hedig was more photogenic than any candidate in recent memory, which wasn't saying much, considering some of the losers the liberals had offered up in past elections. Only a nose that looked like a ski slope stopped Hedig from being pretty. His campaign had floated a story suggesting he'd broken it playing ball, but from the blurred high school photos they had, it looked to Bob like Hedig had been born with impressive equipment up front.

Not that it mattered. Already one of the television stations had run a special about "The Polish Roosevelt," and Hedig's campaign had printed up bumper stickers saying "It's Time" in Polish. There would be more once the campaign heated up.

Still, Hedig had problems. The old guard resented him because he hadn't stood in line long enough, and the liberals distrusted him because he wore five-hundred-dollar suits and smoked Cuban cigars. What was most appealing—and unlikely—though, was the assertion that he got up early every morning to read serious literature before heading off for the Senate. It had been years since Bob had looked at any poetry, but he liked the idea of a mayor who knew something about Modernism. In Milwaukee, of course, such a thing was more likely to turn voters against than for you, but Bob had the feeling that if anyone could make it work, Hedig could. Besides, Milwaukee had changed. The factories were closing down and most of the breweries had been bought by out-of-town interests. It was still a shot-and-a-beer town, but new people were moving in, people brought by the university or business, people who didn't know much about the city's ethnic rivalries and didn't care.

One place Hedig did seem to have some active supporters was in the black community, which was why they had all been in church this morning. The candidate had shared the pulpit of a small B.M.E. on 8th Street, and Bob was impressed with the way he moved among the people without apparent self-consciousness. He made a few self-deprecatory remarks and invoked the memory of Martin Luther King, Jr., before deferring to the minister. Then instead of leaving, as most politicians would, Hedig stayed for both the service and the coffee hour.

On other campaign stops Hedig had seemed awkward and ill at ease, but when his was the only white face in the crowd he was miraculously transformed into a relaxed, gregarious man who charmed the black parishioners after the sermon. If Bob hadn't been there, he would have thought the whole thing was staged, but this was real, though he didn't really understand it. Hedig had grown up around racists on the south side and even his years in the civil rights movement didn't explain it. There were plenty of liberals who said the right things but were uncomfortable around blacks. What was confusing was, why, if Hedig could do this well here, it seemed so hard for him to warm up at plant gates? It was a mystery, but not very important since black support wasn't the key to this election.

Mueller had never had any black supporters and hadn't wanted any because the fact was that no one, black or white, had ever been able to get much going in the Core. The black wards always elected an alderman, had a representative in Madison, and put a few people on the school board. But most blacks failed to register, and canvassing the dark streets was a daunting task for white candidates. Still, there were a hundred thousand people packed into a few decaying miles of the central city waiting for the right person. The unlikely possibility that Andrew Hedig might actually go after the black community and combine it with an ethnic power base from the south side and some lakeshore liberals was exhilarating.

As they were leaving the church, one of Hedig's aides had invited Bob to a cocktail party, and now he considered stopping by. It bothered him that he liked Hedig; the fact that he found the candidate interesting could compromise him, but he thought he could handle it. There wouldn't be any news at a party, but it would be a chance to meet people involved in the campaign who could serve as sources when things got going. If things got going. The bottom line was that bright and attractive as he might be, Andy Hedig was likely going nowhere. It was just hard to imagine a war-horse like Mueller falling to a wine-drinking liberal from the east side who collected Mission furniture and read French poetry, no matter how good-looking he was.

Which put Bob's mind at ease about the conflict of interest, but he still needed a lead for tomorrow's story. He ran a sheet of paper through his typewriter and stared at it for fifteen minutes. He read through the notes again. Nothing. He was about to leave and go for a walk on the lakefront, when the phone rang.

"I'm not here," he told the switchboard operator. "It's Sunday, for Christ's sake. Take a message."

"I already told him that," the operator said. "He says you'll take his call, that it's important."

"Oh, really?" Joseph said. "Who is it?"

"He says his name is Tommy Paley."

Bob remembered vaguely, though not because he wanted to and not because he thought it was particularly important. Someone had gotten killed, but Paley hadn't done it. A black kid, Bob thought, but they let the cops walk, which was not going to shock the hell out of anyone. That wasn't why Paley stuck in his mind. It was more that, like Hedig, Tommy was pure Milwaukee and reminded him of another time in his life, when he'd been new on the paper. Covering cops and courts was every reporter's apprenticeship, but Bob wasn't nostalgic about it. It was necessary, dirty work, and he'd learned a lot during his time in the Safety Building. Still, he had been glad to get on to the city desk.

He stared at the blinking light on the rotary phone, wondering if he should ignore it. He couldn't recall more than two or three conversations with Tommy Paley, and those were twenty years ago. He remembered his watery blue eyes moving nervously around the room during the inquest and an involuntary twitch in his jaw. The district attorney had kept Paley's testimony until the end, even though he was the only witness to the killing and thus the only one who could attest to his partner's innocence. At the time it had seemed strange, but Bob never followed up. There were always plenty of police stories, and once the jury had handed down its decision, his editors lost interest.

Things became clearer in time when Paley was kicked off the force after a bar brawl. Later on, he had been picked up for shoplifting and did two years in Green Bay for writing bad checks. Small wonder Lathrop hadn't wanted to use him as a character witness; Paley had no character. Not long ago, Bob had noticed a one-inch item in the paper saying Paley had been granted parole, and now he was on the phone. A real prince. It was a great way to wreck a beautiful morning.

"This is Bob Joseph," he said.

There was a thin sibilance on the line, then Paley started talking in a halting voice. "This is Tom Paley," he said. "Ah, you remember me?"

"I remember," Joseph said. "What's on your mind." No point in beating around the bush.

"I been thinking," Paley said. "I'm up here in Manitowoc, you know. I got out of jail a couple months ago, and I'm up here training to be a counselor, you know, counsel people on booze and drugs?"

Blind leading the blind, Joseph thought. He wished Paley would get to the point. Unless this was the point, unless this was a social call. God save him from that. "That's good," he said. "We need counselors."

"Aina," Paley said. "That's a fact. So that's what I'm doing up here."

There was a long silence. Bob waited. He found Paley's halting voice to be as annoying and characteristic as he remembered from their previous conversations. A local writer who considered himself an amateur philologist kept track of what he called "Milwaukeese," words and phrases like "over by" and "aina" that found their way into conversation, and listed them in his column in the morning paper. Yet it wasn't really a dialect but rather a collection of shared neologisms and grammatical errors that some people considered quaint. Bob was about to ask again what Paley wanted when the other man spoke. "Look," he said, "you covered the case back then, you know, the one with me and Rogan, right? I was wondering if you could send me the records, you know, whatever you got."

Rogan had been Paley's partner, the shooter. A bad dude with a sheaf full of sworn complaints against him, Bob remembered. He wondered now why they didn't take him down, how Rogan could have been considered innocent of anything. But Paley's question confused him. "What records? The case never went to trial."

"No, no, I mean the stories you wrote, in the paper. That's what I want."

Great, Bob thought. Shoot what was left of the morning looking for the clip file on a twenty-year-old case. But the edge of anxiety in Paley's voice intrigued him. He would have assumed any feelings would have worn off years ago. What a friend had once called the great psychiatric question presented itself: "Why now?" Why had Tommy Paley called him this morning? What was suddenly so urgent about all this? "What do you want with them?" Bob asked.

"Ah, I've been doing a lot of thinking up here, about back then, I mean," Paley said. "In the training they got here, you talk to all these psychologists, and, tell the truth, I haven't been sleeping too good."

It didn't add up. Paley was training to be a detox counselor and he wanted to read old newspaper stories about a shooting? Except for the stuff about psychologists. "You mean what happened then has been bothering you?" Bob said. He was fishing, but Paley responded immediately and seemed almost grateful for the question.

"That's about it," Paley said. "A lot never came out back then."

Suddenly Bob felt hot. He'd been a reporter long enough to sense when something important was happening. He reached for a notebook and tried to think of questions. It was important to keep Paley talking, but his mind was a blank. "Give me your address," he said, stalling. At least maintain contact. "I'll check the morgue and send you those clips. But I'd like to talk. Can I come up?"

"Ah, that's probably not such a good idea," Paley said. "With the training and all."

"Sure," Bob said. How intense could Paley's training be? But he didn't want to scare him. "I just mean if you want to talk. Like you said, I was there. I covered the case. There aren't that many of us left."

"Right," Paley said. "That's why I called." His voice was tense now, his sentences shorter, skipping it seemed, as if he was looking for an escape. Don't press it, Bob told himself. Blow this and he could disappear for another twenty years. Paley had called him, not some other reporter, and he had done it for a reason, even if Bob didn't know what it was. He had to hold on long enough to find out, but he could only do it by appearing casual.

"Look," Bob said, "I'd like to talk but I'm on deadline for another story." It was a chance. He might lose the guy altogether, but now Paley relaxed.

"Sure," he said. "I understand. Maybe I can write you, though. And you'll send me those stories?"

"No problem," Bob said. "I'll do it today."

But later, when he copied the clips, Bob made an extra set for himself and spent an hour reading what he'd written twenty years ago about the murder of a black kid by two white cops. It was all there: names, dates, photos of Paley and Rogan as young men with dark hair and strong chins. He didn't know what Paley meant about the things that hadn't come out in 1959, but he knew that he had let the story go too easily, that he hadn't pressed his editors for space and time to dig. And he knew why. A dead black kid just wasn't that big a deal, unless someone decided to make it one, and doing that could cost you your career. Who elected you? the old-timers would have said. Where's your soapbox?

Bob had avoided all that by going along and taking the easy way to advancement. Yet looking back, the questions he should have asked were obvious. Why had Rogan and Paley chased the kid four blocks and then shot him? If the kid had a knife, why hadn't he come at the cops in the first place? And there was a discrepancy between the two cops' stories as to where exactly Rogan had been when he fired. What was more, the department couldn't wait to get rid of the two once they had been cleared; both cops were off the force within six months for minor infractions of the city's code. Even the protesting ministers seemed to have given up with alacrity after a few mass meetings to draw attention to themselves. And now Tommy Paley was saying he couldn't sleep because of what had happened in 1959.

By the time Bob left, it was four o'clock, and he no longer felt like a walk. There was still time to drop by Hedig's party, though. Somehow Bob sensed a connection between Hedig and Tommy Paley, though he had no idea what it might be. He thought again of his grandfather saying a good newspaperman was always working. If he hadn't been in the office on a Sunday, he couldn't have taken Paley's call, and who knew if that rummy would have called back? The feeling of sad nostalgia was gone now and Bob's mind was sharp. This party might even be more than a chance to develop contacts. Bob felt like a newspaperman again.

Six

Bob was jogging on the lakefront when he literally ran into Andrew Hedig just north of Kenwood Boulevard. "Sorry," Bob said. "I don't know what the hell I was thinking about." They were on a long, wide stretch of sidewalk that ran uninterrupted for five miles north, from Lake Park into Fox Point. A lot of people used it, but Bob had never collided with anyone before.

As they tried to get out of each other's way, Hedig smiled disarmingly. "Maybe it would be easier if we just ran together for a while?"

Joseph might have thought the meeting was calculated if Hedig hadn't looked so awkward in his cut-off khakis and T-shirt. But it was clear the other man was just trying to be friendly, so Bob nodded and went along, though since Hedig was thinner and faster it was hard to talk and run at the same time. When Bob had been on the high school cross-country team he had enjoyed the training runs in Riverside Park and trips to other schools followed by loud bus rides home with the windows misting over and the smell of sweat in the air. What he liked most then was the anonymity of distance running, no one really understanding what they were doing or why. Bob felt vaguely offended when running gained popularity in the sixties and striped track shoes became a fashion statement.

Still, after his divorce, it seemed necessary to do something, and it could have been anything as long as he could do it alone. He had things he needed to think seriously about without interruption, and he found this was impossible when he was sitting still. One day, without knowing exactly what he was doing, he laced on his old Converse racing flats and walked briskly for an hour early in the morning. When he came home he couldn't remember what he had thought about, but he felt relieved, as if he had passed something internally. The next morning, he walked again, and for two weeks he continued this regimen daily. Then he began jogging at a pace so leisurely it could hardly be distinguished from walking, but Bob noticed the difference in his calves. After six months he had worn the soles of the old shoes thin and bought a new pair, white leather with a red stripe. Slowly, he increased both pace and distance and even entered a few races, though at his speed, Bob could hardly have been said to be racing with anyone, except the women who pushed baby carriages at the back of the pack.

They ran together out to Whitefish Bay and then by mutual consent turned back, but Hedig offered little about himself, especially for a candidate. Perhaps this was hard for him too; for a person in such a public position any degree of openness could be a risk. Of course, Bob's colleagues at the Times would consider empathy for a politician to be an admission of weakness or partisanship and a threat to a reporter's objectivity, but Hedig interested Bob.

When they were back in front of Hedig's house, hands on hips, panting, and walking off the run in a camaraderie of exhaustion, the other man asked, "Do you live around here?"

"A few blocks back." Bob was going to add, "In the low-rent district," but thought better of it, in part because he knew there was nothing to be ashamed of in his background. "I inherited the family mansion," he said. And that was how he thought of it, that he was lucky to have such a house; occasionally he felt guilty for liking it as much as he did.

This seemed to interest Hedig, though he didn't appear to notice Bob's irony. "You've lived here all your life then?" He sounded a little envious, as if getting off the south side had been an enormous effort.

"Most of it. I went to high school here and college in Madison. I've been at the Times forever." Bob had actually made it to New York for a brief period ten years before, but he hadn't liked it. He had felt suffocated and tongue-tied around the bright young reporters from Yale and Columbia, though no one else seemed to notice and he won a prestigious award for a series on gangs in the Bronx. Even after two years, however, he felt like an alien in the newsroom, so he was grateful and surprised when the Times offered him his old job with a good raise. He knew people in Milwaukee tended to take things like leaving personally and had assumed he had burned his bridges by trying to move up in his profession. In fact, if he had gone anywhere less prestigious than New York, returning would have been out of the question. As it was, his editors could brag about stealing an ace reporter from the Daily News. His editors installed Bob as their lead political writer, and Bob figured it was an even trade, though it didn't take a lot of savvy to realize that if he was really a star in New York he probably wouldn't be coming back to Milwaukee.

"It couldn't have been that long. You're still a young man."

"Thanks," Bob said. "I'm forty-four." He didn't need to be flattered by a politician. To change the subject, he said, "Do you remember a cop named Tommy Paley?"

Hedig looked quizzical. "The name's familiar," he said. "Should I?"

Bob shrugged. "He was involved in a big murder case years ago."

"A black man was killed," Hedig said thoughtfully. "I do recall it now. Very unfortunate. Very sad."

Though Hedig seemed truly moved, Bob wished he didn't talk like a Dale Carnegie course manual. "That's the one. Paley's partner killed a kid named Jimmy Norman and the coroner's jury let him off. Supposedly, the kid came at him with a knife; except there was some disagreement about that."

"Disagreement?" Hedig said now, interested.

"The family said it wasn't the kid's knife, said he was left-handed anyway and the knife was in his right hand. It was in all the papers at the time, but Paley backed up the shooter on the story and that was all there was to it. There weren't any other witnesses, at least none who wanted to talk."

Hedig nodded, listening. His face was serious as he wiped his forehead with his sleeve. "That's how it would go, I guess," he said. "People were inclined to believe the police in any disputed case."

"It hasn't changed that much," Bob said.

Hedig nodded. Then he said, "I was out of the town at the time. In law school, I believe. I'd have to check." Bob looked away to hide his irritation. He was sure Hedig knew all about Paley, though he pretended to have only vague memories of the case. Even if he was away, this was part of the liberal legacy of the city. Someone would have sent him clips or he might have been briefed later, so why act mysterious? It was as if he were at a deposition, but Bob knew he was partially at fault. The guy had only asked him to go running and here he was being interviewed. You could hardly blame Hedig for thinking he'd have to account for everything. It had to be second nature for a politician to cover up, to feel that nothing would be forgiven by the press, not the slightest memory lapse or misstatement. No wonder he was careful.

"I'm sorry," Bob said. "I didn't mean to give you the third degree."

Hedig smiled again, as if he knew exactly what Bob was doing but appreciated his apology anyway. "It's all right," he said. "It's an interesting situation. I'm glad to be reminded of it." He glanced at an upstairs window of his house, as if someone were there, but Bob didn't see anything and Hedig didn't move. There had been rumors about his private life, about problems in his marriage, but Bob hadn't attached much importance to them. There were always stories during a campaign. Besides, the gossip wasn't about the candidate, but rather concerned his wife, who had supposedly spent time in the kind of private hospital whose patients were all rich or related to someone important. No one could say where this hospital was or why Sarah Hedig had gone there, if indeed she had, and in time the story died a natural death.

And when Bob met her at the cocktail party, she seemed fine, lively and attractive, like her husband. She was a writer, or as she said, trying to be one, which made Bob like her. Writing was enough to push anyone over the line, an occupational hazard. Hedig brought him back to the point. "Yes," he said with certainty. "I was out of town then."

You were at Yale, Bob thought, and now you're back. There was absolutely no reason this should have annoyed him, but it did. It wasn't jealousy, or not only that. But something about Hedig got to Bob, whether it was the self-conscious smile, the big house, or something more subtle. Maybe his lack of ambivalence about it all. Andrew Hedig seemed to be very pleased with himself, with his life, without being cocky. He was the first Yalie Bob had ever met who didn't find an excuse to mention it in the first fifteen minutes of conversation. His manner suggested that he might have been anywhere, that what mattered was Hedig, not Yale. The idea that he might actually feel this way seemed too incredible to be true so Bob didn't pursue it. "The reason I asked," he said, "is that Paley called me the other day."

Hedig looked interested. "Is he a friend of yours?"

"Not even an acquaintance. I might have talked to him two or three times during the inquest." The question made Bob defensive, but he reminded himself that Hedig wasn't accusing him of anything. Hedig had the same pleasant, inquisitive expression on his face as before. "He wanted the clips on the case. I just thought maybe you'd know what it was all about."

Hedig looked at him closely and this made Bob feel stupid. What right did he have to imply that Hedig knew anything about a renegade cop with a drinking problem? He didn't even believe it himself, but now the other man was on guard. They might be standing there dripping sweat in shorts and running shoes, but they were on the record and they both knew it. Hedig could go off, which would indicate that he did know something, or play dumb, or he could do neither, which is what he did. He extended his hand. "What you say is very interesting, Bob. We'll have to talk about it in greater depth another time. Unfortunately, I have a meeting in ten minutes."

Bob shook Hedig's hand with grudging admiration. It was as if he'd arranged to be called on cue. And he had lost whatever advantage surprise would have given him. If Bob had hit a nerve, Hedig hadn't revealed anything.

Back at the office there was an envelope postmarked Manitowoc waiting. Inside, there was a letter from Paley:

Dear Mr. Joseph,

Thanks for sending me those articles. Everything is pretty much the way I remember, except it's
time I started getting honest with myself. I know
this happened twenty years ago, but then that's
how long I've carried it around inside. It's never
too late to stop lying. I'll call you when I can.

Tom Paley

Out of habit, Bob went down to the morgue and checked Hedig's file, but the candidate had told the truth. He had graduated from Yale in 1960, so he would have been away in 1959. Still, he had been involved in the civil rights movement when he was in Washington working for the congressman. Bob even thought he remembered Hedig being in Selma. It just didn't make sense that he wouldn't have known what was going on in his own hometown, especially since the ministers' marches and prayer meetings amounted to the first civil rights protests in Milwaukee's history. Hedig must have been aware of that, so why hadn't he said so? Bob remembered how easily the candidate had moved among the congregants at the church service, the fact that he seemed more at ease with blacks than at plant gates. Andrew Hedig was a complicated man, but he revealed little about himself even when he was pressed.

Bob checked Mueller's file too, but the mayor had been in Madison. Mueller had been elected in 1960 and immediately appointed Tanner chief

of police. Was it a coincidence that he and the chief played baseball together at West Division? Milwaukee was a small town in many ways. So far
all he had were some intriguing bits and pieces, but no solid leads on either
candidate.

He made copies of everything and filed them. It was only August.
There would be many questions to ask between now and the election, especially when Paley started talking for publication.

Seven

Andrew Hedig was reading Tolstoy at his large desk in the front study facing Lake Michigan. It was seven o'clock, the best part of the day, before the phone started ringing and life became crowded with things he wished he didn't care about. It was true, as Bob Joseph had heard, that he read for an hour every morning, but not, as Joseph thought, only poetry. It had started that way when Hedig met a young professor at a Georgetown party who talked passionately about assonance and dissonance. Andy had been so impressed by the professor's engagement with his subject that he had asked for a reading list and over time worked his way through the Cavalier poets and the Romantics before running into a wall with the Victorians, whose optimism he found unbelievable and, worse, boring. He shifted to the Continental writers, reading Baudelaire and Pushkin, but felt he was missing too much by reading in translation. Fiction depended less on music and imagery, or so Andy thought until he read Flaubert. Still, he stayed with it through Stendahl and Maupassant, then moved on to the Russians, though at an hour a day his pace was slow.

Now Prince Andrei had been sent to order Tushin to fall back: "... he was conscious of a nervous tremor running down his spine. But the mere thought of being afraid roused his courage again. 'I cannot be afraid,' he said to himself ..."

Andy sat back, moved by the passage. That was how it was, he thought, mildly amused that Tolstoy had again managed to identify an area of similarity between his life and the Prince's. You couldn't help being afraid, but giving into it was fatal. When you were afraid was the very time you had to fight hardest. He turned back to the novel but was interrupted by a knock and his wife walking into the room.

The bed had been empty on her side when Hedig awoke, and Sarah hadn't been in the house. "Out for a walk?" he asked.

Sarah nodded. "I went to the Pavilion for coffee, but I'm going to have to find a new place. Three people came up and talked to me this morning. I even saw that reporter you ran with the other day."

"Bob Joseph? Did you talk to him?" Joseph seemed to be turning up everywhere, and Andy was experienced enough to suspect coincidences.

"He was with some girl," Sarah said. Then she grimaced. "Listen to me. I mean he was with a woman. She was at least thirty-five. I don't think he even knew I was there."

Andy doubted this, but he was sympathetic. Sarah wasn't running for anything, yet inevitably the campaign had forced her to change her life in certain ways. Though she hadn't had a paying job since they were married, her work mattered to her. She had started out writing children's books for a friend who owned a small publishing house and was working on a novel, but she was having trouble. She had a study as big as her husband's on the other side of the house, but Sarah couldn't work there. Too many distractions. So she had developed the habit of taking her typewriter to the Pavilion, a stately building constructed by some visionary thirty years before and then left to be used almost exclusively by pensioners and park employees on their breaks. There was a snack bar and an unobstructed view of the lake, and except for occasional shouts from the pinochle game in the corner, it was quiet and deserted.

Unfortunately, the Times's Sunday magazine had run an article calling the Pavilion one of the city's unknown treasures and illustrated it with a picture of Sarah. Now curiosity seekers filled the small tables and Sarah felt invaded. Andy didn't understand what was so difficult about sitting in a room and writing, especially since Sarah talked about it so passionately, but he knew he didn't need to understand or question it, so he didn't. "Where will you go?" he asked. "I assume working here is out of the question."

Sarah smiled at his sarcasm. "You're right about that," she said. She thought for a moment, her small, pretty face tense with concentration. "Maybe a condo, you know, for a studio. You've got an office, why shouldn't I?"

Hedig shrugged. "No reason I can think of."

"It'd be deductible."

"If you make any money," Hedig said reasonably.

Sarah made a face at him. "Doesn't matter. I'll take it as a business loss. I can read up on my investments there." She looked pleased with herself, and Andy marveled again at the effect being born with money had had on his wife. She never considered the possibility that someday she might have to do something she didn't want to do. For her, the only problem was decoding her desires from life's elaborate grid and then acting. Yet despite the difference in their backgrounds, Andy didn't think of his wife as spoiled but envied her self-confidence.

"It's worth a try," he said now. "Give Jack Comstock a call. He owns a building down on Prospect. I don't know if it has a lake view, though."

"Got to have that," Sarah said, and Hedig didn't disagree, though he'd been partly joking. He never argued with Sarah, and when she was mad she said it was because he didn't care enough. This disturbed him more than he let on, but he never felt moved to challenge her characterization of him. Maybe this would make her happy, he thought, though happiness had eluded Sarah since he'd known her and he didn't really expect her to change. Still, it wasn't his money. Now she wrapped her arms around his neck. "*War and Peace*? So serious, Andy. Don't you ever just read junk?"

"Most of my life is junk," he said. "Reading in the morning makes it easier to live with that."

He had intended to make a joke and ended up sounding melodramatic. But Sarah nodded solemnly. "I just hate the campaign," she said. "I hate the coffees, I hate the lunches, I hate the cocktail hours, and I hate the dinners. But what I hate most is those old farts pawing me. I just smell death all over them, Andy. Your good friend Jack Comstock tried to pinch my ass the other day."

Hedig put his hand on his wife's behind and patted it. "There doesn't seem to be much to pinch," he said and smiled.

"You know what I mean," Sarah said.

"Be brave," Andy said, thinking of Prince Andrei.

Sarah laughed, and this made Andy realize how much he missed being happily married. It wasn't something he thought about often, and he wasn't even sure when things had changed or what the difference was. He only knew that they were unhappy now and that it had been this way for some time. He remembered long walks in New Haven and in Virginia when they had talked intimately and been excited about the future. Now he was campaigning fourteen hours a day and she was telling her secrets to a psychiatrist. And while they still shared the same bed, they seldom went to sleep or awoke at the same time.

Sarah sat in his lap and combed his hair with her fingers. "I wish we could spend more time together," she said.

Andy felt a sudden urge to retreat. Sarah had moved too close again, and while he was ashamed that he wasn't willing to invest enough time and energy to achieve intimacy, for him this was preferable. He disapproved but had no real desire to change. Had someone asked, he would have said they both wanted the same thing without knowing what it was, yet whenever Sarah approached, he moved away. "After the campaign," he said.

"Sure," Sarah said. "Unless you win. If you lose, maybe." She walked toward the door. "See you tonight."

After she left, Andy sat for a moment, debating whether to go after her and losing the argument. Then he picked up the phone. "May I speak to the Reverend?" he asked. "This is Andrew Hedig speaking."

Andy made a point of placing his own calls and never kept anyone on hold. It was a lesson he'd learned in Washington. Real power is playing into someone else's vanity rather than indulging your own. Control is allowing them to believe they're controlling you.

As Andy waited, the buttons on the rotary began to flicker and die like fireflies as calls were picked up by the answering service and new people came on. Andy had three business lines and an unlisted number, but he never answered them. It was always his decision to speak to someone; he was never at the mercy of a caller's whim or passion. Now Marcus Jackson's powerful voice came over the wire and Andy said, "Peace be yours, Reverend."

Marcus laughed. "Up yours, too. What's on your mind this morning, Andy?"

"I've been reading Tolstoy and thinking about courage."

"But that's not why you're taking up my valuable time."

"Of course not," Andy said. "I was wondering if you remember Tom Paley? He was involved in the Norman murder."

Marcus's voice was suddenly guarded. "Oh, yes, we all remember Mr. Paley down here, Andy. Why do you ask? Is he a friend of yours?"

Andy remembered that he had asked Bob Joseph the same question. He wondered what friendship should have to do with any of this. Still, he couldn't read Marcus's reaction. He had worked with T. T. Lovelace, one of the ministers who planned the march on MacArthur Square. But Andy didn't know the extent of his friend's involvement with the Normans. Someone had told him that Marcus had broken with Lovelace over tactics for the march, but Andy had never asked his friend about this. They had met in Selma, but even as friends Andy and Marcus had always been politicians first. Marc would be willing to share whatever he knew, but he would rather trade.

"No, not a friend," Andy said now. "This might not mean anything, but a reporter named Bob Joseph told me that he'd heard from Paley."

"I thought the dude was in jail," Marcus said slowly. "Just shows what kind of trash they're letting loose on the streets of our city."

"I'll be sure to address that when I'm elected."

"I believe you will," Marcus said. "Yes, I'm certain of that." He was quiet for a moment. "So, Tommy Paley's out of jail and calling members of the media. That's interesting, Andy. What do you think it's all about?"

"That's what Joseph wanted to know. Maybe nothing, but we're all wondering, aren't we?"

Marcus laughed. "Yes, we are. I wonder if that sorry sonofabitch knows how much curiosity people have about him." Andy was about to respond, but someone was talking on the other end of the line. His time was up. "Got to go," Marcus said. "Will I see you at the installation?"

"I wouldn't miss it."

Marcus laughed again. "Thanks for the call, Senator."

Jimmy Keefe was waiting when Hedig came out of the house. Keefe was working as a lobbyist when they met, and now Jimmy was both Andy's campaign manager and driver, the only paid staff member. Jimmy liked to say he had no other life and that this gave him the right to speak his mind.

"When can I schedule something with white people?" Jimmy asked as he put the car in gear. "You want to go to lunch, let's go to Serb Hall and shake hands with Croatian war veterans or take in St. Josaphat's on Sunday morning and say hello to the Polacks. But no, we're down in the ghetto with the Baptists on Sunday, and now we're going to the only black Catholic church in town. You're pissing everyone off trying to prove how liberal you are, Andy."

They were going to St. Augustine's for the installation luncheon of the women's auxiliary of the Guardians of Freedom, a commitment he had made without consulting his campaign manager. Andy didn't expect Jimmy to be happy about it, but he had promised Marcus Jackson. He sighed and looked out the window. "I am a liberal," he said. "I don't have to prove that. And if I tried to hide it, if I mentioned my military record, say, everybody would accuse me of camouflaging my true feelings. Remember Bay View?"

Jimmy nodded. It had been his idea to have Andy announce his candidacy a year and a half before the election and it had been a disaster. They had invited the members of the steamfitter's local, even though Andy's father was a machinist, and his high school baseball coach, which Jimmy thought was a nice touch. But the papers had a field day with it, saying Hedig was an opportunist, an Ivy League lawyer with a big house on the lake masquerading as a working-class candidate from the south side. To make matters worse, the Times had printed a picture of Andy mowing the grass in tailored khakis and French cuffs over the caption "Candidate goes to work."

"Why couldn't you just wear an old T-shirt like everyone else?" Jimmy asked plaintively. He knew it was his fault. He had arranged the shoot thinking the picture would show Andy had the common touch.

"I thought my clothes were up to me," Andy said mildly. "That's my personal life."

"You don't have a personal life," Jimmy said. "Once you decided to run for office you gave that up, just like every other candidate. Now you're mine, at least for the next year. No one held a gun to your head and made you run, but if you're going to do it, for Christ's sake, do it right. We're far enough behind as it is. And don't act like this is some big surprise. You've been running ever since you came back to Milwaukee. That's why you came back."

But Andy hung on stubbornly. "If people want to vote against me for what I am, that's fine," he said. "But I'm through pretending."

This made Jimmy smile. "The whole thing is pretending, Andy. Media events, photo opportunities, speeches, kissing babies, eating kielbasa, even installment luncheons. There's nothing real about the whole fucking campaign. Everybody's tough on crime and no one's ever going to raise taxes again. The voters don't even expect it to be real—just interesting. They go for the guys with the best hair and good-looking wives. If anyone gave a shit about position papers or your voting record, do you think we'd spend money on TV? As long as you don't bore people or piss them off too badly, you're OK."

"Then what are you complaining about?" They'd had this argument before and neither thought seriously about convincing the other. Andy knew Jimmy was right, or mainly right, and Jimmy knew Andy would go his own way, no matter what he said. They respected each other enough to allow tension to exist between them. "Even bad press is interesting, isn't it?"

"Not black churches," Jimmy said. "Then voters—white voters—think you're betraying your race. And that's not interesting."

"OK, I won't do any more after this one," Andy said reasonably. "But after this, let's do what you say, keep it staged. I mean, I've tried. I am from the south side. I grew up there, went to Pulaski High School. I was on the prom court with Mary Ann Dembrowski. What right does some reporter have to say that I'm a hypocrite if I go to my parents' house for dinner?"

"It's not about rights," Jimmy said patiently. "Jesus, I can't believe I'm telling you this. Getting mad at the press is bullshit. It's their job to follow you around and write it down if you fuck up. Rights don't come into it. It's like saying a wolf has no right to attack some sheep."

"I can't argue with the analogy," Andy said.

"Look," Jimmy said. "It's a bitch, but no one's figured out how to run for anything without getting his name in the paper. That's just the way it is and there's no use getting your ass in an uproar about it."

"I know," Andy said patiently. "But let's just do what we have to do. I don't like eating greasy food at street fairs. Some people are good at that—I'm not. If we've learned anything, we should have learned that. Look where we are with me as a man of the people, twenty points down and dropping. Let me give speeches and position papers and they can say I'm stiff, but after a while they might start to listen to what I'm saying."

Jimmy couldn't argue with Andy's analysis, but it was puzzling. He had a good-looking young candidate in great shape with a pretty wife. Any experienced manager would put him out in the street pressing the flesh, but it hadn't worked. And Jimmy knew he wasn't going to have much luck getting him over to the Masonic Temple for the Eastern Star dinner, which was what he had been getting around to. But he still didn't understand why they were going to St. Augustine's. There wasn't much to gain, but Andy didn't seem to care. "Do me a favor?" Jimmy said. "At least keep away from that crazy priest?"

"Father Moretti?" Andy said, smiling. "He's an inspirational leader. Anyway, I can't avoid him. The Guardians are his creation."

"Inspirational, my ass. I'm telling you, Andy, you get tight with him and we won't have to worry about the campaign. It'll be over after the primary."

"You're overreacting," Andy said, but he knew Jimmy was right. James Moretti was the most hated white man in Milwaukee. He had moved to town from Denver a few years back to take a position at a small parish in the Core that no one else wanted and had immediately irritated his superiors by starting a youth council made up of teenage drop-outs. Though he claimed he was just trying to keep the kids away from drugs, Moretti had dressed them in boots, red berets, and kerchiefs, which scared the hell out of everybody. Suddenly the Guardians of Freedom were a presence—and not only at church functions. Television crews filmed them marching in formation up and down the streets of the Core and feeding breakfast to neighborhood kids. Church attendance was up and the school was full, but no one seemed grateful.

"Don't give me that crap," Jimmy said. "Ask your buddy Marcus Jackson what he thinks."

Marc considered Moretti to be little more than a carpetbagger, looking to make a name for himself here before moving on. He might be right, but Marcus and the other black leaders were jealous of the attention Moretti was receiving. It was complicated, as everything always was. "OK," Andy said at last. "I'll stay away from the father. But can I kiss the ladies?"

"Just babies," Jimmy said. "Even black babies are OK, but no pictures of you laying one on the choir."

As it turned out, all Andy had to do was put in an appearance, and he did no more than was necessary. The Guardians marched in and stood sentry duty for the fifteen girls standing on stage. Then the choir sang "Take Me Up, O Jesus," and Father Moretti put berets on the girls and made the sign of the cross. Andy shook hands with each of them, impressed with the serious expressions on their brown faces. It was obvious that the kids loved Moretti and people were just going to have to live with that.

Afterward, Andy looked for Marcus Jackson, but ran into Bob Joseph instead. "Good to see you again, Bob. What brings you down here?"

"It was on your schedule," Bob said dryly.

Hedig looked at Jimmy Keefe. "I didn't know I had a schedule," he said. Bob knew this was bullshit, that Hedig knew exactly where he was supposed be every minute of the day. Scheduling was a fine art, practiced by experts who had a reason for every public appearance, but he played along.

"Sure." Bob pulled a card from his pocket. "You've got handshaking at Ladish at three, then coffee at the Union. I don't know about tonight." He offered the schedule for Andy to examine. "It's all right here."

Andy feigned interest, then handed it back. "Will you be joining us for these events?"

The reporter shook his head. "Jeez, I'd like to, especially the coffee. But I'm on deadline. Got to get back."

"I'm sorry to hear that," Andy said. He looked around the room. "I'm afraid there isn't much here to write about."

Joseph shrugged. "Moretti's always good for a quote. Maybe I can even get him to endorse you."

"Save us from that," Jimmy broke in. He grinned at Bob. "We're late," he said. He grabbed Andy's elbow and steered him toward the door.

Bob watched them go. Politicians were always late; it was part of their appeal. Their managers would announce a time they couldn't possibly make and purposely book a room too small for the event. Then they'd make the candidate wait in the car for fifteen minutes so the crowd would really be crazy by the time he came in, out of anger at being kept waiting as much as anything else. But the television cameras just recorded the frenzy. Bob knew all this, but he still liked politicians because, unlike most people, they accepted the crap of life as being necessary and were generally good-humored about it. What's more, you had to admire people who put themselves in front of a group as ill-mannered and unpredictable as the voters at regular intervals.

Moretti was still surrounded by kids and their mothers. The idea of waiting around for a quote made him tired, so Bob shoved his notebook in his pocket and turned to go. If he got stuck, he could do a recap or an analysis of the campaign thus far. They had a new editor from the East who considered himself an intellectual and went for thumb suckers.

Bob found his car in front of an auto parts store with windows and wheels intact. Then he drove south, down Third. It was a part of town that had never come back after the riots in 1968, when whole blocks had gone up in flames. The merchants couldn't be convinced to rebuild, and while Joseph didn't blame them, he regretted losing the neighborhood. There were only boarded-up windows where Schuster's had been, but Bob remembered going there with his mother, his hand tightly clasped in hers, as they made their way down the crowded sidewalks. Third Street was more colorful than Wisconsin Avenue, and more fun. There weren't any push-carts, but the area was alive with noise and movement and nothing had a fixed price. His mother always came home with more than she had intended to buy. Now the Jews had moved out and just walking down the street was an adventure.

During the riots, the mayor had gotten a lot of ink for the way he'd handled things. Cities were exploding all over the country after King's murder and everyone was looking for a panacea. Time and Newsweek had reporters in town for a week writing about the "Milwaukee Solution" to urban unrest. All Mueller had done was ban the sale of alcohol and erect a tight perimeter around the Core. No one was allowed in or out except the cops, who went block by block looking for snipers. And while Daley had told the Chicago police to shoot to kill, Mueller's cops had done it and people cheered them on.

Not that Bob had been very heroic during this period. The press wasn't allowed in the Core, but he could have found a way. The press was the activist's ally, and blacks were understandably eager to have white reporters around. Instead, Bob drove to the Shorewood line, where a friend handed across a bag holding a couple of bottles in it. Then he and Margie sat on the back porch drinking pink gin as the crackling sound of gunfire drifted across the river. The fighting went on for two days, after which the police withdrew like an occupying army. There had been snipers and some cops had been killed, but the real damage was done to the Core, which had never recovered economically.

White Milwaukee had changed little since then, although it was a little less prosperous, which meant things were worse than ever in the Core. Factory closings didn't directly affect blacks since the unions wouldn't let them in. But cuts at A. O. Smith reverberated throughout the economic chain. If whites had smaller paychecks, there was less to spend on eating out or going to the movies. Middle managers had to do without their cleaning ladies or yard men, and busboys and ticket takers were among the first laid off, which meant there were fewer jobs in the inner city than there had been before.

The mayor started a "black capitalism" program, which lasted as long as the federal money did, but now the despair was palpable. You saw it in the graffiti-covered walls, broken windows, and boarded-up shops. The only businesses that seemed to be thriving were taverns and funeral homes, for the last indulgence a black person would give up was a stylish funeral with a parade down Fond du Lac Avenue to the cemetery. For all the bullshit surrounding the Guardians, you had to credit Moretti for giving the kids something to be excited about, and Joseph liked seeing all the old racists in the Catholic church upset.

He stopped at a light and sat facing a storefront with a sign reading "Paint Box Art Center." He remembered the story. Some lady artist from the university had come down here to rent a studio, and kids kept coming inside and interrupting her. Instead of calling the cops, she started teaching them to draw. Word spread and before you knew it, she was holding classes for their mothers too. Then she got a government grant, opened the store-front, and talked the dean into giving college credits to the adults. She brought in some graduate students who did internships, and soon the project was taking up a good part of a building. It was the only one spared when the rest of the block went up in flames. Bob thought Marcus Jackson was involved somehow, but he couldn't remember the connection.

The light turned and he was past the art center going downtown. Joseph stopped at North and then came up on Wright Street. He was only a few blocks from the spot where Jimmy Norman was killed. Without thinking, he turned west, just as Tommy Paley might have done twenty years ago. He drove down to Eighth, took a left, and went around the block. No one was on the street. There had been abandoned houses then and there still were.

Bob turned again on Seventh, then took a right, going east on Wright, and now he realized he was retracing Jimmy Norman's route exactly. The kid had been driving his car that night and this was what he had seen: nothing and then, suddenly, John Rogan behind him on his motorcycle, motioning him over. Bob remembered the police report on this; originally, Rogan had pulled the boy over for a broken taillight, and then Norman had run away. For no reason Bob looked in his rearview mirror, but the street was empty. Like Norman, he turned north on Sixth Street and after a block found himself in front of the little white house where the chase had ended. Bob remembered the address from the clips: 2650 North Sixth.

There was no snow, but now Bob had the illusion that it was all happening again. He saw Jimmy Norman turning the corner, running like mad, and Rogan and Paley after him, firing their guns in the air. No one could know what had been going through Jimmy's mind, why he had really run, and why the cops had gone after him. Why chase someone for three blocks only to shoot him at last? But Bob felt the panic of being pursued, of being trapped in the cold, lonely street. Then the feeling was gone and the street was clear.

Bob wondered how it felt to be a killer, if Rogan was the psychopath the police reports made him out to be, or just another fucked-up kid who'd been brought up to hate anything he didn't understand. He got out of his car and walked over to the service entrance. There was no sign that anything unusual had ever happened here. And if anyone lived in the house, he didn't care enough to come out and ask Bob why he was snooping around. Because that's what he was doing, he realized, looking for something, even if he had no idea what it might be. Again, he imagined he was back there. Norman turned sharply and started down the walk with Rogan right after him. This was where the cops had gotten in trouble contradicting each other. Rogan said he was fifteen feet away when he shot; Paley originally reported he was closer. Then they got together on a story with the help of one of the detectives. Or that was what Bob heard later on. One cop refused to go along, Bob remembered, but they managed to lose his testimony by the time they got to the coroner's jury.

Bob wondered again why he had been so willing to let the story go. Was it the temper of the times or some deficiency in him? It was hard to believe he had ever bought the official line, but he didn't like thinking of himself as a flack for the cops. Of course every other reporter in town had done the same thing, but that was no excuse. Now he was standing at the exact spot where Jimmy Norman got it. He could see the kid's eyes, wide and scared as Rogan raised his gun, swearing, ready to shoot. What had the cops said Jimmy did, threaten them with a knife? It was a joke, so why hadn't Bob seen it then? The feeling was so intense, so real, that he dropped his eyes to the pavement, expecting to see blood, but the walk was clean.

Bob shook his head. It was a long time ago, but he knew this was a story that wouldn't go away, even if it had taken someone else to bring it to mind. It was two weeks since Paley's call, a week since the letter. He felt the hot August sun on his shoulders as Jimmy Norman's image receded. Maybe Paley had changed his mind and wouldn't call again, but Bob didn't think so. None of this was dead for him either. The only real question was what Tommy had wanted to come clean about and how long it would take him to work up the courage to do it.

Eight

The next morning Bob's knee was tender to the touch. He figured it was just more evidence that he wasn't twenty anymore, but after a few days he went to the clinic at Mt. Sinai, where he waited for twenty minutes in his underwear until a small dark man in a white coat came in. Bob had no family doctor because he had no family and was seldom ill.

The doctor told him to take aspirin and stop running. Then he was gone. Except for the running, Bob found this a small price to pay for comfort. Maybe, he thought, running was an expression of arrogance in forty-year-olds, an unwillingness to accept the passing of time, yet he liked the feeling of freedom, the wind in his face. For now, walking would have to do. Most mornings, he would go three miles out along the lakefront. Afterward, for a reward, he treated himself to breakfast at the Pavilion.

Without admitting it to himself, he knew he went there to see Sarah Hedig, though he hadn't really spoken to her, except to introduce himself at the party. Since his divorce, Bob tended to hang back around women, waiting for them, but Sarah was different. There was a bruised diffidence in her manner, a feeling that while she expected little from the world she needed something. Bob thought she was lonely. Today, after ordering eggs and toast, he paused momentarily on his way to the porch and caught her eye. There was a moment's irritation, but then she gestured to an empty chair.

"You could get a better breakfast at the Coffee Trader," she said.

Bob nodded. He didn't know what he was doing here, now that he had achieved his goal. She was not only married, but married to a mayoral candidate whom he was assigned to cover for the paper. Being friendly at social gatherings was one thing, but this didn't feel friendly. It was something else and whatever it was, was wrong. That much was obvious, but things seemed out of his control. He settled into his chair with mixed feelings of anxiety and resignation. Whatever was coming, if anything was, seemed inevitable. "You meet a better class of people here," he said.

Sarah smiled. She was casually dressed in jeans and a red sweatshirt, but she seemed elegant to Bob with her black hair and long legs. The place was nearly empty and their voices echoed in the big room, making them shy. Two old guys in green work clothes were nodding off over a card game, and an off-duty cop sat watching target practice down at the lakeshore range. "We were overrun for a while," she said. "After that story in the paper."

Bob wondered if this was a dig because he was a reporter but decided to ignore it. "What are you working on?"

Sarah's hand rested on her manuscript. "Nothing. A novel. I mean, it was going to be a novel. Now, I'm not sure it wants to be anything."

Bob liked the way she talked about writing, as if it was something outside of her and she was just the transcriber of a foreign intelligence. "Is that how it works?" he asked. In a college literature class, he had learned that Hemingway got his start as a journalist, and as a young man Bob had assumed the same thing would happen more or less automatically to him. Later he discovered that every reporter at the Times had an unpublished novel in his desk drawer. Genius turned out to be harder than it looked.

"I don't know how it works," Sarah said. "Obviously." Then she leaned toward him. "Are we off the record?" She was smiling, but Bob knew this was serious for her, that she wanted to know where they stood.

"We're off the record permanently," he said, not knowing exactly what this meant. It was important to gain Sarah's confidence, to reassure her.

Something happened in her eyes and then she looked relieved. But a simple act of consideration didn't explain Bob's feeling of tenderness. Now she sighed, nothing dramatic, just a small exhalation of breath, but an expression of vulnerability, and Bob, who hadn't been able to care for a woman since the first years of his marriage, found it terribly appealing. It was pathetic that such a small thing could matter so much, yet it did.

"This sounds crazy," Sarah said. "But I thought you were coming here in the mornings to get something on Andy."

It was crazy, but he understood. There was nothing newsworthy about Sarah Hedig's mornings at the Pavilion, but a lack of significance had never stopped reporters from writing about family members of politicians. His kid editors called them "people-centered" features, but it was just gossip. Bob favored the old journalism, before reporters got bylines and considered themselves professionals. Now the people's right to know got confused with simple voyeurism in every edition and they all used the First Amendment as a shield. "I probably shouldn't say this," he said, leaning toward her. "But the truth is I thought if I came here often enough you might invite me to sit down and talk about your novel."

Sarah looked skeptical, but she was pleased. "Just an insatiable interest in fiction, then?"

"No," Bob said recklessly. "Pretty women."

By the time Bob got to his desk, pink message slips had started to pile up, including one from Jimmy Keefe, whom he had always liked. When Jimmy was lobbying for the county hospitals, he'd always been straight with Bob. He'd never try to convince a reporter to write a story about his project for the good of mankind. Instead, he would make it personal. Jimmy would say, "I need some positive press on this," and let Bob decide if he wanted to help. But before he could return the call, the phone rang.

"I'm in town," Tommy Paley said. "Actually I'm at Krause's."

Bob could hear alcohol in his voice and wondered if the other man was drunk at nine o'clock in the morning. "What are you here for?"

"Not over the phone," Paley said. "Can you come down?"

"Five minutes," Bob said.

Reporters from both papers were drinking coffee in the crowded restaurant when Bob arrived, but none apparently had noticed Paley. They were too young, he decided, as he slid into the back booth, but even if they weren't they could be forgiven because the changes in Tommy Paley were amazing. Part of it was that Bob had been looking at twenty-year-old pictures, but life had beaten the other man up pretty well. They were about the same age, but Paley seemed like an old man, fat and gray with islands of yellow pus swimming in his blood-shot eyes. He was wearing a shiny double-breasted suit and had missed a few spots shaving. The guy was a mess.

Bob ordered coffee. Then Paley said, "I got something to tell you, but I need immunity or whatever you guys call it."

It amused Bob to think that he'd had the same conversation with Sarah an hour before, but he didn't smile. Everyone wanted what he couldn't

give: protection, shelter from the awful things they knew, the things they had
done. Perhaps because of Paley's appearance, he felt obliged to be straight
with him, to explain the ground rules. He was going to have to guard against
being soft on this man. "What we call it is going off the record," Bob said.
"What you mean is that you don't want me to quote you, right?"

Paley shook his head. "No, that ain't it. At least not all of it. I don't even
want you to write about what I say. It ain't I don't want you to quote me—
I got to keep this out of the papers period."

Bob felt tired. This wouldn't even be background. If he agreed to
Paley's terms, he couldn't write a story citing unnamed sources or allude to
things he knew to be true, couldn't do anything at all with whatever the
other man told him. Why had Paley even bothered? What they were doing
here?

Bob slapped his notebook closed. "Look, I'm a reporter. This isn't a
social call. I wouldn't be here if I didn't think there might be a story in it."

Paley nodded equably. "Sure, I can see that. You got to get something.
How about down the line then?"

"How far down the line?" Bob asked. He still didn't know what they
were talking about, but his instincts told him to push on. While he wanted to
avoid scaring Paley, Bob didn't want to get beat by someone else on this,
whatever it was.

"A month, maybe longer than that."

"OK," he said. "I can wait that long, but just so we understand each
other, this is the way it works. We're off the record until you say you want to
go on. Then I can quote anything you say that I think is newsworthy and
identify you as the source, unless you ask me not to. If you want to be
anonymous, you're giving me background and I'll quote you without revealing your name. When we're on the record, if I see anything, and I mean
anything, a letter, a note, some personal belonging that's relevant for any
reason I decide it is, I'll use it. If I'm in the room and I overhear you talking
to someone on the phone, then that's on the record too. You're on until you
say out loud to me that you're off and I hear it. So be careful because there
are no slips, no mistakes, and I won't forget anything."

Paley listened carefully. Then he said, "OK with me."

Bob almost sighed out loud. He had been tougher than usual, tougher
than he needed to be. As a rule, he wouldn't even have bothered to explain
things. If someone got burned on a quote, to hell with him. He should have
kept his mouth shut. But he felt the need to explain himself now, even to
justify what he did, and because he wanted to hide his sympathy toward

Paley, he was unnecessarily abrupt. "One other thing," Bob said. "You asked me to hold off, and I will, but only on condition that I get this exclusively."

"I can't talk to the Post?"

Bob was glad he had said something. He had a vision of Paley shopping his story to everyone in town. "Right, but not just the Post. The television stations, the radio, high school papers, shoppers, the works. You don't talk to anybody else and I'll keep quiet as long as you say."

Bob knew Paley could just tell him to shove it and walk away. Every news outlet in the city would be interested in him and might not make the same demands. He was taking a chance, but they had a sort of history together going back to the night of the murder. Besides, when Paley called, Bob had responded and that had to be worth something. These young kids with their blow-dried hair wouldn't have known what Paley was talking about. He'd have to take them to school before they could do anything for him. Age had its advantages. Paley extended his hand. "It's a deal," he said.

"OK," Bob said. "But I'm curious. Why me? You could have called Cameron at the Post or anyone else."

Paley looked into his coffee cup and took a deep breath. He looked uncomfortable and Bob wondered if he had pushed too far. "I don't know any of them," Paley said hesitantly. "And back then, it wasn't like you and me knew each other exactly, but you asked me once about a traffic case, interviewed me. You remember that?"

Bob had no recollection of this. He'd talked to hundreds of cops over the years. "Sure," he said, guessing, "A hit-and-run, wasn't it?"

Paley brightened. "Yeah, that's it. You quoted me, and the other coppers said you were a right guy. That's why I called."

A right guy. Cop talk for a reporter who didn't press too hard and would hoist one with you after your shift. If he had been less of a right guy he might have done a better job on the Norman story. But, hell, that was then. "So what's this all about, Tommy?" Bob asked.

Paley looked away, as if he thought someone else might be listening. "Those stories you sent me, about the Norman kid. The thing is," he hesitated now. "The thing is," he repeated, "there never was a knife."

Bob was careful. "No knife," he said softly.

Paley shook his head. "I never saw one. I said I did, but it wasn't true. I went to call in the shooting, and when I come back there's a knife in Norman's hand. I always figured John planted it on the kid. They taught us that shit at the Academy. No point in going down over a dead nigger."

Bob took this in. It was important not to put words in Paley's mouth. "You're saying you saw no knife when Rogan first shot Norman, and you think the one he found was planted, but you don't know for sure?"

Paley nodded. "That's it. But I was back of them quite a ways."

"All right," Bob said. "But what about the rest? Did Rogan think the kid was armed, was that true? Did Norman come at him like he said? Did he threaten you?" The original reports had linked Norman with a robbery a few blocks over on Brown Street. Norman had supposedly yelled, "I'm a holdup man" and waved his knife around.

Paley shook his head. "I didn't even see why John pulled him over in the first place. It was cold as hell and we were just sitting on our bikes having a smoke. Next thing I know, Rogan's going after this old Dodge. I knew he hated niggers, but it didn't make sense. First John had the kid spread-eagled against his car and next thing you know we're chasing him down the street. Rogan was practically on top of him, holding onto his collar, when he shot him. All that other stuff was just a bullshit story we cooked up after."

Cops had killed black kids before, though it wasn't as routine as some of Bob's liberal friends thought. Taken all together, the police did pretty well, especially considering their racial attitudes and the difficulty of the job. But there was something different about this, about Paley's intensity, that intrigued him. "So it was homicide, not self-defense?"

Paley nodded. "I don't think John meant to do it. He was telling the truth there. Things just got away from him. It was cold as a sonofabitch and we were scared and excited. You don't know what that's like, but any copper could tell you."

Bob knew Paley was right. He'd seen cops on crime scenes so high on what had happened that they'd start fighting with each other or laughing hysterically or, less often, crying. Calm reflection about what might be the right thing to do was a luxury no street cop ever had. Which was why their training was so important. Still, there were cops who'd been on the force for twenty years without firing their guns. "What happened after that?" Bob asked.

"John got real calm, you know, he wanted to save his own ass. He just said, 'We've got to figure out something here, Partner,' and I don't know why but I thought I had to do it, had to back him up, even though he wasn't really my partner. I mean, I'd just been war-horsing out there."

"War-horsing?"

Paley nodded. "I didn't have a regular beat then. The captain had taken me off mine because I got drunk, so I was just pulling whatever was left after the guys went out. I just ran into Rogan. I was just there."

So it was an accident. Dumb luck that Paley happened onto a situation that ruined his career and sent him into a tailspin that hadn't stopped twenty years later. "Let's go back to the scene. Rogan shot the kid, and then he told you the two of you had to come up with a story as to why it happened. Is that it, Tommy?"

Paley shook his head. "It's not the way it sounds. I mean, we were out there and the kid was on the ground already, and it was like there was no connection between us and him, but there was. John did it and now he's looking like he'd do me if I gave him anything back."

"You were afraid of Rogan?"

"Not afraid maybe, but he was a mean sonofabitch. Everyone knew that. Anyway, the point is I went along with it, and I shouldn't have. That was my fault, that I didn't just say then and there, no way."

Bob still wasn't sure exactly what Paley was saying. If everyone knew Rogan was a bad cop, why should Tommy have felt the pressure to back him up? "Went along with what, Tommy?" He encouraged familiarity with people he was interviewing. They were just friends talking, trying to understand, and with Paley it worked. He seemed to relax.

"All the suits downtown. And Charlie Moran, the detective sergeant at the scene, I tried to tell them."

"What did you try to tell them, Tommy?"

His eagerness made the other man wary. Paley held up his hand. "This thing goes a long way up the ladder," he said. "I got to talk to the D.A. before I say anything else."

He wanted to make his own deal, make sure he had immunity against prosecution as an accessory before he went public with it. Bob could understand that. But what Paley was talking about was a cover-up, one he had been brought into against his will. And that's what he wanted to talk about now. Bob needed more, but already he knew this could be politically explosive in the middle of a mayoral campaign. Milwaukee was no bastion of liberal values, but even here you couldn't get by with what had been acceptable in 1959. Emil Mueller may not have been elected until 1960, but cities didn't change that much in a year. You had to assume Mueller knew what was going on, if not in the Norman case, then in the police department in general, and the mayor hadn't changed a thing.

But the more important question was what would happen now. Paley could come in and tell his story, but what was the district attorney going to do with it and to what extent would that be determined by the political realities of the city? Bob had been off cops and courts for years, but he knew there was no statute of limitations on first degree murder.

Fishing, he said, "Wasn't Chief Tanner captain of detectives in '59?"

Paley seemed uninterested. "Tanner? Yeah, he was the night shift captain. We seen him that night and then again the next day."

"Was he in on the cover-up?"

But Bob had lost him again. Paley sat back in his chair, his eyes clear now. "I don't want to say no more. I just called to thank you for sending me all that stuff. I went to a priest up north and he said I should come down and talk to the D.A., make amends, so here I am. You know, I lost everything because of this. Before that night, I was doing OK. All the time I was growing up, all I wanted to do was get to be a bikeman. You don't know what that meant where I grew up. Those guys were fucking studs. Big strong guys, always there when some hot shot visited the city, always with the mayor. I mean, we were the best, and I sat for the exam and qualified when I was only two years out of the Academy. I was married and we were going to have a kid, buy a house, all that. I thought I had it knocked." He sighed and exhaled. "Then because of one fucking night, everything goes down the toilet. My wife left me, I got put in the drunk tank, and I ended up doing time for kiting checks. I got to tell the truth now."

Bob listened, knowing that a big story had just fallen into his lap, but realizing too that it went beyond a story, or even justice finally being done after a long delay. He was looking at the human cost of deception reflected in Tommy Paley's face. In his dewlaps, veined nose, and nervous, nicotine-stained hands, in his greasy, thinning hair with his scarred scalp visible underneath. And though Bob was reluctant to give the cop too much credit, he was even looking at a kind of courage, morality if you wanted to call it that, because when you got down to it, Paley didn't have to do this, no matter what the priest said, and the poor sonofabitch was going to get fried, immunity or no immunity. Bob could write a good story on the crime-and-punishment theme, playing all the right notes, making Paley the hero, and in the end no one would give a shit. People weren't going to admire a cop rolling over on his partner after years of silence. Bob hoped the knowledge that he had followed his conscience and done the right thing would give Paley a lot of satisfaction because when it was all over he wouldn't have many friends left in town.

"Go see the D.A.," he said. "We can meet and talk like this, whenever you want, off the record, until you're ready to go public. I won't write a word until then. But you know all hell's going to break loose when I do."

Paley nodded, his expression serious but calm. "I know that," he said. "But I'm ready. It's been hell inside my head for twenty years."

Bob left the restaurant and went back upstairs, but instead of going straight to his desk in the newsroom, he turned right off the elevator and walked toward the managing editor's office. About halfway down the hall, the linoleum changed to plush burgundy carpet. He pushed through the oak double-doors and approached the secretary's desk. "I've got to see Mike," he said.

The walls of the outer office were lined with pictures of former editors and publishers of the Times as well as some framed awards. Among them were three Pulitzers, although the last had come years before and had been for editorial cartoons. The Times, like a lot of papers, was riding on its reputation, which in any case, rested more on local reporting than on national or international coverage. They did a good job covering the city and the state. Not long ago, the metro editor had told Bob earnestly, "Our readers don't give a shit about what's happening in Liberia and, tell the truth, neither do I." But Bob didn't let this bother him. It was still possible to do good work here.

The past executives were a serious group, dressed in expensive business suits with a variety of props, ranging from a book to a telephone. For a moment, Bob reflected on the unlikeliness of Myron Klein's being in such company. Mike had come to Milwaukee to work on one of the socialist papers during Heinz Josef's heyday and had stayed on after the paper folded, catching on at the Times and rising in the ranks but never losing the sense of moral outrage that had brought him out from New York thirty years before. Like a lot of people, Mike had been attracted to the University of Wisconsin because of the Progressives and to Milwaukee because of its tradition of Socialist mayors.

Unlike the others, Mike stayed on after learning Fighting Bob La Follette was really a Republican and that in Milwaukee socialism meant good parks and municipal services, not revolution. He bought a home on the east side and in time allowed Bob Joseph to marry his daughter. Mike maintained a proper distance after the divorce until one day he decided to give Bob a call. "Look," Mike said. "I can't disown my daughter, but I don't see why I should suffer for her mistakes. Let's have lunch."

Now he stood smiling over Bob. "Taking a rest?" he said. "Come on." The managing editor turned and led Bob back to his office. The older man was tall and thin with a fringe of gray-white hair over small brown eyes. He was in shirt-sleeves and his tie was tucked into his shirt military style. Bob was amused to see that his father-in-law no longer wore clip-ons, but otherwise he hadn't changed much. There was a large desk submerged in paper and a conference table with two full ashtrays on it. In front of the desk sat two padded chairs. The walls were bare except for a framed Pulitzer citation, which Mike had won for public service. Bob remembered going shopping with Margie for the frame and hanging it while Mike was at lunch.

Klein collapsed into one of the chairs and indicated the other. He patted his knees. "It's been a while," he said.

Bob nodded. He didn't say he'd been busy. They both knew it wasn't that. "How's Margie?"

Mike had red knobs for elbows and a high forehead. Now he rubbed it with both hands to wipe away unpleasant thoughts. "I never understood you kids. One minute you're happy as anyone has a right to be, the next my daughter's moved out and is dating guys named Bruce."

Despite himself, Bob smiled. For five years he had tried to understand what had happened between them. In her own way, he knew, Margie had tried too. Finally, the inevitable truth sank in: they had lost the intimacy of marriage and it was too late to do anything about it. They weren't kids, but they had fooled themselves into thinking they had all the time in the world. Or perhaps the passage of time was just their way of acting, because doing anything would have been too hard. You couldn't really blame anyone, couldn't say whose fault it was because fault didn't matter in the end. The only thing left was to get out with as much good will as possible. Still it hurt like hell, hurt for a long time. The remarkable thing to Bob was that eventually it went away, because he had thought it would be with him for good. Little by little, over years, the pain diminished, and now it only hurt when he thought about it, so he tried not to do that. "I never got it either," he said simply.

Mike nodded sympathetically. Then his expression changed. "You didn't come here for counseling," he said. "What's on your mind, Bobby?"

Bob told Klein about Paley's phone call and letter and walked him through the case, laying the clips from 1959 on the desk as he talked. Then he mentioned the deal he had made with Paley at their meeting in the restaurant.

The managing editor took it all in, listening without interrupting, his small eyes attentive but wary, always ready to question. He turned the clips over in his hands as if they were money, then he read through them quickly. "I remember this story," he said finally. "I wasn't involved in it. I was over on the state desk, and we had that mass murderer up in Marshfield, the one who liked little boys. I wanted to nail that sonofabitch and we did."

Mike nodded ruefully, remembering what it was like to be out on a story, because to a reporter something was either a story or it was nothing. Mike wouldn't talk about a killing or even a natural disaster like an earthquake as anything but a story. His limitation was the same as the newspaper's, the transience of it, the dailiness of its interest in anything. Others might have said Mike lacked imagination, but that wasn't true. Mike Klein didn't value such things. He thought imagination was for birdwatchers or poets, whom he put in roughly the same category. It wasn't much use to a newspaperman.

"So, you think you've got something here?" he said now. His eyes were suddenly very serious.

Bob nodded. "A cop comes forward after twenty years because he can't live with himself. Homicide's always important, especially when cops are involved. And in the middle of a mayoral election. Yeah, I think it's big."

Mike Klein scratched his head. "Let me play the devil's advocate, especially since at the end of this you're going to ask me for something.

"Assume for the moment that this putz is telling the truth. I'm capable of moral indignation. I say find the bastard and make him pay. But it's not news that cops hate blacks. Hell, we've been doing stories about police brutality for years." He shrugged. "Have you got anything fresh?"

"This isn't about individual cops. Paley's not a model citizen, but what's important is the cover-up, the fact that the highest officers in the department were in on it. Isn't a racist police department news anymore?"

"Can you prove it?" Klein asked mildly. "We've all suspected this for years. Martin, Tanner, they're both scum, and so are the rest. You don't have to convince me—you're preaching to the choir. To the guy working at A. O. Smith, the cops are all that stand between his family and the Mau-Mau. If we could change that guy's mind, we'd be doing something. But what have you really got? Some broken-down rummy saying he's better than the others because he wanted to blow the whistle." Mike let the clips fall in a pile on his desk. "I don't know, Bobby. It doesn't look too solid to me."

Bob sat back in his chair. The way Mike put it, Tommy Paley's story didn't sound like much. People lied to reporters all the time, but Paley wasn't lying. You couldn't fake a face. "Let me follow it for a month."

Klein smiled. "If that didn't knock the wind out of you, maybe your hunch is right. Take two months, but stay in touch." He reached across the desk and patted Bob's face. "Now get the hell out of here. I've got work to do and so have you."

Nine

Tommy couldn't figure out where he was. The sensation wasn't new, but he hadn't been drinking and now he wondered if his mind was starting to go. Then he saw the hotel sign outside the window and it all came back: the bus trip down from Manty, his meeting with Joseph, and checking into the fleabag yesterday afternoon. He had decided to give himself a day before going in to see the D.A., but this morning he felt worse than last night. He was like one of those sand timers that you see in stores, except that it was his life that was running out and the only question was whether he could slow things down in time to start over again.

He lay back and closed his eyes. In the dream he had been back in the apartment with his wife. They were young and things were good between them, yet nothing dramatic had happened. They'd been eating breakfast, poached eggs and toast, and reading the paper. Lu was nervous about catching the bus for work and running around the room the way she always did. But that was all: a normal morning. Except that Tommy hadn't had a morning like that in years, one when he didn't wake up drenched in sweat, his head pounding, thinking of Jimmy Norman lying dead on the sidewalk and Rogan over him with the gun. For years, Tommy had treated the dreams with booze, but it worked imperfectly, sometimes bringing forth nightmares far worse than those he suffered from habitually.

He'd been sober for two years, and the priest said he had a chance—if he told the truth. Not to get Lu back, though. She was remarried with kids and had hung up on him the last time he called. A chance at an ordinary life, though, free of night sweats and visions. Cornflakes and the morning paper instead of three fingers of Old Crow. Even Tommy didn't think it sounded that great, but he was a realist; this was all he had a right to expect.

He threw his legs over the side of the bed and felt a wave of nausea. Tommy barely made it to the bathroom. It took ten minutes for the dry heaves to slow down. Raising his head over the sink, he peered into the mirror. "You look like shit," he told his reflection and put his head under water.

At least the nightmares had improved since he'd been in Manty. The ones about Jimmy Norman's shoes, those patent leather Stacies, had been replaced by a kind of dumb show where Tommy would be standing off to the side watching Rogan pump bullets into the kid's lifeless body. Then he would flash on Norman's right hand. First it would be empty. Then a knife appeared, but not the switchblade, more like a fucking machete. It jumped out of the kid's hand and came after Tommy, whirling around in the air like a helicopter blade.

Tommy had had the dream so often it no longer surprised him, but it hadn't lost its effect. He remembered screaming his head off night after night in the joint until the other prisoners complained and he got moved to a private cell. It was funny. You could do almost anything in there and no one gave a shit. Drugs, ass-fucking guys, even murder, and the guards looked the other way. Have a bad dream and you were moved out of the general population. Tommy did the rest of his time in solitary, which turned out to be OK with him. The first few months he heard voices, then everything quieted down. Because it was dark most of the time, he lost track of days and nights and never knew the date or the month. It was all the same to him. When he was released he had the illusion that he'd actually shrunk a few inches and he had trouble talking to people after all those silent months, but it gave him a chance to think. One way to look at it was that if he hadn't had that time he probably wouldn't be doing any of this. The months in the hole taught him that he could stand more than he had imagined. It made him stronger.

Tommy shaved, showered, and put on the gabardine suit he'd bought at Sears. Before leaving, he looked to see if he'd left anything. Then he remembered. He'd checked in without a suitcase and paid cash for the one night. He considered taking the toothpaste and razor, but decided against it. Let the next poor bastard think he got lucky.

Tommy walked up State Street, breathing a little more heavily now, past the Times and the Arena, where he used to watch Marquette play basketball.

He entered the Safety Building by a side door, brushing against two blues and a plainclothes detective as he went inside. The corridors were crowded, as always, but Tommy didn't need directions. He could've found the D.A.'s office in his sleep. For a moment, he stood outside the frosted door, catching his breath, then he went in and told the secretary who he was.

They didn't keep him waiting. The district attorney was a tall, dark-haired man named Timothy Dolan and looked to be around forty. Tommy had heard about him, heard he was fair but no pushover. The word was he wasn't a great fan of Tanner's. Dolan wasn't friendly or unfriendly. They didn't shake hands, but what the hell, it wasn't a social call. There were three other people in the room, a legal secretary, a young kid who must have been Dolan's assistant, and against the back wall a man who looked familiar but whom Tommy couldn't place.

"I asked agent Magnusen to sit in," Dolan said, "because most of the people involved with this case aren't with us anymore."

Tommy wondered if Tanner knew about him coming in. Although the Police and Fire Commission was officially in charge of police in Milwaukee, everyone knew the guy with the power was Tanner and the department had become increasingly isolated from the rest of the city hierarchy. The talk was that Tanner had more clout than the mayor, though that was hard to believe. But there was no doubt that the chief was the most feared man in Milwaukee, and Tommy didn't like the idea of going up against him with no protection.

Now he placed the guy in back. Magnusen had been the cop who stood up to Tanner and refused to rewrite his report when Tommy and Rogan came in with different versions. He had been a detective but young, like them, only recently promoted out of a uniform. Tommy remembered thinking he had balls. Now he spoke to the agent. "So you're with the FBI?"

"Fifteen years," Magnusen said.

As long as Tanner had been chief, some coincidence. But Tommy didn't say anything, and Dolan cleared his throat. "The reason we are here today," he said formally, "is that Mr. Paley requested a meeting. We have a court stenographer present, and you'll all have a chance to check the minutes for accuracy. The whole proceeding will be on the record. If that's acceptable to you, Mr. Paley, why don't you tell us why you called in the first place?"

Tommy had already told Dolan, but he ran through the story again. The three men listened patiently, taking notes occasionally, but showing no particular interest. It took Tommy about an hour, and when he finished he was surprised to see that his hands were shaking.

Dolan gave him a minute, then said, "So, twenty years after this alleged obstruction of justice, having known the truth of the matter from the beginning, you've come forward now because you have a guilty conscience?"

The way he said it pissed Tommy off. Dolan made it sound like he and Rogan had farted in Sunday school. What did these suits know about his life and what he'd gone through trying to be a stand-up guy? But even in his anger he understood the D.A. was just doing what he had to do, covering his own ass, like everyone else in the world. Losing his temper wasn't going to help. He was in too deep for that already. "What else?" Tommy said coolly.

The D.A. shifted in his chair, turning slightly toward the others now. "Isn't there something you want for yourself?"

"Sure. I want immunity."

"From what?"

"Like you said, obstruction, whatever."

The district attorney made a brushing motion with his open hand, as if the question of Tommy's responsibilities was too trivial to discuss. "Whatever you might have been charged with in the past, you're not liable now," he said. "The statute of limitations is long past. The question is, what should we do with this information you've brought us?"

Tommy figured that was obvious, but he wasn't the one being paid big money to make legal decisions. "What do you do?" he said. "I just told you a cop murdered someone in cold blood. Why am I down here, for Christ's sake? I rat on a fellow officer and you fucking ask me what to do?"

"Relax," Dolan said, but Tommy had the feeling his outburst had served the other man's purpose. "It was a rhetorical question," Dolan went on. "I wasn't really asking you." He said this as if to suggest that even a moron wouldn't ask Tommy's opinion about anything. "And I didn't say we wouldn't do anything. I'm just thinking out loud, really, wondering how to proceed."

Dolan sounded like a professor at the university, one of those guys in tweed jackets with bread crumbs on their ties. Wondering—wondering what, for Christ's own sake? Tommy couldn't believe the way this was going. "You go out and grab Rogan and bring him back here and put him on trial." Tommy talked slow, as if he were speaking to someone who was deaf and read lips.

"That sounds simple," Dolan said in a tone of voice that implied it wasn't. "Do you know where he is?"

They had been in touch over the years, and Tommy had even visited a few times. He was impressed with the way Rogan had put the murder behind him and started a new life. He drove truck and had remarried, a nice girl from Wyoming. Everyone where he lived knew what had happened, but no one cared. "As far as they're concerned, one less nigger in the world is nothing to cry about," Rogan told Tommy. "I never killed anyone out here."

Dolan turned to the others. "Gentlemen?" he said.

The young kid spoke first. "I'm not crazy about this case," he said. "Why didn't the D.A. call Paley twenty years ago? Because he was a lousy witness. And he's worse now, an ex-con who got kicked off the force for alcoholism. I wouldn't be thrilled about going into court with that."

"Hey," Tommy said. The kid spoke as if he weren't even in the room. Dolan put his hand on Tommy's arm to shut him up. Then he looked at Magnusen. It was hard to see what the feds had to do with any of this.

"Maybe you've got interstate flight," Magnusen said. "That gets Rogan back here. But it's tough to see how you're going to get first degree. Timmons is right. Paley's not going to be the strongest witness, but he's the only one you've got. Nobody else was there. I don't even see manslaughter without some kind of confession. Otherwise, it's his word against Rogan's."

"Isn't the statute of limitations past on second degree?"

Timmons shook his head. "Rogan's been in and out of the state since he moved. You've got to be gone for seven consecutive years."

Tommy remembered hearing from Rogan when he came back for his mother's funeral. "How much time do we have?"

"About five months," Timmons said. "Four and half, to be safe."

Dolan exhaled. "We've got to extradite Rogan, get a confession, and charge him all before the statute runs out? His lawyer could piss away that much time with motions."

"Sure," Magnusen said. "Except for one thing. They don't know you're not going for first degree, and there's no statute of limitations on that. What's more, that's what you'll have to go for if you can't get him to cop. But if you get a confession before you charge him, Rogan might agree to plead to man or reckless endangerment. That's what you've got to bargain with."

Dolan looked interested. "How do we get a confession before we charge him? He's in Colorado. How are we going to talk to him?"

Magnusen looked at Tommy and shrugged. "I don't know."

"The mayor doesn't want a long trial," Dolan said. "No one needs publicity on this case."

Tommy thought it was interesting that while the mayor knew what was going on, Tanner wasn't there. Magnusen was talking again. "OK, try it this

way. You bring him in, he cops, the judge sets the sentence according to
whatever agreement you make, and it's over. Rogan's in and out of town
before anyone knows what happened. Frankly, I'd rather see the bastard go
down for first degree, but that's probably the best you could hope for."

"So it all comes down to the confession?" Dolan said. "It depends on
that. What if he decides to fight?"

"Then we're fucked anyway you look at it," Timmons put in. "Worst
case, we don't make first degree but it's in the papers for six months about
everyone in the Department conspiring to cover up a race murder. To top
it all off, Rogan walks in the end because we can't make the case. I like it."

"That happens in an election year and we're all looking for work."

Tommy felt irrelevant to the conversation. Lawyers could talk, he knew
that, but he felt as he had twenty years ago, like it was all a chess game. Move
the pieces this way and get one thing; move them another way and you end
up with something else. And no one seemed to care that people's lives were
involved. Tommy felt bad thinking about Rogan's new life and the fact he
was rolling over on him. Still, the way things were going, it almost seemed
like his testimony didn't matter. Though he didn't like to admit it, the D.A.
was right: he was a shitty witness. Unreliable. When it came down to it, he
could hardly distinguish between his dreams and what had actually happened back there. That's why they had to have a confession. Tommy didn't
know for sure what they had done, only that it was wrong and that he
couldn't live with himself.

The other men in the room seemed oblivious to Tommy's feelings. All
they cared about was what deal they could make to fuck Rogan. Nobody
seemed to give a shit about what was right and wrong. It was different
when Tommy was talking to the priest. Doing the right thing seemed kind
of noble up there, when they were talking in the church with the white walls
and stone floor. He remembered the priest's soft voice urging him to listen
to his conscience. But the priest had never been on the job, and he'd never
had to testify against his partner in court. Noble causes weren't where these
guys lived. To them, Tommy was just shit under their feet and the whole
case was a big pain in the ass. If they could use him, fine; otherwise, get the
hell back in your hole. Tommy's mouth was dry and he wanted a drink.

Magnusen spoke again. "We could put a tap on Paley's phone and he
could contact Rogan. They talk and we get Rogan saying he did it—that's as
good as a confession."

The atmosphere in the room changed subtly now. "Can we get an
interstate tap?" Dolan asked.

"No problem," Magnusen said. "The only thing that worries me is whether Rogan would admit anything. I mean, why would he do that?"

Tommy started to sweat in his cheap suit. It pissed him off that they were putting him on the spot, because he hadn't agreed to any of this, calling a guy up, a friend, and trying to get him to bury himself. He thought he'd come down, tell his story, and that would be that. On the other hand, what kind of friend would be here in the first place? He'd made that decision in the joint or with the priest or somewhere, that friendship wasn't enough to help him, that he had to get this out, no matter what happened to Rogan. After trying it the other way for twenty years, he had come here today out of guilt, out of pain, out of the wreckage of his whole fucking life, but not out of friendship. And he was in too far to back out now. "I don't know," he said. "We don't talk that much about the murder, I mean, like I'd just ask him out of the blue. Like Magnusen said, why would I just bring it up?"

No one answered. Magnusen shifted his weight in an oddly menacing way. "OK," Tommy said finally. "I'll try. I can't do more than that."

Dolan patted the table with satisfaction and Tommy felt like a jerk. They'd probably already talked it over at breakfast, but he couldn't do anything about that. "That's what we'll do then," Dolan said. "Magnusen, you work with Paley to set it up. Timmons, you're the liaison with this office. For now, none of this goes outside this room." He paused and looked seriously at each of them in turn. "I mean nothing."

Ten

Bob was walking down Prospect Avenue after lunch at the Shorecrest when he saw Sarah Hedig getting out of her car. She was showing a lot of leg as she bent to lock the car, and since she hadn't seen him, he had a chance to study her. She was taller and thinner than he remembered, the black dress accentuating her slender waist and long legs. But her posture seemed agitated and Bob wondered what was bothering her. Now she straightened and noticed him. Flustered, she dropped her keys along with some files she had been gripping with her elbow. Bob had imagined that women like Sarah were always in control, but obviously he made her nervous. She stood hugging herself, her mouth in a tight smile. He picked up the files and handed them to her.

"What are you doing here?" she asked, and Bob smiled at the bluntness of the question.

"Following you, of course," he said. When she seemed to take this seriously, he added, "Actually, I just had lunch." He gestured vaguely in the direction of the restaurant.

Sarah seemed relieved, as if she thought someone would really assign a journalist to shadow her as she ran errands. "I don't know how I'm going to get all this stuff in there," she nodded toward the back seat. There was a typewriter, a cardboard file cabinet, books, and several reams of paper.

"Where are you going?" For a moment he wondered if she had moved out, if she and Hedig had split up.

Sarah indicated one of the high-rise buildings that lined the street. "In there. I just bought a condo. I can't work at the Pavilion anymore."

She said it defiantly, as if she expected him to challenge her. Bob tried to think of something glib to say, but thought better of it. He didn't really give a damn. He had to admit that the idea of buying a condo as a solution for limited office space had never occurred to him, but then he wouldn't have thought of a mansion on the lake as being unsuitable for work either. Anyway, it wasn't about him. If Sarah Hedig wanted to spend her father's money on condos, why should he care? It was a relief to have to make no judgment of Sarah. He smiled reassuringly. "I'm going to help you," he said.

As it turned out, the apartment was surprisingly modest. One large room with a daybed, a desk, bookshelves, a comfortable chair for reading, and an alcove kitchen. But it had the best lake view in town. Standing at Sarah's window Bob could look south to the harbor or go the other way and follow the long sweep of the shore north, up past Bradford to the private beaches of Shorewood, Whitefish Bay, and Bayside. At Riverside, they had called these exclusive suburbs Whitefolks Bay and Bagelside, but that was a long time ago.

Cars sped silently down Lincoln Memorial Drive far below and a large ship sailed diagonally across the horizon, coming in at port. It was easy to forget all this existed when you were spending your life covering installment luncheons at inner-city churches. Bob thought he should have some socially relevant reaction to the casual display of wealth, the beat-up Eames chair in the corner, the ratty antique Persian carpet. But to his surprise, he didn't.

Instead, he remembered sitting on the bluff near the water tower as a kid with his grandfather watching with his binoculars ships that had come through the St. Lawrence Seaway to the Great Lakes and copying down the odd foreign spellings in his notebook. Invariably, this would set off nostalgic reminiscences about good times in Göteborg or Hamburg, and the old man would drink more schnapps than he should from a leather-covered flask. They'd return home stiff and sunburned in the late afternoon and catch hell from his mother. With a sadness that surprised him, Bob realized that he had never made it to those European cities. The ships had sailed, but he had never made the Grand Tour and now chances were he never would.

But he didn't reveal this to Sarah Hedig, who was standing behind him. All he said was, "That's a hell of a view."

Sarah came close and he smelled her perfume. Violets, he thought, but her proximity made him tremble. It had been a long time since he'd been

alone with a woman, a long time since he'd wanted to be, or at least alone
with a woman he wanted to be with. Now he realized with astonishment
what was going on, what the perfume and the view added up to. It seemed
funny, not because Sarah wasn't desirable, but because she had been so ill at
ease when he had seen her on the street. But he knew instinctively that she
was serious, so he didn't smile. "Was this supposed to happen?" he asked.

She nodded, surprisingly sure of herself. "Maybe not today, and maybe
not exactly this way, but something similar and soon. I knew when you sat
with me in the park." Then he was pulling her down to the bed. There was
only a moment's hesitation, before he gave in, when Bob thought that he
really liked Andrew Hedig and wouldn't have wanted to do this to him if
there had been a way to avoid it. But it was only a moment because Bob
knew that he wanted Sarah more than he cared about hurting her husband,
and that with a woman like this you weren't going to have more than one
chance.

Afterward, she made tea and they sat for a long time watching the lake
and not talking. Then Bob said, "Look, I've never done this before, so is it
all right if I'm real stupid about it?"

Sarah smiled. "What do you mean?"

"You know, like I feel bad about your husband, but I figure you
wouldn't be here if everything was great between you. And I was married
for ten years, and it was never this good in all that time, even when I thought
it was, which is probably why I'm going to fall in love with you, and when
I do I won't be very suave about it. I'll send you flowers and little cards with
just my initials on them so the doorman won't know. And I could be a real
pain in the ass about wanting to see you a lot and not realize that for you this
was just something that happened spontaneously. So I'd appreciate it if you
could just tell me how it is and then I'll see what I can do about dealing with
it."

He could have gone on, but stopped because he had started out trying
to be charming but had gotten serious along the way. He had wanted to
provide an escape route for her, but then he realized that he was telling the
truth about most of it. He really wanted her to tell him where they stood.

Sarah listened carefully and then put her cup down in its saucer. When
she spoke, she sounded hurt. "Is that what you really think of me?" she said.
"That I'm just a bored housewife with nothing else to do than screw my
husband's friends, some kind of dime-store Emma Bovary?"

Bob had been thinking about himself. He hadn't read *Madame Bovary*
since college, but he knew that wasn't what he meant. The problem was that

he couldn't imagine himself being with Sarah, couldn't imagine why she'd be interested in him. It was really a failure of imagination, his failure, and now he felt it, felt her pain and embarrassment and regretted having said what he did. "I'm sorry," he said. "Maybe I should go."

But Sarah stood up with him and took his face in her hands, cradling it, ignoring what he had said about leaving. "Look, I am bored. You're right about that; it just hurts to hear someone else say it. And I'm unhappy in my marriage too. I don't think I love my husband anymore, and that's sad because there was a time when we were happy together. But the rest is bullshit. I've never had an affair with anyone else; I mean, I don't do this. I'm not that sophisticated—dishonesty bothers me too much. This was wonderful; you were. And you can see me whenever you want. I love flowers and cards and I don't give a shit what the doorman thinks."

This time when they made love it was leisurely, even luxurious. Less hurried and uncertain. He traced the outline of her body, cupping her breasts in his hands and limning the large brown areolas of her nipples with his tongue. Then he moved lower, kissing the stretch marks on her abdomen and the slight give at her hips, finding them endearingly imperfect. He buried his nose in her stomach, inhaling her woman's odor as if it were perfume.

Occasionally he would look up, unsure of himself, as if to ask permission to investigate further. But Sarah didn't speak. Her head was thrown back, her arms clutching the sides of the mattress as if it were a raft. She abandoned herself completely to the pleasure of love. Bob licked her inner thighs, her knees, her toes, then he spread Sarah's legs gently and tongued her until he heard her groan. He elevated her legs, resting them on his shoulders, and balanced her hips in his hands. He flattened his tongue on her, feeling her writhe beneath him, and then she screamed, screamed so loud that it seemed impossible that it would go unnoticed. He imagined the police kicking the door in, but this only increased his pleasure. She screamed again; then she shuddered, her whole body shaking in his hands. Then she was silent.

He felt her fingers dig into his shoulders now and he rose and inserted himself. Sarah's eyes widened and filled with tears. Watching her, looking into her was surprisingly intimate, more personal than sex had ever been before. Bob realized he was crying too, not just because of the power of it but because of the realization that he might never have had this, might never have even known it existed except for her, and then he was grateful, crying for what he had nearly lost, which didn't make much sense, but there it was.

Deep within Sarah he felt himself give and he heard her say, not really to him, "Where have you been?" As if she were asking herself where she had been, as if she had somehow gotten lost along the way. Not to answer, he said, "Oh, Jesus. Jesus Christ." Then neither of them said anything.

The nature of his work took Bob out of the office frequently. There was no news being made in the city room, and while the campaign hadn't gained momentum yet and wouldn't until the mayor announced, there were ribbon cuttings, lunches, and "major" speeches to be covered every day. Andy Hedig's campaign issued position papers on every conceivable subject, and while most reporters ignored issues this early, you could call the contact person if you were on deadline and hard up for a quote. It made it possible for Bob to cover Hedig without going to the speeches. In fact, this was what candidates wanted, to control the flow of news through releases. And while it made Bob uncomfortable to be cooperating in this way, it served his needs.

Mike Klein had released him from his routine duties, but reporters were required to check in with their editors every couple of hours even if they were on assignment. Most newspapers had grudgingly accepted the idea of reporters being professionals when they started giving bylines, but at the Times everyone punched a clock. In Milwaukee, it was important to remember you worked for the company, no matter how many degrees you had. Bob was on a longer leash than most, but he wouldn't have felt right doing nothing while waiting for Tommy Paley. Besides, he had a hunch all this would come together eventually and he wanted to be on top of things when that happened.

Occasionally, Bob was struck by the irony of his situation. Hedig's having announced early necessitated coverage by the paper, which gave him an excuse to get out of the office to see Sarah. His sense of caution told him he was running a risk if anyone found out, not for himself but for Sarah. Mike Klein didn't tolerate conflicts of interest among his reporters, but the worst that could happen was that Bob would be reassigned. For Sarah the stakes were a good deal higher. Still, he wasn't ready to give up either his new lover or the assignment. So he compromised by being careful and rationalized that he wasn't supposed to write about Sarah but about her husband. No one cared about her, except him. It would not be easy to keep his feelings out of his work, but it not impossible either. It was the best he could do for now.

Once, it seemed Jimmy Keefe was on to something. It was Columbus Day and Hedig was making the most of it since the Milwaukee Italian community was small and discrete. In the morning he marched in the parade, after which he went to the Italian Workingman's Club for lunch. Bob spent the day in bed with Sarah, who providentially had brought along a copy of her husband's speech. After reading Bob's story the next day, Keefe said, "I don't get it, Bobby. How can you do such a good job covering us when you're never around?" But Joseph just smiled and Keefe didn't mention it again.

Sarah never felt at ease seeing Bob in town, so he would meet her at a commuter lot on the North Shore and then drive to Port Washington for lunch. Afterward, they'd spend the afternoon in a motel under an assumed name. Sarah liked literary figures, Bob politicians. Already the names of Willa Cather, Edith Wharton, and Emile Zola had been entered in Wisconsin hotel registers along with Ben Disraeli and Henry Wallace, but Bob doubted they were fooling anyone. They didn't act like they were married, falling all over each other, kissing openly, laughing delightedly at each other's jokes. You didn't have to be an expert in American literature to guess they weren't who they said they were, but in the rush of early love they didn't care.

What Bob found most amazing, though, was not the fact that they were getting away with their affair, but that they continued to be so happy. He would have expected small irritations to surface, to chafe at them. His table manners should have grated on her; her upper-class values should have annoyed him. If nothing else, the strain of deception should have been brought to bear on their feelings for each other. None of this happened. They were relaxed and accepting of the inconveniences their situation made necessary. They understood if one or the other had to cancel unexpectedly, and there were no hurt feelings. As October turned to November this consideration seemed to deepen rather than deteriorate, and Andrew Hedig noticed nothing unusual.

"Doesn't he wonder why you're not more responsive to him?" Bob asked after a French meal in Fond du Lac. "I damned well would."

"You'd notice if I looked up at the waitress while you were talking," Sarah said, smiling. "But he's not like you. He doesn't expect as much. That's why I'm here," she said, softening the implied criticism.

Bob shook his head. "That's not what I'm talking about. I know I expect a lot, maybe too much. I realize that I'm demanding and Andy's not. But he's got to want something. You're a beautiful woman and you're not really there for him anymore. I mean, you're not sleeping together, right?"

Sarah smiled indulgently because she understood the question behind Bob's question, understood that he was actually jealous of her husband.

"That's nothing new," she said. "But you don't understand. He doesn't see me the way you do. He loves me in his own way, but he doesn't think I'm beautiful, or interesting, or any of those other things. He feels sorry for me and wants to help solve my little problems. I'm grateful for that, even though I don't think I really need the kind of help he can give. I mean, he's a decent guy. But when Andy gets home after campaigning all day, he's usually too tired to wonder about anything. I'm sure he's relieved that I'm not bothering him anymore."

Bob didn't see how anyone could feel bothered by Sarah and resented the time she spent with her husband, though he felt guilty at the same time. "What's going to happen with us?" he asked suddenly.

Sarah sighed. "Probably you'll get bored with me and find some young tootsie. Isn't that the script?"

"Seriously."

She looked at him. "Seriously seriously?" He nodded. "OK, I'm married and I don't hate my husband; I already told you I don't love him either. I know women who have worse marriages. Like I said, Andy's a decent guy. He treats me well enough, or as well as he knows how."

"I know," Bob broke in. "He's a fine man, a credit to his community. But I asked about us."

"So impatient," Sarah said, patting his hand. "What do you want to know? I was serious. I think there's a good chance you'll get tired of me."

Bob felt like a teenager, his tongue so swollen that he wasn't sure he could force air and sound over it. "I just want to know where this is going."

"Does it have to be going somewhere?" Sarah asked.

Bob hadn't thought about that, about the possibility that things would just continue as they were for an indefinite period until they had had enough. "Yes," he said, surprising himself with his decisiveness. "For me, it does. This is great, all of it, the lovemaking, the secret lunches, the way we talk to each other. But if this is all we're going to have, then I want to know."

Sarah was touched. She traced an invisible line on the tablecloth with her finger. "So it's up to me? I thought men always got tired of women first. That it was women who wanted commitment and men who were afraid."

"Don't give me that bullshit," Bob said. "This isn't *Ms* magazine, Sarah. This is my life, our life, and it's important."

She looked at him again, impressed. His anger was always serious, especially when it was directed at her. Andy never got mad, it was one of the problems she had with him. When Bob raised his voice, it made her feel important in a new way. She spoke softly now. "I understand you want to know things," she said. "But you've got to see that this is hard for me. I've been married to the same man for over twenty years. I have two grown children and my family has always acted like marrying Andy was the only thing that made sense in my life. I don't agree with that, but it pulls on me, so it's hard to break away, even if there isn't much to break away from anymore."

"Fine," Bob said. "That's your answer, then. We both know your marriage is lousy, but because of your parents, you're going to stay with it."

"No," Sarah said. "But you act like it's easy."

"Please," Bob said. "I'm already divorced. Don't talk to me about how easy it is to end a marriage."

"All the more reason you should be understanding," Sarah said.

She had a point, but Bob was afraid she'd come to her senses and realize that a life with him wasn't what she really wanted. If that was what she was going to come to in the end, he wanted it to happen now, before she cut her lines. Better for her, but better for him too. Why get his hopes up? Except that they were already, and going back to life before Sarah seemed impossible. "How much time do you think you'll need?"

Sarah took his hand in hers. "I don't know. I just met you, really, and this is a big decision. I want to take Andy through the campaign. That's only fair. And we can go on like this. If things are still good in the spring, I think I'll want to move out and file for divorce then."

The word "then" hung between them. If . . . then. It was conditional, but Bob felt freer than he had in years. It wasn't a guarantee, but he wasn't buying a refrigerator. He didn't a need guarantee, didn't want one. They just had to go on like this, and then—there was that word again—then everything would be all right. She would leave her husband and they'd have a life together. He had no doubt they'd continue to feel the same way. Being in love with Sarah was easy, the easiest thing he had ever done. "April then?"

She smiled. "April." Worry passed over her face suddenly, or maybe concern. "What about your life, Bob? Milwaukee is a conservative city. What would the paper think about your breaking up the mayor's marriage?"

"Great story," Bob said, thinking of Mike Klein. "I heard once about a reporter who got fired for getting caught giving some alderman a blow job, but I don't see how anyone could accuse me of being biased in favor of Andy if I'm screwing his wife. He might not win. But then there's no problem; anyway, I hope he does. It wouldn't be fair to lose both you and the election."

"He'd still have Tolstoy."

"And a big house on the lake full of Mission oak."

"You're terrible," Sarah said, but she was laughing. "Andy would get along fine without me. Just fine."

They didn't discuss it after that, but the tension was gone. They had an understanding and this made balancing the different parts of his life easier. He would cover the campaign while Tommy Paley negotiated his deal. There was a lot going on, love and work, which made life interesting, more interesting than it had been for a long time.

He would bide his time because there was nothing else to do. Waiting wasn't hard if you were waiting for something. For years he had been waiting without knowing what he was waiting for, which was closer to despair than anticipation. At least there was a limit. April. His mother's birthday had been in April. The baseball season began in April. It was a time of hope and renewal. He could wait that long.

Eleven

Tommy rented an efficiency on Wiel Street from a widow who asked if he'd shovel the walk when it snowed and mow the grass in the summer. He said he didn't know how long he'd be there, but that he would help out if he could. It took a week to get a phone because Lu had never paid the bill at the old place, then more time to set up the tap. When they were finally ready, Tommy put in a call to Rogan, but his wife said John's business had gone to hell so he was working as a long-haul driver, making the L.A. to Chicago run. She expected him to come through in a week or so. She asked Tommy when he'd be coming to see them again. He remembered her vaguely, a short girl with brown hair, freckles, and a crooked smile. He didn't like to be rude, but it made him uncomfortable having this friendly chat, considering what he was trying to do. Rogan's wife asked if Tommy wanted to leave a message. He looked across the card table and Magnusen shrugged. What the hell. Tommy asked that Rogan give him a call. After that, they waited.

Tommy would have preferred to catch Rogan in. They hadn't talked in three years and it would seem strange to just call out of the blue and act like it was urgent. One thing you learned from being a cop was to trust your instincts; if you thought something was funny, it probably was. Rogan would catch on pretty quick. But with the FBI breathing down his neck, Tommy was under a lot of pressure and Magnusen wasn't the friendliest guy he'd ever met. One day, as they were sitting together in the room waiting for

Rogan's call, Tommy tried to get the guy to loosen up by talking about football. "So," Tommy said. "You been away, you still follow the Packers?"

Magnusen looked like Tommy had insulted his mother. "Look, Paley," he said. "This isn't a social call. I mean, we're not buddies hanging out together here. I thought you were an asshole in '59 and I haven't changed my mind because you finally decided to tell the truth. I got out of the department because of guys like you, so let's sit here and think our own thoughts, OK?"

Which is what they did. For five days. The first time Rogan called, Magnusen was out eating. At least they figured it had to be Rogan because no one else had the number. Tommy could've picked up, but he wanted Magnusen to be there. Otherwise, there would be things he missed, questions he didn't ask, some way he'd fuck up. The agent was pissed off anyway, which went to show you couldn't win with these guys. What Magnusen said about Tommy might be true, but he was no prize himself. They were a hell of a team. Magnusen gave Tommy a typed Q&A. "In case I'm not here. All you've got to do is read what's written down. Think you can handle that?"

"Got it," Tommy replied. Get fucked, he thought.

But most of the time he didn't let Magnusen get to him. During the long days when they sat waiting, Tommy thought about fate, something he'd talked about with the priest, who said there was no such thing, that God had everything planned right down to a T. Tommy wasn't so sure. Take the night Norman was killed. If he hadn't been driving up Wright Street at exactly the time he was, he wouldn't have seen Rogan, and if he hadn't pulled over, if he had just gone on and made his mark like he was supposed to, then they wouldn't have been together when Norman cruised by, and he wouldn't have gone along when Rogan started after the kid. If he hadn't joined the chase and seen how Norman was pulling away, Tommy wouldn't have pulled the Chevy over, and if he hadn't done that, Rogan would never have caught Norman and there wouldn't have been a killing that night.

But there was more to it than that. Tommy had had a lot of time to think it all over in the joint. With no booze in his system to blur his thoughts, he figured he got it all pretty clear in his mind. The way Tommy saw it, it had to be him on the bike or nothing would have happened. Another guy might have just waved and kept on going even though the rules said you had to stop when you saw a fellow bikeman down. You had to be as dumb as Tommy to think Rogan could be in trouble and that a fucking rule was worth getting off your bike when it was freezing cold. Because that was why he had done it, not because he liked Rogan or wanted to stand around in the street and shoot the shit. He had done it because he thought it was something he had to do, that it was part of his job, something he wanted to do well. Beyond that, there had to be a car going down the street at the right time. If any one of those things hadn't happened, Jimmy Norman would be fat and middle-aged and Tommy wouldn't be sitting in this crummy room waiting to double-cross his friend. You couldn't convince Tommy Paley there was no such thing as fate.

The second week, the phone finally rang. "What's the big emergency?" Rogan asked. "I've been getting messages in every truck stop from here to Santa Barbara."

Rogan's gravelly voice brought the other man back in a visceral way, and though there was no reason for him to be nervous, Tommy started to sweat. He remembered Rogan's late-night calls, which always started the same way: "How are you, Partner? Hanging in there for me?" And Tommy had hung in and things had gone their way, or so it seemed at the time. But he was through hanging in for Rogan. That was over.

"No emergency," Tommy said, trying to hide his anxiety. "I just wanted to talk about something with you."

"I don't hear from you, what, in four years and we've got to talk now? I'm standing in a phone booth in the middle of Missouri and I've got a load that's got to be in Oklahoma City tonight. Talk fast."

Tommy thought, trying to bring it up in a way that would sound natural. "That whole business with the Norman kid, it's come up again."

Rogan was immediately suspicious. "Come up? The hell you mean it's come up? How did it come up, Tommy?"

"I was talking to some people . . ." Tommy began.

"You out of your fucking mind, Tom?" Rogan broke in. "What people? Who're you talking to about that stuff?"

"A priest, " Tommy said.

Rogan exhaled, relaxed now. He wasn't worried about priests. Very patiently, he asked, "What the hell are you worrying about?" As if he were talking to a child. Tommy could hear truck engines revving over the phone.

"I'll be honest with you," Tommy said, knowing he wasn't being honest at all; honesty had nothing to do with this. "I haven't slept too much with this. I just think we should have told the truth in the first place back then and now it'd be over and done with." He looked at Magnusen, hoping for some encouragement, but the detective was doing something with the tape recorder.

"It is over and done with," Rogan said. "It's been over and done with for twenty years, you know that."

"Yeah, well, the thing of it is, it isn't really, not for me it ain't." Tommy could feel sweat dripping from his armpits. His hands were so slick he could barely hold the phone. Magnusen was staring at him, quiet but intense. He wanted something he could use to nail Rogan and despite the way the agent had treated him, Tommy wanted to perform. He couldn't fuck up now.

"What are you telling me?" Rogan said. There was an edge in his voice, and Tommy could sense the old menace. Maybe he was wrong. Fate had nothing to do with it. Rogan was just a bad-ass. Maybe it didn't make a dime's worth of difference if Tommy was there or if he'd hailed the car. Maybe Rogan just wanted to waste some niggers. If not Norman, then some other poor sonofabitch who just happened along. Wrong place, wrong time.

"I'm saying we ought to tell the truth, get it over for good and all."

"That's great, Tommy," Rogan said. "That's the best idea I've heard in a long time. You're a real deep thinker. I always said that about you. And what do you think would happen if we went out right now and told everyone what happened? You think they'd say, 'Oh, that's very interesting. Thanks for coming forward'? You think we'd get a commendation for honesty? Fuck no, not for me, anyway. They'd have my ass in a sling. And not just me. I wasn't the only one in that whole deal; you were in it too—you covered for me. And it doesn't stop there. Everybody who backed us up along the line'd be in the soup with us, count on it. The whole goddamned thing would come out."

Tommy was getting tired of everyone saying he was stupid. He'd had to take it from the D.A., but he didn't have to listen to this shit from Rogan. No one had ever accused him of being any kind of genius. He was about to say something when he noticed Magnusen had suddenly come alive. Animated now, he was weaving his hand around an imaginary spool and Tommy knew this meant he was supposed to keep Rogan talking because this stuff would hang him. But there were only so many questions he could ask and still sound anywhere close to natural. He was doing his best. "I know," Tommy said, temporizing. "I understand that. Everyone else would be in it too."

"Well, if you understand so goddamned much, why are we having this conversation? That's what I want to know. Why am I standing out here in the rain, when my rig's supposed to be in Oklahoma in six hours?" Rogan's voice rose, but Tommy could tell he was trying to keep a lid on it. "It's over and done with," Rogan sighed, as if the conversation demanded great patience. "The best thing with a sleeping dog is to let it lie there, know what I mean?"

Magnusen was spooling his arms like mad, and Tommy knew the agent was afraid Rogan was going to hang up, which would be bad. He hadn't confessed to anything specific yet and he'd know enough to avoid picking up the phone again. This was their chance, and it was important not to blow it. For a moment, Tommy felt relaxed, even languorous. Screw Magnusen. Let him track Rogan down on his own and get him to talk about murdering a black kid twenty years ago. He'd see how easy it was. Still, the whole thing held a kind of dull fascination for Tommy, like a ball game on a hot afternoon. He wanted to follow it through, just to verify his own sense of what had actually gone down, just to hear Rogan say it. He tried a new tack. "Jesus," he said, "don't you ever wish that it'd never happened? That you just never did it?"

"Sure, I do." Rogan's voice was softer now. "It's goddamned unfortunate, even if it was an accident. But they taught us to do it right in the Academy, when we were full of piss and vinegar. Remember what-the-fuck's-his-name became a captain later? Sprague, Steckel, something like that."

"Yeah." Tommy had no idea who Rogan was talking about, but Magnusen was pumping his fists up and down, like he was at a football game.

"I can still see that sonofabitch," Rogan said. "Big guy with a butch haircut and a gut on him. You know, 'You guys ever get in a deal and you have to put one down, protect yourself. Stick a knife in his hands, stick a fucking gun if you have one. You're innocent, sure, but protect yourself.'"

Tommy waited. He didn't remember anything like that from the Academy, but why bother making it up? Rogan didn't know he was on tape. "So right there in the beginning they fucking taught us the whole thing. I remember Sprague talking to us guys just like I'm talking to you, saying to carry those little throwaways because you never knew what niggers were going to do. And that was just how it was. We didn't make the world, aina?"

"Sprague," Tommy said, just to keep Rogan talking. He didn't know any Sprague; he'd never even heard of him. Of course, he'd been in the bag the whole time they were training. He didn't even remember graduation.

"Yeah," Rogan said, remembering. "Big sonofabitch. Tall—know who I mean? Sprague, something like that."

"So that's what you did, that's why, I mean."

"You were there," Rogan said. "You saw everything."

"Right, right," Tommy said, even though he had never seen a knife. This was Rogan's game now: his memory, his truth. Magnusen was giving the high sign, but they weren't through yet. Rogan hadn't confessed, not quite. Suddenly, Tommy felt powerful, in control. His voice took on a casual ease. "I still think we should just go in and tell the truth about this, John."

Rogan's voice was hoarse with emotion. "Look, Tom, this whole deal is just so unfortunate. I'm not a killer. I never killed anyone before or since. It just happened. I mean, it was an accident, you know that."

So now it was Tom, not Tommy, not the asshole who had lied for him, but a man to be reckoned with, a man of respect after twenty years. But the problem was Tommy believed him, believed it had been an accident. It didn't make sense that even Rogan would have wanted things to go as far as they had. What Rogan wasn't saying, though, was that what had happened had a lot to do with who he was. Even if what he said about the Academy was true, all cops went through the same training and most didn't come out carrying throwaways. But that wasn't really the point and Tommy tried to drive it out of his mind. "I just think we got to go to the D.A. with this," he said. "We got to come clean."

"Tommy, I'm pleading with you," Rogan said. "Don't tell a fucking soul. Come out here and we'll go fishing. We'll talk it out, everything, but don't go to the goddamned D.A. Who'd believe it was an accident now? Things are different. Black this, black that—they'd have a fucking field day with a white cop who shot an unarmed nigger kid. No matter how you punish yourself, you got to live with it. And on my own point, I lose my job, I lose my home. I made a new life and worked hard to forget about all that bullshit. Now I'd lose everything, and why? The kid's dead. It's over. Finished."

Tommy almost laughed. Here they were talking about not telling any-one and Magnusen was sitting across the table with his headset on. It was finished all right, but not the way Rogan meant. Hearing Rogan try to talk him out of it, Tommy didn't feel so bad. He knew if he went out to Colorado he'd be just as dead as Jimmy Norman. He could hear it in Rogan's voice. John Rogan could say he wasn't a killer, but he had killed once and he'd do it again. Like he said, he stood to lose everything. Tommy shivered. He was glad he'd gone to the D.A., glad he had this tape. "It won't be over for me until it's over," he said.

"Just don't fuck me then, Partner," Rogan said, resigned now. "Do what you think you have to do, but keep John Rogan the hell away from it."

Tommy didn't know how Rogan thought he could keep him out of it, but he didn't say anything because it didn't matter. The deed was done. When he hung up, he looked over at Magnusen. "That OK?"

For the first time in weeks, the agent smiled. "Rogan's ass is mine now," he said. "All we've got to do is go out to Colorado and pick him up."

Twelve

Andy was still reading Tolstoy, but it was slow going. Morning had always been sacred; even when he was driving back and forth to Madison, he had always found time to read before going off to the legislature. But the campaign had bogged down and he couldn't get it out of his mind, which disturbed him. Perhaps he was more ambitious than he had admitted to himself.

Though Jimmy was frustrated by his apparent inability to get through to Andy, his criticism actually had more effect than the campaign manager knew. Andy wanted to do the right thing and he wanted to win. It was just that Jimmy's practical suggestions always presented themselves to Andy on a philosophical level as well. Thus, it wasn't only a question of his willingness to adapt, but his ability to, and then finally the question of whether change truly existed or if there were only differences in perception. Not that Andy thought this helped—he didn't—but he knew he couldn't do anything about that.

He closed the book and looked out the window. The wind was whipping the water into whitecaps out beyond the bluff. Where was Sarah? He couldn't remember the last time he had seen her, and this made him vaguely anxious. Even when things weren't going well between them, they had always talked. Now he felt as if he had lost his compass. Something was wrong, he knew that. He told himself it was the campaign, but the truth was he didn't want to think about Sarah's problem. He just wanted it to go away. What he needed from Sarah was stability, support, someone to bring his troubles to. But she wasn't there.

All fall she'd been increasingly distant. Pleasant but absent. She no longer complained about his being gone or about her own political duties. In fact, she didn't complain at all, which wasn't like her. At first, Andy thought perhaps the new apartment was the answer. Was it possible that for once they had identified a problem and solved it? Could it be that having a quiet place to work was all she had truly needed? He couldn't believe this, but there was no other logical explanation. Of course it was ungrateful of him to consider Sarah's apparent satisfaction to be a problem; it wasn't that, not really. She did seem to be happy, or happier, but more important, she seemed content, at peace. And while this should have pleased him, it didn't, because her happiness had nothing to do with him. What was it, he wondered, that made her sing to herself in the morning while she worked in her garden?

He had probed gently, asked about her writing, how the apartment was working out. But while Sarah wasn't exactly evasive, she wasn't forthcoming either. Things were fine. She didn't have anything to show him; maybe in another month. He remembered a Polish proverb: Beware a happy wife. He had never thought much about it, but his mother never smiled and his parents had been married for sixty years. Sarah's behavior concerned him, but he didn't have time to think about it seriously now. Jimmy was coming by in a few minutes.

As he was dressing, he got a call on his private line from Marcus Jackson. "Isn't it early for you, Reverend?" he asked, but Jackson wasn't in a joking mood.

"Never mind that. We've got to talk."

Andy had never heard Marc sound both upset and excited. He balanced the phone between his shoulder and jaw as he worked cufflinks through his sleeves. Andy dressed conservatively, J. Press and Paul Stuart as a rule. But recently he had ordered a few suits from a tailor in Chicago and their cost had made him feel daring. He laid a gray pinstripe on the bed and searched his closet for a tie. "What is it?" he asked.

"Not on the phone," Jackson said. "Can you get down here in half an hour?"

Andy placed a burgundy foulard inside the lapels of the suit. Good clothes made up for some of what life did to you, he thought. "See you then," he said.

Jackson's office was crowded when Andy arrived. It was only two rooms and then a large open lounge where some teenagers wearing earphones and high-top leather sneakers sat in broken-backed chairs. Andy wondered how they could talk and listen to music at the same time, but the question became academic as all conversation ended when he entered the room. Everyone waited in awkward silence until Jackson's secretary motioned Andy inside.

Marc was seated behind a desk that took up most of the office. He was a small, lithe man and wore an open-necked shirt and no tie, and Andy noticed his hair had begun to gray. Marcus stood to shake hands but didn't come out and join him in the other club chair. Instead, he stayed behind the barrier of the desk, as if this were a formal meeting. "What's going on, Marc?" Andy asked. "What's all the mystery?"

"Remember a month ago you called me about this cop, what's-his-name, who was involved in the Norman murder?"

They both knew his name, but Andy went along. "Tommy Paley." He hadn't heard any more about it since his conversation with Bob Joseph. In fact, he hadn't seen Joseph, which seemed strange. Now Marcus's manner, the fact that he didn't want to talk on the phone, piqued his curiosity.

Marc smoothed the desk blotter, patting it down. "I put the word out after you called, no big thing, just 'what have you heard?'" Marc stopped and looked at the ceiling. "At first, I didn't get much. Someone saw Paley at a tavern on Third putting them down pretty good, but nothing unusual about that. Then I got a call from a friend of mine, a black cop, who said he heard Paley'd come in."

"Come in?"

Marcus nodded. "Right, as in the front door of the Safety Building. Going to see Tim Dolan, my friend says."

"The district attorney?"

"Shit, yes, the district attorney. How many Tim Dolans you know, Andy?"

Andy ignored this. He was getting the chills. "When was this?"

"Last month." Marcus held up his hand for peace. "And I didn't tell you then because there was nothing to tell. He was in town, which you told me, and people saw him. That's all there was to it. For all I knew he stopped in to have coffee with Dolan."

Andy smiled indulgently at this. There was no point in losing his composure; this was politics in the inner city. Still, it seemed unlikely that even Marcus could think white people were so insensitive that a cop who had been kicked off the force would drop in for a social call on the new D.A. twenty years later. "And now you do have something to tell me, Marc? Or more likely, something to trade."

Marcus was enjoying his edge. Andy knew that information was what put you up on other people, the way you got the things you needed. What you knew and how soon you knew it were often your only leverage. "I'll get back to you on that," Marcus said. "Promise." He shifted his weight and looked at Andy with a slight smile on his face. "Like I said, all we had was Paley coming in and even that was just a rumor, so really we had nothing. But it put a flag on the thing, made me want to pay closer attention. And the next week things got really interesting because Paley rented a crib on the north side, Wiel Street."

Andy raised his eyebrows. "Moving back to town? So what? A man has a right to rent an apartment."

"Sure he does," Marcus said. "Even a scumbag like Paley has rights in our great nation. But why would he share it with an agent of the Federal Bureau of Investigation?"

Andy didn't understand, didn't understand Jackson's sudden interest, didn't understand the FBI's being in Paley's life. "They're living together?" he said.

Marcus laughed. "Not like that, at least not as far as I know. Thing is, my man made the agent 'cause he used to be a Milwaukee police detective, arrested him once back when. So we checked, and what do you know, this dude was the one who fingered Rogan back in '59. Quit the force. Now he works for the Feds, name of Magnusen."

Andy felt like a slow child. He still wasn't putting it together. "This man, Magnusen, was involved in the Norman investigation?"

Marcus nodded. "Big time. He was first on the scene, testified before the coroner's jury. He was the only one who didn't go along with that bullshit about Jimmy having a knife. Kind of funny he's suddenly tight with one of the perps? And that's not all. They put some fancy phone equipment in. And not to tap Paley, because they're in there together."

"Together," Andy said to himself. "Listening to what?"

Marcus pointed his finger at Andy. "Very good. That's exactly what we want to know. What's more, they got a third man now so they can cover the phone twenty-four hours. No one goes in or out, and the landlady doesn't say shit except that Paley won't shovel the walk. Something's going down, but we can't figure out what. Which is why I called you."

Andy sat silently, thinking it over. He remembered his conversation with Joseph and how he seemed to think Andy might know something, but why? Of course, Joseph could have been fishing, but what was he looking for? And why had the FBI gotten involved? Whatever Paley might have done, he hadn't broken any federal laws; he hadn't even been charged. Jackson was right: something was happening, something important, but Andy didn't want to betray too much interest. "I'm late," he said. "But let's stay in touch."

Marcus wasn't fooled. "Just remember who you heard it from," he said, smiling.

Tommy Paley's behavior didn't remain a mystery for long. Three days after Andy's meeting with Jackson, he picked up his morning paper and read the headline: EX-COP ADMITS HOMICIDE. There were grainy pictures of Rogan, Paley, and Jimmy Norman above the fold along with a sidebar under Bob Joseph's byline explaining how Paley had sworn the reporter to secrecy in an August phone call. Now Andy realized that their conversation must have taken place just after Joseph had heard from Paley.

The story went on to say that Rogan had been charged and brought to town on a private plane accompanied by a Denver attorney and had already pleaded guilty to homicide by reckless conduct and perjury for having lied to the coroner's jury. Andy noted that he had been charged and convicted the same day.

Joseph's column recounted Paley's battle with alcohol, which had ruined his personal life and eventually sent him to prison. "'I couldn't live with myself,'" Joseph quoted Paley. "'Every day seemed like a lie; I couldn't accept what we had done to that boy. The only way out was to finally tell the truth, even if it took twenty years to do it.'"

Which was affecting, but the importance of the case went beyond melodrama. Paley's struggles with his conscience didn't really matter to anyone else. The real story was the cover-up of the murder and the obvious corruption of the coroner's jury. That the police made mistakes was inevitable. Official complicity in concealing a murder made it more serious. Standing on his front steps in his bathrobe, Andy wondered how long it would take for the press to realize this and start pushing the mayor.

Jimmy was not as calm when they met later. "They're trying to get Rogan sentenced and out of town before anyone knows what's going on," he said. "We can't let them."

"You can't blame them," Andy said. "It's bound to be embarrassing to the mayor. But I don't think there's much chance they'll succeed." He looked at the paper again. "The television reporters will be furious at being beaten by the print media, and the other paper will be looking for its own story, if it isn't already."

"Maybe we should put out a release," Jimmy said. "You're horrified, you can't believe such a thing could happen in Milwaukee, you want an investigation."

Andy smiled tolerantly. "But, of course, I don't blame the officers on the street, who were only following orders, because I don't want to alienate the union? I'm surprised at you, Jimmy. Usually you have such good instincts." He shook his head. "I don't see how we can help ourselves by jumping in before we know more. Let's wait and see what the mayor does. Of course, we should also keep in touch with our friends in the black community. I'll have something to say sooner or later. I don't want to focus on Rogan or the murder."

"What else is there?"

Andy shrugged. "How does something like this happen? Rogan didn't invent racism. Every kid in my high school was a racist according to today's standards. Prejudice was something we breathed growing up in my neighborhood. We were afraid of the blacks and they were afraid of us. The cops kept us apart and it was probably a good thing. So when you look at a man like Rogan, you have to ask about his background. What did his parents do? Where did he grow up? And what made him so different from the other cops who trained with him at the Academy—or was he really very different at all?"

"I'd say he was different," Jimmy said. "He shot a kid in cold blood and then planted a knife on the body. And no one's ever said he showed any remorse about it. To John Rogan, the whole thing's just a run of bad luck, like losing money at poker." Jimmy shook his head. "This wasn't your average south side racist telling nigger jokes in the barroom, Andy. You didn't go to high school with this guy."

"Let's say you're right," Andy said. "And it wasn't Rogan's background or his training. Let's say he was as bad as everyone says. That still doesn't let the department off the hook. They should have picked up on him. There was a detective involved, and a captain, the chief of police, and the district attorney too. There was an inquest, with a citizens' jury chosen by the county sheriff. Rogan couldn't make the ruling of justifiable homicide himself. He needed help. It's too easy to say that it was just some crazy cop out shooting people. And if there was a cover-up, it's pretty obvious that Rogan wasn't smart enough to engineer it alone."

Jimmy nodded. "No argument there, but that's how they'd like it to look."

"Damned right. Maverick cop, everyone's very sorry, but justice delayed is not justice denied. One bad apple and that's all. Easy. It's our responsibility not to let them get by with that."

Jimmy looked at Andy with new respect. "Maybe you've got some political instincts, after all," he said.

Andy smiled. "It's good to know I can still surprise you now and then."

Joseph's phone was ringing off the hook and he'd been in meetings all morning, first with Klein, then the editorial board. At noon the New York Times called. They were sending a reporter up from Chicago, but in the meantime could Bob do something for the paper? They had run his original stuff and now they wanted a second-day story. When Bob hung up, Newsweek called. A writer was on his way, but they needed background. There was a rumor that *60 Minutes* was doing a segment on the Norman case.

When he told Mike, the older man grinned broadly. "Everyone is going to be all over this now," he said. "But we've got the advantage because we were there first. We'd be crazy to keep trying to top everyone else with reaction stories. Let the Post do that. Our job is to tell people what all of this means, what the story's about."

"That's pretty obvious, isn't it?"

The managing editor shook his head. "Not really. Not to me. Like I said when you first told me about Paley, I'm not all that excited about the shooting. We had to report it and we did. But that's not the story I'm interested in. I want to know how that got hidden so easily in a city like Milwaukee. Why wasn't anyone asking questions, and I don't the mean just the black community or the aldermen or the mayor, I mean us too. Where was the press on this one? And why is everyone so eager to have Rogan cop to a lesser plea? I know it's hard to be shocked by the death of one kid, but maybe we should try a little harder. In Israel when a soldier is killed, the whole country goes into mourning, and they've been at war for twenty-five years. Think about that for a moment."

Mike paused. Bob didn't know what to say. It was true. Death wasn't shocking; nothing was shocking anymore. They had stopped being shocked sometime after Vietnam, after the Kennedy assassinations, and Martin Luther King. "You're right," he said.

"There's something wrong with a society that just shrugs when a kid is killed by a cop," Mike said. "We should take a good long look at that."

"Still an idealist, Mike?" Bob said. "I wish I was."

Klein smiled, his teeth a jagged line in his mouth. "Work on it, kid," he said. "You're good at everything else. When you write your story, think about how we got so tolerant of murder. And when. I'd like you to think about an old-fashioned word: outrage. Things used to outrage us; it wasn't just religious fanatics that talked about morality. We don't have any goddamned standards anymore; it's whatever you can get away with." Mike smiled sheepishly. "I need a soapbox. Maybe I should go back to writing editorials."

Bob shook his head. "Sure, except you're right. It's fine to blame TV or the movies. Maybe they concentrate whatever's out there. But I can't remember the last time I heard someone take responsibility, say something was their fault or apologize."

Klein pointed at him. "Exactly. Well, go out and write that story for me. Where the hell did decency go in this town? If we could get the people to do a little soul-searching, we might really accomplish something."

Listening to Mike, Bob wondered why he hadn't seen as much. To him, the story was more than cops and robbers, but not that much more. Still, he was excited. There weren't many days when he came to work thinking what he did mattered to anyone except himself. Mike made it all seem crucial again. "I'll try to get some of that," he said.

"See that you do," Klein said.

At three, Sarah called. "I'm insulted," she said. "All the time we've spent together and you never said a word about Tommy Paley."

"Not to you, but I mentioned something to Andy that first day. I guess he didn't tell you. He probably doesn't remember."

Sarah laughed. "Andy never forgets anything, but that's no excuse. I told you everything." Her voice dropped. "It's a wonderful story, Bob, but does this mean I'll never see you again?"

"I haven't had lunch."

"Do you think your public will tolerate your being away?"

"Let me worry about that."

"Fifteen minutes," she said. "At the apartment."

They were holding Rogan in a cell at the Safety Building, away from the other prisoners. A white cop who had shot a black teenager wouldn't last long in the general prison population. Tommy hadn't been in court when Rogan arrived, but Dolan had left word for him to be admitted.

A guard brought Rogan into a conference room in handcuffs, which Tommy thought was excessive. The guy wasn't going anywhere—why play games? Rogan was dressed in gray prison dungarees, and when he sat down he centered a pack of cigarettes on the table in front of him like a deck of cards. Then he looked up, as if he were surprised anyone else was there. "You got this room bugged too, Tommy?" he asked, but John didn't seem angry, merely resigned.

On television, Tommy had thought Rogan looked like a dude in his checked sport coat, bolo tie, and cowboy boots. He was showing some attitude too. But in jail in the middle of the night, he was just another tired, middle-aged guy with more hair on his chest than on his head. "I'm sorry, John," Tommy said. "I tried not to tell anyone, to live with it. I tried like hell and I did it for twenty years, but it was just too much."

Rogan nodded and dragged on his cigarette. "So now you're a hero and I'm in here waiting to get corn-holed by every nigger in the joint. Great."

"They're not putting anyone in with you," Tommy said quickly. Dolan had assured him that they understood the risks of Rogan's situation.

Rogan shrugged, unimpressed. "Tell the truth, I don't give a damn. I really don't. I just think I got a shitty deal, that's all. Back then, the whole fucking city was behind me, including you, Tommy, whether you wanted to be or not. But it wasn't just you. The detectives, the chief, the fucking D.A. I even heard the mayor was in on it, you know, on the qt. But think about it: We had no fucking evidence to support our story. So how do I get off so easy if the higher-ups aren't in too? It doesn't take a genius to figure that out."

He grimaced, showing Tommy his yellow teeth, and repeated, "The whole fucking city. Goddamn. They all hated the niggers back then. I used to get money in the mail every week, remember? And now it's like I'm fucking Lee Harvey Oswald and no one else knew anything." He laughed silently without moving his lips, smoke punctuating his breathing.

"I told them about the others too," Tommy said. He knew it was hopeless, but he wanted Rogan to understand his position. He didn't care about the others, what they thought. But he wanted Rogan to know what he had gone through.

"Yeah?" Rogan made a pretense of looking around the room. "Funny, I don't see anyone else in here taking the heat with me."

He was right. Even Joseph's stories in the Times described the cover-up only in vague terms. The reporter hadn't named names, and so far Dolan had refused to talk to the press. What's more, the deal Rogan's lawyer had accepted specified that he wouldn't talk about the case publicly or testify. Dolan had really pressed the point, Tommy remembered, and now he wondered where the pressure had come from.

"Is there anything you need, anything I can get you?" Tommy asked now.

Rogan lifted the pack of cigarettes. "More of these. If I'm lucky, maybe I can kill myself before sentencing."

"OK," Tommy said. "You want me to come back or should I have them delivered?"

Rogan looked at him. He seemed irritated by Tommy's hesitant manner. Then he sighed. "Shit, I want you to come back. I always liked you,

Tommy, and I still do, even if you turned me in. You're probably the only friend I've got left in this town. If you'd moved to Colorado like I wanted you to, maybe none of this would have happened."

Tommy nodded. "Maybe." What a pair of losers they were, sitting in jail in the middle of the night. If it weren't so sad, he would have laughed. When all was said and done, they were friends, weird as that seemed. But while there was no point in contradicting Rogan, he was wrong about Colorado. It wouldn't have mattered where Tommy was. There was only one way for him to begin to get straightened around. It was too bad about Rogan; he was sorry to be the one to put him away. Which was easy to say, but it was the truth. Still, Tommy wasn't confused about what he had done. Say what you want about the chief and the mayor and the coroner's jury. Tommy agreed they were all scumballs. But no one else had pulled the trigger. John Rogan had done that all by himself. Tommy had held the line for twenty years, and if that wasn't good enough, then that was too goddamned bad. Everyone was a genius at living other people's lives, but living was hard. If Tommy had learned anything, he had learned that. He had done what he needed to do. That was it and that was all.

He stood and pushed his chair back. Rogan remained seated, smoking. "Take it easy, then, John," Tommy said. "I'll be back."

Thirteen

Olivia Norman Brown knew she made a strong impression on people. Even just riding the number fifteen bus back home from her job at the telephone company, she could always feel the others looking at her, wondering who she was. Because it was obvious she was somebody. It had always been that way. And it wasn't just because she was a statuesque black woman in a brilliant royal blue coat and the wife of T. O. Brown, who owned the Rocket Car Wash on Third Street. It wasn't just that at all.

T. O. was important in the community—Olivia knew that—but her husband's stature had little to do with the way she felt about herself. Even as a little child back in Alabama, she could remember the preacher coming to Daddy to talk about her, saying, "Watch now, that Olivia is something special. Be careful with her." And even if there was nothing so unusual about answering telephones, Olivia still felt she was different and that sooner or later something would come along and declare itself and show this to everyone.

Of course, there was Jimmy and everything that had followed from that. Thinking of it, Olivia put a hand to her heart. For it had been a heartbreak, the actual thing, a rending and tearing away of a part of her. And even if things had gone better since then, and even if Olivia now had money to buy whatever she needed and some things she didn't need, it couldn't change the fact of that loss. She had never gotten over Jimmy, not really, even if she didn't cry anymore or talk about it, and she knew part of the reason was that she didn't want to get over him.

Olivia always sat in the back of the bus, as she had back home, and though she knew people noticed her, she tried never to draw attention to herself. She always had a smile for the driver, but just a small one, not enough to encourage casual conversation. Olivia valued her privacy. And it worked. Folks respected her and left her alone. When T. O. practically begged her to let him buy her a new car so she wouldn't have to stand on the corner waiting in the cold, Olivia refused. She liked to be out among the people.

She had been the first in her family to come to Milwaukee in 1952, and because she liked the city and was happy there, the others had followed, all except Daddy, who said he was too old. He wouldn't come no matter how hard she tried to convince him.

"I want you to find some different kind of life," he'd said. "But the change would be too much for an old nigger like me."

And so they had all come, even Jimmy, who was only thirteen years old. Olivia remembered going down to the bus terminal on Michigan Avenue to meet the Greyhound and seeing this little boy in a man's overcoat, his hat falling over his eyes, which were just as wide as they could possibly be. She had to laugh, and he looked so hurt that she hugged him to her and cried with happiness because at last the family was reunited. She had taken Jimmy home, but they didn't have any money then, so at first he slept on a blanket in the kitchen next to the stove. After a few weeks, T. O. found a rollaway that they put in the living room behind a screen along with a small chest of drawers. And that was how it was until the troubles began.

Olivia tried and tried to get Jimmy to go to school; she wanted him to be the first one to go to college. She bought him a new suit and a brown leather briefcase. She bought spiral notebooks in different colors and a pencil case and a plastic ruler and a protractor. But nothing seemed to make Jimmy like school. He came home the first day with his suit torn and dusty, and he had lost the briefcase. Finally, he said, "Sister, I just can't go back there. My hands and feet sweat too bad, I get headaches, and the boys beat on me."

So Jimmy left school and that was the beginning. First, he worked as a carrier for a man who owned a contracting business, but he was fired for being late. Olivia didn't blame the contractor because she knew you had to be on time to your work, but it had a bad effect on Jimmy. After that, he just sat around the house all day, staring out the window and not talking. Then he started getting arrested. It was never anything bad, like they made out. But things happened and Jimmy always seemed to be in the wrong place, which grieved Olivia, who loved him like a son. She sat him down with T. O. and together they tried to talk to Jimmy, and at first she thought they were successful. But then Jimmy got picked up again, and she saw that something hard had dropped between them—she could see it in Jimmy's eyes—and after that she couldn't get through anymore. Still, she wanted to help. She explained to the policeman that he had only patted that little girl's head and nothing more. And she told the girl's mother that, but the woman filed charges anyway, and that was when Jimmy went away the first time. Olivia and T. O. visited Jimmy at the Boys' Home, and she wondered if this was actually for the best, if it was something he needed. But a week after he got home, Jimmy showed up with a car, and when Olivia asked where he got the money to buy it, he just said, "Isn't it beautiful, Sister?"

The car bothered Olivia, bothered her more that she let on, because she knew Jimmy didn't have a job and he couldn't have come out of prison with any money. So how could he afford to buy any red Pontiac? But Olivia always tried to make the best of things, to see the good side, and since she couldn't return the car, in time she accepted it as Jimmy's new passion, and she was happy that something made him happy. Maybe the car would keep Jimmy out of trouble, because that was what worried Olivia most. She feared that Jimmy would cross some invisible line beyond which no one would be able to reach across and pull him back. Maybe, she told herself, he'd be more careful now that he had something he loved.

But things just got worse. Jimmy said that trouble always found him, but even if Olivia would never talk against her baby brother, she knew that Jimmy had something to do with it when the police came by to say he had been picked up for driving without a license. Still, she couldn't help defending him, because at base she believed in his goodness. How was the boy supposed to get a license, she asked, when he couldn't read the rule book to pass the test? They let him go, and Olivia begged Jimmy not to go out again in that car, at least at night, but he had said, "Sister, I've just got to." And so he had. But Olivia knew that if Jimmy had had that license when he was stopped, he might not have run, and maybe that man wouldn't have shot him dead.

It may as well have been her, but Olivia didn't blame the police entirely. There was just something in Jimmy, something wild, and Olivia knew it would have found its way out eventually, even if she never said this out loud to anyone. She had done what she could back then. She had gone to the papers with pictures and called the reporters, trying to get the truth out about what had happened, because even with all Jimmy's problems she knew he would never have gone at the policemen with a knife. He just wasn't that kind of boy. But everyone she spoke to told her it would do no good, and of course in the end they were right. Get yourself some comfort, they said, and Olivia had, though she kept it to herself. Even so, the heartbreak was still there, and having a little money and some standing in the community did nothing to heal the pain.

When the newspaper articles about Tommy Paley's confession first appeared, Olivia felt good, like it had taken a long time but at last they had Jimmy's killer and justice would be done. But the more she thought about it, the worse she felt, for it turned out they weren't even going to put the man on trial. Everything had been set up ahead of time, decided in a closed room downtown by a bunch of white men who couldn't have cared less, so now Jimmy's side wouldn't get out at all. Which just went to show what came of trusting white people to turn on their own, no matter how bad they said they felt. They treated the one cop like a hero for doing what he should have done twenty years ago and the other one just seemed to have disappeared.

Olivia thought of Daddy coming north all those years ago to bury Jimmy and then staying on for months, trying to get some justice by suing the people in charge downtown. How he fainted in court from his grief and aggravation and them acting like he was just some crazy old nigger, but in that way they had so you couldn't really say that's what they were doing and hope to ever prove anything. And after it was all over and done with, Daddy getting only twenty-five hundred dollars, as if that was all a son could ever be worth, at least a black one. And stubborn and bitter as Daddy was and had a right to be, how he would never cash that check no matter what Olivia said about how they could use that money and looking at a check pinned to the wall would never bring Jimmy back to them. And even that wasn't all, couldn't ever be all, for weren't two of her brothers out to County in that mental hospital, and didn't the rest of them suffer every day of their lives with all their pain and remembering?

Olivia thought about nothing else for a week, all day at the telephone company and then alone in her room at night, rocking back and forth by the window, her head aching as if something bad were growing inside. And what she finally came to was like a revelation, that sudden and undeniable: she needed a lawyer. But not one like that old man Daddy had, with the bald head and big belly, who called everyone downtown by his first name. No, she needed a lawyer good enough to fight the white man and fight him hard.

When she told her family, T. O. and her brothers were against the idea. The boys didn't want any more trouble, and T. O. said he had a business to run. But when they saw her eyes, they went along because there was no point in arguing with Olivia when she was bound and determined. So she had called Mr. Jackson, and he gave her this man's name and now they were down here in his office waiting and had been for thirty-five minutes.

Actually, Olivia was worried about the office, and the longer they waited the more worried she became. At first, when Mr. Jackson told her, she had been happy because the lawyer was a Jew and everyone knew they were the smartest and made the most money. She didn't want a black man, because the judge wouldn't listen to him, but now this man's office worried her because it was only upstairs of a drug store and the furniture wasn't very good and the magazines were old. Olivia wondered why the man didn't have better things and how good a lawyer could he be if he didn't make enough money to have a nice office. What's more, he had a black receptionist, a little snip of a girl who hadn't even offered them coffee. But she had to trust Mr. Jackson, had to believe he would do his best for them. She knew he wouldn't recommend a man who didn't know what he was doing.

That was the thought she was holding in her mind, but just when she had settled down and wasn't worried so much, this young man came out not even wearing a suit, just some kind of sweater and pants, like he was going to the ball game. And as good-looking as he was and as nice as he seemed to be, Olivia just found it hard to believe that he was any kind of lawyer at all. This man didn't seem to have any mean in him, and they needed that, needed a real man to go up against all those cops and lawyers downtown. Olivia had seen enough to know how bad they were. If he wasn't careful, they'd chew this fraternity boy up and spit him out. And now Olivia was really worried, but she went inside anyway, just to talk, she told herself, just to see, because they had come all this way and they owed Mr. Jackson that much as a courtesy.

Charlie Simons hadn't grown up in Milwaukee, so what he knew about the Normans he had read in the newspapers, but that was enough to convince him that this was the case he had been waiting for since he went south to law school. Even though Vanderbilt could not be said to be typical of the Deep South, Charlie was glad he had gone to school there because his experiences had validated his nascent ideas of what his life would be about.

He had come to Milwaukee to join a firm that represented draft resisters, but Charlie's practice changed after Vietnam. He now spent most of his time on cases involving employment discrimination, which he liked and which he thought was important, but this could not conceal the fact that he had begun to drift. Charlie had started to wonder if he was doing the right

thing in the right place, because it was characteristic of Charlie that he believed there was a right place—if not for everyone, at least for him—and
that he was obliged to spend his life looking for it.

It was also characteristic that whenever life became too easy or predictable, whenever he was making enough money to support his family, whenever he was getting along too well with his partners, that Charlie would then
decided he was in the wrong place and move on. So far, he had quit two
good jobs and given up a chance at partner in his own firm because things
hadn't seemed right, and while this drove his wife to distraction, Charlie
couldn't help it. Which was why when Andy Hedig called to say the Norman
family was looking for a lawyer, Charlie was immediately interested.

Now he wondered if he might have been mistaken. The two men
were large and silent, and Mrs. Brown looked as if she was angry about
something. Charlie had to remind himself of his tendency to take responsibility for things that had nothing to do with him. Anyway, Mrs. Brown had
reason to be angry, considering everything. But it had nothing to do with
him. He invited them into his office and offered coffee. Then he asked how
he could help.

Mrs. Brown did all the talking, and Charlie could tell that she would be
a difficult client and a worse witness, if they got that far. She held herself as erect as an African princess and acted as if his questions, no
matter how perfunctory, were personal insults rather than simple requests
for information.

"We're here for justice," Olivia said. "Just like I told Mr. Jackson."

"I think we can all agree on that," Charlie said.

"Not some people don't," Olivia said.

"I meant all of us in this room," Charlie said. "But perhaps you could
tell me exactly what you mean by justice, Mrs. Brown?"

Olivia looked at Charlie as if he were deranged. "Justice for my brother
Jimmy," she said. "And justice for my poor dead daddy. Justice for all my
living brothers and justice for me for bearing up with it all these years."

That seemed to cover everyone, alive and dead, but it was hard to
know exactly how to respond since most courts considered justice too
abstract for their deliberations and concentrated instead on legal procedure.
Still, Charlie had read about Aesculapius "Cap" Norman and remembered
his suit against the city. "I might be mistaken," he said, "but I thought I
understood that your father had already settled his case with the city attorney."

"Never cashed the check," Olivia said firmly. "We sent it back after he
died." Charlie nodded. He decided not to tell Mrs. Brown that this would

have no bearing if Cap Norman had previously accepted the terms of the settlement, as he suspected. Res judicata was an unforgiving legal principle. In general, you couldn't ask for another judgment on the same matter just because later you decided you could have made a better deal. Unless, of course, Cap Norman had been obstructed in some way, unless some piece of evidence had been withheld by the city, which was certainly a possibility.

"Were you thinking of a civil rights action, then?" Charlie asked.

"That sounds good," Olivia said.

Charlie nodded. It was the first time she'd seemed pleased since she came in the room. "We might be able to initiate an action on your brother's behalf, claiming his civil rights were violated by the murder."

"Which they were," Olivia said triumphantly. "A man don't have no rights once he's dead."

Charlie smiled slightly. Actually, it was quite possible that Jimmy Norman possessed more rights dead than he ever had alive. But even if that were true and it turned out they had sufficient grounds to file suit, he wasn't sure about the sister, wasn't sure he could work with her. "With Rogan's confession, you might have a case," Charlie said carefully. "Assuming we could show there was a cover-up. Were you thinking of asking for damages?"

"Damages?" Mrs. Brown looked suspicious, as if Charlie were suggesting she had damaged someone. He would have to be very patient with this woman, slow down, explain himself as clearly as possible, in order to ever win her confidence. For he could tell that she was both very intelligent and verging on paranoia, which was not the best combination he could think of.

"Money," Charlie said. He didn't want to be indelicate, but he needed to be understood and was getting tired of Olivia's querulous expression. "Do you simply want the court to say that what happened was wrong, or do you want to ask for money to alleviate the pain and suffering your family has undergone?"

Olivia wasn't put off by his bluntness. For the first time, Charlie thought he saw respect in her eyes. Then she smiled, as if pleased with what she had learned. "Damages," she said. "Definitely."

Charlie hadn't studied this area of the law recently, but he thought loss of companionship would apply only to parents or children of the deceased, not brothers and sisters. And it would be hard to prove cause and effect for the brothers in the mental hospital. On the other hand, the cover-up the papers were hinting at gave them an opening. There was the chance that they could persuade a judge to set aside Cap Norman's settlement because the city had withheld crucial facts of the case. Then they could initiate a new action on behalf of Jimmy's estate with Olivia and her brothers as beneficiaries. He couldn't see any other way to go.

Charlie pushed back from the table. "I'll need a week to study this in order to better advise you. And I'd like to discuss it with my colleagues."

"How long?" Olivia said, as if she hadn't heard.

"A week," Charlie repeated. Then he smiled.

"No more than that, though?"

"That should be enough." Charlie shook hands with everyone and walked them to the door. When he returned to his office he dialed Andy Hedig's number. "I just saw the Norman family, and I think I'm their lawyer," he said when Andy answered.

"You think so?" Andy sounded amused.

"Mrs. Brown wasn't exactly enthusiastic. I don't think she liked my clothes. Anyway, thanks for the referral."

"I've always had doubts about your wardrobe myself," Andy said. "Sounds like a perceptive woman. But thank Marcus Jackson—I was just the conduit."

"You thank him," Charlie said. Then he sat in the late afternoon calm, looking out his window at the street below and the people passing by, ordinary people, people without problems, or at least problems with which he had to be concerned. The malaise was gone. Now he knew he was where he was supposed to be again, doing what he was supposed to be doing.

He remembered that while he had promised Mrs. Brown money, they hadn't actually discussed his fee, and he wondered without being very concerned about it whether or not he had just taken on another pro bono case, something that would please neither his partners nor his wife. He smiled at the thought because this didn't matter to him, didn't matter at all. What mattered was that passionate sense of mission he always looked for in his work. This case would provide plenty of that. He shook himself out of his reverie and called his secretary on the intercom. He'd be working late and needed some case files from the city. He asked her to have a sandwich sent up from the cafe on the corner before she left for the day.

Fourteen

Though the Times had the advantage, the rest of the press was all over the Norman case now, leap-frogging each other daily with new revelations. Someone went out to Colorado and interviewed Rogan's friends and co-workers. Olivia Brown was the subject of profiles in both papers, and Tommy Paley had become a media figure. A week after Rogan's appearance in court, Tommy called Joseph and said he'd received a call from a Hollywood agent.

"What did he want," Bob asked, bemused.

"It was a she, and she wants to represent me," Tommy said. Joseph could hear both pride and amazement in his voice.

Bob was always willing to be surprised by life, but he couldn't see Tommy Paley with dark glasses and a sun tan. "What exactly does she want to represent?" he asked.

Tommy seemed insulted by this, as if it should be obvious. "She wants me to tell my story," he said. "She says I should concentrate on the crime and punishment thing."

There was something ludicrous about a broken-down ex-cop with a high school education talking this way. Bob doubted Tommy was familiar with Dostoevsky, but he had been wrong before. "Stage, screen, and television?"

"The whole shot is what she says."

"Well, you'd better start typing, Tommy. You know what they say about yesterday's news."

"That's just it," Tommy said. "I can't write. So I was kind of wondering if you'd do it for me."

Joseph laughed. "I've got a job."

"I was going to pay you," Tommy protested. "You know, after it gets published, then you get some of it."

The idea of being involved with Tommy Paley and his agent on a book project held a kind of seedy fascination for Bob. He didn't want to waste time on this, but it didn't seem right to discourage Tommy. "It's not that. I just I don't think my boss would like it. Conflict of interest and everything."

"OK, but there's some things I ain't told anyone yet." He sounded cagey and Bob liked it. It was nice to hear Tommy feeling good for a change.

"Just don't forget your old friends."

Tommy took this seriously. "I'd never forget you," he said. "If it wasn't for you I'd still be back on the slag heap drinking Thunderbird."

After Tommy hung up, Bob looked at the afternoon paper a copy kid had laid on his desk. Someone had found the old chief of police up north. After reminiscing about the old days, Martin claimed he remembered no cover-up. Across the page was an interview with Tanner, who didn't know anything either. Neither Martin nor Tanner had ever heard of throwaway knives, and both said Milwaukee cops were the envy of every other city in the country. Circling the wagons. Bob wasn't surprised. What could you expect when they had given their lives to the department, no matter what kind of cesspool it was?

Meanwhile, Dolan still refused to release the names of the detectives, living or dead, who had worked on the Norman case, and the mayor's office was silent. What you had when you got down to it were denials from everyone involved, except Rogan, who had been allowed to cop to a lesser charge instead of going on trial. Olivia Brown had hired a hotshot lawyer, and Tommy Paley was looking for a ghostwriter. Bob remembered his grandfather saying, "It's all part of life's rich pattern," whenever something unexpected came up. He smiled at the idea that he had something to do with creating this particular variation. Then he flicked off his desk light and headed out.

Andy Hedig was standing in the small lounge at Marcus Jackson's headquarters waiting for the meeting to begin. Marcus had invited Andy over ostensibly to discuss the Norman case with black leaders, but they had discussed their positions privately beforehand. The meeting was really for the press, who filled the room beyond the small fringe of community organizers.

When the television lights were switched on, Marcus announced that a march was being planned for the following Sunday. "It's an outrage that a crime of this magnitude should be treated with indifference by the elected officials of this city," he said. "You know and I know and everybody else knows that if a white policeman had been shot in the street by a black man, no stone would remain unturned in the search for the truth about what had occurred. Yet here we are twenty years after Jimmy Norman's murder still asking questions.

"We are told that the mayor is satisfied the truth has come out, the chief of police is satisfied, and so is the district attorney. There is no need for a special investigation, they say. Everything is fine." He paused dramatically and looked directly into the cameras. "Well, we are not satisfied, and we won't be satisfied with glib assurances. So on Sunday we're going to march for justice, just as the black people of this city should have marched twenty years ago. And we'll keep on marching until we get some answers."

There was a general murmur of approval, but Andy was struck by the absence of passion in the room. These people were regulars, committed to the cause. They would turn out to support Jackson, just as they had supported others over the years, but few in the room would remember Jimmy Norman. While the reporters scrambled to get down what Marcus had said, Andy looked at his friend, who had mentioned only one march to him. Marcus just shrugged, embarrassed but excited. He'd gotten carried away.

Now Andy stood to make his statement. Though he disliked public speaking in general, Andy preferred news conferences to informal gatherings at people's homes. He was used to dealing with the press and found the artificiality of the situation oddly comforting. He wore a dove-gray suit he had bought in London and wondered if he was over-dressed, but no one seemed to notice his clothes. While he was paid the polite attention generally accorded a candidate for public office, he sensed a certain boredom in the hall. Whatever news there was here had already been made.

"Are you going to march?" a reporter Andy recognized from Madison yelled from the back of the room.

"Nice to see you again, Phil," Andy said. "I had a feeling you'd have a question." He hesitated, as if searching for the words to express his feelings, though his statement was printed in speech ball and lay front of him on the lectern. "I've been marching for the rights of black people most of my adult life. In fact, I first met my good friend, the Reverend Jackson, on the Selma march. So, yes, I expect to march on Sunday, and I know I'll be joined by hundreds, perhaps thousands, of concerned Milwaukeeans of all races."

Andy paused. The audience was restless, and he didn't want to lose them. "I was going to read this statement," he said, indicating his notes. "But I don't really think this is the venue for speeches, at least not from me. It's a time for conscience, and we must all attend to those demands as best we can. I know I will. I do want to say that, like Reverend Jackson, I am concerned that Mayor Mueller and Chief Tanner do not believe this tragedy is worthy of their attention. Unfortunately, this is not an isolated incident, and those in positions of responsibility should address publicly any questions regarding the conduct of Milwaukee police officers. I too find it very peculiar that no investigation has been authorized into the alleged conspiracy to cover up the actions of those officers involved in the death of Jimmy Norman."

"I thought you weren't going to make a speech," Marcus Jackson said afterward.

"I couldn't help myself."

Marcus laughed. "Don't bullshit a bullshitter."

"Speaking of which, what about these marches?" Andy asked. "Or was that just rhetoric?"

"People are upset," Marcus said. "If we don't have marches, we might have riots. We could have them anyway."

Andy searched his friend's face for the ironic detachment that was usually present, but Marcus was serious.

"This happened twenty years ago, Marc. As bad as it was, who really remembers now?"

"No one, but that's not the point; Jimmy's not even the point. Every black man in town knows that if he takes a walk after dinner to clear his mind he could be stopped and frisked on suspicion of something. Any black kid is automatically a suspect in any crime committed within five miles. And the women are all whores or welfare mothers. It's been this way for years, so you're sitting on a lot of resentment. Add to that unemployment, poverty that won't quit, a cracker police chief, and top it off, Norman's killer is going to a country-club prison when any black kid who holds up a 7-11 does hard time at Green Bay."

"They haven't sentenced him yet."

Marcus nodded. "They made a deal, didn't they?"

Marc was right, but any indignation Andy felt was mixed with presentiments about the future. He remembered the riots of the sixties and was glad he wasn't mayor. Yet even in his moment of empathy, he realized this would affect the campaign. Just as Mueller couldn't appeal openly to the racists, he couldn't seem to capitulate to the blacks. And there was the legitimate issue of a police chief who was the supreme power in an internal hierarchy that could sweep even murder under the rug.

Mueller wouldn't admit that he couldn't control his own city, but the fact was that, at least in matters involving the police, Tanner seemed to be more powerful. The uproar over the Norman case gave Andy an obvious opening, and besides it was the right thing to do.

"Are you inviting Father Moretti?" Andy asked.

"Don't have to. He's like a roach—just shows up."

He understood Marcus's resentment, but Andy didn't mind the priest. Moretti's intensity made people uncomfortable, but they were people who should be uncomfortable. "At least his kids are organized," Andy said. "Otherwise, all you've got for crowd control is the police."

"And who's going to control them?"

"My point. We'd better make sure we control ourselves."

Fifteen

The thought came so suddenly to Sarah one morning that it made her suspicious of its simplicity. Andy was in his study reading, and she was drinking coffee and looking at the papers when she thought, "It just is what it is." Immediately, she felt embarrassed and somewhat annoyed with herself, as she would with a friend who had just discovered astral travel and had come breathlessly to tell her. It would be one thing if she were high or drunk, but it was seven o'clock in the morning, an odd time for The Answer to present itself.

Except that Sarah never thought of Bob as the answer. There was no answer, no explanation for what she was doing to her life. Still, instinctively she kept looking for reasons. Bob was good-looking and talented enough, but the most important thing was that he had fallen wildly in love with her for his own reasons. He didn't see her either as Andy Hedig's wife or a neurotic middle-aged woman whose ego needed a boost. Which was amazing enough without his also having to be the messiah. What was remarkable was that Sarah saw this clearly, knew Bob for what he was and accepted him. Satisfied? The truth was she was ecstatic. She took a deep breath and wondered if she could tolerate being happy.

She tried to think back to when she had first been in love with Andy, but it was hard. They had just been kids when they met, so delighted with what was happening that they never thought of analyzing it. She remembered noticing Andy in history lecture and being struck by how smart he was and how badly dressed. He wore white socks with black shoes and his pants were long and baggy, which made him look like a clown. But his eagerness to impress the professor and meet Sarah made him irresistible.

She had taken him home for Thanksgiving and was nervous about it since her parents had wanted her go east for college so she could meet someone with tone. But when Andy showed up wearing a suit and tie, called her father sir, and complimented her mother on her cooking, they were won over. Sarah's father had asked what Andy wanted to do in life, and he answered, "I want to marry your daughter and go to law school." Sarah remembered Daddy smiling at this, even though it was plain that Andy wasn't joking.

Afterward, Sarah's mother took her off alone and said, "That boy is a gem. Don't you lose him." Which struck Sarah as being odd and prophetic, as if even then the issue was what she might do wrong. Sarah wondered about her parents, since they had never been like this about anyone else. But in the end she did exactly what her mother told her to do.

They were married a week after graduation, and Sarah was pregnant by the time they loaded their car for the trip to New Haven. She remembered waving to her mother and crying until they passed Chicago, when she straightened in her seat and thought, "Well, that's over."

They found a flat near the Yale Bowl and she enjoyed walking the baby in the park while Andy studied. Daddy made sure they had money for weekend trips to New York, and Andy did well in school. Sarah thought of it as a bargain: he would work hard and succeed while she provided moral and financial support. It was like the Medicis or the Elizabethan Court, even though Andy wasn't an artist. And if this arrangement troubled Andy, he never showed it, just as he never asked directly for anything. He had a gift for making people want to help, and when he graciously accepted, they were pleased for being allowed the pleasure of contributing to his life.

Andy made law review, but more important, the people he met at Yale liked him and recommended him for jobs. His earnestness might have been questioned if someone had been so inclined, but with Andy it just seemed organic, not something he cultivated to impress anyone. Things mattered to him in a way they didn't to most people. When President Kennedy was killed, Andy took it personally, as if the assassination had occurred within his own family; it made him question his own life, though Sarah couldn't really see what it had to do with them. Later on, he felt the same way about Bobby Kennedy and Martin Luther King, Jr., as if each successive murder had taken something from him that could never be replaced.

Yet along with his seriousness, Andy had a capacity for delight that Sarah prized. She remembered taking him to J. Press and explaining about patterns and stripes and English shoes, and afterward Andy seemed as interested in his new clothes as he might have been in an unusual case. He learned how to dress and how to talk, and exceeded his teacher in each area, so that in the end the only thing Sarah could regret was that in breeding the awkwardness out of her husband she had also lost the thing she loved about him. Sometimes now she found herself wishing Andy didn't dress so elegantly or know so much about wine and antiques. She missed those black shoes with the pointed toes, the pegged pants, and the white athletic socks. But what was gone was gone forever. There was no changing that.

After they returned to the Midwest, things were good for a while. They walked on the lakefront and went to film revivals at the Oriental. Andy took her to ball games and taught her to keep score, and she showed him the Impressionist addition to the art center. It was a nice time. They weren't in school anymore, and they were new enough to the city that their phone didn't ring constantly. If it had stayed that way, life could have been very different.

But then Andy decided to run for the Senate, and of course he was elected, which meant commuting back and forth to Madison. What made things worse was that Sarah felt she had no right to complain. After all, she had help, and Andy was encouraging her to go back to school. But she didn't want to take more classes; she wanted their old life back. She missed his relying on her, but the fact was that other people needed Andy now and those people were more interesting to him than his wife.

Her mother was no help. When Sarah confided in her mother, she said this was just the way men were, especially ambitious young men like Andy. He had to be out meeting people, impressing them. It was exactly what he should be doing at this point in his career. Sarah had to understand that what he was doing now was really for both of them. But Sarah already knew this; Andy had told her. Understanding was never the issue; it was just that the life that had grown up around them wasn't what she wanted and she couldn't remember anyone ever consulting her.

For a while she did take classes and go to poetry readings at the university because she had to do something with her time. Sometimes she'd stay afterward, even though the others were all ten years younger than she was. They'd be passing a joint and she'd take a toke, but it was all pretty innocent, so she was surprised to come in one night to find Andy and her parents waiting for her in the living room.

They made her feel like a child with their long faces and sincere voices. She cried and told her parents to go away, but they insisted that they just wanted to help. In the end, everyone decided all Sarah needed was a good rest. She hadn't done anything to need a rest from, but there was no use protesting that her inaction, her lack of a life, was the real problem. Arrangements were made with a private hospital where the staff was very discreet. All the rich women from Wisconsin who might embarrass their husbands in some way seemed to be in attendance, and in retrospect, Sarah wondered why the place wasn't more well known. But it worked. Andy wasn't embarrassed by Sarah, because no one knew what had happened, not even her closest friends.

The only problem was that it was hell for her. When she was in the hospital her head felt as if it were packed with cotton. Twice a day a nurse gave her a Dixie cup full of pills, and when she asked what they were, Sarah was told they were vitamins. After a week, she refused to take any more, and slowly things became sharper, though no less painful. The fact was that her husband had committed her against her will, put her in a rest home for rich drunks and lunatics. Sarah's only relief came, paradoxically, when Andy drove up on weekends. He was always very sweet, apologetic about the situation, but firm in his insistence on its necessity. They would have a picnic in a nearby park and Andy would give her the Milwaukee newspapers. It was more time than they had spent together in years, but it seemed somewhat extreme to check into a mental hospital just so she could have lunch with her husband.

After six weeks she was discharged into Dr. Jamison's care, and she saw him twice a week for the next three years in his paneled office in the Plankinton Building. She never saw anyone she knew coming or going in all that time, but the experience was degrading. Jamison seldom made eye contact with her and spent the sessions working on model railroad cars or cleaning his pipes with a small metal tool. Sarah talked on anyway because she supposed that was what the treatment was meant to be, and in time she came to understand her situation without anyone actually saying anything: she was important not because of anything inherent in her but because she was married to an important man and she had the potential to harm his career, which was unacceptable. It went beyond manners, beyond being willing to pour at campaign functions and knowing which fork to use. She could no longer be allowed a personal life, at least not one that might be seen as reflecting badly on Andy. So without ever discussing it with anyone, Sarah stopped taking classes and going to parties, and everyone said Jamison had worked miracles.

After that, there was affection between Sarah and Andy but no real closeness. Sarah told herself she didn't hold anything against him, but it was hard to trust someone who had committed you for smoking pot at a poetry reading. Still, life went on uneventfully. They were kind to one another, respectful, and Andy's personal conduct seemed to be above reproach. Sarah wondered from time to time if there were other women. It had been so long since there had been anything sexual between them that she wouldn't have blamed him. If Andy did have lovers, however, nothing ever came back to her, and since Milwaukee was in many ways a small town, Sarah thought she would have heard if there was anything to hear. She assumed he was faithful, and if he was frustrated, he never let on to her. They had made an accommodation not dissimilar from other couples in public life; he supported her and she respected the demands of his work. If their life wasn't wonderful, it had been adequate, at least until Bob Joseph came along.

Yet, after the first surge of passion, Sarah developed doubts about Bob too. He had grown up on the east side, after all, and graduated from Riverside. But he was much too talented for anyone to patronize. It wasn't only that he had worked in New York and was the lead political writer for one of the best newspapers in the country. What made Bob unique was that he didn't care. Nothing impressed him, including his own accomplishments. He was satisfied with the clothes he wore, though he didn't pay much attention to them. And he liked the old house he lived in, even if the wallpaper was stained and the roof was falling down. He enjoyed going to the stadium to watch the Brewers and drink beer with friends from the paper. Still, there remained something innocent about him, something sweet. After they made love, he'd say, "I just can't believe I'm here with you."

But Bob hadn't been sweet when she showed him her novel, which hurt because there was not a shred of malice or jealousy in what he said. "You shouldn't have asked me," he said. "I'm just not very good at flattering people."

"Couldn't you be more encouraging?"

"Sure, but writers don't get better because their friends pat them on the back. They improve because they can't stand being bad, because it's too damned painful. If a writer can be discouraged because of what someone else says, he should give it up. There are easier ways to drive yourself crazy."

After that, Sarah didn't ask him to read anything for a long time and Bob showed no curiosity about her writing. In this, he was completely different from Andy, who read everything she did and gave her long notes written by hand with his Mont Blanc pen. Finally Sarah worked up the courage to show Bob a new story, and he seemed to like it a little better than the novel, though he had really only grunted in the right places.

Most of the time, though, they didn't talk about writing. More and more, in fact, they didn't talk at all. Instead they listened to opera, took long walks, or went to matinees in obscure movie theaters on the far south side, where they sat in the dark holding hands. Yet Sarah was calmer than she could ever remember being, and so when Bob had asked how she felt about him, her first thought had been that of course she would leave Andy. Since then she had considered more carefully what leaving would mean, but she hadn't changed her mind. For while it made her sad; she knew that her pleasant, muted life with Andy was going to have to end, no matter how painful that might be. Because suddenly, at the age of forty-three, Sarah had a chance for something more than she had ever expected. What was re-markable about it was how unambivalent Sarah felt; she supposed she was going to have to become accustomed to that along with everything else.

Now Andy's door opened and Sarah was amazed, as she always was, at how youthful her husband was, how boyish when he smiled, as he did now. She felt something around her heart give. "You look thoughtful," he said.

"How's Tolstoy coming?"

"I'm learning a lot about Russian history."

Andy was so good at learning that Sarah had no doubt he'd be teaching a seminar before long. "What's on the schedule this morning?"

"Today's the march to protest inaction in City Hall."

"Watch that irony."

"You're right," Andy said. "I've got to be very serious about this."

"See that you are. But be careful too. I'm serious about that."

He bent over and kissed her forehead lightly. "The police will be there, but I'll watch out."

Andy turned and Sarah watched him go, slim and graceful. She felt enormous tenderness for him along with regret for what would soon hap-pen. She wondered briefly if she'd discover later that she'd made a terrible mistake. But tenderness wasn't the same as passion. And regret wasn't the same as remorse. There would be something seriously wrong with her if she didn't feel bad about leaving her husband. It should hurt. It should make her question herself. In the end, she had to trust her own instincts.

The plan was for the marchers to set off from Marcus Jackson's headquar-ters and walk down Third Street toward City Hall. But while the television stations all had trucks out and the pencil press was out in force, Bob knew the organizers would be disappointed in the number of marchers who had assembled this morning. There were a few white people from the Unitarian Church mixed in with the Guardians and street people, but the masses hadn't made it. Charlie Simons, whom Bob had known for years, stood off to the side. Bob walked over to join Charlie.

"Will your client be joining us today?"

Charlie smiled. "I have more than one client, but, yes, the one you're thinking of will be at the head of the line."

"You don't look like you're overjoyed about that."

"Actually, I'd rather be over at the Speed Queen having lunch, but I figured I'd better see what was going on."

The Speed Queen was a rib joint that had opened on the edge of the ghetto and become an immediate success with both the neighborhood residents and some white journalists and politicians who frequented the area. Before becoming a restaurant, the place had been a Laundromat with Speed Queen washers and dryers. The new owners had never taken down the sign. Bob hadn't been there for a long time and now he felt nostalgic for his old life. "How's it shaping up?" he asked. "The case, I mean."

"I won't try a suit of this magnitude in the press," Simons said.

Bob put his notebook in his pocket. "Same old bullshit, Charlie. So how's your life?"

Simons shrugged. They had been divorced at the same time, but Charlie had remarried within a year, a woman with two young children. "It's a bitch being a stepfather," he said. "I pay the bills and make sure the kids get to bed on time and off to school in the morning. But whenever her asshole ex-husband decides he feels like being a father, I'm out of the picture. How about you? Are you seeing anyone?"

"Actually I am," Bob said, "but I don't want to talk about it."

Simons raised his eyebrows. "So, it's like that? A married woman. I wouldn't have expected it of you, Bobby."

"Neither would I," Bob said, which was the truth. "That's probably why I'm doing it. I've got to get some good therapy one of these days." But in the moment of saying this, he felt guilty for joking about Sarah. Still, he knew there was some truth in what he said. "Think there'll be trouble today?"

"Are we off the record now?"

Charlie liked to give Bob shit about his job; it was a ritual with them. "For Christ's sake, we're just two old friends out for some sun."

Simons blew out some air. "I told Olivia not to come and I wish she hadn't. It isn't like she's been involved in the movement before and people expect it of her. She'll draw press attention, especially without more people around for camouflage. They're just using her for her name anyway."

"Who?" It seemed obvious, but Bob asked anyway.

"Who do you think? Jackson, Andy Hedig, and the rest of them. They don't give a shit about Olivia or her brother, for that matter."

"To them this is bigger than that?"

"You've got it," Charlie said. "But for Olivia there's nothing bigger than this case, there couldn't ever be. Of course that works to her advantage too. As far as the court is concerned, especially in a jury trial, she's much better off looking like an aggrieved sister than a civil rights activist. But maybe I'm wrong about all this. There's been a lot of grieving over the last twenty years and where has it gotten anybody?"

"About as far as a march will, if you ask me."

Simons hunched his shoulders. "Probably, but I can't blame her for being here. It's just that this should have happened a long time ago, and it would have if those ministers hadn't lost their nerve."

"You think that's what happened back then? That's why they never marched on MacArthur Square in 1959?"

Simons shrugged. "I wasn't here, but that's what I heard. Anyway, Olivia needs to feel important and the way I build the case isn't her problem."

"Unless she wants to win."

Charlie smiled. "Well, it's true that the client can help," he said. "But a lot of times they don't."

The doors opened behind them now, and Jackson and Olivia Brown came out arm in arm. Flanking them were several other black ministers and, to the rear, Andy Hedig and Father Moretti. Bob got his notebook out again, but there were no speeches. The leaders just started walking south down Third, followed by perhaps fifty marchers. The Guardians walked in formation on either side of the line while the television trucks drove ahead at a stately pace.

Joseph followed for a few blocks and noticed that the marchers were picking up stragglers at every intersection, but if it got no larger than this they were going to embarrass themselves, especially on a slow news day. Mass movements needed to be massive, and the side streets were empty. He circled back to his car and drove to the Times building. It would take half an hour for the leaders to walk down Third, so he went in to pick up his messages.

Tommy Paley had called but left no number. Joseph wondered what he wanted, but the story seemed to have passed Tommy by, or it would very soon. The question of guilt had been answered, at least for the murder. What people wanted to know now was whether anyone who was still alive had been involved. No one really cared about Martin off in retirement, but if Tanner had been in on it, then Mueller would have to act, or explain why. Yet no one was saying anything openly, not even Paley. He had been coy when Bob asked how high the cover-up went, which meant either there was nothing more or Tommy was afraid to talk about it. Olivia Brown's suit might bring everything out, but if Charlie Simons thought so, he had been careful not to say anything. Bob decided to press Paley harder about the cover-up.

The Times lobby was a large open area making the corner of Fourth and Kilbourn and was usually filled with people trying to place ads or get past issues of the paper. Its large picture windows faced the arena and offered various inducements to bring people in, but today the lobby was empty except for a guard reading the paper who hardly noticed Bob. He went down to the corner but still couldn't see any marchers, so he walked across the street. As part of the downtown revival, someone had put benches along a fringe of grass on the riverbank. Bob took a seat and watched the water.

Milwaukee was not a river city in the way that Cincinnati or St. Louis might be. The Milwaukee River had no colorful history and had never served as an inland railway, but it was important to Bob. He remembered what it had been like twenty years ago higher up, near the high school, when they had rented canoes and gone swimming in Gordon Park. In those days, the river was a dividing line between rich and poor, black and white, and people on the east side had panicked when the first black kids walked across the Locust Street viaduct to attend Riverside. He remembered the boys with their slick, processed hair and bright tuxedo shirts and the girls in party dresses for the first day of school. Nothing earth-shaking had happened, but there was some tension in the lunchroom for the first week, after which time everyone settled into a pattern of distrust and avoidance. Because he ran track and played basketball, Bob had come to know some of the black kids slightly, but their personal lives were separated in an almost surgical way. For no reason he thought of his wife, wondered where she was and what she was doing. After all these years, he still thought of her that way, as his wife.

He lay his head back on the bench and listened to the water flow and the low hum of traffic from the street behind him. The memories just came, unbidden and sometimes unwelcome but always unavoidable. The smallest thing, a song, a familiar face would remind him of Margie and he'd be locked up in the past again. He had even gone to a therapist, a small gnome-like man whom he had talked to for a year and then asked how he could forget about his marriage. "Tolerate it," the therapist said. "The memories, I mean."

"Then they'll go away?" Bob asked.

The man shrugged. "Maybe," he said.

Bob and Margie had known each other at Riverside but didn't start dating until college. After graduation, they had been married farther up the river, in Shorewood. It had rained all day and then miraculously cleared in time for the wedding, which everyone said was an omen. Some omen, Bob thought. He remembered writing their vows together, making chains of flowers that were supposed to be symbolic of fidelity and candor. It was painful to remember, but he couldn't help it. He let the past wash over him.

The wedding dinner had been at the Pfister, and the hotel threw in a room with a canopy bed and a bottle of champagne for the bridal couple. But sex had never been easy for them, and the champagne didn't help. They went to sleep turned away from each other in the king-size bed on their wedding night, and Bob remembered thinking it was like being alone. Though neither ever mentioned it again, he knew the beginning of their marriage was also the beginning of the end. It wasn't so much that things had gotten bad but that nothing ever improved as much as it should have. They never learned what they needed to know to make each other happy.

Oh, he had loved her; he would never love anyone with that desperate intensity again. But he had known, almost from the beginning, before the fights even began, when they were happy, that something was wrong, something basic. Now he watched the brown water flow south, and he felt inexpressibly sad, though not because he had lost the marriage. He was glad that was over. But he felt sad for the pain life seemed inevitably to bring to everyone, deserved or not. His affair with Sarah would hurt Hedig, who was a decent guy, but it was unavoidable. Unless of course things didn't work out, in which case he would be hurt. No one ever set out to fuck up his life; it just seemed to happen. But it happened a lot. Bob tried to think of someone he knew who had been treated well by life, but his mind was a blank, though he was willing to believe there were people like that. He threw a rock and watched it skip across the river. Then he returned to the corner.

In the distance, Bob could see flashes of red from the bikemen and a large crowd edging up against the curbs on Third Street. Somewhere along the way Marcus Jackson had found some people, and Bob felt a shiver of anticipation. He went to call a photographer, and when he got back, he could see them clearly, stretching all way back to the north side and chanting rhythmically, though he couldn't make out what they were saying. Jackson, Hedig, and Olivia Brown walked past arm in arm. Then Bob was part of a scramble of reporters trying to get to City Hall Plaza ahead of the marchers.

A platform had been erected, and the cops had cordoned off the area so that no cars were moving on Wells, but an unfriendly crowd had gathered behind the barriers and were waving flags. Bob saw only a few mounted cops and a couple of squads parked on the corner of Water Street, hardly enough for crowd control. He didn't like the way things were shaping up, but by then marchers were everywhere and he was looking for a place to stand.

Hedig joined Jackson and Olivia Brown on the platform, but he stood slightly in back of them, hands crossed in front of him, which Joseph thought was a good move. Solidarity was one thing, but if it looked like he was trying to take over it would hurt him. Of course even being there would alienate some people, but Mueller probably had those votes already.

The Guardians were walking a perimeter, and to his surprise Bob found himself inside their circle. One woman in a leather jacket stared at him and screamed, "Nigger lover!"

Someone was waving the Stars and Bars, and now Bob noticed that the Nazis had decided to put in an appearance. Nothing like a race riot to spice up the weekend, he thought, and started edging toward the back. But the circle tightened, and the surrounding city seemed eerily empty.

Jackson was conducting a contrapuntal chant: "Ain't gonna kill black folks . . ." one group of marchers shouted, while the others responded, "No more!" Hedig moved to the side of the platform, looking for an escape. Then there was a kind of brutal rumbling, as if a stampede had just begun.

Jackson moved forward to quiet the crowd, but before he could speak, rocks were flying. Now the mounted cops appeared from nowhere swinging their billies, but they seemed interested only in the marchers, who cowered in the middle of the plaza. Then a rock grazed Bob's forehead, and he ran to find cover. There would be time to sort things out later.

The door of the Pabst Theater was providentially open and Bob ran inside, where he stood in the ornate lobby watching the stream of blacks going by. He wondered what had happened to Andy Hedig, but then his instincts took over. He went to a phone on the mezzanine. His office was only a block away, but it was safer to call. When the desk editor came on, he was ready.

"This is Bob Joseph," he said calmly. Then he began to dictate his story.

Sixteen

Emil Mueller always read the paper before coming into the office, but this morning his executive assistant had left a copy of the Post lying open on his desk with its banner headline: RIGHTS RIOT INJURES 30.

There had been reports all night of snipers firing at squads patrolling the Core, and now Father Moretti was promising another march. They planned to go right over the Sixth Street viaduct and meet the Polacks head on.

Mueller switched on the intercom: "Get Tanner's ass in here," he told Fischer. "And you'd better get Dolan too."

He looked at the paper again and swore. Then he went into his private bathroom and rinsed his face. There was a small dressing room leading off it with a couch, and when Mueller was going through his divorce, he had spent more than a few nights there. That was the low point, the mayor of a major city sleeping in his office. But after he got divorced and met Tracy, things began to settle down. Now he had a lake condo and could look into his mirror with satisfaction. At fifty-five he was the longest-sitting mayor in America. He got a respectful audience from the national press when he went to Washington, and at Tracy's urging he had given up cigars and had himself photographed with a pipe in his hand whenever possible.

Mueller often said he thought no more of Andrew Hedig than a horse would think of a fly on his ass, and for the most part this was true. But it was hard not to be affected by riots. People would be hurt and property destroyed. It wasn't the way he wanted to go out. One more term was all he asked, and he thought he deserved that much. The liberals might have had their problems with him over the years, but the fact was that Emil Mueller had brought Milwaukee to a position of national prominence it had never known. The Socialist mayors and all that Progressive crap was fine, but when Mueller took over, the city was falling apart. There were no decent hotels or shopping downtown, and you had to go to Chicago to hear a concert. Mueller had rebuilt, bringing in new business and passing a bond issue for the civic center. Some wise-ass critic for the Times complained that the building looked like a crematorium, but it was better than the warehouses that had been there before. Along the way Mueller had made some deals to get things done, but the city was better off and everyone knew it. He wasn't going to let a little shit like Hedig ruin that. Not that he blamed his opponent for the riots, but he knew Hedig would use them in the campaign, because if their positions were reversed Mueller would be holding press conferences every day. That was politics.

By nine Tanner and Dolan were sitting in the mayor's office looking edgy and ill at ease. Mueller looked at each in turn. "OK," he said patiently. "Who wants to tell me what the hell's going on in my city?"

Tanner flushed and shot his cuffs. He was a large man, about the same age as the mayor and wasn't used to being called to account for his actions. "We didn't think it'd be that big," he said at last.

"You didn't think what would be that big?" Mueller said.

Tanner looked surprised. "The protest, or march, whatever you want to call it."

"They had a parade permit, didn't they? Which means they were entitled to a police escort, am I right?"

Tanner shifted uncomfortably in his seat. "We had some bikemen along the route and some uniforms out there too."

"Well, they sure as hell disappeared once the march hit City Hall Plaza," the mayor said. "Tell me, did you know there were going to be a thousand crazy Polacks there to meet them? Did your intelligence cover that?"

Tanner nodded. "We heard something about it."

Mueller seemed to think this over. In a soft voice, he said, "Why didn't you have more cops on hand, then?"

Tanner reddened, angry now but uncertain of his ground. "We just didn't think anything was going to happen."

Mueller looked disgusted. "That's very interesting. Look at it from my point of view: I'm out on the lake with my bride, fishing, drinking a few beers, getting sun-burned, having a good time. It's the weekend, so I have a right. By the time I get into the dock every TV station in town wants to know what I'm going to do about these race riots. Now my police chief tells me he knew about it ahead of time but didn't do anything because he didn't think anything was going to happen. Am I right so far, Tanner?"

"They weren't really riots," the chief said quickly.

"Close enough. Thirty people hurt and snipers on every roof in the Core. To me, that's a riot. That goddamned priest wants to march again, and this time the whole south side will be waiting. Mitchell Street is going to look like the Maginot Line." He pointed at Tanner. "I want you to close it down."

"You can't really do that," Dolan said. "They got a parade permit."

"I can shut the whole fucking city down if I want to," Mueller said, hitting the desk. "I did it in '68 and they wrote me up in Newsweek, put me on Walter Cronkite. The 'Milwaukee Solution' they called it, remember, Fischer?"

His aide nodded without enthusiasm. What the mayor said was true, but the situation was different now. Sealing off the Core wouldn't promote the image of peace and prosperity the mayor wanted. "Sixty-eight was special," Dolan said slowly. "There were riots everywhere after King's death. It was a litmus test for the black community. There's nothing national going on now. The cops would be out there by themselves and we'd get crucified by the press."

"It'll be OK if I get more men out on the street," Tanner said.

"On both sides of the bridge," Dolan added.

Mueller wasn't convinced. He didn't like Tanner, never had. He'd been thinking about other things when he first took office and had hardly noticed as Tanner solidified his position and then managed to isolate himself from the city hierarchy. But he'd always distrusted the chief and thought he was a suck-ass with dirty hands. They said a lot of things about Emil Mueller, but he had never taken bribes or covered up a murder. Playing hardball was one thing; corruption was something else. Still, what Dolan said made sense, and Mueller wanted to preserve his position as a peacemaker. He pointed at Tanner again. "Just remember, it might only be me and Dolan who are up for re-election, but you can bet your ass Andy Hedig's going to be looking for a new police chief if he gets in."

Tanner nodded but maintained a dignified silence. He considered himself above partisan politics, no matter what Mueller thought. Now Fischer went to the door and spoke softly for a minute. Then he turned to the mayor. "Norman's family has just filed a civil rights suit against the city," he said.

"Shit," Dolan said.

"That's not the worst part." Fischer hesitated for a moment. "They're asking for $100 million in damages."

Charlie Simons asked his secretary to hold his calls. The phone had been ringing off the hook, and he had called a news conference for that afternoon. Enough was enough. For the fact was he was annoyed with the kind of attention they were getting, though he couldn't blame the press. While the $100 million hadn't been his idea, he thought it was his fault. He should have known better when he invited Bill Isaacson to join the case.

Isaacson had run unsuccessfully for attorney general and in the process became a high profile lawyer who handled a lot of liberal cases. Charlie hardly knew him, but he thought they might make a good team, Mr. Inside and Mr. Outside. Isaacson had a reputation for being good with the media. What's more, it would spread case staff-support over two law firms.

When Charlie had visited his office Isaacson was wearing red suspenders and looked like somebody's idea of Clarence Darrow in mid-life. Heavy, with a florid face, Isaacson gestured with a cigar as he paced. "Terrible what these people have gone through," he said. He hadn't mentioned money until they were with the Normans, and then it was too late.

Charlie tried to argue with Bill and the family anyway, pointing out that they would never get a fraction of what they were asking and might be thrown out of court, in which case they'd get nothing. Even if they went to trial, the city would appeal until they were all dead and gone. But Isaacson said that didn't matter and Olivia's eyes shone. Charlie imagined she was thinking, This is a real lawyer—not some kid in topsiders and a sweater.

Charlie went along because he had no choice. He had little experience with this area of the law. Most of the people he represented were trying to avoid doing time and couldn't care less about million-dollar settlements. But now that the story had broken, Bill was off in Washington testifying about acid rain while Charlie looked to all the world like a shyster chasing his fee. It was a bitch, but there was nothing to do but bear with it.

Andrew Hedig had retreated into the deep doorways of city hall when the rocks started flying and remained there until the square emptied. Then he walked past the fallen barricades east on Kilbourn, away from the crowd. It took an hour to walk all the way up Prospect to his home, but Andy didn't mind. He wasn't so much angry as puzzled about what had happened.

It was obvious that the protest had exceeded Marcus Jackson's expectations and that the police had set them up, as if they thought letting some angry whites loose would end the uproar over Jimmy Norman. Andy found it hard to believe that the sixties had taught Tanner so little.

As he walked, Andy pondered how much he could make of this, or if he wanted to make anything of it. For he had never thought of himself as an opportunist. His heroes were not politicians but people like Thomas Merton, odd as that might seem. Yet even if had not created this situation, he felt obliged to use it. Like it or not he was a politician, not a moralist, and this would probably be his best chance against an entrenched mayor. Most politicians would be grateful if a twenty-year-old scandal surfaced unexpectedly, and Andy knew that with Bill Isaacson involved they were going to be hearing a lot about the police cover-up in the months ahead, which happened to coincide with his campaign.

In one sense, it didn't matter what Andy did. Charlie Simons was the smartest liberal lawyer in town and Isaacson was the most political. They knew the mayor would be more inclined to bargain during the campaign. Once the election was over, there would be no pressure on Mueller, win or lose. Andy could take the high road, attacking Mueller's record, and Isaacson would take care of the rest.

Of course, Marcus Jackson would want him in the middle of things. He had been in City Hall Plaza today, and it wasn't too far-fetched to think some of those rocks were aimed at him. What it came down to was how badly Andy really wanted the office. He was mulling this over as he unlocked his front door. Sarah wasn't home, and when he checked his messages, Andy found all the television stations had called.

His private line rang. It was Jack Comstock, who hadn't heard what had happened downtown. Andy had known Jack for years and depended on him as a fund-raiser, but Jack's voice sounded thin. "I don't know if I should tell you this, Andy," he said. "We've been friends a long time."

Andy rearranged the pens on his desk. He wondered if he still had time to get on the six o'clock news. "It's all right," he said. "Go ahead, Jack."

"It's about that condo I sold your wife?"

"I remember," Andy said. Sarah must have missed a payment and Jack was embarrassed at having to ask for it.

"Thing is," Jack said now, "it looks like she's sharing it with someone."

"Sharing it? Another artist?" Andy paid closer attention because it didn't make sense. Sarah had what amounted to a fetish about her privacy.

"It's not that," Jack said, his voice serious now. "Thing is, she's playing house in there. I don't know what you want to do, Andy, but that's how it is."

Andy heard relief in his friend's voice at having got it out and felt for him. This wasn't Comstock's fault. "I'm glad you did," he said. "Do you know the man?"

"Yeah," Jack replied. "I recognized him from his picture on the tube. It's that newspaper guy."

Andy knew instinctively this was the truth and was amazed he hadn't suspected before. "Bob Joseph?"

"That's the one," Jack said.

There was an awkward silence on the line. Andy and Jack Comstock didn't trade such confidences as a rule. The closest they had come was when Andy attended Jack's wife's funeral, but this was different. "I want to thank you for this, Jack," he said now. "I know it wasn't easy for you."

"Sure, Andy," Jack said. "I'm sorry I had to be the one. Hell, maybe the guy's interviewing Sarah."

"Is he there often?"

"About every day the doorman says."

"That's a hell of an interview then, Jack, wouldn't you say?" There was an edge in Andy's voice; he didn't want to be patronized. Then he heard Jack's labored breathing. "You did the right thing, but let's keep this to ourselves."

"You can count on me," Jack said. The last thing he wanted was for some action to result from what he had done.

After he hung up, Andy was surprised at his lack of anger. He felt something like hurt, but he didn't really blame Sarah. He hadn't been attentive to her for a long time. But the affair itself wasn't what bothered him. He was just amazed that she could have been so stupid. How could she think she could carry on an affair with someone as well-known as Joseph without being noticed? That worried Andy because it spoke of an arrogance that could be out of control. He let the feeling wash over him and then it was gone. Something had shifted inside and now his head was clear.

He dialed the number of the political reporter at Channel 4. When the call was answered, he said, "This is Andrew Hedig and I have a statement about today's events at City Hall Plaza."

Seventeen

It snowed. November storms were unusual but not unheard of, and it allowed Emil Mueller to show off. Both papers ran pictures of the mayor in Sorel boots and a down vest at his command post in the basement of city hall. The city's entire fleet of snowplows were on the streets all night, though the weather report did not call for another major storm. But the snow was wet, heavy, and difficult to move. To make matters worse, a hard freeze followed, leaving the streets nearly impassable.

Father Moretti and the Guardians marched anyway, going straight down Sixth and over the viaduct, penetrating the south side at its strongest point even though the enemy was home watching the march on television, in comfort. A squadron of police officers kept a small band of hecklers at a distance, and the marchers returned to the north side an hour later, chilled but determined to march again.

"How about taking a snow day?" the reporters asked.

But the priest was not known for his sense of humor. Pale and ascetic, with thinning red hair and heavy black glasses held together with adhesive tape, he had championed a variety of causes throughout his career, and it hadn't gone unnoticed in the church hierarchy. Moretti had been moved frequently, from Philadelphia to Detroit, Denver, and now Milwaukee—in each case to avoid embarrassment to the church. But in each new city Moretti found some group that needed his energy, and since priests couldn't be fired, the church had to live with him. "Freedom can't take a day off for the weather," he snapped. "We'll march all winter if we must."

Yet as November turned into December, it seemed that Mueller might have succeeded in deflecting public attention from the Norman case. Moretti's marches continued nightly, as the priest had promised, but the lack of response made the media tire of the story. Bob Joseph was no different from his colleagues in this. What if you gave a war and no one came, he thought. But he knew that Moretti's wish to prolong things for his own purposes was at least part of the reason for continuing the nightly vigils. It was easier to organize around a march than to get people involved in the daily, grinding work of fighting poverty. The week before Christmas, Bob gave Charlie Simons a call.

"How's the girlfriend?" Charlie asked. But there was no news on his end either. The lawsuit was mired in pre-trial negotiations, and Charlie didn't expect anything to happen until after the first. Given the dearth of news, the papers ran releases manufactured by the city's public relations office.

TANNER SAYS HE WOULD HAVE TAKEN ACTION, said one, skirting the issue of whether Tanner was involved himself. The Times took pains in an editorial to point out that Mueller had been in Madison the night Jimmy Norman was shot. Even if there had been a cover-up, the paper suggested, it couldn't be considered his responsibility.

Yet Andy Hedig was confident the mayor had been hurt whatever the papers said. It was all people wanted to talk about, and the depth of sympathy for Olivia Norman among young people was surprising. Andy didn't believe that a snowstorm and a few puff pieces in the papers would be enough to rescue the mayor. He also knew Charlie Simons and Bill Isaacson wouldn't go away. If Mueller somehow managed to ride to victory on a snowplow, he would accept it, but Andy found himself feeling uncharacteristically optimistic.

Work absorbed most of his time, but in the few hours that remained, Andy kept to himself. He needed to be sure how he felt about the things that had happened before he said anything to Sarah. In the meantime, they were polite but distant, and if Sarah suspected anything she didn't give it away. It was a breathing space Andy thought they both needed. He hadn't seen Bob Joseph in weeks when he ran into him at a Christmas party.

Andy felt more curious than angry, and he wondered if he had lost his capacity for outrage. Instead of wanting to hit Joseph, they shook hands. "I haven't seen you around," he said. "Not covering politics anymore?"

"They had me working on a thumb-sucker about the Norman case," Bob said. "Now they're holding that until something happens, if it ever does."

"If?"

The man seemed so at ease that Andy wondered if Jack Comstock had been mistaken. But this was the way he would have acted. It would have been a point of honor not to avoid his lover's husband, to look straight into his eyes. It was unsettling to recognize his own duplicity in someone else.

"There's been talk about a settlement," Joseph continued. "Makes sense. Mueller wants this to go away."

Andy was sure this was true. A long trial would make the city look bad, and while some people would consider a settlement to be admitting guilt, no one would remember it by April. If they settled, Andy could forget about winning. There were other issues, but no one cared about them. "What do you think?" Andy asked.

The reporter had intelligent eyes, and he was reading Andy as if they were talking about something else. "I doubt it'll happen. Simons doesn't want to let go because of the civil liberties issues; Isaacson needs the ink. It's an unbeatable combination. What's more, Norman's sister is after the money."

"You can't blame her. They've been through a lot."

"I don't blame anyone," Joseph said. "That's not my department. But the city's saying that before they pay anything they want back what the family got over the years in welfare and hospitalization costs, which turns out to be a couple hundred thousand. Olivia says her brothers wouldn't be crazy if Jimmy hadn't been shot by the cops."

Andy suppressed a smile. "I like her logic," he said.

"Me too," Joseph said. "She's sharp and she's willing to fight. She figures this has been around for twenty years, why give up just when you have the chance to get something? And no matter how badly Mueller wants out, just giving money to a welfare family would be political suicide."

"So it sounds like they're going to court," Andy said, trying not to sound eager. "Tell me, do you ever hear from your friend Mr. Paley?"

Bob smiled. "Tommy's writing his memoirs. He's got an agent and 60 Minutes is coming in next week to interview him."

"I'm glad someone's going to profit from all this," Andy said.

"You're doing OK," the reporter replied evenly.

Andy searched for irony in his expression, but Joseph's eyes were clear. His composure was impressive, which made Andy like Bob and regret the fact that they wouldn't be friends. At least Sarah had good taste, he thought. "Let's hope you're right," he said and offered his hand. "I've got to work," he nodded toward the room. "Good to see you again."

"I'd like to sit down sometime and talk about the campaign."

"Jimmy can set it up. Give him a call." Andy was suddenly annoyed with himself for making things easy for his wife's lover, for recognizing that Bob could help him. "See you," he said brusquely and moved away.

Tommy Paley would have been surprised to learn that Bob Joseph and Andy Hedig were talking about him at an east side party. Tommy had lived on the north side all his life, and even walking across the Locust Street viaduct was an exotic and daring thing to him. As kids, he and his friends had driven up North Avenue to the lake, but they seldom deviated from their route or explored the serpentine streets lined with large, gracious homes that wound their way back from the park. Tommy didn't resent as much as envy the people who lived there, but for the most part he didn't think about them any more than he thought seriously about the pretty girls with long legs and country club tans whom he saw at Bradford Beach. Their lives had nothing to do with his.

Now the small apartment on Wiel Street was filled with newspapers and dirty clothes. Dishes caked with grease were piled on every available surface, and rather than trying to clean up Tommy went out to eat. Considering the interest he was getting from Hollywood, he figured he shouldn't have to worry about these things. It was only a matter of time before he would cash in and move out of this dump anyway. Maybe the Morley Safer interview would do it. But despite the attention his story had received nationally, Tommy was curiously alone in Milwaukee. He had an answering machine, but the light indicating messages seldom glowed. Which was OK because Tommy no longer trusted the press. Once word leaked about the agent, the papers ran stories implying that conscience had nothing to do with his coming forward. Which was a joke. It was all right for the Normans to go for the bucks but just because he wanted something too, he was dirty. And what had it gotten him anyway? All he had so far was a room full of bills and no job offers. And while he had gone out and bought a Big Chief tablet and a box of #2 pencils, nothing came out right when he tried to put it down on paper. To top it all off, he hadn't heard from California since that first call. Life was weird.

Tommy zipped his coat and walked three blocks to Webb's, where he sat at the counter and ate a couple of gut-bombs. The cook was a skinny guy named Buzz, who must have been wearing the same gray T-shirt for years. He nodded but Tommy didn't feel like talking, especially to a loser like Buzz. A copy of the Post lay open on the stool. RIGHTS TRIAL TO BEGIN, the headline read over an account of the attorneys' maneuvering.

Neither Tommy nor Rogan were mentioned, though there was a picture of Olivia Brown. The story had gone right by the two of them, like some bizarre parade.

Two cops came in and sat next to Tommy, hitching up their belts but not taking off their short jackets. They didn't wear the Bennies anymore, those coats the bikeman wore when Tommy was on the job; they buttoned up around the throat and went down far enough to protect your ass from the cold wind. These guys had razor-cuts and carried little walkie-talkies. The coppers showed no sign of recognizing him, but why should they? They were babies when Tommy was on the force. He thought about saying something, but to them, he'd just be some old fart trying to make conversation, which was pretty close to the truth. Tommy put a dollar on the counter and walked out.

Tommy caught the bus on Holton and stopped to buy Rogan a carton of cigarettes when he got off. Then he walked to the Safety Building. His visits had taken on a rhythm. He usually came on weekends when no one was around, or sometimes he came at night. Generally they avoided talking about the case, but today as soon as Tommy walked in, Rogan said he'd gotten a call from CBS. "They want me to go on TV, tell my story," he said.

Tommy nodded. "Me too. What are you going to do?"

Rogan shook his head. "Fuck them. What's in it for me, you know? The way I look at it, I've got my sentencing coming up here in a week."

"So?" Tommy didn't understand.

"Maybe my lawyer can get me a reduced sentence, if I play along." Rogan blew smoke at the ceiling. "Mainly I just don't give a shit. For you, it's different. You could make a few bucks, what the hell. I don't hold it against you, I don't. But I know where I'm going; it's just how long I got to be in there."

The way everyone kept talking about money made Tommy feel crazy. Now he thought he should have gotten the agent to handle the 60 Minutes thing. Maybe she'd have gotten him something, at least a little respect. "You ought to talk," he said now. "You'd get a lighter sentence if you did. There'd be more pressure on the city if you talked."

"That ain't what my lawyer says. Besides, you're my friend and all, but when you think about what's happened, I'd be a real asshole if I took any advice from you. No offense, but isn't that right, Partner?"

Yet when Rogan's sentence came down, it wasn't lenient. Seven years of hard time. Tommy was sorry to see him go. It was strange to think that the only friend he had was the guy he'd betrayed, but that was the way it had turned out. Tommy wondered if he'd ever see Rogan again.

Eighteen

The judge they drew was William Alberts, a former governor whom Charlie Simons had known slightly in the sixties. He had a vague memory of an anti-war fund-raiser organized by Alberts's wife at which he had met the governor. They had spoken briefly, but all Charlie remembered of the conversation was Alberts's alert gray eyes. Still, he hadn't been surprised when the governor was defeated for re-election. Even then he hadn't seemed like much of a politician.

Since being appointed to the federal bench five years before, Alberts had built a solid, if unspectacular, liberal record. The word was that he was slow and wrote long, carefully reasoned opinions that often made their way into law review articles, which didn't encourage Charlie. Since his plan was to push the administration into making concessions because of the campaign, a long trial wasn't in his interest. But he would have to make the best of it; political exigencies meant less than nothing to the judge.

Both sides met in Alberts's chambers on an overcast morning that promised a long winter. But the weather wasn't getting Dolan down. The city attorney seemed ready for a fight. He announced that he planned to ask for dismissal and if that failed for a summary judgment. Charlie didn't respond directly. Instead he asked for an early scheduling order.

"Are you in a hurry, Mr. Simons?" Alberts asked.

"My client has waited twenty years for her day in court," Charlie said. "I don't think she should have to wait any longer than necessary now."

"You're not in the courtroom yet, Charlie," Alberts said smiling. He looked at his calendar. "There's an opening next week. We can do the hearing in January. But assuming we go to trial, I can't fit it in until May or June."

The primary was in April and Charlie knew there could be more delays. "We'll take May," he said.

Alberts looked at Dolan. "Is that acceptable to you?"

Dolan shrugged. He couldn't appear to be dragging his feet, but he had to be thrilled. "We'll try to be ready," he said. "Assuming we have a trial."

"That's it, then," Alberts said, closing his book. "I'll make sure each of you receives a schedule. And I'll hear your motion next week, Mr. Dolan."

So far everything was running Mueller's way. The city had hoped Rogan's sentencing and the trial's beginning would occur during the holidays, but this did not dampen interest in the case. "Jesus Christ," Dolan said looking out the window. "Don't they have families, shopping to do?" The sidewalks were packed, and vendors moved among the crowd selling photos of Jimmy Norman and buttons that had been made up to take advantage of the moment.

When Charlie arrived at nine-thirty, the Guardians were outside keeping a corridor clear for witnesses. Still, Charlie was grateful for the crowd, which would be sure to be noticed on television. And though they had been assigned one of the larger courtrooms, all the seats were taken. In the press row, there were people Charlie didn't recognize and he assumed they were from out-of-town papers. Even though interest would drop off once they were underway, the pre-trial attention would put more pressure on the city to settle.

Bill Isaacson was seated when Charlie arrived. They had agreed that Charlie would handle this part of the trial. "Ready?" he asked.

Isaacson smiled. "You're doing all the work today."

Charlie shook hands with Olivia. "Mrs. Brown," he said.

She nodded her head, still not exactly friendly but more respectful than before. Charlie wondered if perhaps she was just reserved, but the fact was that Olivia was beside herself with excitement. She had awakened at four, and after lying in bed unable to sleep for an hour, she rose and made herself tea and sat alone in the kitchen thinking her thoughts until dawn came slowly over the city. Despite what others considered to be her demanding ways, Olivia had never believed this day would come; she had never expected a new trial for Jimmy. Sitting with her two white lawyers in the large, wood-paneled room filled with reporters, it was hard to believe it was all happening.

Dolan was dressed in a brown pinstripe and wore an aggrieved expression that Charlie figured he'd been working on for some time. All trials were theater but some lawyers were better actors than others. Alberts entered and everybody stood up. When the judge was settled Dolan made his motion. "Your Honor," he said. "I speak as a public servant representing the people of Milwaukee when I say that this suit is frivolous and a waste of the court's time."

"You let me worry about the court's time," Alberts broke in testily.

"I apologize, Your Honor," Dolan said. "Our motion to dismiss is based first on the principle of res judicata, that is, this case has already been finally adjudicated and a judgment has been handed down; second, the city should not properly be the defendant in this case because the action was originally taken on behalf of the state of Wisconsin; third, the brothers and sisters of Jimmy Norman are not eligible under the law to recover benefits even if it were ruled that his was a wrongful death; and fourth, that in any case, the statute of limitations has long since passed. We ask the court to save the taxpayers the expense of an unnecessary trial by dismissing this complaint."

The district attorney looked calm and unassailable as he returned to his seat. Charlie didn't blame Olivia for whispering, "Is that right?" even though he had explained the whole process. Isaacson was looking straight ahead, his blond head in sharp profile as Charlie approached the bench.

"Your Honor," he began, "the district attorney, in the name of the city, has managed to withhold justice from my clients for twenty years. He should not be allowed to do so any longer. He knows that this action, far from being frivolous, has profound implications, not just for Milwaukee, but for our nation, as is shown by the presence of representatives of the national press."

Alberts smiled slightly. "That may be true, but confine your argument to the case, Counselor." he said.

Charlie nodded. Alberts had to say this, but he had hit a nerve. Any judge would welcome national attention, and there was nothing wrong with reminding Alberts of it. "On the city's motion," Charlie said, "we assert first and foremost that under Wisconsin law, a defendant may not plead the statute of limitations where his own fraudulent conduct has prevented the plaintiff from filing suit within the allowable or permissible period of time.

"Clearly, this is such a case. For Tommy Paley, a former patrolman in the Milwaukee police department and a principal in the Norman killing, has testified that a cover-up conspiracy existed in 1959 to prevent the truth about Jimmy Norman's death from getting out. Mr. Paley has further testified that this cover-up reached into the highest echelons of city government. In the absence of this crucial information, my clients could not possibly have pressed their case at that time.

"The conspiracy denied them equal protection under the law in that, unlike white citizens, the person responsible for the death of their brother was never brought to justice. Yet, the fact that a racially based conspiracy prevented a finding of wrongful death and the awarding of appropriate damages to the family in 1959 does not mean justice in this case should be further delayed now, no matter how inconvenient this is for the city. We have the opportunity to redress the injustices done then and we must take it."

Charlie waited for a moment, giving his words a chance to circulate in the room. Then he returned to the plaintiff's table. Judge Alberts called for a recess before ruling on Dolan's motion. People were milling around the table, but Olivia tapped Charlie on the arm and put her mouth close to him. "You're good," she said, her breath hot in his ear. "You're real good." Despite himself, Charlie smiled, feeling that he might have reached his client at last.

When he stood to walk out into the hall, he saw Isaacson looking at him critically. Despite the other man's vanity, Charlie had never doubted his intelligence. He raised his eyebrows in question, but Isaacson patted him on the shoulder. "You've got him," he said. "Nice job."

"Anyone could have done what I did just now," Charlie said modestly. But he was pleased. A lot of the lawyers in town avoided going up against Dolan because he was tough and smart and he usually won. Charlie had done better than most, breaking even over the years, but he respected his opponent and knew this was going to be a fight. Which made him appreciate Isaacson's support even more. Bill knew what he was up against.

He saw Joseph in the hall, but the crush was too intense for speaking and back inside the crowd seemed even larger. The bailiff called for order and Alberts re-entered the courtroom. The judge was wearing half-glasses and along with his robes, this gave him the appearance of a scholar. He nodded at Dolan and at Charlie. Then he began reading in a soft, firm voice.

"The defendant's motion to dismiss can essentially be broken into four components," Alberts began. "First, they argue that the claims of Jimmy

Norman's estate did not survive his death. Second, that Jimmy Norman's brothers and sister do not state a cognizable claim under the Federal Civil Rights Act. Third, that in any event all claims are barred by the statute of limitations. Finally, that the complaint filed by Mr. Simons and Mr. Isaacson on behalf of the Norman family fails to state a cognizable claim against the city.

"In order to address the issue of the claims of the estate, it must first be recognized that the estate may litigate only those claims that Jimmy Norman could claim on his own behalf if he were alive. If Norman himself would have had no claim, then the estate has none as well. In my judgment, however, there are three possible claims available to the plaintiffs: Jimmy Norman may have been subjected to an unlawful search; he may have been subject to invidious racial discrimination in violation of the equal protection clause of the Fourteenth Amendment; and he may have been deprived of his right to due process by being subjected to excessive force in the course of an arrest. The estate seeks to recover for the deprivation of Jimmy Norman's civil rights before his death. Thus I will permit them to litigate those claims.

"Under Wisconsin law, brothers and sisters may not recover for loss and companionship, but these damages are available to the estate of Aesculapius Norman, whose trustee has joined the suit." Here, he nodded in Olivia's direction. "Finally, there is the statute of limitations."

He stopped and drank some water, and it struck Charlie that the judge was nervous. Then Alberts put his glasses aside and addressed the court in general, looking at the audience, as if for posterity. "The facts from which this action arises are, alas, not in dispute," the judge said. "Both sides acknowledge that John Rogan unlawfully shot Jimmy Norman, who was unarmed, and that he and his partner and officials of the Detective Bureau of the City conspired to withhold this evidence from the general knowledge. I must add that neither the press nor the community at large were particularly aggressive in their search for the truth, but they are not liable. Moreover, none of this would have been known had Thomas Paley not gone to the authorities with the true story last fall after twenty years of silence, depression, and guilt.

"John Rogan has pleaded guilty and is presently serving his sentence in a federal penitentiary. Though we have more to learn about the extent of official cooperation in this cover-up, we must assume these to be the facts of the case: that is, there was a cover-up involving officials of the city of Milwaukee and it seems to have been racially based. Mr. Simons is quite correct when he says that under Wisconsin law a defendant may not plead the statute of limitations when his own fraudulent conduct has prevented the plaintiff from filing within a reasonable period of time. As he points out, the Norman family can hardly be blamed for not filing suit against the city when the true facts of the case were not available to them. Given what they knew, no reasonable person could find fault with the family for acting as they did. Moreover, once they possessed relevant information about the case, they took action in a timely manner. Defendant's motion is denied. Court is adjourned."

Pandemonium broke out. Olivia threw her arms around Charlie's neck but was borne off by well-wishers. Charlie knew it was hopeless to try to talk to her now, to tell her that all they had won was the right to move on to discovery, to take depositions and prepare for the real trial. That Dolan would have other motions. Yet small as this victory was, Charlie couldn't help smiling at Olivia's happiness. He looked up at the judge, who hadn't moved to try to control the celebration though he was known for running a tight courtroom and hadn't yet left the bench. Alberts looked bemused, but that was all right. That was fine. They made eye contact briefly, and Charlie thought the judge might have winked at him, but then Alberts was gathering his papers together and Isaacson was saying something and the moment was gone.

Tim Dolan was standing at the defense table, hands on hips, shaking his head. Charlie offered his hand. He liked Dolan, though they were never on the same side. "Better get control of your client," Dolan said.

"She'll be all right," Charlie replied. "Can we move this along?"

"Smelling a fee?" Dolan smiled to show he was joking.

"Bankruptcy's more like it."

"We both agreed to the schedule, Charlie."

"I just thought maybe we could use some common sense here. You heard what he said about the facts of the case."

Dolan smiled again. "You know better than that. So we lost a motion to dismiss—so what?" He patted a thick file. "I have a few more ideas for Judge Alberts to consider. You understand that, don't you, Counselor?"

"It was worth a try," Charlie said. He moved away from the table and headed out of the room. He did understand. He would do the same thing if he were in Dolan's place. Delay long enough and people would die or lose their memories; they would move away or get re-elected. The world of the case would change, and it might very well benefit the defense. Given the leisurely pace of Alberts's calendar, it didn't really matter to the city who won as long as it happened after the election. Unless, of course, the publicity generated by the trial was bad enough to affect the mayor's chances, in which case he might order Dolan to settle. But press coverage seemed to have a rhythm all its own. Reporters would get aggressive, then lose interest when something more timely came along. Weeks of motions and delaying tactics would dull even the most determined observers. Dolan knew what he was doing and he would do it well. Charlie decided to discuss it with Isaacson.

When he got outside, however, Bill was surrounded by cameras. He was in his glory. Charlie didn't resent this, but it didn't seem like the best time to talk. He stood on the edge of the crowd for a moment and watched the other man work, but Isaacson didn't see him. Then Charlie walked away from the courthouse unnoticed, alone and happy for his solitude.

Nineteen

Charlie need not have worried about the press. After Christmas, coverage of the candidates increased as the campaign gained momentum, and despite Mueller's attempts to minimize the importance of the Norman trial, the story was in the papers every day. "Questions have to be answered," the Times editorialized, "about the extent of the conspiracy to cover up Jimmy Norman's brutal murder. As Judge Alberts noted, the facts of this case are not in question. It is no longer enough for Mayor Mueller to protest his own innocence or plead ignorance. What is needed is a thorough investigation of the police department and, if necessary, a complete housecleaning as well. As time goes by, many are wondering if this administration is capable of that."

"Comes close to an endorsement," Jimmy said.

"That doesn't mean much," Andy replied. "Everyone knows the Times hates the mayor. They'd endorse Mrs. Brown if she were willing to run."

"There's an idea," Jimmy said. "I'll bet she'd be willing to shake hands at church bazaars too."

Yet the growing public awareness of the trial helped. Private contributions were increasing, and there were now enough volunteers to staff a couple of storefronts in strategic neighborhoods. Encouraged, Andy picked up the pace, doing plant gates in the morning and then talking to community groups in the afternoon. As a matter of principle, he never ate alone. Jimmy said his downtime was when he was asleep and that was only because he couldn't help himself by sleeping with anyone. It was still too early for people to be thinking seriously about the election, but excitement was building. There was something different about the audiences; they were larger and more interested in what Andy was saying. And there was no longer any problem with name recognition. Wherever he went, people offered support, which in turn stimulated Andy. In January, he told Jimmy to schedule more meetings.

"You want appearances?" Jimmy said. "I'm beginning to believe in the power of prayer." Andy just smiled. He was in a good mood these days.

Perhaps because he noticed Hedig's growing popularity, the mayor announced his candidacy, surprising no one, but this did little to stem the tide against him. No one was in a hurry with endorsements considering the situation. Instead of defending his record, Mueller attacked his opponent, which pleased Andy because previously the mayor hadn't deigned to notice him. Now he was important enough to be defamed. The Times noticed too.

"In his announcement, Mayor Mueller criticized Andrew Hedig for sowing discord in our city," the paper wrote. "But as articulate as Mr. Hedig is, he could never have done as much damage to the administration as the mayor has himself with his record. The winds of change are blowing in Milwaukee."

The next morning, Jimmy came in with the paper. "More good press," he said. "And Bob Joseph called again. He wants an interview."

"Can it wait until I make the transportation speech?"

"Use the interview to set it up," Jimmy said. "Then it gets covered twice. Unless you've got something against Joseph. The Times is important."

Andy didn't answer for a minute. Things were going so well that he hated to be reminded of Bob Joseph, but asking for another reporter would make it an issue. And there was the chance that any residual guilt Joseph might feel would help. But somehow Andy doubted that would happen. "Put him down for the weekend," he said. "I'll talk to him Saturday or Sunday."

Marcus Jackson was surprised but not annoyed when his secretary told him Olivia Brown was waiting. "Always a pleasure, Olivia," he said, steering her into his office. Marcus smiled at Olivia. He had hardly known her before Tommy Paley's confession, but now they were linked together in people's minds because of the protest marches.

"How can I help?" Marcus asked. "That lawyer doing all right?"

"Got two lawyers," Olivia said. "That Mr. Isaacson, he's a talker."

"Yes, he is," Marcus agreed. He'd never liked Bill Isaacson, but he understood why Simons had brought him on. The man had his uses, as long as they could keep him under control.

"And the other one's real smart," Olivia said. "I wasn't sure at first, but now I like him fine."

"That's good to hear, Olivia. It certainly is." Marcus was pleased, and not just because he had recommended Charlie. He had come to Milwaukee to work with poor people, but Olivia was not part of that constituency. Her husband was a successful businessman, and they lived out on Capital Drive. But the Norman case had revitalized civil rights in Milwaukee and provided the first real chance to beat Emil Mueller. Which made it important to keep Olivia happy.

But Marcus could see something was bothering her and he knew she had come to tell him what it was. He waited. Finally, Olivia said, "I just got to tell our story. Jimmy's, I mean."

"Of course you do," Marcus said, trying to sound sympathetic, though he had no idea what she was talking about. They were in the papers every day, and profiles of the whole family had run on television. Except for sports stars, black people just didn't get that kind of attention. How much more could there be? "Tell me what you want," Marcus said patiently.

Olivia was a big woman, and when she stood and spread her arms she seemed to draw to herself all the available light in the small office. "I mean, get it out," she said, squeezing her hands into fists. "All of it—where we was brought up, who our momma and daddy was. What all the kids was like, especially Jimmy, on up to right now."

Marcus was getting the picture. "You mean like a book or something, Olivia?"

"That's it," she said. "I read in the paper that that cop's going to write a book and all he's done is kill folks."

So that's where this came from, Marcus thought. Tommy Paley hadn't killed anyone, but he didn't bother to correct Olivia. And he had heard nothing about Paley's literary career since the story about his having an agent appeared. But what really bothered him was that a book about the Norman family wasn't going to help things. No matter how they dressed it up, her brother had been a common thief; her father had collapsed in court; and she had two brothers in a psychiatric hospital. They needed to bury the unsavory details beneath the rhetoric of injustice and hope people would forget the rest. But he couldn't think of a tactful way to say this.

"That's a wonderful idea," he said. Maybe she'd just forget the whole thing if he went along.

But Olivia wasn't easily put off. She raised her hand like a crossing guard. "I can't write," she announced.

Marcus looked at her warily. If she wanted to be immortalized, it was only fair that Olivia be willing to work at it. But clearly she wasn't asking about adult education classes. "That's going to be a problem," he said carefully.

"Uh-huh," she said. "That's what I thought, why I didn't say anything until now." She reached into her purse and pulled out a copy of a magazine. "Says here your friend's wife is a writer."

Marcus didn't understand for a moment, then he saw Sarah Hedig's byline. "Oh, now, Olivia, I don't know about that," he said. "I truly don't."

"Could be some big money in this for someone, Mr. Jackson." Olivia drew her coat around her. Marcus didn't say anything. He doubted there would be any profit in this project, and Sarah had no need of money. But he knew the risks of telling people things they didn't want to hear.

"You know, Olivia. Sarah's a good person, but I don't think she's very experienced. I mean, she's done some articles for the paper and all, but she's never written a book. And she's not really a journalist, so she's not used to interviewing people." He didn't want to come on too strong and say Sarah was a beginner. He didn't really know much about it, but none of Andy's friends took his wife's writing seriously.

Olivia wasn't convinced. She pointed to the paper. "Says right here she's working on a book. And her husband's going to be mayor." She pursed her lips and said, "I want you to call this white lady for me."

Marcus sighed. He found her attitude demeaning. He had already found her a lawyer, now she wanted a ghostwriter. It was as if he were her errand boy. But he knew that if he refused, the word would get around that he was trying to suppress the family's story. And steering her to an amateur who would never write anything would be the best thing to do. At least that made him a broker. And there was the slight possibility that he was wrong. So Marcus took Olivia's hand, "I'd be honored to call Mrs. Hedig for you."

Bob and Sarah lay pleasantly exhausted in the aftermath of passion, not speaking, barely touching, on the disordered daybed in Sarah's studio. Their lovemaking had become more leisurely and assured with time, yet it was no less intense. Sometimes, in fact, Sarah's sexual abandon frightened her. She never seemed to get enough of her lover. Bob would arrive with a basket full of cheese, wine, and bread. Before they ate they would make love. Then they would eat and make love again, unless they fell asleep. Occasionally, Sarah wondered if there was something wrong with this, not only the sexual frequency but her ardor. They were mature people, after all, not teenagers. Yet it was so wonderful that she couldn't seriously question it.

What was equally surprising was that they hadn't been found out even though they no longer took elaborate precautions. Andy hadn't come by or even called in all the time that she and Bob had been together. Her husband had visited the studio only twice since she bought it, respecting her need for privacy. It made her feel vaguely guilty to use her work as a cover for the love affair. There was probably a logical explanation for all this. Still, it seemed odd. Sarah didn't know her neighbors, wouldn't have even known she had any if she hadn't read their names on the doors. But she wouldn't have expected them to be so incurious, or maybe she hadn't noticed. When she was with Bob, there was no one else in the world.

Now he propped his chin on one hand. "You're incredible," he said.

Sarah blushed instinctively. "To you," she said, unused to praise.

Bob smiled. "I hope it's only me, but actually, you're right on schedule. Women reach their sexual peak in their forties; men are on the way down, no pun intended."

Sarah looked at him. "How do you explain it then?"

"I take no credit. You'd get a reaction from a rock."

Sarah kissed him and got out of bed. Even when they were young, Andy hadn't flattered her this way. He was always preoccupied, or so it seemed. He loved her, but never seemed to put much feeling into it. That wasn't Andy's style. Bob seemed to feel obliged to tell her every thought he had, a kind of openness her family had considered bad taste. While she couldn't remember anyone ever saying so exactly, Sarah guessed her mother thought this was the way minorities acted. Jews, Italians, perhaps. But in any event, if you loved someone there was no need to be saying it all the time. Yet Sarah had discovered that she liked being told that her breasts were beautiful, the breasts of a twenty-year-old, was the way he put it. She liked having him say her body was voluptuous and that he couldn't get enough of her. She thought this grew out of exuberance rather than insecurity. However daring this seemed to her, Bob seemed to take it in stride. "Sure," he said when she told him about her mother's attitude. "If you're not exuberant about love, what would get you excited?"

Still, Sarah couldn't help doubting herself. And she worried about Bob. How could he do his job when he was with her so much? He didn't even

call in to check with his editors anymore. Yet everything seemed to be going
well. The paper had nominated Bob's series on Tommy Paley's confession
for all the big journalism awards, and he'd been getting calls from other
papers asking if he was interested in moving.

She put on a robe and poured some wine. "I want to talk to you about
something," she said and settled herself on the bed again. "I got a call from
Marcus Jackson this morning."

Bob slipped on a sweater. "What did he want?"

For some reason this annoyed Sarah. Marcus didn't have to want anything; they were old friends. But the fact was he had wanted something, so
why should she react this way when Bob asked? "Jimmy Norman's sister
wants me to write her memoirs—well, not hers exactly. She wants me to
write about the family, a book about them."

"They want you to be the official biographer?"

"Something like that. What do you think?"

Bob sensed that she was edgy about something, and he knew his opinion was important to her, probably more important than it ought to be.
Skepticism was natural to a journalist, a way of keeping your distance from
the world. Doubting everything made you right some of the time and
seldom embarrassed. Still, he trusted his instincts and wanted to protect
Sarah. The world was crowded with hustlers. "Have you talked to Andy?"
he asked.

"He's against it," Sarah said quickly. "That's not what he said exactly, but
I could tell he didn't like the idea and I can see why. How would it look if
the candidate's wife is involved in a lawsuit against the city?"

"You wouldn't be suing the city."

"That's how it would seem to some people."

Sarah was probably right about that. Being Olivia Brown's ghostwriter
would complicate things. "But it interests you?"

She nodded. "And not just because I can't really get this novel going. It's
a fascinating case. Look how much of your time it's taken up."

Bob smiled. "It sounds like you've made your decision."

"You still haven't told me what you think," Sarah said.

Bob wanted to support Sarah, but Olivia Brown made him uneasy.
"Do what you want, but make sure you get a contract," he said.

Back at the office there was a message saying he had an appointment
with Andy Hedig. The office was empty but the pink message slip made
him feel oddly vulnerable, as if it might have communicated something to
someone. His colleagues wouldn't care, but it bothered him. He knew he

was coasting on Paley's confession and he didn't like it, didn't respect it. Or maybe it was just that Andy's gracious response to his request made him feel guilty.

Bob put the slip of paper in his pocket and headed out. Rather than face his empty refrigerator he went around the corner to Mader's and was pleased to find the old restaurant little changed. He ate too much sauerbraten and drank German beer, and later he was sick. Sitting alone on his bathroom floor in the middle of the night washed any remaining traces of shame or sentimentality out of him.

Twenty

On Saturday, Andy broke his morning routine of reading in his study. Instead, he walked the four blocks to Downer Avenue, where he ate breakfast at the Coffee Trader and then shopped either there or up the street at Sendiks before returning home. He read the out-of-town papers or the New Yorker and made notes of books or plays that interested him.

He valued this time not only because it was diverting but because he realized he would soon lose it. The waiters at the restaurant protected his privacy by putting him at a back table, but inevitably someone would approach apologetically to shake hands or offer advice about the campaign. Andy didn't object to this, but he found it embarrassing because often these were people whom he had met but whose names he had forgotten. He tried to cover by clasping the person's elbow and addressing him as "my friend," but this was seldom successful. The fact that other politicians handled this sort of thing with ease only increased his sense of exposure. Andy thought now of FDR with his jaunty cigarette holder and Nelson Rockefeller calling steelworkers "buddy" and going out with them on a job for the benefit of photographers. Whatever had made him think he was suited for public life? And yet here he was, and so he made the best of it, smiling awkwardly until the people retreated to their tables, satisfied that at least they had made contact with the candidate.

After breakfast, he selected a dozen oranges and some mixed nuts and walked home through a pleasant drizzle. The January thaw had set in, and

Andy enjoyed the brief respite from the cold. Sarah was reading the paper when he came in and put the fruit on the counter. She looked up and said, "Jimmy called to remind you that you've got an appointment at eleven."

"Bob Joseph is coming over. From the Times." Andy thought he saw a slight tightening around the corners of her mouth and felt a momentary rage, an urge to slap her, but he turned away and it passed.

"I remember," Sarah said. "You went running together."

Standing there in his raincoat, Andy was amazed at her insouciance, but he couldn't think what to say about it. She remembered her lover indeed. He wanted to have it out right now for good and all. He wanted to lose his temper gloriously, as he was never able to do, to yell and scream and throw things. And he thought he wouldn't have felt this way if Sarah had seemed the least bit uncomfortable or exposed by the thought of Joseph's visit. But she continued to read and drink coffee. Only the slightest rustle of paper hinted at any emotion she might be feeling, and Andy couldn't even be certain if it was nerves that made her fingers tremble, a slight muscular tremor, or nothing at all. She was so calm that he considered again whether he was doing Sarah a disservice by not accusing her openly and then allowing her to defend herself. Eventually, unproven suspicions would harden into fact and then bitterness, whether or not what he believed was true could be shown. In time, that wouldn't matter, and then it would be impossible to talk at all. He would have lost his chance. And Andy's silence was serving the function of allowing him to begin to hate his wife. Yet he couldn't help it. He didn't want to discuss Sarah's affair; in a sense he could manage only if they didn't talk about it. And Sarah seemed content to leave things this way. "So he's coming here?"

Sarah looked up, amused. She glanced at her watch. "In twenty-three minutes," she said. "You OK?"

Suddenly Andy felt like crying. He wanted to hold her to him in a death grip because absolutely nothing was OK between them. But with an effort he overcame the impulse. "I'd better get dressed then," he said.

The interview was uneventful, though neither Bob nor Andy had expected it to be very exciting. Joseph asked dutifully about the city's shrinking tax base and problems in keeping heavy industry in town, giving Andy a chance to attack the mayor. Andy floated a few ideas about attracting business to Milwaukee. They discussed health care, the urban crisis, education, and the environment, which in Milwaukee meant blowing the tubes to clean factory furnaces at night so the citizens could remain unaware of the soot and grime that paid their bills. The interview reminded Andy of a chat

between two friends, which was surprising considering the anger he had felt
an hour before. Andy considered the other man and wondered if Sarah
was choosing Joseph's clothes now or remodeling his house. But try as he
might, he couldn't understand the attraction. Slight, with wispy blond hair,
an aquiline nose, and stooped shoulders, Bob Joseph looked more like a
college professor than an investigative reporter. Certainly he couldn't be
anyone's idea of a matinee idol. Sitting together, with rain running down the
window panes and tea in their hands, it seemed incredible that this was
actually Sarah's lover, that this man had cuckolded him, and yet Andy knew
it was so.

Bob put his notebook aside. Hedig seemed distracted. So far he hadn't
asked any hard questions, allowing Hedig to create the shape of the interview. Control inhered in being able to appear not to need it. This was the
moment when he would characteristically bore in, having previously lulled
the interviewee into complacency with his easy manner. But something held
him back. Finally, he asked, "How do you want to handle the Norman case?"

Hedig raised his eyebrows. "Handle it?"

"We don't have to talk about it all," Bob said. "I've already got enough
for my story. The paper's on record asking the mayor to come clean and so
are you. We can skip it unless there's something you want to say."

Andy looked thoughtful, as if he were considering this possibility, but
when he spoke he wasn't really responding to Joseph's question. "Did you
know my wife has agreed to be the Normans' official biographer?" he
asked.

This was in its own way a trick question. The Normans didn't put out
press releases. The only way Bob would have known was through Sarah.
For a moment the two men looked at each other openly with knowing,
unspoken candor. "Is that for publication?" Bob asked, breaking the spell.

"Why not?" Andy replied. "It won't be a secret for long. Starting next
week she'll be attending the trial."

Bob made a note of this. "You want to comment on that?"

Andy was enjoying the conversation that was going on beneath the
interview. He felt an odd kinship with the reporter; after all, they had both
slept with the same woman, and the fact that he was married to her seemed
incidental. He wanted somehow to let Joseph know this, that he understood, but he didn't really know how. Maybe there was no way, he thought
sadly, for the two of them to talk about Sarah. "My wife lives an indepen-
dent life," he said carefully. "And she's not running for anything. I'll leave
judgments to others, like you perhaps, who are better qualified than I am."

Andy's high-mindedness was impressive and had a predictable effect
on Bob. By saying he wanted his wife to live independently Hedig was
sending an ambiguous message. For he didn't necessarily mean he was setting her free, only that periodically she would go off on her own. But Bob
didn't respond directly to this. Then Jimmy came in to end the interview.

Walking home, Bob was left feeling admiration for the other man, though
he couldn't articulate even to himself exactly why that should be. Hedig had
done nothing out of the ordinary. And the most surprising thing Bob had
learned had nothing to do with politics and was something he could never
print. "How did the son of a bitch find out?" Bob asked himself. "How
could he?"

Charlie Simons was not thrilled to learn about Sarah's new assignment either
and called a meeting with Olivia and Isaacson immediately. When Olivia
came in, she looked submissive, almost meek, as if she knew she had done
something wrong. But Charlie had been around her enough to recognize
this as a ploy and it irritated him further. Charlie held up a copy of the
Times.

"I don't think I should learn about things like this in the paper, Mrs.
Brown." He pointed to Bob Joseph's story. "I don't think that's fair to me."

Olivia shifted in her chair. Despite her outward appearance, she really
didn't care what Charlie thought. White people were always upset about
something, and she was used to their lectures. "It's about my family," she
said. "Why do I have to tell you?"

"Because I'm representing your family," Charlie said. "Bill and I are
both trying to do that. We're working very hard, spending a lot of time on
this."

Olivia looked around the book-lined office. She didn't want to argue,
but she found it hard to take Charlie seriously because she had never seen a
white man even brush up against hard work. They left that for the colored
folks. This man should have been out in the cotton fields with her daddy if
he wanted to talk about working hard. But it wouldn't have done any good
to say this. "You're going to make a lot of money on it too," she said.

Charlie shook his head wearily. "Even if we win, which isn't at all certain, we may not receive any damages. Those are two separate considerations. We certainly won't receive the ridiculous amount we're asking for."
Isaacson was gazing out the window. "And whatever I eventually receive as
a fee will be far less on an hourly basis than I ordinarily charge for much less
complicated cases in which my clients are willing to cooperate."

"A lot of money," Olivia repeated, and Charlie felt his indignation begin to recede. Because she was right. To her, whatever they got in the end would be a lot of money. The fact was that he had been hurt that neither Olivia nor Sarah had thought to consult him, but being left out wasn't really an important issue, and, in any event, he regretted referring to his fee. It wasn't what he had meant to say; money had never been a motivating factor for him. He took a deep breath and started over.

"You're right, Mrs. Brown," he said. "It is a lot of money, even if we don't get what we're asking for. But the amount of the settlement isn't the main thing for me or Mr. Isaacson. We want to help you get justice."

Olivia listened stolidly to this. She nodded as if she understood, but she didn't believe this. It was just like when the man was talking about how hard he worked. If white people didn't care about money, how come they had all of it? But then let a black woman try to put a little aside for her own life and they were calling her downtown. "Why then?" she asked, going along.

Charlie breathed deeply. "You have something to say about this, Bill?" It wouldn't help to lose his temper, and she respected Isaacson.

Isaacson stretched his long arms over his head and cracked his knuckles. "There's the issue of client/attorney confidentiality, Olivia."

"What's that?" Olivia asked.

"That means that what you tell me or Mr. Simons is privileged information; it stays here, between us, and no one else can know about it. But how can we have that if you're repeating everything we say to Mrs. Hedig— nothing against her." He looked at Charlie. "I don't know the woman myself."

Charlie wanted to hug the man. It was brilliant, and he would never have thought of it, would never have chosen an indirect way to achieve what he wanted. He nodded to indicate that he agreed with Bill.

Olivia didn't like to admit it, didn't like to give up control or even share it, but the man had a point. "Maybe she won't say nothing?" she asked hopefully. It changed things for her to think that what she said to her lawyers was important to anybody. It made her wonder if she had sold herself cheap by signing that contract without even reading it first, but it was too late now.

"You want her to say something," Charlie exploded. "That's why you hired her, for Christ's sake. To write everything down so that other people would be interested enough to buy a book about it. Isn't that the whole idea?"

Olivia seemed shaken by this, and Isaacson moved to smooth things over. "Let's take it easy here, " he said. "No point in getting upset."

Charlie wasn't really upset and he knew Isaacson understood this. He liked the way they were handling the interview. But he made a show of regaining control just the same. "OK," he said. "I'm sorry I lost my temper. I trust Sarah. She's an old friend. But Bill's right. We've got a very sensitive case here, a case that has already received too much publicity. The city could claim pre-trial prejudice because everyone in town has an opinion about your brother's murder. Dolan could ask for a change of venue, which might put us in Green Bay in front of an all-white panel. If that happens, I don't like our chances very much." He stopped and looked at Olivia, who was paying rapt attention now. Isaacson was intent on what he was saying too.

"What can we do about that, Charlie?" he asked. "If we hadn't had the press in on Paley's confession we wouldn't have a case at all. And the fact that they wrote about a cover-up might be the only reason Alberts is letting us go to trial. Otherwise, he might have given on Dolan's motion for dismissal."

"That's right," Charlie said. "That was a necessary evil. But we can try not to make things worse. There's nothing more for us to gain from additional publicity. Our best bet is to just keep our heads down, do our homework, and hope we get lucky." He looked at Olivia purposefully. "But I'm not going anywhere on this if you continue to make important decisions without consulting me. That happens, you find yourself another lawyer. From now on, you understand that anything you do can affect the case we're trying to build. The way you dress, your personal conduct, what movies you go to, who you see in your spare time—anything. You've got to accept that or I'm gone."

Olivia looked at Isaacson but Bill looked away. It didn't make sense to her that someone would give up the chance to make money because she hadn't told him something, but the other man was serious. And while she liked the blond lawyer, Mr. Simons was smarter. "You'd quit?" she said.

"Damned straight," Charlie said. "Today."

"What do I got to do then?" At base, Olivia was a realist. It no longer mattered what she wanted, as long as they could reach an agreement.

"Just clear everything with me before you talk to Mrs. Hedig. Some detail that might seem completely innocent to you could hurt us if it got out."

"She made me sign a paper," Olivia said.

"A contract?" Charlie asked.

Olivia nodded. This was giving her a headache. Suddenly she was in a lot of trouble without understanding why.

"I'll talk to Sarah about that," Charlie said. "I'll promise her an exclusive look at everything if she waits until we've gone to trial. As long as no one else gets there first, I think she'll go along."

Isaacson nodded, but the atmosphere had changed. Everyone understood that this was Charlie's case. He was the one they needed in order to win. Without really planning it, Charlie had made himself indispensable.

"OK," Olivia said, smiling, because she liked strength in a man, liked it a lot. "That sounds OK to me."

Mueller and Dolan met the day before Judge Alberts was scheduled to reconvene. Things weren't going well. Even if they hadn't drawn a liberal judge, the district attorney didn't like the way public opinion was running. The plan had been to get Rogan out of town before anyone noticed, and it might even have worked if Paley hadn't shot his mouth off to that reporter. Mueller didn't blame Bob Joseph. He had only done what reporters do. It would be like blaming a dog for pissing on a tree. And, based on the laws of pack journalism, what happened after that was mathematical. Mueller had yet to meet a reporter with an original mind; the cardinal sin of journalism was missing something. The practical effect of this was that if one reporter wrote something, the rest had to follow for fear of making a mistake, which would get their editors on their asses. And if there was nothing to write, you had to invent something, which meant raking over the ashes of an old story.

The mayor didn't resent Hedig either. No politician would pass up the opportunity to use a story like this. Mueller just regretted what had happened, as he regretted other mistakes in his life. The important question was what to do now. Due to some changes in the judge's schedule, the actual trial was now set to begin two weeks before the election. Mueller knew Alberts well enough to realize that he wouldn't have done this to help Hedig, but that was the effect it would have, just as the original schedule had been to their advantage. Alberts would move heaven and earth to appear impartial, but he was damned either way. And if Dolan objected to the timing it would open them up to new charges of conspiracy or foot-dragging.

Yet Mueller thought the case was distorting his record. He would have freely admitted that he had never cared much for blacks, but in his heart he felt he had been fair. Tough but fair. Now he was in the position of catching heat for someone else and appearing to be a part of a conspiracy to obscure a race murder. He didn't like this at all, but it was a hard position to defend. He had the choice of claiming ignorance of the goings-on in his own police department, or accepting responsibility for something that turned his stomach. Which, to the mayor, seemed like no choice at all.

Dolan sat down heavily and Mueller told Fischer to close the door. He looked at the district attorney. "Mr. Dolan, you look tired and that worries me because we've got a hell of a lot of work to do in the next few months."

"I'm all right," Dolan said. "It's just been a tough few weeks."

"It's going to get tougher," Mueller said. "But I want you to tell me what the hell's going on. I hear Mrs. Hedig is writing Norman's memoirs."

Dolan nodded obediently. "That's right," he said.

Mueller sat back and looked around the big room. There wasn't an inch of wainscoting that wasn't covered with a plaque, an honorary degree, or a picture of the mayor shaking hands with someone. He had met four presidents and the heads of state from thirteen foreign countries, but that wouldn't help now. His large desk was bare except for a paperweight recognizing him as president of the National Council of Mayors and a Blue Book. He smoothed the desktop with his large hands. "Well, that's wonderful," he said. "That's just great. Mr. Fischer, would you tell the district attorney what you told me a minute ago?"

Fischer looked at some notes. "According to a private poll we had taken last week, Hedig's coming up," he said.

"Coming up," Mueller thundered. "I'll say he's coming up. Fifteen points in one week. Coming up, my sorry ass."

Fischer blinked behind his glasses. "You're still well ahead."

Mueller snorted. "He keeps gaining like this and I won't be in two weeks." He blew out some air, which seemed to relax him. "But he won't. I know that." The mayor grimaced at some private pain. "He won't because he can't; no one could. Something will happen; he'll fuck up. Maybe I'll even do something right, you never know. And his wife might hurt him by hanging around with the Normans. I'm surprised he let her do that." Mueller looked thoughtful for a moment, as if he were pondering the changing rules of marriage. Then he was back, fingering his collar nervously, his leg bouncing beneath the desk. "What we've got to do is stop making it easy for them. My Aunt Sally would look good running against me with this goddamned trial in the papers every day." He looked at Dolan. "What's your plan for tomorrow?"

"We're asking for a summary judgment."

"Refresh my memory." Though Mueller had graduated from Marquette law school, he'd never actually practiced and didn't regret it, but it put him at a practical disadvantage now.

"Basically, it's a way of admitting that the facts in a case aren't in dispute, just like Alberts said. We all agree about what happened, the circumstances of Norman's death, I mean. But we still say they have no case."

Mueller's eyes opened wide. "You lost me. If we admit they're right on the facts, why don't they have a case?"

Dolan shrugged. "Lots of reasons. We say, yes, the kid was killed and that's unfortunate, but there was no conspiracy. Or we say OK there was a conspiracy, but it didn't damage the family, just Jimmy, who's already dead. Even if we agree that it did damage them, we disagree as to how much. We claim they're exaggerating the amount of the damages, which as a matter of fact they are. I think the judge was offended by the $100 million."

"Offended?" Mueller said eagerly.

Dolan nodded. "I could be wrong, but I don't think so. Alberts wants to take the high road and hear this as a civil rights case. But asking for damages that high seems like bad taste to him. This is a guy who drives a ten-year-old Plymouth and shops at Montgomery Ward."

"Thank God for Judge Alberts's innate sense of decency."

"Amen. So what we end up with is that all this happened twenty years ago and is regrettable but shouldn't be adjudicated now. It's over."

Mueller waved his hand in the air. "Hold it. You already got beat on the statute of limitations."

Dolan shook his head. "No, we didn't. The judge just said he wouldn't dismiss because of it, which is a very different thing. I also think the judge would have dismissed because of res_judicata if it weren't for the conspiracy charge. He didn't like the fact that Norman's old man accepted a settlement and now they're back asking for more."

"Kind of a puritan, the judge?"

"Exactly, but that's to our advantage. We say, fine, don't dismiss. But it's not worth going through a trial. It's going to waste thousands of the taxpayers' dollars and a hell of a lot of time. Decide who's right and wrong based on what you already know. We'll put our faith in your judgment."

"Isn't that a risk?" Fischer broke in.

Dolan shrugged. "Sure, but it's in our favor. If Alberts rules against us, we'll appeal. And it'll slow things down. But what's important is that it's finished. We've got three months to regroup before the election, and the papers aren't going to devote a lot of space to explaining the legal niceties."

Mueller thought this over. "What are the chances of your getting this summary judgment? Not winning, just getting Alberts to move on it?"

Dolan looked at his assistant, who had been sitting quietly in the back of the room. "Probably not very good," Timmons said. "It's pretty clear Alberts wants to know more about the cover-up."

"So what it comes down to, we're just delaying?"

Dolan nodded, but he was annoyed. Delay was their whole strategy, because the facts were against them. Despair blanketed the room until finally the mayor went into his private bathroom where he urinated loudly. He took his time washing his hands.

The mayor emerged renewed. "OK," he said. "Suppose we lose this one too, and from what you say, we will. What then?"

Dolan took a deep breath. He had thought this through carefully, but he wasn't sure how to read the mayor. Dolan wasn't a career politician; in fact he didn't think of himself as a politician at all. Elections were simply the price one had to pay in order to hold office. Over the weekend he'd even thought about not running for re-election, but then he'd be leaving under a cloud. And if he somehow managed to win, the Norman case would be a cornerstone in his career. "We've got to assume they'll want to depose everyone associated with the case," Dolan began. "They may even interview you."

"Me?" Mueller protested. "I was in Madison. I didn't even know anything was going on." This wasn't entirely true, and everyone in the room knew it, but their public position was that Mueller was so busy with Senate business that he wasn't even aware that the kid had been killed.

"Doesn't matter," Dolan said. "They'll argue that you have relevant knowledge about the way the city and the police function. We can object and make things difficult, but basically Timmons is right: Alberts wants this to go to trial, and the way the system works is the judge gets what he wants. If we throw up too many motions, he might decide we're being dilatory and press harder. And, worst case, they could find someone during discovery who says there not only was a cover-up but that it went higher than the Detective Bureau. If it's out there, Charlie Simons will find it, trust me. He's a damned good lawyer. So we've got to know what there is to know before they do."

The mayor understood. "I didn't ask Tanner here for a reason. What do you think, Tim? Was he in on this, the cover-up, I mean?"

"He's covered his tracks pretty well," Dolan said. "But we know he came in ten minutes after the shooting and he was night chief of detectives. If there was a conspiracy, it's hard to see how it could have worked without Tanner's knowing about it. I'd say he was probably involved."

"Suppose that's true," Mueller said. "That's bad, but what else is there? Who could we give up? What about Martin? We know he was there."

"We don't have to worry about Martin," Dolan said. "Most people have forgotten him or don't care. But if it went to the mayor's office, that would be different. It might not seem fair, but even if no one remembers who was mayor, they'd throw it to you and you'd have to respond."

Fairness seemed irrelevant. Politics was war and you made your own rules. Still, he had to admit that the possibility of the mayor's office being involved changed things. Mueller's predecessor had been an old Socialist named Karl Schulz, whose great passion in life was garbage removal. It was hard to imagine Schulz covering up a murder. "That's impossible," he said.

"For what it's worth, I agree," Dolan said. "We'll try to limit the damage, say Rogan was a bad apple. If the chief's story holds up, it's their word against his, and they have lousy witnesses."

"Say it works. What then?" Might as well look at the bright side.

"We luck out," Dolan said. "If it's no worse than we already know, Alberts does his duty getting the truth out. History records the fact that it happened in his court and he's in every law review. The $100 million is a joke. I think Charlie Simons is embarrassed. It's not like him to go for that kind of money. I figure Isaacson pushed him into it, and Alberts hates Isaacson."

Mueller nodded. "So if everything goes just right, and that's no sure thing, I've got a fucking trial running through my whole re-election campaign. If everything goes as well as it can possibly go, I've got stories in the papers every day about corruption and brutality in my police department, and in the end the city gets socked for a couple million in damages. That's the best case, am I right?"

Dolan smiled grimly. "That's about it. Best case. You hit it right on the head."

Twenty-one

Sarah was up early. She dressed conservatively in a gray suit and pink blouse and was sitting at the kitchen table when Andy came in. "Any last-minute instructions?" she asked. He hadn't said anything about the trial.

He poured a cup of tea and sat down. "I'd appreciate it if you didn't give interviews. You'll attract attention, and you're not an impartial observer."

"Fairly impartial," Sarah said. She didn't like to think of herself as a hagiographer, though there was no question about her sympathies. "I promised Charlie I wouldn't talk about the case," she said. "I'll just try to blend in."

This turned out to be easier than Sarah expected. By the time she reached the courthouse, the plaza was full and she had to push through the crowd to get to the door. Several fights had broken out, and the police were doing their best to keep the antagonists apart. No one noticed Sarah as she made her way up the steps to the courtroom. Inside, she showed her pass and was admitted to the section reserved for the press. Though she felt somewhat counterfeit, Sarah was glad she didn't have to wait in line. She saw Bob talking into his tape recorder as she came in, but they had agreed not to talk. He looked over now and raised his right hand before turning back to the machine.

Charlie watched the courtroom fill up, feeling a corresponding rise in his spirits. The moments before a trial began were tonic to him. Anything seemed possible now, even justice. He was like a kid waiting for the parade to begin: the air was fresh and the horses hadn't yet crapped in the street. Soon enough, this euphoria would be corroded by passion, and in the end he would leave the room spent and disheartened. But what was remarkable was that hundreds of trials over twenty years had done nothing to dissipate his optimism.

He had met with Isaacson this morning and came away impressed with the other man's savvy. The question they had to consider was how they were going to proceed together, assuming they were allowed to begin discovery, which was hardly a sure thing. Isaacson wanted to depose everyone, including the former mayor, who was eighty-five years old and senile.

"That'll take a lot of time," Charlie said.

"It might be worth it," Isaacson said. "You never know what you'll find. And it'll make them nervous as hell, especially if the press gets onto it."

Charlie knew whose time it was going to take, but he didn't object because he agreed with Isaacson. Even if Bill was only going to be the front man, there was no question about his political instincts. If he said more depositions would make the mayor more likely to settle, Charlie believed it.

He had noticed in a distracted way when Sarah Hedig came in, but now he looked at her. Thinner and more attractive than he remembered, she looked tentative as she made her way into the press section, and Charlie wondered if he had made a mistake in helping her get credentials. She had been cooperative when he explained the legal problems the book presented, but it was in her own interest to draw as little attention to herself as possible. What she might write later, if she wrote anything, didn't concern Charlie. He just needed a clear road through the trial.

Now Charlie noticed that Sarah was looking intently across the room. She raised her hand slightly and there was something so touching in the gesture that it held Charlie's interest. Her expression communicated longing and regret, and these were emotions he didn't associate with Sarah Hedig. Out of curiosity, Charlie followed her gaze down the row and found himself looking at Bob Joseph, who raised his hand briefly in response and then turned away.

Suddenly, everything was clear. Sarah was the married woman Bob had mentioned. Her look said everything. While he was getting ready to try the biggest case of his career, they were making like Keats's lovers in the courtroom. And though it had nothing to do with him, the discovery made Charlie queasy. Nothing good will come out of this, he told himself. Nothing.

Then he was aware of Isaacson talking and Olivia asking questions. The bailiff called for order, and Alberts walked in, stooped as always and expressionless, as if he were going to the store for milk. In the moment before the hearing began, Charlie wondered if he should say anything to Joseph, some cautionary word, but he decided against it. What good could it do? Charlie didn't want to be anyone's confidant right now. He put the lovers out of his mind and focused on Dolan.

What the district attorney was saying sounded like a reprise of his previous motion to dismiss. He cited res judicata and the statute of limitations again in asking Alberts for a summary judgment. The only difference was that this time he brought in Cap Norman's wrongful death suit as further evidence that the matter had already been settled. Otherwise, it was the same, which made the strategy clear: delay by introducing as many motions as possible. The judge might give on something, and, if not, they would have moved the trial closer to the election. It made sense, though it was risky, because if they were too close, the trial would overwhelm the campaign and sink Mueller.

When Dolan was through, Charlie rose to respond. "Your Honor," he said, "the district attorney has told us nothing new. Res judicata did not apply two weeks ago, and it doesn't today because of the conspiracy to withhold the true facts of this case from my clients, hindering their ability to make a case for themselves. We urge you to allow this matter to go to trial without any further delays. We plan to depose all those still alive with knowledge of the cover-up and reveal the truth about this sad episode in our city's history.

"Mr. Dolan's reference to a settlement is cynical and disingenuous. He knows that Cap Norman never signed the agreement or cashed the city's check. He further knows that Olivia Brown and her brothers didn't accept the official version of their brother's murder and would not have submitted to an attempt to cloud the issue with a settlement even if their father had felt differently."

During the recess, Sarah ran into Bob at the water fountain. "Is it all right to talk to each other?" she asked.

He smiled. "Why not? We're both members of the working press."

They walked down the hall and leaned against a wall. "I just feel so visible," she said. "As if everyone must know."

"Can you smell adultery, feel adultery?"

"Something like that," Sarah said. "It just seems so obvious." She laughed out of nervousness and embarrassment. "I imagine the people sitting between us getting hot just because of what we send off."

"Then they should be grateful," Bob said.

"I know, but I'm scared, Bobby. Maybe I shouldn't be, but I am."

They were quiet for a moment. He didn't know how to help her not to be afraid. It seemed like an appropriate response. He was scared too, but he had gotten used to it. People moved around them in the crowded hallway, and Bob felt like a stranger, though he knew everyone in all the courts and offices. His old life seemed foreign now; only Sarah was familiar, and her eyes were round with fear. He wanted to take her hand, but he controlled himself. "No one cares," he said as softly as a crooner. "Try to remember that. This is the biggest thing in the world to us, but everyone in this room is much too involved in his own life to pay attention to us."

He felt her relax. "You sound so sure of yourself."

"That's because I am," he said, sounding more certain than he was. He imagined everyone looking too. "Trust me. I'm right about this." A bailiff appeared, and the crowd started moving sluggishly toward the courtroom. He patted her awkwardly on the shoulder. It was hard not to be intimate, hard not to embrace her, to try to seem instead like a casual acquaintance. "Better get back," he said. "You don't want to miss anything your first day."

Sarah followed Bob inside. The morning had been so confusing that she wasn't sure she'd know if something important did happen. But she was smart; she'd take notes and ask questions and she'd learn.

Alberts re-entered the room. He was wearing the half-glasses again. Charlie was impressed with the care he was giving the case, but he wasn't really worried. He couldn't imagine the judge granting Dolan's motion.

"Defendant's motion is based on two principal arguments," Alberts began. "That this action is barred by the doctrine of res judicata and by the statute of limitations. I am persuaded by Mr. Simons's argument in rebuttal that where crucial evidence is withheld from the plaintiff these doctrines do not apply.

"The matter of Cap Norman's acceptance of a settlement is somewhat more complicated than Mr. Simons is willing to allow, however, and consequently more troubling to me." Alberts paused and looked over his glasses at Charlie. Something about his mien made Charlie suddenly nervous, but there was nothing to be done. "The fact is that Mr. Norman or his representative and the city did enter into an agreement to set aside the wrongful-death suit filed on behalf of his son. The size of that settlement and the question of whether Mr. Norman cashed the check is, it seems to me, largely irrelevant as are the statements attributed to other members of the Norman family, who were neither parties to that suit nor entitled to act in it.

"If Cap Norman truly felt as Mr. Simons now says he did, it could be argued that he should not have accepted a settlement. If Jimmy Norman's family did not believe the story of the police officers involved in their brother's death, it could as well be argued that they should have fought to bring out the truth. Since neither of these occurred, statements about contrary opinions held twenty years ago by principals in this case must be treated as speculation. They may be true, but they are certainly very convenient to draw upon today. Since on the one hand the family accepted the settlement and on the other kept silent, this argument would assert that they should not be allowed to set aside one settlement merely because it may be possible to win a larger one today."

There was some stirring in the audience, and Alberts cleared his throat to indicate that he wasn't finished. He resettled his glasses on his nose and looked again into the crowd. Charlie saw something new in the judge's expression, perhaps annoyance with the general perception of him as a liberal, and this scared him. He didn't see how Alberts could grant Dolan's motion, but he had no idea how they could finance an appeal if the judge surprised them.

"Against these thoughts," Alberts continued, "is the overwhelming fact of the appearance of an official conspiracy, which we must now take to be true. And this is the single most important consideration before the court. Whether the Norman family was wise in entering into a settlement with the city is finally not ours to determine. What is clear is that Cap Norman and his family made their decision without being in full possession of the facts. Had they known then what they know today, they might well have acted differently. For the sake of justice, this court must not deny them the opportunity to redress past mistakes. Motion denied."

The celebration was more restrained this time, if only because everyone had been through it before. But Isaacson understood, even if the others didn't. "We almost lost it," he whispered to Charlie. He hadn't expected Alberts to make so much of Cap Norman's settlement and had underestimated Alberts's intelligence; they would have to work harder in the future.

Dolan walked over. "Want to meet?"

"Don't tell me you're going to offer us a deal?" Charlie said, smiling.

"In your dreams," Dolan said. "I'm going to kick your ass, and you know it. But we've got to schedule depositions."

"I'll be in touch," Charlie said. As Dolan moved off, Charlie saw Sarah Hedig leaving the room, books clutched to her chest like a sorority girl. Perhaps he was wrong about her and Joseph, but even if things weren't what he thought, something was going on, something he wasn't going to like.

After the brief thaw the weather turned cold and the sun disappeared. Andy kept to his hectic pace, moving not only with greater ease, but often with enthusiasm from one appearance to the next. Although most of the scrambling for endorsements had occurred during the early stages of the campaign, various polls had decided Mueller was on the ropes and Andy was picking up support as people decided they'd better get on board. Depending on the person's importance, they might even have to dream up an appropriate title. There was a limit to the number of campaign chairs they could list, but Jimmy had created Lithuanians for Hedig for the benefit of one supporter, and now he wanted to name a new convert head of something called East Europeans for Hedig.

"Isn't Lithuania in Eastern Europe?" Andy asked.

"Most of our supporters aren't geography nuts, like you," Jimmy said. "Titles are important, and it means we can do a press release."

The liberal groups had been supporting Andy since the beginning, but today he had a small rubberworkers local on his schedule and later he would visit a temple brotherhood on the east side. Neither he nor Jimmy would have chosen this kind of strategy. Both would have preferred to run a media campaign, putting Andy on the tube every day. If you had youth and a pretty face, common sense dictated that you go with your strength. But they didn't have the money for this, so they had decided to organize the city, precinct by precinct, and put campaign workers on every block three times before April. Organizing around a relatively unknown candidate was difficult, however, because until now there hadn't been enough volunteers to do it effectively. But the phones were ringing off the hook. "We say yes to everyone," Jimmy said. "If there's nothing to do in the office, they can run errands for shut-ins or give old ladies a ride to the market."

"They'll remember this on election day?" Andy said.

Jimmy smiled. "Some of these codgers can't remember their names. So we'll help by picking them up at home and taking them to the polls."

"What about inside the booth?"

"Then they're on their own. It's an imperfect system."

Even in an organizational campaign, however, most managers would have considered going door to door a waste of the candidate's time. There were too many other things to do. Yet here it was essential. Milwaukee was less a city than a collection of small towns, each proprietary and suspicious of the others. So contact with the people was essential. Attending a street fair on the south side got you nothing on Brady Street, even if it made the five o'clock news. And doing a plant gate at A. O. Smith would only make the workers at Ladish feel ignored if Andy didn't stop there as well. Everyone wanted to see the candidate for himself and look into his eyes. Milwaukeeans had great faith in their political acumen, and local political traditions had led voters to expect nothing less than this from candidates for city-wide office.

Still, Jimmy argued, a lot could be accomplished by walking into a corner tavern, buying a round and leaving Hedig buttons at each place on the bar. Word got around, and this might mean more than being endorsed by some C.Y.O. leader. Andy resisted at first, complaining that such a cynical approach would hurt them in the long run. "I feel like a race horse," he said one day. "Next thing you know they're going to want to examine my teeth."

"Then smile," Jimmy said.

But as his crowds grew larger and more enthusiastic, Andy responded. Now they were waiting when his car pulled up and they listened with respect when he attacked Mueller. The Norman trial never failed to come up, no matter where he was or who he was speaking to. It was too easy to assume everyone south of Mitchell Street was a racist. They tended to assume the police were innocent in normal circumstances, but their faith had clearly been shaken by the trial, and every mother in town could sympathize with Olivia Brown. It was something worth noticing, and, encouraged by the response he was getting, Andy started to work it into his prepared speeches.

They saw polls every day, but these were less important than the feeling Andy had of momentum growing. It didn't matter now that his clothes were too expensive or that crowds made him uncomfortable. Something new was going on and it was exciting. He had the feeling that Mueller was on the run and that he was going to catch him, and this drove him to put in even longer hours. And when he came home late at night and saw Sarah's closed door, it no longer mattered as much. Maybe when the campaign was over they would sit down and talk, assuming there really was something to talk about, and assuming Sarah was still there. Andy had the vague feeling that this should concern him, but it didn't. Right now, there just wasn't time.

Twenty-two

Charlie and Isaacson decided to depose Tanner first, though they didn't expect the chief to be very cooperative. "Might as well see what we've got," Isaacson said. Lawyers were like archaeologists searching the rubble for valuable clues—a rune, a piece of a vase, something. But there was no other way. If Tanner wasn't going to be useful, they were better off knowing.

They met in a room in the Safety Building, supposedly because of the press of Tanner's responsibilities. Charlie's office would have been more convenient, and it was his right to name the site, but there was no point in making an issue out of this. It was unlikely that the chief would be intimidated by his office anyway. It certainly hadn't had that effect on Olivia Brown.

Charlie and Isaacson were seated when Tanner came in, which seemed to give him an advantage. He was a big man with thinning hair and towered over them. But Tanner didn't seem hostile or even wary. Perhaps a little tired, but they were all tired. Although they knew each other, introductions were made and the interview began in a falsely congenial manner. Dolan was present as Tanner's counsel. Charlie had agreed to let them tape the session. "Chief Tanner," Charlie began, "can you tell us where you were the night of February 8, 1959?"

"At home," Tanner said, "watching television with my wife. She passed away ten years ago. At 10:30, I came in to work."

"You were captain of detectives at that time?"

"After my promotion, I was in charge of the night shift."

Charlie checked a note. "You were promoted in 1958?"

"Actually, it was in December of 1957," Tanner said.

"Thank you," Charlie said dryly. But Tanner seemed unaware of the irony. "Now," Charlie continued, "could you describe the atmosphere in the Safety Building that night?"

"Atmosphere?" Tanner was a veteran witness and he wasn't going to make things easy for his interrogators. He wanted to know exactly what Charlie meant before he agreed with his characterization.

"Did you notice anything unusual that evening?"

"Unusual?" Tanner had a look of such complete innocence on his face that Charlie had to remind himself that this man had been interviewing witnesses for thirty years. Tanner shook his head. "It all seemed pretty normal to me," he said. "Of course, it's, what, twenty-some years ago."

Charlie pounced on this. "But you said you remember that night, February 8, didn't you? Even if it was normal." He emphasized the word, as if anyone who considered that night to be normal was either a liar or a fool.

If Tanner felt threatened, however, he didn't show it. He pulled out a battered logbook and held it up for the lawyers. "I keep a diary every night I'm on duty. I went back and checked because I thought you might ask."

"I see," Charlie said. He was beginning to feel exasperated, which was exactly what Dolan wanted him to feel. "Surely, Chief, you're aware that February 8, 1959, was the night Jimmy Norman was killed."

Tanner didn't falter. "I am aware of it, but that wasn't the question. You asked if that night was unusual."

"Do you think the murder of a boy by two police officers is unusual, Chief? Or does that happen often?"

Tanner had a bemused expression, as if to say Charlie should know better. "There was no murder. There was a death; it was regrettable."

Dolan broke in. "Object to line of questioning. There has been no proof of murder in this matter." Which was true. Rogan had pleaded guilty to reckless endangerment. "Ask question be stricken," Dolan said.

"OK," Charlie said. "You made your point. Strike it." He was annoyed with himself for letting them bait him this way. He looked at his notes for inspiration and tried again. "All right, Chief, the death occurred at 8:30, and you stated that you entered the building two hours later. Perhaps you were made aware of what had happened after you came in?"

"I heard something." Tanner said with the slightest hint of irritation.

"Could you tell us what you heard?"

"I don't remember exactly. A black kid died, something like that."

"Black? Isn't it more likely they would have said 'Negro,' Chief?"

What they would have said was "nigger, " but Tanner seemed bored. "Maybe," he said. He was skating through this, but Charlie pressed on.

"Isn't it true that you were told a nigger kid had been killed and that you had to do something to cover it up?" This was what Paley had told them, but Dolan handled it like a hanging curve on an August afternoon.

"Objection. Charlie, you're putting words in my client's mouth."

Tanner didn't seem upset, however. He ignored Dolan and answered. "No," he said equably. "I don't remember anyone saying that."

Tanner was lying and everyone in the room knew it. This was the point at which the chief was supposed to start slurring his words and lose control. He should be sweating profusely, his eyes darting wildly around the room. But he seemed at ease, almost nonchalant. Only in movies did justice prevail. In the real world, witnesses lied through their teeth, lied stupidly all the time and then dared you to do something because they knew you couldn't.

"Chief," Charlie said. "Were you aware in 1959, or are you aware now, of a conspiracy within the department, and perhaps in even higher city offices, to cover up the true facts of Jimmy Norman's death?"

"Only what I read in the papers."

"So you personally concealed nothing about his death?"

Tanner shook his head. His face had the innocence of a child, but Charlie didn't expect anything else. What was Tanner going to do, admit everything? This was just for the record anyway, so there would be no surprises in the actual trial. A dress rehearsal of sorts.

"Did you ever meet with Detective Moran, Inspector Halloran, or Chief Martin to discuss this case?" Charlie asked.

Tanner shifted in his chair and shot a look at Dolan. "I might have," he said. "I saw those guys every day. We talked about a lot of things."

"Would that be in your logbook?" Charlie asked.

The question caught Tanner off balance. He hadn't expected his log to be used against him. For the first time in the interview he appeared uncertain of how to respond. He looked at Dolan again, but the district attorney said nothing. The question wasn't objectionable. "I don't know," Tanner said.

"Could we examine the book then?" Charlie asked. "Maybe we could find something you've overlooked."

"You're deposing the chief." Dolan said, "not his reminiscences."

"Unless they bear on the case," Charlie said. "Of course, I could subpoena the logbook."

"You could do that," Dolan agreed, but the interchange had given Tanner time to recover.

Charlie started in again. "Is it fair to say you don't remember if you met with these men to discuss the Norman case, but that you might have?"

Now Tanner was stuck. He had just said he didn't remember, and that lack of memory cut both ways. "I might have," he said speculatively.

Charlie pushed the pace, speaking quickly but emphatically. "So while you don't remember exactly what was said, in these discussions you had with Moran, Halloran, and Martin, the subject of a cover-up might have arisen?"

"I didn't say that."

"That's right," Charlie said. "But you did say under oath that you met with these men every day, men who have been positively identified as being involved in the conspiracy to cover up the facts of Jimmy Norman's death. And you can't remember what it was that you talked with them about?"

Tanner's face was red. "It's not how it sounds."

Charlie sat back in his chair and spread his hands in a gesture of infinite patience. "Then tell us how it really was, Chief. That's what I'm after. That's why we're here. Tell us what did happen, if memory permits."

"I don't remember," the chief said petulantly. "I told you that."

"Even with the help of your diary?"

Tanner was no longer tall and proud, and Charlie thought Dolan would accuse him of brow-beating the witness if he pushed any further. But he had learned something about the chief's vulnerabilities. He looked at Dolan. "I'm not through with this witness, Tim," he said.

Outside, Isaacson was excited. "You really nailed him when he admitted meeting with those guys but said he couldn't remember what they talked about. Couldn't remember, my ass. Good work, Charlie. Real good."

But Charlie wasn't certain. "All he really said was he couldn't remember conversations he had twenty years ago. Some people would be sympathetic. Hell, I can't remember what I was doing Saturday night."

"Come on, give a jury some credit," Isaacson insisted. "He'd remember whether he was involved in a conspiracy to cover up a murder."

"We both know that," Charlie said. "But Dolan's whole case is going to be built on making this look like a liberal witch-hunt. It's not going to be enough for us to be sure in our guts about what happened. We need to prove it. Unless we can put Tanner in a room with the others talking about covering up the murder, it's going to be a bitch to convince the jury. You know what they say, you've got to knock out the champ. You can't win on points."

Isaacson thought this over. "Who else was there?" he asked.

"That's the problem. We don't know. And most of the people who could tell us are dead. Even Paley isn't cooperating the way I'd like. He says there are names he doesn't want to mention. Like this detective, Moran. Turns out they're from the same neighborhood. Even though he's been dead ten years, Paley says he doesn't want to dishonor the dead. In another situation you'd think that was kind of touching, but it's a big pain in the ass for us."

"A kid's dead because of his partner and Paley's talking about fair?"

Charlie shrugged. "Tell the truth, Paley's about as noble as everyone else in this case. I think the sonofabitch is just covering his ass."

"Why? You think he's afraid of something else coming out?"

"Maybe someone is putting on the pressure."

"Like Tanner?"

Charlie shrugged. "Who knows? Anyway, Paley's in California being a movie star. I doubt he's thinking about Milwaukee much these days."

"You could squeeze him, couldn't you?"

"Like a goddamned grape," Charlie said. "But what's it worth? The guy's a shitty witness. The most Paley can do is point a finger at someone."

"What about Rogan?" Isaacson said.

"Same thing. He's a murderer, for Christ's sake. Besides, Rogan already made the best deal he could. It's pretty hard to threaten a man with contempt who's already doing hard time in Terre Haute."

As they talked, cops pulled up in their black-and-whites and walked past them, casual and incurious. They had all seen lawyers before and they didn't like them. Well, Charlie thought, the feeling is mutual. At the same time, he felt an odd sense of identification with the bikemen. Despite the bravado they cultivated, Charlie knew what they went through on a daily basis and knew too that the intuitive response that came forth whenever a cop was killed was due in large part to their shared vulnerability. The leather jackets, jodhpurs, and white helmets made them seem almost inhuman, and their toughness was legendary in the city. But the masks of imperturbability they wore couldn't completely hide the fear they lived with every day on the job.

"What are you going to do?" Isaacson asked now, interrupting Charlie's thoughts. He was like a law student. The guy didn't have a clue. All Isaacson really knew how to do was get in the papers.

"Just go down the list and hope we get lucky," he said. "I was serious about wanting to get Tanner again, push him a little more. The only time he lost it was when I went at him about his memory. Who could predict the guy would get pissed off like that? But it's good to know. It gives us a chance. If we can throw him something else, we might get lucky."

"You pushed him pretty hard already," Isaacson said.

Despite Isaacson's inexperience, it was pleasant going over it like this. He didn't know why he didn't like Bill more. He just rubbed Charlie the wrong way with his shoulder-length hair and fancy suits. There was something soft in Isaacson's manner and he chewed his words. But they weren't dating, so who cared? "Yeah, he's tough," he said. "But we knew that."

"That's something then." Charlie realized with some surprise that the other man was trying to please him, to make him feel better.

"Sure," Charlie said, cutting it off. "Not much, but something."

Olivia Brown lived in a bungalow near Sherman and Capital, and Sarah's first impression was that the house was neater than hers. The living room furniture was covered in plastic, so she followed Olivia into the kitchen where the white linoleum floor shone so brightly that the harsh light hurt her eyes. Mrs. Brown's husband wasn't home, and Sarah didn't know if there were children. In fact, she realized now that she knew almost nothing about this woman. Yet she had agreed to write a book about her life.

Sensing Sarah's discomfort, Olivia smiled. She watched the other woman's nervousness with interest. Though she was tall and elegantly dressed, Sarah's teacup rattled when she picked it up, and Olivia knew she had the upper hand, even if Sarah's husband was a powerful man. Sarah would write what Olivia wanted her to write and not ask questions about how she had the money to live as she did. Such questions would not even occur to her.

Yet while control was important, Olivia found herself liking Sarah. She respected her for coming down here even though she was nervous, fighting through it; she respected white people who did things they didn't have to do for black folks. She had the best of both worlds. A woman she liked and respected was going to tell her story just the way she wanted it told. "Relax, honey," she said, reaching for Sarah's hand. "I won't bite."

"I've never done this before," Sarah said.

"But you're a writer. I saw your name in the paper."

"Yes," Sarah said. "But I've never written a book about anyone."

"Well, then, we're even," Olivia said. "Because I never had no one write about me before." Her laugh was so appealing that Sarah relaxed and laughed at herself. Then she felt less strange about being here with this nice black woman in the brilliant white kitchen in the heart of the city.

She didn't ask, but Sarah assumed the living room was reserved for ceremonial occasions, though her experience was so far removed from this woman's that she couldn't imagine what such occasions in Olivia's life might be. What did she know about poverty, prejudice, or murder? All her life she had been fawned over, often by black people hired to look after her. She had never even known anyone who owned a gun, much less anyone who had been shot at. And if she had evinced the slightest interest in such things, which she had to admit was unlikely, the man who was watching over her would have said, "Now you don't have to worry about things like that." And this was important because it was true. She didn't. She had never had any reason to be concerned for her safety or that of those close to her. But Olivia had to think about guns and violence every time she or a member of her family walked out the door.

Sarah realized suddenly that Olivia had probably known this, that it was the reason she had been asked to write her story. The vast differences in their lives was the point. Sarah's experiences couldn't get in the way and distort Olivia's story because Sarah had no experience. Sarah looked at her hostess now with new respect.

Olivia watched Sarah watching her, working things out, her large brown eyes interested but not intrusive. Sarah thought she saw a hint of humor in the other woman's expression, but she wasn't sure. She wondered if Olivia would have called if Andy wasn't running for mayor, but she didn't care. Other people would have their reasons, but she had gotten involved and now she was going to follow it through. Whatever the motivations of others in bringing her here, staying was up to her, not Andy, Bob, or Marcus Jackson.

Which helped her feel settled. Sarah took a deep breath and picked up her notebook. "OK, Mrs. Brown," she said. "Tell me about Jimmy."

Twenty-three

Bob hadn't seen his father-in-law since the Paley story broke, so he wasn't surprised to get a note one day asking him to stop by. He wondered idly if they had heard about one of the prizes, but it was probably too early. He returned a few calls, then walked down the long hallway and stood in front of the secretary's desk. In a moment, she motioned him inside.

The office looked the same, if a little dingier. A tie was draped over the lamp and Bob was going to say something sarcastic, but Mike's face was serious when he looked up. "Happy New Year," Bob said.

"Same to you. Sit down. We've got to talk." Then Mike lapsed into a long silence, punctuated only by the occasional shaking of his head.

Bob didn't know what to make of this. He'd seen Mike angry and confused before, but never depressed. Maybe it was just age, some mid-life thing. Come to think of it, Bob wasn't feeling so lively himself. "What's going on?" He had the feeling he might not want to know. "Something with Margie?"

Mike shook his head and smiled ruefully. "No, it's not Margie," he said. "For a change." Then he was silent again. At last, he cleared his throat. "There's no good way to say this. But I've got to anyway." The older man shrugged his shoulders to ease the tension. Bob wondered irrelevantly why he was wearing short sleeves in January. Then Mike said, "I heard something about you the other day and now I've got to ask if it's true."

"What did you hear?" Bob was beginning to get the picture.

Mike colored in embarrassment. "It was about Andy Hedig's wife. The two of you, I mean." Bob thought Mike's eyes had begun to tear but he couldn't be sure. He knew his father-in-law wanted to be reassured, and he also knew that Mike would defend him up and down if he denied being involved with Sarah. He knew he could stall or challenge Mike's source. There were things he could do. He could ask exactly what it was Mike had heard. Who could have told him anyway, and what could he have said? Or he could defend his right to a private life and walk out of Mike's office without saying anything in his own defense. But Bob didn't do any of these things because he cared too deeply about Mike to bullshit him. "It's true," he said simply.

Mike looked hurt and surprised at the same time. And Bob knew that in part it was because to Mike this meant giving up the illusion that Bob and Margie would ever be reunited. Mike had never said this in so many words, but it didn't take great insight to know that this was what he wanted. "You don't even know what I heard," he said plaintively.

"I can imagine," Bob said. "Why fuck around? We've known each other too long, and I like you too much not to be straight about it."

Mike nodded. "Thanks, Bobby. I appreciate you making it easy on me." They sat silently for a while, allowing themselves to get used to knowing what they knew.

"What happens now?" Bob said finally. "Rogan got kicked off the force for adultery."

"I'd lose half my reporters if I did that," Mike said. "And what's the point? You'd have ten offers by the time you got home. I don't want to lose you, but I've got to think about the paper. " He looked at Bob, his expression caught between sympathy and exasperation. "Is this thing serious, Bobby?"

Bob knew it was more than concern for the paper that made Mike ask the question. It was personal, though he had always considered Mike to be remarkably incurious about love. Having been married to the same woman for forty years, he considered marriage to be simple, the answer to the problem of loneliness. A good thing. The only mystery to Mike was why anyone would do anything different. "Yeah, I think so," Bob said. "At least it's serious for me."

Mike sighed heavily and rubbed his face. "Then I've got no choice but to pull you off the story. You can't cover Hedig now; I don't know what ever made you think you could."

Mike was right. There was no choice. "I can see that," Bob said. "OK, I'm off the campaign, then?"

"Sure, the campaign. The Norman trial too."

"Why?" Bob protested. "The trial's got nothing to do with Hedig."

Mike looked at him. "Are you kidding? Everything in this city has something to do with Hedig while the campaign's going on, especially a rights trial big enough to knock Mueller out of office. Hedig's making statements about the Normans and going on marches, for Christ's sake. He's involved every which way, and his wife's the family's official biographer. How's the paper going to look if you two are holding hands in the press box?"

Bob hadn't really thought about it from Mike's point of view before, or from that of the Times. It was his life they were talking about, and he couldn't imagine his feelings for Sarah compromising his work. But he understood, even if he didn't like it. The only thing that surprised him was that his response wasn't more complicated, that he didn't feel obliged to defend Sarah. Of course, Mike hadn't attacked her. "It's my story," Bob said.

Mike's avuncular tone disappeared now. "Like hell it is," he snapped. "No one owns the news. Anyway, you should have thought of that before you started shtupping the candidate's wife. All the women in this great city and you've got to pick Sarah Hedig in the middle of the mayoral campaign. Great timing." Mike shook his head in disgust, and Bob knew the editor was right. It was a stupid thing to do, unless you were in love, in which case it didn't matter whether it was stupid or not. "Tell you what I'll do," Mike said. "Break it off and I'll keep you on the story. Otherwise, report to the metro desk in the morning for your new assignment."

Bob wanted to object, but he stopped himself. Though he was mad, he could see Mike was right. How was he going to cover the story if he was the story, and he would be if it became common knowledge that he and Sarah were lovers. Which was just a matter of time. If Mike knew, others did, at least in political circles. There was a chance people would keep quiet if he was off the story; if not, he and Sarah would be fair game. He patted his knees and rose to his feet. There wasn't anything more to say, but for some reason he felt like apologizing. "OK," he said instead. "First thing in the morning."

No one had ever handed Emil Mueller anything, and he wasn't afraid of a fight. His old man had worked on the line at Harnishfaeger, and Mueller grew up in the old Third Ward and went to Lincoln High School before the niggers ruined it. Because there was no money and his father didn't believe in education, Mueller had worked on a lathe after graduation rather than going off to the university in Madison. At night, he took the trolley up

Oakland Avenue to attend the old normal school, where he earned high honors, which won him a scholarship to study law at Marquette. Since the grant was more than he had been taking home from his job, his father grudgingly admitted there might be something to education and allowed his son to give up his position at the plant. Then Mueller made law review and worked representing his father's union before going off to the state Senate at the age of thirty.

Mueller had no false modesty about him, but he never thought there was anything extraordinary in this. His family wasn't really poor, and he knew a dozen guys from the neighborhood—wops, Polacks, and Germans like himself—who had gone on to college and graduated, mostly from night school. Only rich kids from the east side or the suburbs went off to Madison. Mueller and his friends didn't even consider it and thus didn't resent it. The truth was that they seldom thought about the hand life had dealt them, good or bad. It was just there and it was all right. But even considering this, Emil Mueller was thought to be a comer by people who cared about such things. And his steady rise in the Senate and then to the mayor's office only bore this out. Moreover, it had given him confidence that he could handle whatever life might throw at him, or walk away if he decided the fight wasn't worth it.

Now, however, the developments in the Norman trial and the effect this was having on his re-election campaign had made him question himself, and doubt was so unfamiliar to Mueller that he gave it more credence than a less successful person might have. It wasn't Hedig that bothered him, though he disliked the other man. The recent series of events had upset Mueller's understanding of the world, his sense of fairness. Try as he might, he couldn't see the justice in blaming him, or even the city, for the kid's murder. In his mind, he deserved four more years and then a dignified exit from public life. He had given his life to Milwaukee, and the city owed him that.

Six months ago most of the electorate would have agreed, would have responded to the sentimental appeal that Mueller had planned. Posters and campaign buttons would say "One More Time" over his picture. Nothing more would have been necessary. But this trial had changed all that. What had seemed inevitable was now problematical at best, and though he knew it wasn't personal, Mueller felt insulted by the polls that showed him losing support in a city that had always returned majorities of seventy or eighty percent for him. He had assumed the papers would support Hedig; that was no surprise. They attacked him because he refused to kowtow to anybody. But he had always been able to count on the people before, the ordinary joe in the factory, and his wife too. It hurt Mueller that this seemed to be changing.

And even though he was mayor of the goddamned city, he couldn't seem to get a very good idea of what was going on. No one wanted to tell him just how bad it was. He had advisors and consultants coming out of his ass, and not one of them had anything useful to say. It was no longer acceptable to explain that he had been in Madison when the murder occurred—he understood that. People would see it as passing the buck, even if it happened to be true. And it wouldn't work to deny that a cover-up had existed, even if so far no one had been able to nail it down in testimony. Denials sounded weak; there was no use kidding himself. He had to prove Charlie Simons's accusations to be wrong, and the fact was he couldn't. He didn't even believe it himself.

Mueller figured Martin and Tanner had gotten the rest of them in a room and cooked a story that would work for the coroner's jury. Of course, almost anything would have worked for them. He knew how those guys put together a jury and none of them was above obstruction of justice, especially when niggers were involved. Back then, it didn't matter how dirty a white man was; you hung together on matters of race. Even if no one was willing to come out and say so, it was the truth. But whenever Mueller talked to Dolan it seemed as if the district attorney was holding something back, perhaps to protect himself, as if he didn't know that their futures were linked.

Mueller got up and walked to the window. All around him, there was evidence of progress. Beneath his window was a new office plaza and beyond that hotels, a downtown shopping mall, and the convention center. He had instructed Fisher to start referring to Milwaukee in press releases as the City of Fountains, though Mueller knew that there hadn't been any until he started requiring them in each new development contract. But who had a sense of history these days? Besides, it was good for the city. Mueller had also built fairgrounds along the lake, and now a series of ethnic festivals kept the tourists coming in all summer. They had their own symphony, an art museum, two major universities, three ball teams, a marathon named after the local basketball coach, and a triple-A bond rating. And all of this had happened since he became mayor. So why wouldn't they let him ride off into the sunset with a smile on his face? It didn't seem like a lot to ask.

Mueller had earned the right to feel fulfilled, but he was haunted by the past. Things he had nothing to do with were threatening his future. Still, it was not in him to give up. He pushed the button on the intercom, summoning his assistant. When Fischer came in, the mayor said, "I want Tommy Paley."

On Trial

Twenty-four

Charlie adjusted the knob on the handlebars to simulate an uphill climb and got on the exercise bike. He had started riding forty minutes a day after his second knee operation. Although tennis had been a lifelong obsession, he had no difficulty giving it up when the doctor told him he could choose between a few more years on the court and being able to walk for the rest of his life. Besides, there were advantages to the bike. Charlie never had to make a reservation at a club, and he had come to enjoy riding.

They had built onto the house when his wife was pregnant with their third child and they needed more room. As he rode, Charlie thought of that time, that baby, whom they still couldn't talk about without Donna breaking down. They had named the baby Nate because Charlie thought a kid that small and frail needed a tough name to get a break in life. But Nate's name hadn't helped, or it hadn't helped enough, though there was no question about his fighting spirit. After one hundred days and three operations to repair an incomplete digestive system, they had given up and let Nate die.

Donna had never been able to use the new addition, and so while they called it the sunroom, it was seldom occupied. At least until Charlie turned it into a small gym with a rowing machine and free weights in addition to the bike, but this metamorphosis seemed to help them both. It was hard to feel bad when you were working hard. Now Donna stuck her head in the door. "Where are you?" she asked. It was their morning joke, a way to get things going. As Charlie rode, he imagined he was traveling west toward Madison, always trying to get farther than he had the day before.

He checked the odometer. "Nowhere," he said. "Five miles. I'm not even out of the city limits."

Donna walked in and hefted a five-pound barbell. "Maybe if I worked out I could intimidate the kids at school."

"I doubt it," Charlie said. "How's it going anyway?"

Donna taught special education in the inner city, but she was getting tired. Every kid she met seemed to have special needs, and recently the courts had started calling juvenile delinquents emotionally handicapped. Donna spent most of her time trying to convince them not to kill each other. It wasn't the way she had imagined her life. "Same old shit," she said.

"I love it when you talk dirty," Charlie said.

Donna's face changed when she laughed. "You're irresistible." She put her arms around Charlie and kissed him.

"I can't ride if you're going to make love to me."

"Sorry, I couldn't help myself. Fight the good fight." Then she left.

Talking improved Charlie's bleak mood, and he got into the rhythm of the ride, feeling his muscles shift and pull as sweat ran down his back. He was ten miles out now, into Wauwatosa and well on his way to Waukesha.

The tension receded in his neck, and he started thinking about the Norman case and the difficulties it presented. He knew it was the biggest rights trial in the history of the state, and a great chance for him to distinguish himself while still doing the right thing. But he shouldn't have let Isaacson talk him into the $100 million, not because he found it personally offensive, but because he had only done it to keep his client. Olivia cared about justice, but if there were ever a conflict between money and justice, her choice would be easy. She had grieved, but she was no longer grieving. What was left was hard, calculating. Charlie knew life had made Olivia that way, but it was still troubling.

Beyond these concerns, Charlie was worried about the case itself, because winning wasn't going to be easy. Alberts had been lenient regarding the statute of limitations but Charlie knew that if the city lost, Dolan would appeal. More important, the family hadn't contested the settlement until now. They had managed to avoid summary judgment because Alberts wanted the case to go to trial, but Dolan's argument made sense. If the Normans' lawyer gave them bad advice, it wasn't his problem. Sue your lawyer, not the city.

Distracting as these things were, however, Charlie had to push them out of his mind and continue with discovery as if his case were perfectly solid. They had asked for and received every piece of paper the police had that was relevant to the case, and so far nothing incriminating had turned up. Charlie hadn't seen all the interrogatories yet, but the witnesses' responses to his questions hadn't yielded much. The only thing he could do was keep on trying, but for some reason everything seemed pointless this morning.

When he reached Oconomowoc, Charlie got off the bike and started doing sit-ups. He was sweating freely and his thoughts flowed more easily. He was flying to Sarasota later in the day to take Chief Martin's deposition. The chief had a retirement home there, and you couldn't require a witness to travel for a deposition. They had no money for plane fare, but since discovery had yielded so little, it was necessary. They were going to trial in March, and Charlie had to know where he stood on witnesses.

He had sent out a trial subpoena ad testificardun on Rogan, and the marshal in Indiana called to say he need $1,800 to fly Rogan and two marshals first class for security. This was bullshit, and Charlie knew it, but he agreed because he had no choice—they were scrambling.

He finished the sit-ups and regarded himself in the mirror. At forty-six he was 5'10" and weighed a hard 158. There were some miles on his face, and he had never made more than fifty thousand dollars a year in his career, but things could have been worse. He loved his wife and he still respected the law, even if he disliked most lawyers. He should be happy, he told himself, yet melancholy kept tugging at the edge of his mood.

Then he understood, though Donna hadn't said anything. Today was Nate's birthday. Their son would have been sixteen years old. In the brilliant sun-lit room, filled with equipment testifying to his good health, Charlie's eyes filled, and for once he didn't dry them immediately or jump up to do something else. He sat on the mat and bowed his head. Alone in the sunroom they had meant for Nate, Charlie mourned his son.

Sarasota should have been a welcome contrast after the January chill of Milwaukee, but Charlie wasn't on vacation. He rented a conference room at the airport and waited for Martin. After an hour, the chief's attorney called to say they'd rather meet at his office. Raising hell over this would just take time and Charlie didn't want to stay over, so he rented a car and drove to the lawyer's office, arriving in a downpour, which didn't improve his mood.

Dolan hadn't come down, and Martin's lawyer knew little about the case. He was a big man wearing an ice-cream suit who probably spent most of his time putting together real-estate deals. The lawyer shook Charlie's hand vigorously and led him into a wood-paneled conference room.

Martin was dressed in a blue sport coat and bolo tie and looked like a conventioneer. He stood and shook hands, but the sour look on his face made it clear that he wasn't happy to be here. Charlie didn't blame him. Martin had been a career public servant, rising through the ranks to become chief of the department, which he served without distinction or disgrace, which was more than you could say for some people. Now ten years into retirement, this had come up and he didn't like it. As far as Charlie could tell, Martin's attitude was "I didn't shoot the kid—what am I doing here?" Which made a kind of sense, but didn't change anything. Martin had been around when Jimmy Norman was killed and might actually remember something about it. If he didn't like it, tough shit. Charlie didn't expect hostile witnesses to like him.

"Chief," Charlie began, emphasizing the title, "I'm going to ask you some questions about the Norman case."

"I figured," Martin said. The man was fat and despondent, which expressed itself in sarcasm.

Charlie nodded. "Good. No surprises, then." He looked at his notes. "On February 8, 1959, you were chief of police in the city of Milwaukee. Is that correct."

Martin just shrugged. "Sure," he said.

"Was there anything unusual about that night, Chief?"

"Yeah. The Norman kid got shot," Martin said.

"And how did you learn about this, Chief?"

"The officer on duty called me," Martin said.

Charlie looked at his notes again. "So you weren't directly involved in questioning the officers that night?"

"I told you, I was at home."

"That's right, you did say that," Charlie said. Lots of television that night. He wondered if Martin and Tanner had talked about this. "Let me ask you, then, about the two officers involved. Did you know them?"

Martin shrugged. "How can I know every patrolman in the division? I think I'd heard of them."

"And why was that?" Charlie asked. "Why would you have heard of these two. Was it Rogan's record that you had heard about?"

Martin yawned. "Maybe. I heard he had some trouble."

"That's right. He had a folder full of complaints for assault. But Paley had nothing. How had you heard of him?"

"Maybe I didn't. Maybe it was just the other guy."

"In any case, they were both off the force six months after the Norman killing, isn't that right?"

Martin indicated that it was.

"So you got rid of these bad apples. Is that it, Chief?"

"Something like that."

"How about the rest of the department?"

"What about it?"

"Were there any other bad apples, or was the department made up of good men, in your opinion?"

"It was the best in the country. Everyone knows that."

"Maybe not quite everyone," Charlie said. "In any case, you'd agree, wouldn't you, Chief, that the motorcycle corps, the bikemen, were the best? They had to apply for the corps, pass an exam; they were an elite group."

"Damned right they were," Martin said.

"Well, then, how do you explain the apparent contradiction? The two officers whom you called bad apples had been selected from among the officers assigned to your elite corps. Rogan and Paley. How did that happen?"

"Somebody screwed up. We're not perfect," Martin said.

"All right, I think we can all agree to that," Charlie said. "Nobody's perfect, including the police. Very good."

"Why don't you make your point, Counselor," Martin's lawyer interjected. "We haven't got all day."

Charlie wondered what pressing business the man might have, but he wasn't going to argue fine points of the law with a resort attorney. He nodded. "Just a few more questions, Chief," he said. "It has been reported that there was a conspiracy to cover up the truth about this death and, further, that the true facts were concealed by members of the police department administration. Were you aware of this cover-up?"

Martin looked at his lawyer, but the man was out of his depth. "I don't know nothing about that," Martin said.

"Well, if there had been a cover-up, would you have known about it?"

Martin looked wary, as if Charlie were trying to trick him into saying more than he wanted to. "I was in touch, sure."

"Then we can conclude that either the newspaper reports are inaccurate, because you would have known about the cover-up, or you're not telling the truth and do know. Is that a fair statement, Chief?"

"Wait a minute," Martin's lawyer said, but Martin was on his feet. His bolo tie had come loose and spittle formed at the borders of his mouth. "Those sonsabitches don't give a rat's ass for the truth," Martin said. "Especially when a cop's involved. Everyone knows that."

Charlie waited to see if Martin would come completely unglued, start yelling, maybe lunge at him. But with an effort the chief regained control. Still, Charlie could see he would be able to use him as a witness, which was the reason he had come down. He closed his file. "We'll leave it at that, Chief. But I'll tell you one thing." Martin's eyes were slits. Charlie doubted he wanted to hear another word, but he was listening. The sleepy indolence was gone. "If I were you, I'd get a better lawyer."

He smiled at both of them. "Have a nice day," he said.

Twenty-five

It was New Year's Day, and Andy watched the mist rise over the lake. On cold days it was as dense as fog and he could hear the ice cracking like brittle bones far below. He felt warm and safe in the study. He hadn't spoken to Sarah and knew he should check in with the office, but he was reluctant to break the peaceful spell. He had been reading about Napoleon's disastrous attempt to invade Russia in the winter of 1812 and the unwitting brilliance of the Russians' victory:

> Napoleon began the war because he could not resist. . . . Alexander refused all negotiations because he felt himself personally insulted. . . . And in the same fashion all the innumerable individuals who took part in the war acted in accordance with their natural dispositions, habits, circumstances and aims . . . they argued and supposed that they knew what they were doing and did it of their own free will, whereas they were all the involuntary tools of history, working out a process concealed from them but intelligible to us. Such is the inevitable lot of men of action, and the higher they stand in the social hierarchy the less free they are.

Now Andy got up and walked to the window. The glass was cold against his fingertips. He thought of Napoleon, invading Russia in his omnipotence, and thought he understood the general from the distance of 150 years. To Napoleon it must have seemed impossible that he could fail. And why not? He had the greatest army in the world, the most brilliant generals, and the Russians were in complete disarray as they retreated. It was far-fetched, but in this frozen winter of 1980, the message of 1812 came through clearly if you were inclined to see it. Paradoxically, it was the illusion of freedom that made you less free. The idea that you controlled your destiny only ensured that you would actually be controlled by it. But if you embraced the historical necessity of the situation, accepted it, then some motion was possible.

The fact of the Norman trial coming now rather than two years before or five years in the future was out of his control. There was no point in even thinking about it, but it had given him an opening to exploit. Mueller was the Russian bear, huge and somnolent, apparently disorganized and on the run, while he, aristocratic and detached, was venturing into dangerous territory in the belief that he was smarter and stronger than his opponent.

Andy stepped back. On the other hand, maybe it was simple arrogance to make an analogy between one of the world's great military battles and an obscure mayoral election in Milwaukee. Maybe this was no more than it seemed to be. In the last month, he had been rising steadily in the polls, but now he had leveled off and was afraid he might have peaked two months early. Perhaps this would be the wrong time to press ahead. By giving himself more chances to make points, he was also increasing the chance he'd fail, and that would be to Mueller's benefit. If he were to draw back, on the other hand, and consolidate his resources instead of going in for the quick kill, he might be more successful. With the trial about to begin, there was at least an even chance that events would defeat Mueller and save him the trouble. In the cold morning, with the mist rising off the lake, it seemed like the right thing to do.

Sarah was drinking coffee when he went into the kitchen. "Happy New Year," he said, and she nodded in assent, though they hadn't done anything the night before or even seen much of each other. He missed the friendly companionship of their marriage but had no idea how to retrieve it, considering the circumstances. He wanted for her to be curious about his life, to ask questions. He thought he deserved that at least. Curiosity.

But Sarah was incurious. Friendly but distant. She rinsed her cup in the sink and put her arm on his shoulder. "You look tired," she said. "Why don't you get more sleep?"

"I'm all right," Andy said, and he realized that he was tired, though he wasn't sure why. Neither of them commented on the irony of her advising him to get more rest when they no longer slept together. It was all either very civilized or pathological.

Sarah smiled at him. "Well, you take care of yourself, Andy, because Jimmy will run you to death if you don't say no."

"I'll be careful," Andy said. Then Sarah was gone.

As it happened, Sarah had not seen much of Bob lately either. She had asked him to come by the apartment several times, but he put her off.

"You're not avoiding me, are you?" Sarah asked. She was joking, but Bob heard the anxiety of a person who used humor as a defense.

"Why would I do that?" he said. But Sarah was right; he didn't want to see her until he figured out how he felt. He didn't really blame her, but getting taken off the Norman story had hurt. He knew he should discuss it with her, at least tell her what had happened, but he didn't want to say anything he'd regret. He and Margie had talked about everything and considered it one of the strengths of their relationship. Now Bob wasn't so sure. He hadn't talked about anything with anyone for years, and it was some comfort not having to explain every reaction to someone else, even someone who loved him. Bob thought communication was overrated, just as simple respect for privacy was probably not valued as much as it should be.

He slept badly and awoke at six with the cotton mouth of a hangover, though he hadn't been drunk the night before. He remembered an old college friend who gauged the success of his weekend by how bad he felt on Monday. By that standard, Bob had had a hell of a night.

He washed his face and pulled on his old Riverside windbreaker. Then he walked for an hour along the bluffs, returning under Andy Hedig's windows and up Newberry Boulevard and back to the house. He remembered Newberry being the boundary between rich and poor when he was younger and how pleased his mother had been to buy a house just off the boulevard. Now these distinctions seemed to matter less, though the mansions were still there with their fluted columns and coach houses extending down to the street, the huge wrought-iron gates protecting them from the lower classes. Perhaps they mattered as much as they ever had, and it was he who had changed, who was less attuned to social gradations than he had been as a younger man.

He wanted to go out for breakfast, but nothing was open on Downer, so Bob went home for coffee and a stale English muffin. Margie had always stockpiled Thomas' whenever they went east, and Bob had continued the habit after they separated, though he couldn't remember the last time he had been out of the state. Muffins lasted a long time when you lived alone.

Then he sat and looked out at his yard, aware of the silence of the house and the beating of his heart. Like most reporters, Bob thought of himself as being tough and unsentimental. It was protective coloration, considering the way he lived. Things happened, people came into your life and left, and you adjusted and went on. It had helped when he lost Margie. Or so he thought. What he realized now was that it was only a means of delaying grief, a way to rationalize loss. The result was that emptiness had lodged deep within him and stayed there for years. Being with Sarah these past months had the unexpected result of making him realize how much he missed Margie. And while he regretted the admixture of sorrow in the joy he thought he had a right to feel, it was only Sarah who had allowed him to feel this delayed pain.

Still, some things didn't bear close examination, and he rationalized the fact that he lacked family, friends, and even outside interests by telling himself that he didn't have time. As you got older, Bob told himself, everything shrinks, not just your body—your mind, your interests, your whole experience of life. When he died, he imagined a cigar box would be large enough to hold everything of value he had accumulated, with room left over.

It was a self-enclosed system and it worked as well as anything else. Yet falling in love had also had the effect of making Bob more optimistic. He found himself unexpectedly interested in people, their family peculiarities, likes and dislikes. Food tasted different now; the fact that he tasted anything at all was different. He couldn't remember eating a meal in the previous five years, but now suddenly he was a gourmet, savoring every sauce and wine. The fact that he was stupid in love and knew it changed nothing. Being stupid was all right. He was amazed by Sarah's love, but more astonishing was the fact that he could return it. He had assumed that was gone forever and because of this, he hadn't previously considered the cost of love.

Because of course there was a cost. It wasn't that he hadn't expected people to find out; he had just assumed his love affair wouldn't matter to anyone else. It had even occurred to him that some friends might be happy for him. Among other things, Mike Klein's lecture had made him feel foolish. Mike had embarrassed him, though really Bob had embarrassed both of them with his naivete. It was one thing to be taken off a good story. More important was the fact that he hadn't really thought about Mike, or the paper, or even Sarah. Now it seemed incredible that he could have imagined no one would care that he was sleeping with the wife of a mayoral candidate while he covered the campaign. The only thing that had really mattered was the giddy excitement of being in love. Even teenagers had more sense than that.

The kitchen had large, leaded windows that looked out on a back yard a friend had once characterized as being like something out of Faulkner. Some friend, Bob thought, but he had to admit Yoknapatawpha was never quite this forlorn. In a weak moment last summer, Bob had spent several hundred dollars on lawn furniture, chaise longues and web chairs, imagining friends coming over for beer and barbecue after work. But the parties hadn't materialized and now the chairs sagged under a foot of old snow. On the porch, a couple of stools, some logs, and a rusting Weber grill were all bounded by a decrepit wooden railing with peeling gray paint along which squirrels ran.

Bob went outside carrying the remainder of his breakfast. He broke up the muffin and set the pieces on the railing. "Time to eat," he muttered. Then he walked down into the yard, hands in his pockets. The branches of the fruit trees his mother had planted ten years before were heavy with snow, and though he was wearing only the white shirt and jeans he had slept in, Bob picked up a stick and started knocking snow off the branches. First he worked on the plum tree, then the apple behind it. He was aware of his ears feeling so brittle that he imagined them breaking off and leaving him with symmetrical holes in his head. But he didn't care. He worked for nearly an hour, snow falling around him in a steady shower until finally the trees were clear.

Then he went back inside and stood at the window watching the squirrels attack the feast he had left. At eleven, Sarah called. "What are you doing today?" she asked.

"Yard work," Bob replied without thinking.

"I know a good doctor for cases like yours," Sarah said. "I'm seeing Olivia Brown, but I'll be done around two."

"On New Year's Day?"

"Neither of us likes football," Sarah said.

Bob thought for a moment. He had to cover a night meeting in the suburbs, part of his penance, but he was free until then. It was surprising how badly he wanted to see her. The time alone had served its purpose, and now whatever had been holding him back was gone. "That's fine," he said.

"Such enthusiasm," she said.

"Sorry," he said, and meant it. "I'd like to see you. Really."

"That's better. The apartment at two, then?" Her voice was brisk and businesslike. She was a woman of the world arranging an assignation with her lover. First the appointment, then lovemaking, and home in time for dinner. Bob envied her.

"See you then," he said.

Twenty-six

Tommy had rented a room from a widow in West L.A. when he first came to town, and though he didn't like the smells that emanated from her kitchen and found the old lady's decrepit furniture and yellowing, picture-laden walls depressing, he stayed on because the price was right. The widow was pleased to learn Tommy had once been a cop and whiled afternoons away reading lurid descriptions of murders from tabloids she bought at the supermarket. Occasionally, she would try to engage him in conversation by encouraging him to reminisce about his days on the force, but the fact was these were things Tommy didn't really want to remember, so he took to staying in his room with the door closed.

After he was settled, Tommy called the agent and made an appointment, which her secretary—they called them assistants—canceled twice before finally giving him a firm time. When the day came, Tommy awoke early and put on his drip-dry suit. Then he sat waiting patiently until it was time to go. He went by bus and had to change twice, but he still arrived early, which gave him fifteen minutes to walk around Sunset Boulevard looking for the office.

Like everyone else, Tommy had heard the names so often on TV and in the movies, that the streets seemed familiar, though he'd never been in California before. Still, he was disappointed to find the address the agent had given him painted on a shabby wall next to a souvenir shop. He didn't believe in signs or portents, but after all his anticipation, it was hard to get excited about an agent who offered special deals on models of Shamu.

When he climbed the stairs, the actual office was no better, consisting of a couple of cluttered desks pushed together and a few broken-backed chairs. A girl with a pouty mouth, frosted-blond hair, and secretary's spread was on the phone. Between calls, she worked her nails. Tommy figured this was the assistant. She indicated one of the chairs. As he waited, Tommy tried surreptitiously to see whether or not he had sweated through his armpits.

Tommy started to feel better when the door to the inner office opened and the agent came out. Her name was Tami DeBerg and she was short with a lot of red hair piled on top of her head. She smiled and actually seemed glad to see him, though she thought his name was Pooley. Tami told the blond to hold her calls, which Tommy thought was a nice touch, but once she took him inside, he could tell she wasn't that excited by what she saw, and Tommy couldn't blame her. He knew he looked exactly like a thousand other overweight middle-aged guys with a widow's peak. But he couldn't help that and it wasn't the point anyway. It was just hard to see how this woman in her dumpy office was going to be able to introduce him to anyone important. If either of them had better options they'd probably be pursuing them, but there was no point in finding fault, especially since Tami hadn't said anything yet. Tommy decided to be positive about it.

Tami threw out a lot of names Tommy didn't recognize. He smiled and nodded as if they were having a real conversation. Everyone seemed to be called Brent or Cliff or Sasha, and Tommy found himself wondering if anyone in L.A. had a normal name. The bus stations were probably on alert for any Margies or Susies arriving from Omaha and they were held at customs until appropriate names could be found.

But Tommy tried to look interested. What did he know? At least this Tami had gone to the trouble to call, which meant she had her ear to the ground enough to read a paper. Most people in California didn't even know what state Milwaukee was in. And she was making nothing by having this meeting, so why not give her the benefit of the doubt? Still, when he found himself back on the street he wasn't sure what had happened. He didn't even know if Tami was actually representing him, though she had said she'd be in touch, which seemed to mean he was still in the game. And she liked his screenplay idea. "Wonderful," was what she had said. Even though Tommy figured this translated to "OK" in Hollywood, it was better than nothing.

For the next few days, he hung around the house waiting for the phone to ring until he figured out that it wasn't going to and he was wasting his time. When Tami said she'd be in touch, he should have understood she was letting him down easy instead of getting a hard-on. Which was OK, but Hollywood wasn't turning out the way Tommy had expected. He thought he'd draw some attention; he had thought being on '60 minutes' would matter. He had imagined that by this time he'd be having lunch with producers while starlets went down on him. Which was a joke. If he was lucky he might get a table at the Farmer's Market and avoid the bag ladies for a day. That was about it.

Tommy hadn't even seen a producer, and while the streets were full of pretty girls, none of them would give him the time of day even if he tried, which he didn't. In the Midwest, people usually greeted strangers on the street, but here Tommy felt invisible. If it weren't for the TV the widow kept going night and day, he wouldn't have even known movies were being made. But Tommy was determined not to give in to self-pity. What did he have to feel sorry about anyway? Worst case he was avoiding the midwestern winter, and at $50 a week you couldn't beat the price. He still had his return ticket in case he got an uncontrollable urge to go back and freeze his ass in Milwaukee.

To cheer himself up, Tommy bought ban-lon shirts in three different colors at a discount store and, to top it off, a pair of shades with mirrored lenses. Maybe it would help to look the part. And because everyone seemed thin, he decided he'd better do something active. He couldn't see himself running around in short-shorts, however, and golf and tennis were rich guys' sports. Here, the weather was always good, so Tommy started walking again, sometimes even getting on the bus and going over to Griffith Park or Beverly Hills High School, where women in tight gym suits lapped him as he made his way decorously around the oval. After a week, he got on the old lady's scale in the john and saw he'd dropped a few pounds, which made him feel more a part of things in the Golden West.

There was a big pinochle game in a nearby park and Tommy started stopping by. When the old guys who ran the game found out he was an ex-cop, they dealt him in, saying Tommy could protect them from the niggers shooting hoops across the way. But the kids never said boo, and Tommy didn't know what he could have done if they had. After a while, no one mentioned it anymore. The conversation centered around the old guys' health problems or declining morals of young people with an emphasis on the girls who walked around in public with their asses hanging out of their shorts.

When he wasn't walking or playing cards, Tommy was a tourist, visiting the studios, Grauman's Theater, and even the La Brea tar pits. He lost a few more pounds, worked on his tan, and one day picked up a light blue blazer at the discount store for $24.99, but which looked like it cost a lot more. The next time he met the agent she seemed friendlier. They should have lunch, she said. There was someone she wanted Tommy to meet. Which set Tommy up pretty good. He told his buddies in the park that he might have something big cooking but he couldn't talk about it yet, which seemed to impress them. It had taken a while, Tommy thought, but when you got down to it, L.A. was no different from any other town: you had to know your way around. As an experiment, he tried working Malibu into his conversation. He had a friend with a place out on the beach, he told the old guys one afternoon, though the closest he'd ever come to Malibu was when his old Chevy was repossessed. Still, he liked the way the words dropped off his tongue, liked the way such talk made him feel. And the old guys nodded knowingly, as if they were between deals themselves and hung out in the park just because they liked it. On the way home Tommy bought himself a pair of tennis shoes with stripes on the sides and trotted for a block without collapsing.He was headed for his afternoon nap when he saw a note his landlady had pinned to the door: "Please call Ameel Mueller," it said, with a Milwaukee number underneath. Suddenly Tommy was wide awake, his breath coming in little gasps. For a minute Tommy had thought some Arab was after him, but then he recognized the mayor's name and the feeling of well-being that had been building drained out of him like water. His fucking luck. Just when things were getting started, this had to happen. What the hell could Mueller want with him and how had they tracked him here?

It was five o'clock in California, which made it seven in Milwaukee. Too late to call, Tommy thought with relief. It gave him time to think, make a plan. He went into the kitchen and made himself some beef stew, which he washed down with a can of beer, then another. He started to feel better. So Mueller had called, so what? He had no obligation to the city and he wasn't on anyone's fucking string. He'd talk to them OK, see what they wanted, but he wasn't wasting any money on long distance. Let them find him. Of course, he liked the idea of holding up the mayor for the price of a call by calling collect, and there was no denying that along with being annoyed, he was flattered that Mueller had called. But why go looking for trouble? He was starting to like his new life. If he let it alone, maybe they'd forget all about him.

Making the decision improved his mood. Tommy checked the papers for a movie. He'd heard about a new one, with Audrey Hepburn, who was a little skinny but still good-looking. He figured it would help with his screenplay to see all the movies he could. He looked at his watch. With luck, he could make it over to La Cienaga in time for the discount show at six.

The streets were deserted as Sarah drove to meet Bob, but her meeting had gone reasonably well. Olivia always set out petits-fours and tea, which both charmed and irritated Sarah. Still, she knew the most important part of an interview was winning the other person's confidence. Olivia was feeling her out, and Sarah had decided to let it go for as long as the other woman needed. They couldn't really start working until the trial was over anyway.

Sarah parked in the underground garage and took the elevator to her apartment. When she opened the door, she saw Bob lying on the couch. "Been waiting long?" she asked.

"I don't know," he said and smiled. "What's long?"

Bob seemed different, thinner maybe, though that seemed unlikely. But wistful, not as intense. He was wearing jeans, a hooded sweatshirt, and red socks. Though it had only been two days since they had been together, it seemed like weeks and she felt oddly nervous, tentative. "Are you all right?"

"As all right as you can be covering night meetings in Brookfield."

Sarah was still wearing her coat, but she felt her good mood evaporating. Something was going on. "Brookfield?"

Bob nodded. "Klein pulled me off the Norman story, so I'm covering night meetings. Makes me feel young again."

Sarah felt chilled. "Why? What is it, Bob?"

He got up from the couch and faced her. "Mike found out we were together and fired me off the story."

"Because of us?" It seemed incredible. "I thought everyone did it."

It was some comfort to Bob that she was as dense as he had been. "I guess not. At least not at the Times."

"Jesus," Sarah said. "I'm sorry. I don't mean to sound stupid, but what does this have to do with your job?"

Bob shook his head. "Nothing. It's not that, at least I don't think so. Mike's a prude and he's probably offended by the whole thing. But that's not why. If he had a choice he'd leave me on the story because I'm a good reporter and it's my beat. I know it better than anyone else. But they say it's a conflict of interest for me to be involved with you while I'm covering your husband, and I probably agree with them."

Sarah didn't understand exactly what this meant, but she knew it changed things. The funny thing was that no one had accused Bob of being impartial when they were driving to Port Washington and making passionate love in motels. No one had said a word. But now that they were being honest, there was a conflict of interest. "Who told him?" she asked.

Bob shrugged. "It doesn't really matter. Mike was embarrassed even talking about it and I was too. The thing is, if he knows, other people do too. Mike's part of the inner loop, but it's a big loop, especially in politics. People could have been talking for weeks, even if we didn't know."

"How?" That was the important question. How did it happen? Sarah wasn't ready to even talk about what to do yet.

"Think about it. We haven't exactly been discreet."

This hit Sarah like an accusation. "You think I've been flaunting it, kissing in public, leaving lipstick-stained notes around, all that?"

He smiled. "Not exactly, but someone could have seen us in a restaurant or on one of those trips. I wasn't paying attention. I hardly knew if there was anyone else around half the time. And Mike didn't tell me exactly what it was that he heard. It could have been anything. It doesn't matter."

"Why not?" It mattered to Sarah. This wasn't some passing thing; they had fallen in love. The difference between that and whatever people were saying was crucial. Then she had a sudden realization. "Andy must know."

Bob nodded. "Probably. There was something the day I interviewed him at your house. Nothing specific, just the way he acted, the things he said. I'm pretty sure."

Sarah felt intensely guilty because her husband had known that she had taken a lover and hadn't yelled or thrown her out. He had just lived with it, and probably suffered too. Then she was annoyed. Why was she always so willing to punish herself? If Andy had paid more attention to her and less to politics they might not be here. But he hadn't, and now Bob was looking thin and worried. That was what was mattered. She took him in her arms and they stood watching the lake together. Then she said, "What happens now?"

"It kind of upsets our timetable," Bob said. "April just came early."

Sarah shook her head. "It doesn't have to change anything," she said. "I think you're being gallant and I don't like it. You've essentially lost your job because of me. There are worse things in the world, but that's bad enough. And you don't have to do it. Not for my sake. We never said anything about your giving up your career for this. You don't have to hang around."

Bob was impressed, though giving up his career sounded a little grandiose. This would pass. It would just take time. After the election, he'd be back downtown as if nothing had ever happened. Still, it amazed him how right she was. He did feel like a martyr, and though he was ashamed to admit it, he had been blaming her. "It isn't that," he said weakly.

"Sure it is," Sarah said. "You're an honorable guy in a traditional way. I know how it works. When you were in high school, if you knocked a girl up, you forgot about college and married her. This doesn't have to be the same thing. We've always been honest with each other, let's be honest now."

"You mean you don't care?" Bob asked.

"I didn't say that," Sarah said, and suddenly she was angry, not just at Bob but at all the clumsy attempts of men to protect and limit her. "Of course I care. I care more than anything. Just don't think you've got to save me. Andy is being very civilized about this; even if I didn't realize it before, I do now. I wouldn't blame you if you didn't want to give up that story. I'm not sure I would if I were in your place. I just want to know that if you do, it's for your own reasons. It's whatever you want to do." Bob looked so stunned by this, that she softened. "I really mean it, Bobby."

Bob had walked through the situation in the yard when he was working on the trees and thought he had made his peace. It was a sacrifice he had to make for love. Now Sarah was telling him to do whatever he wanted but to leave her out of it, which wasn't in the script. She should break down and cry, and then he'd take her in his arms and feel good. Except that Sarah had seen his ambivalence so she'd set him loose, but to his surprise he had no desire to go. Brookfield could be OK. Brookfield looked better all the time.

He locked his hands behind his head. "OK, you're right. The only reason to do this is because I want to. But now it's got to be out in the open. No more bullshit. I want everyone to know whatever there is to know."

"You mean Andy." Sarah smiled at him.

"That's right. But I don't think he'll want to put out a press release."

"He won't have to. I'll talk to him." Then tears started down her cheeks. Bob took her in his arms and they were silent for a long time.

Finally Sarah said, "I was just so afraid." Which was odd because she hadn't really been aware of fear as an important part of the whole thing.

"Of what?" Bob asked.

"Oh, you know. That you'd rather have the story than me."

In his world this was reasonable, even predictable. Bob knew reporters who had given up marriages for less. In fact, he had surprised himself with his reaction. "Don't worry, I'm not going anywhere," he said. "Except Brookfield." He looked at his watch. "I've got an hour."

Sarah wanted to laugh, to hold him, to make love, but she was drained. She wiped her eyes with a handkerchief. "I'll make some coffee for the drive," she said.

Twenty-seven

"You want to do what?" Jimmy asked. They were sitting in Hedig head-quarters on Plankinton. The office couch was partially covered with a che-nille bedspread and some throw pillows and looked as if it had been slept on. "Run that by me again," he said. "I don't think I heard you right."

Andy looked for a place to sit. The three chairs were piled high with papers. The surfaces of two desks held typewriters and ditto machines along with a coffee maker and several jars of instant standing open. He leaned against one of the desks. "I just think we should slow down, pull back," he said gently. "Why don't we let Mueller make the mistakes for a while."

"You think we've been making mistakes?" Jimmy's voice had an edge of hysteria. He didn't look good. His long nose was red from a constant cold and his hair was matted on one side. His collar was gray and he had grown love handles that caused his shirt to gap in front.

Andy looked outside, giving himself time to gather his thoughts. Pedes-trians were skidding along the sidewalk on Wisconsin Avenue, and cars moved slowly on the iced street, their bodies nearly hidden by plumes of exhaust. "You've done a great job," he said. "No one could ask for more. In fact, you should go somewhere for a few days. You look like hell, Jim."

"What are you, my doctor?" Jimmy said. "This isn't about me. "Who rests during a campaign, for Christ's sake? The point is we've got Mueller on the run and that wasn't an easy thing to do. We fought for months and nothing happened. Finally we begin to move, about five minutes before I have a nervous breakdown, and the staff quits. It's amazing. We come up fifteen points in two weeks and Mueller's shitting in his pants. It's a big story, the papers are paying attention again, and the TV guys are with us all the time. So you come in and say let's take a break? Am I stupid, Andy? I don't get it."

"That was three weeks ago," Andy said, his voice even. "We've been flat since then. And don't forget, Mueller's still ahead by ten points."

Jimmy waved him off irritably. "Don't tell me about polls. I read polls every day of my life." Andy knew what really irritated Jimmy was that he couldn't argue with the facts. "One good week we'll make it all up."

"That might be true," Andy said. "But we'd need a very good week." He decided not to mention Napoleon, but he remembered a picture of the French retreating in the snow with boots and helmets lining the road. It was easy to be over-confident when the other side was in disarray. Looking at Wisconsin Avenue in the frozen twilight, the comparison seemed inescapable.

Jimmy poured cold coffee from a carafe and ran his fingers through his hair. "This have anything to do with your wife and that reporter?"

They had agreed not to do anything publicly until after the election. Sarah was spending more time at her studio, but otherwise things were the same, if not better. Now that there was nothing to hide, they had no reason to feel awkward. They spoke daily on the phone, though Bob Joseph was conspicuously absent from their conversations. Andy had told Jimmy immediately, but oddly, there had been no gossip or at least none he was aware of. There had always been talk about Andy before, for no good reason except that it wasn't true, which could have been reason enough, given the social ethos of the east side. There was no pleasure for some people like causing chaos in a friend's marriage. It amused him that now that there actually was something to talk about, people were being discreet.

"No," he said. "I've just been thinking about it for a while. I wanted to be sure before talking to you."

"Well, I certainly appreciate that," Jimmy said. "It would be embarrassing if you just started skipping lunches and I didn't know why. Now I can tell people you were home reading some hot novel." Jimmy looked at a sheet of paper. "I've already got you committed to forums all over town for the next month. You've got a press conference on the Norman trial today. There's plant gates, coffees, the usual. What do you want to cut?"

"How far out does that take me?"

Jimmy checked the list. "Into February anyway. People ask us all the time, but there's nothing solid past that."

Andy nodded. They were intimate in a peculiar way without really being friends. Jimmy was the first person he had hired when he was able to hire anyone. They met when Jimmy showed up and asked to do a remote for an FM station with a five-hour broadcast day. He introduced himself as the news director, which was funny since the station consisted of three guys and a transmitter, but Andy admired the younger man's bravado. After talking for fifteen minutes, he offered him a job as his administrative assistant.

For the next three years they sat a few feet apart in an office that barely had room for two desks. As Andy moved up, Jimmy went with him, moonlighting at the station until the leadership made him quit. "I guess they thought this would give you control of the playlists," Jimmy had complained. But it was a crossroads for him and he had chosen to stay with Andy. They had shared meals and motel rooms over the years, but there were things they didn't talk about, like Jimmy's girlfriends and Andy's literary tastes. Andy smiled now. Jimmy was right in thinking it wouldn't make sense to anyone that they were changing their campaign strategy because of a Russian novel.

"I've got to do the forums," he said. "And hold onto anything else you've scheduled. After that I'd like to ease up. Not stop, just slow down."

Jimmy tried again, almost pleading. "You've got him on the run, Andy. Don't let him get back up. Mueller's not a gentleman boxer like you; he's a street fighter. Give him a chance and he'll cut your heart out."

The snowy street was fading in the winter afternoon. Andy recognized a shade of purple that you saw only at this time of the year and then only at twilight. He remembered what it was like to be standing in line for a job, what it felt like to pound your feet on the sidewalk, too tough or proud to give up. Give up and give in, they had said, and no one was going to give in. But no one who knew him now would believe this about him, so he kept quiet. Jimmy might be right about Mueller, but he didn't know Andy as well as he thought he did. "Don't worry, Jim," he said. "I won't let him up. Trust me."

Bob stamped his shoes as he entered the house and skated on the kitchen's slick linoleum floor to the dining room. The drive from Menomonee Falls had taken forty-five minutes, but this didn't bother him. Nothing did. He wondered how he had managed to be unhappy for so many years.

Every morning he went into the office at eight to get his assignment from the metro desk before heading out. Though it was hard to admit without embarrassment, he felt excited about his job, much as he had when he was a cub reporter twenty-five years ago. Everything seemed fascinating and new. He liked sitting at the small-town lunch counters, talking with the regulars. No one in the Falls was in a hurry and, for the first time in years, neither was he. It made Bob appreciate what he had forgotten in his rush to importance: life is always complicated and difficult, no matter where you happen to be living it.

Bob had known Mike would keep the reason for his reassignment to himself, but everyone knew. It was hard not to notice when the star political writer was suddenly covering Boy Scout jamborees for the zoned editions. But on the whole Bob's demotion had drawn little attention. Few people said anything at all, and in time this would simply become part of the legend of the newspaper. The story would be elaborated and improved upon even as the principals were forgotten. Journalists were too caught up in the present to have much of a sense of history.

Which was fine. Bob did his work and went home and didn't think about it until it started all over again in the morning. There was a comforting dailiness to small towns that was different from covering a developing story. Usually, he purposely planned nothing for the evening. Often, he would have dinner with Sarah, but sometimes they needed a rest. On these occasions, Bob would heat something up and walk around the corner for a movie, not even checking to see what picture was playing. Anything was fine. It was as if a string had been cut, removing all tension from his life. He saw no one socially except Sarah, and this had the effect of making him feel oddly remote in the city, alone in his weathered cocoon. For he loved the house, loved its age and fragility and the fact that it was his free and clear and always would be.

Now he opened a can of beer and sat at the kitchen table to consider the possibilities. There was chicken pie, pizza, or the Tuxedo, a neighborhood bar. The wind was blowing and Bob enjoyed listening to the creaking storm windows rattle. He became aware of a tinny quality at the edge of the noise. The phone. Sarah, he thought hopefully and hoisted himself, carrying his beer carefully as he navigated the familiar corners of the old house.

But it wasn't Sarah. A male voice he vaguely recognized said, "Bob Joseph?" as if there could be some question. Bob found this mildly irritating, but with the wind, he could barely hear. Probably an anonymous tipster who hadn't heard he was off the Norman story. Pain in the ass. He mashed the receiver against his head and plugged his ear. Maybe he'd stay in tonight. "This is Bob Joseph," he said. "Who's calling?"

"Tommy. Tommy Paley. You remember?"

It seemed like years but had actually been only a few weeks. How the hell could he not remember? His whole life had changed since then, but Paley wouldn't know or care. "Of course I remember. You sound like you're at the bottom of the river." Considering Paley's life, that would make a lot of sense.

"I'm in L.A.," Tommy said, and Bob could hear pride in his voice. You couldn't say too much against the land of opportunity when a low-life like Paley could get kicked off the force, spend time in prison, and still end up on the West Coast saying he was in El Lay. "I'm out here talking to producers," Tommy added. Bob sensed this was a conversation he should avoid.

"Good luck with that," he said. "Look, I'm off the Norman story. I can give you the number of the guy who's working on it." Brisk, that was the way to handle Paley. Pass him along to someone else and go to the movies.

"That ain't why I called," Paley said, and Bob felt rather than heard the other man's fear. The mannered quality disappeared and miraculously he was the same north side loser he'd always been, producers or not.

Bob wanted to bang Paley's head against the wall, or failing that, his own, but when Tommy didn't say anything, he asked the obvious question. "Why did you call then, Tom? What's up?" He should just hang up, but he couldn't do it. What hooked him was his curiosity, he couldn't help it. He'd spent too many years snooping into other peoples' lives to be incurious.

"Mueller called," Paley said, as if this explained something.

"The mayor," Bob said and felt stupid. Of course the fucking mayor. But why would Mueller call Tommy Paley? "What did he want?"

"We didn't talk. My landlady took a message."

It had nothing to do with anything, but Bob was interested to learn there were landladies in Los Angeles. Without consciously thinking about it, he had assumed everyone out there lived in a beach condo or in one of the canyons, though he had always had trouble visualizing canyons in the middle of a city. Now he had a new image of middle-class life in tinsel town. They probably had milk delivery and duplexes too. Fathers played ball with their kids after work and wives had kaffeeklatsches in the afternoon. There was a dime store on the corner and you could get the paper delivered. Amazing, but Paley hadn't called to talk about this. "He'll get back to you," Bob said.

"You don't understand." Tommy's voice was urgent. "He already did. Three times. I figured I'd ignore it, but now the D.A.'s calling too."

Bob knew Tommy was scared, but he wasn't working on this any-more. And they weren't personal friends. Paley was just a guy holding up his dinner. "I don't know what to say," he said. "Why don't you take the call?"

"I'm afraid, goddamnit," Tommy said. "You would be too if you'd been through it like I have. You think I want to end up like Rogan? These guys are fucking after me."

Paley's whining made Bob's reply tougher than he meant it to be. "Is there something you want me to do?"

"I didn't know who else to call," Paley said miserably, and then Bob was hooked. He couldn't help it; he felt for the poor sonofabitch. Just as poor blacks in the South relied on their white folks, he was the one Paley would call if he was in trouble. And Bob couldn't refuse because he had brought Tommy back into the world.

"Look," he said patiently. "You haven't broken any laws. You've got nothing to be afraid of. You plea-bargained out of the Norman thing. Rogan's in the can, but you're clear. They can't do anything to you."

"Sure they can," Tommy said, and Bob knew he was right. Guys like Tommy Paley were always vulnerable. No education or family, a bad work history, and a prison record. A few phone calls from Mueller could ruin the poor bastard, if he wasn't ruined already. Growing up on the east side with parents who were professionals, Bob had always known that compared to the children of factory workers he was a prince. Milwaukee was a city with a strict hierarchy, and if the blacks were untouchables, poor whites weren't much better off. Bob had spent his life trying to forget this, but Tommy Paley couldn't.

The beer was warm in his hand and now the house seemed devoid of charm. He wondered why things affected him so deeply, even things he didn't need to care about. Why couldn't he discriminate, spread his empathy around? But he had only gotten older, not smarter. Lights went on in the house across the street, and Bob imagined a family sitting around a cozy fire and popping corn while they watched television. He had wanted his life to be that way, or at least he thought he had, but things hadn't worked out. The image faded slowly, but regret lingered and Tommy Paley was back in his ear.

"What do I do?" Tommy asked plaintively.

"OK," Bob said, summoning as much authority as he could. "You haven't talked to anyone else yet, right?"

"No, they just keep calling."

Bob tried to filter out Tommy's crying. It made it hard to think. "I'd say let them call," he said. "It's their nickel, so they can do what they want to do.

But don't pick up. Have your landlady take a message; you're never home. If you don't talk to them, you can't refuse whatever they want you to do."

"Is that legal?"

"Legal? Jesus, I don't know. You were a cop, you tell me."

"OK," Paley said. "Sorry."

Bob wondered if he was obstructing justice. Then he decided he didn't care. "I've got an idea," he said. "Go away for a few days."

"Away?" Paley said. It was a foreign concept; he *was* away.

"Sure. Take a trip."

"A trip?" Paley said.

Couldn't this guy do anything but repeat? "That's right," Bob said patiently. "Go away, on a trip somewhere."

"Where would I go?" Paley was like a child.

"Sea World, Disneyland. I've never been to California. People go there on vacation, so why can't you? Disappear. Just don't talk to Mueller."

"What if they serve me?"

"For what? The only thing they can do is subpoena you as a witness, but the trial isn't until March. Have you got money?"

"Some," Tommy said. "Enough for a while. I'll buy a bus ticket and go somewhere. I knew a guy up to Santa Barbara once."

"Don't tell me where you're going. Just get the hell out of town. And stay in touch." But after Tommy hung up, Bob stood leaning against the wall holding the receiver in his hand until it started beeping and a recording came on. He was annoyed with himself for getting involved, but the more important question was what to do next.

Finally, he dialed a number. When Klein answered, Bob said, "I just a call from Tommy Paley in Los Angeles."

"El Lay?" Jesus, Bob thought. He's doing it too.

"Right. Paley says he's out there meeting with producers and banging starlets and suddenly he starts getting calls from our mayor."

"Interesting," Klein said. "What do you make of that?"

"Nothing," Bob said. "I'm off the story. But I thought the *Times* should know."

Twenty-eight

The intense cold finally lifted, but the sky remained gray as February moved in. Those who could afford it went to Florida or Arizona. Everyone else stayed home and complained about the weather. The January thaw had warmed things up just enough to turn the dirty snow lining the streets into slush, which the buses, moving sluggishly around the city, threw up on passing cars. The residue froze on the sidewalks, causing any number of nuisance suits from old ladies with broken hips who now crowded the wards at Columbia and St. Mary's. The Scandinavians called it suicide season, but to Wisconsin natives it was just winter.

Mueller had held staff meetings on Monday morning for years, but now the mayor's personal staff was focused entirely on the campaign. Dolan and Fisher sat facing the mayor along with a young woman they had hired to handle scheduling, which was more important than it sounded.

With dozens of requests for Mueller's presence coming in every day, someone had to decide what was crucial, what could be postponed, and what should be passed up altogether. It was more than a secretary could handle, even a good one, because political decisions were being made every time they said yes or no to anyone. Decisions as to which appearances would yield the most publicity and which might generate the largest contributions or cement political alliances were all within the purview of the scheduling coordinator. She had to understand the complicated political machinery Mueller had created and the ways the ethnicity of the neighborhoods had shifted over time. It was remarkably easy to insult leaders since everyone seemed to be leading someone. Yet as important as all this was, Mueller couldn't remember his scheduler's name, and this made him feel old. For a moment he imagined he was safely at home, sitting in front of the fire with a warm drink in his hand, the campaign over and Hedig gone. But this was just self-indulgence.

Fisher tapped his pen, but the others continued talking. A word from the mayor would produce immediate silence, but Mueller let it go on. He thought of his assistant as a young man because he had been young when he joined the staff, but Fisher had aged in the job. Now his shiny scalp shone through the few strands of hair artfully combed across his head and his eyes were weary. Mueller had known his grandfather, who had been one of his ward captains and worked in Transportation. The kid started hanging around the division over the summers during law school. They had him drive around the city to make sure all the stoplights were where they were supposed to be—a make-work job if Mueller had ever heard of one. The old guys used to say there were no small jobs, just small men, and Milwaukee could have been a showcase for that bromide. Every guy pushing a broom needed a helper according to the unions. But in time Fisher had been noticed and moved up, first in the division, and then onto the mayor's staff. Then suddenly it seemed it was fifteen years later and the kid wasn't a kid anymore. A filigree of dandruff lined the worn collar of his pin-striped suit. This city would wear you down, but it bothered Mueller to see it because he had always liked Fisher.

Now the younger man smiled, though it was closer to a grimace. "We just got a new poll," he said. "It's the same as last week, which is good news. Hedig's stopped gaining." He looked around the room for affirmation, but no one said anything. Yet Fisher was right: staying even was all you had to do. Do nothing more than hold your ground for two months and you won. Hedig had come up suddenly, which created expectations, especially among the press. The fact that he had leveled off might mean he had shot his wad or it could be a plateau. There was no way for them to tell right now because nothing was happening, good or bad. It was too damned cold. All people cared about was getting the car started after work and getting home. Still, the hard fact was Mueller's lead would be gone in a week if Hedig got going again.

"We've got captains in every precinct now," Fisher continued, "and our fund-raising is bringing in money. Our TV and radio spots start in a couple of weeks, and everybody except the *Times* has endorsed us. It looks good."

Fisher actually seemed to believe what he was saying, which was amazing. You had a sitting mayor of a city with a triple-A bond rating and they were celebrating because the opponent had stopped knocking twenty points a week off his lead. Acid shot up into Mueller's throat.

Now the scheduling girl was talking, running through her arrangements, checking to see if anyone vital had been ignored. She was smart and energetic, but that didn't help Mueller's stomach. He had shaken every hand in the city three times but increasingly he couldn't see the point. Everyone kept repeating this fiction that politics was a science. Some science. The truth, which any ward-heeler could tell you, was no one knew why people voted for anyone. Unless you paid for the vote; then you knew.

He remembered being button-holed once by a man at a Serb Hall smoker who said, "I been hearing a lot about this incumbent who's running for mayor, Emil. Bad things. So I'm not going to vote for that incumbent. I'm voting for you." And Mueller said, "You go ahead and do that, my friend." The story always got a big laugh at political dinners, but it didn't really seem funny anymore. Mueller had lost his enthusiasm for the fight, the office, the whole damned thing. More often, he looked at the gray winter sky and wondered why he had poured his life into this city. He had sacrificed a marriage, his children, and so little had been accomplished. But whether or not it made sense, he wanted a last term. He didn't want someone else telling him when to quit.

The staff looked at him expectantly. He had missed something when he was daydreaming, but Mueller recovered instinctively, shooting out a question. "Anyone know why Hedig's stopped campaigning?"

This caught them off-balance. Fisher looked at his notes. The young scheduler opened her mouth to speak, then thought better of it.

"Well, you've noticed, haven't you?" Mueller said. "I mean, this great thing we're talking about—holding even in the polls—it's a hell of a lot easier if your opponent decides not to campaign. You might even say the fact we haven't come up this week shows how bad things are. Hedig does nothing and stays even. Meanwhile I'm working my ass off going to everything from B'nai B'rith to the Eastern Star banquet. But forget that for a minute. Can anyone answer my question? Why's Hedig gone into hiding?"

The room was silent. They had all been so intent on their own work that they hadn't paid much attention to Hedig's tactics. "Overconfidence?" Fisher ventured, like a kid hoping to get lucky on the chemistry quiz.

Mueller nodded. "Maybe. But I wouldn't be all that confident if I was ten points behind even if I was young and good-looking. Anyone else?"

"Maybe he's saving his energy and resources for later," the scheduling girl said hopefully.

"That's good," Mueller said, trying to encourage her. "But it doesn't explain his disappearing. Plant gates don't cost anything." Finally Mueller waved his arm to break the tension. "OK, relax," he said. "I don't know the answer either. But I learned a long time ago to keep an eye on the other guy. Sometimes that'll tell you more than the best poll."

He pointed at the scheduler. She was tall, blond, and dressed in a blue business suit that was supposed to let him know she was serious and not some bimbo. Mueller still couldn't remember her name. Liz, he thought. He was almost sure it was Liz. But rather than make a mistake he just nodded in a friendly way. "I want you to keep a record of every appearance Hedig makes; if he doesn't do anything, I want you to write that down too." The woman nodded. Then Mueller looked at Dolan. "What about that cop, Paley?"

The district attorney had been quiet all morning. He looked uncomfortable. "We haven't been able to contact him."

"You don't know where he is?" Mueller asked.

Dolan shook his head. "That's not the problem. We've got an address and phone number, but we haven't spoken to him."

Mueller looked amazed. "He won't come to the phone?"

Dolan nodded. "And now he's gone on a trip. His landlady doesn't know where he went."

Mueller couldn't believe it. A disgraced cop wouldn't take his call and now he'd vanished. He was getting too old for this. "So now we've got a relationship with this landlady of Paley's, is that right, Dolan?"

"That's about it," Dolan said.

While Mueller had been irritable before, this latest development made him feel impotent. He was the mayor of an important city, but he couldn't get Tommy Paley on the phone. "Did he call Simons?"

Dolan shrugged. "I don't really see why he'd do that. Charlie didn't list him as a witness. Paley's not going to make anyone's case look good."

"What's going on, then, in your opinion?"

"I think he's just scared and looking for cover."

Mueller understood this. He wouldn't mind a little cover himself. "OK," he said. "Then we'll keep on doing what we've been doing because I don't know what else to do, if that makes sense. Fisher, try to figure out what Hedig's up to. And, Tim, if Mr. Paley doesn't pick up the phone in the next few days, you're going out there to talk to him."

The district attorney looked at Mueller, a hint of defiance in his expression. He was an elected official, and he didn't take orders from the mayor. Except, of course, he did. Everyone did. That's why they were in the room. "Why?" Dolan asked.

"Because I'm telling you to," Mueller said. "This meeting is over."

Charlie arrived early at Mitchell Field and nursed a ginger ale in the lounge as he watched the big planes move around the tarmac. He liked coming to the airport, though he didn't get there very often these days. Twenty years ago it had been different. He remembered driving out on Sunday mornings for the out-of-town papers. They were new to Wisconsin then, and Donna thought Milwaukee was the end of the earth, which wasn't far from the truth. Having a drink in the airport lounge was no permanent cure, but it helped create the illusion of freedom. They would sit holding hands and watch the sun fade. Then the small blue runway lights would come on, making the world seem more manageable. The airport had been a tentative connection to a more exciting life, but the romance was gone now. The place seemed about as exotic as an enormous bus station filled with screaming children and people moving aimlessly along the concourses, loaded down with luggage.

Charlie forced himself to think about the trial. Progress had been slow and jury selection was only beginning. He was waiting now for a specialist, though it was only in the last five years that anyone even thought about juries as a legal specialty. Charlie had rebelled against the idea initially, feeling as if his judgment were being brought into question. But he had to admit that nothing was more important than the jurors you got in a race trial.

If they ended up with a pro-cop panel, they could forget about winning, no matter how good a job he did. And it was hard to tell about a juror's sympathies during selection. Some considered it patriotic to disguise their loyalties because for zealots defending the police was a kind of secular religion. Charlie had come to understand that people who thought cops could do no wrong were really defending themselves. It terrified them to think of the police being out of control. But understanding this didn't help. Which was why Charlie was spending his afternoon at Mitchell Field. They needed help.

The flight was announced. They were working with a big New York firm, and Charlie's anxiety irritated him. When he had noticed that he was taking more time than usual dressing, he ripped off his tie and put on an old cardigan. Now he felt self-conscious in the sweater and battered raincoat.

Charlie held up a hand-lettered sign that read "Marge Pancost." When all the passengers had passed by, he felt foolish holding the sign, but he didn't see how he could have missed anyone. Then a red-haired woman carrying a stuffed briefcase walked slowly through the tunnel. He smiled and held up the cardboard again. "I'll bet you're Marge Pancost," he said.

The woman held out her hand. "I've never had a sign before," she said in a way that pleased Charlie. She was not what he had expected. Tall and thin, Marge Pancost wore blue jeans and a green turtleneck under a tweed jacket. She carried a knapsack and wore jogging shoes. He wanted to know if these were all her clothes, but wasn't sure how to ask. "Baggage is over there," he said, pointing down the concourse. "Do you have a suitcase?"

Marge laughed. "Sure. And don't worry, I brought a dress. It's just more comfortable to travel this way."

As they stood in front of the baggage carousel, Charlie looked her over furtively. She was about thirty-five and attractive, though not beautiful, and she had a nice figure and no wedding band. It always surprised him when people with no obvious flaws were unmarried. He assumed it was a choice; certainly a woman like Marge would have had offers. Unless she was divorced, which was a distinct possibility these days. But then there'd be a story in the divorce. Come to that, there was always a story. When Marge noticed him noticing, Charlie asked. "Are you a runner?" he indicated her shoes.

"Most people wouldn't call what I do running," she said. "It's more like crawling, but I ran in college and it's hard to break the habit. You?"

"My knees gave out. I ride an exercise bike."

Marge looked sympathetic. "How the mighty have fallen," she said and smiled to show she wasn't serious.

Charlie carried her bags to the parking lot and put them in his car. Once they were on the freeway, he said, "We've got you at the Pfister."

"Is that close to the courthouse?"

"Close enough." It was the most expensive hotel in town, but Charlie liked the fact that Marge was incurious about it, wanting only to know about the courts. As they drove downtown he was aware of her beside him, of her perfume and the rustling of her clothes. It had been a long time since he had driven to a hotel with an attractive woman who was not his wife, and he found it exciting. He took the freeway loop east toward the lake to prolong the drive. When he pulled up in front of the hotel, he said, "You're probably tired."

"I slept on the plane," Marge said. "Why don't we get started?"

Charlie gave his keys to the doorman and followed Marge inside. Charlie always felt cosmopolitan when he walked into the ornate lobby of the Pfister, and being with a strange woman only increased the illusion. Did the desk clerk look suspicious? Had the bellboy taken notice? But this was ridiculous. Even if they had been there for other reasons, no one would care. It wasn't as if no one had ever taken the day rate at the Pfister. Marge didn't seem to notice. "Why don't you wait for me in the coffee shop?" she said.

In fifteen minutes, she came in and ordered a salad. Then she looked at him, her eyes clear and questioning. "So what's going on?"

"Do you know much about the case?" Charlie asked.

"Just what you sent. I'd already seen it on TV. Seems pretty solid."

"It probably looks stronger than it is," Charlie said. "Especially in Milwaukee. People here support the police and hate blacks. It would be going against the grain to find for a black family against the police."

"That's not so different from a lot of cities," Marge said quietly.

"Maybe," Charlie said. "It's more intense here."

He liked the fact that she didn't disagree. Being willing to grant that he knew more about his city than she did was a small thing, but it was more than most hot-shot lawyers would do. "So you've got committed racists?" she asked, just to show she hadn't bought his story entirely.

Charlie laughed. "Actually, it's a historical thing. The Klan was big in the twenties, and Wallace almost won the presidential primary twice."

"That's interesting," Marge said. "I always think of Wisconsin as being liberal. The LaFollettes and all those Socialist mayors here in Milwaukee."

Charlie was impressed because most New Yorkers didn't know what side of the Mississippi Wisconsin was on. "A lot of people don't know the Progressives were Republicans," he said. "And the Socialists were mainly interested in sewer lines and parks. But the LaFollettes were all right. It's just that we had McCarthy too. Somebody who was supposed to know called Milwaukee the most racially prejudiced city in the country."

Marge took this in without saying anything. People who travel are always being told that whatever city they're visiting is nationally known for one thing or another. In Milwaukee it was just race hatred instead of beauty roses. "So you want me to find out which ones are the racists?"

The way she said this made it sound childishly easy, but they both knew the job would be more complicated than that. That's why she had come. In a good trial, jury selection might take three to five hours, but in a case like this they'd be lucky to get through it in a week. "They could all be racists. What we need to know is which ones are capable of being open-minded."

"Open-minded racists?" Marge said smiling.

"That's it," Charlie replied.

Marge shrugged her shoulders. "Then that's what I'll look for. How are you going to handle the interviewing?"

"We filed for individual, sequestered voir dire."

"That's good," Marge said. "Better to get them away from the others if you can. What about strikes?"

Each side had three peremptory challenges, which were called strikes. You could strike a potential juror for any reason, but since you had a limited number it was always better to strike for cause. If you could establish that a person was a racist, for example, and the judge decided racism was fair cause for removing someone from the jury, it wouldn't count as one of your unquestioned strikes. Of course, the other side would try to force you to use your peremptory challenges. It was a chess match that took a lot of time. "We're hoping to get lucky with the judge on striking for race," Charlie said.

"That sounds reasonable." Then they sat looking out at the street. Men in topcoats moved back and forth, looking busy and self-involved. The workday was ending and people were going for a drink or heading home. Charlie was struck by the compartmentalization of his life. The way this piece he was living now fit in some unknown way with everything else. It amazed him that they could be discussing something tragic—a boy's murder—so calmly and in such a civilized setting. Yet it needed to be this way, unemotional, calm. Peace and decorum were the necessary companions of this kind of outrage; it was what had drawn Charlie to the law, its orderliness. It reaffirmed the idea that there was a measured way to express the anger and frustration he felt.

"So where do I start?" Marge asked.

Charlie reached into his briefcase. "These are the people they're going to call," he said. There were sixty names on the list. The judge would let some go because they'd admit they couldn't be fair in a police case. Others would be excused for health problems. That would bring it down to fifty, fourteen of whom would be pulled out of a hat. But they weren't going to know which fourteen, so they had to assemble files on everyone. That was where Marge came in. Assuming Alberts granted individual voir dire, each side could ask questions for thirty minutes. The hard part was knowing what to ask. Charlie was afraid Isaacson would go crazy and alienate everyone.

Marge looked up. "These addresses are all over the place. Cedarburg, Germantown, Greendale. I'll need a car."

"Why do you have to go out there?" Charlie asked.

"To check them out, look at their cars, see if they have any good bumper stickers, lawn signs. Some things are clear. Fundamentalists and racists tend to hang together. I'll ask the neighbors if I can find a way without looking obvious. A person says a lot about himself in the way he takes care of his yard, the kind of car he drives."

"We're looking for pro civil-rights people too."

Marge nodded. "Sure, fanatics either way piss everyone else off."

Something about this bothered him. Reducing jury selection to a pseudo-science took away from the process. Charlie wanted to decide if a person was fair by looking into his eyes. Peremptory challenges had been around since the inception of English common law, but driving surreptitiously past a man's home seemed unsavory. Why hold it against a guy that he drove a Buick? He could have been working double shifts at American Can for five years to pay for the damned thing. The idea of a jury made up of people who drove Volvos with Greenpeace bumper stickers wasn't entirely pleasing.

Marge patted him on the shoulder. "This bothers you, doesn't it? Well, it shouldn't. Maybe I won't see anything you wouldn't, but I'm coming into it fresh and jury selection is what I do. I'd be surprised if the other side hasn't brought in their own specialist already."

Charlie was always underrating Dolan, and the district attorney had a bigger budget to work with than he did. "You're probably right," he said.

"No 'probably' about it," Marge said. They shook hands. "I'll be in touch."

Twenty-nine

Jimmy would have derived satisfaction from knowing Emil Mueller was devoting his staff meetings to an analysis of their strategy, but Andy wasn't thinking about the mayor these days. He had been spending more time alone, as he was this morning. Often, he would go out in jeans and a sweater to the Coffee Trader. Or he'd just turn off the phones and read. This drove Jimmy crazy, but Andy couldn't help that. The campaign was simply less important to him now, being mayor was less important. Jimmy would have to understand.

Too often, Andy thought, politicians cared only about winning and not about what it was they would gain if they were successful. Though Andy knew his decision to pull back from the daily round of plant gates and ribbon cuttings might have an effect on the election's outcome, he had become increasingly fatalistic. Mueller's problems, for example, had much less to do with Andy's strategic brilliance than with bad timing. If the Norman case had not come up when it did, the mayor would be pulling away. Andy could use the trial to his advantage, but first it had to be there. Whatever happened, win or lose, he would not fool himself by forgetting that much of it was luck.

Andy wasn't sure why Tolstoy gave him such a feeling of peace, but he no longer questioned this and gave himself up to it instead, reading with growing amazement of the slaughter of the Russians at Borodino and Napoleon's willingness to sacrifice thousands, as long as they didn't happen to be French.

He imagined that the war with Russia came about by his own
volition, and the horror of what was done made no impression on
his soul. He boldly assumed full responsibility for what happened,
and his darkened mind found justification in the fact that among
the hundreds of thousands who met their deaths there were fewer
Frenchmen than Hessians and Bavarians.

Andy wondered about his own darkened mind. His vulnerability was
that he thought too much and treated every coffee as if it were a step on the
road to Moscow instead of an event in a relatively meaningless campaign in
the frozen heart of America. The big issues came naturally to him. Questions concerning good and evil or free will versus determinism were the
grammar of his life. It was the middle ground between superficiality and
profundity that troubled him. But that, of course, was where he spent most
of his time.

Sarah and Olivia had reached an accommodation that was less a working
relationship than a friendship, though one with ground rules. Two or three
times a week they met, ostensibly to gather background information, but
Sarah had begun to doubt she would ever write anything. They were simply
two dissimilar women drawn together by mutual interests.

Today, as Sarah waited in the living room, she ran her fingers along a
bookcase containing a shelf of *Reader's Digest* condensations, an encyclope-
dia, and a collection of almanacs, none of which showed signs of having
been read. Sarah reminded herself that this was a middle-class bias, not only
that books should be read but that reading made one superior. She remembered her mother's book club and how the ladies saved most of their
enthusiasm for the refreshments. Sarah then noticed that the little secretary
was open. Usually it was locked, but apparently Olivia had been working
because a green ledger with several columns filled with numbers lay open.
At the top, someone had written, "Hometown Properties."

She was ashamed of herself for snooping, but Sarah's curiosity overcame her guilt and she was about to turn the page when she heard Olivia
coming with the tea. Sarah thought of asking about the ledger, but the other
woman closed the desk decisively and locked it. Sarah didn't know if Olivia
had noticed her looking at the book or not, but neither of them said anything.

Olivia patted the chair next to her. "I don't know about this lawyer,"
she said after Sarah sat down. "The smart one, I mean."

"What don't you know?"

Olivia shrugged. "He's just got a bad outlook, like he's thinking we'll lose, planning on it almost. I've been losing all my life, don't need anyone telling me that. We never had nothing, and all we want now is justice."

Over time, Sarah had come to understand why justice equaled money in Olivia's mind. It was fine for liberals like Charlie to belittle a cash settlement or to suggest that accepting one would be selling out because they had no comprehension of Olivia's life. Neither she nor her brothers had been surprised by Jimmy Norman's murder, horrified as they were. Blacks were murdered all the time, not infrequently by police officers. And Jimmy had been in trouble before. Whether such a murder occurred during the commission of a crime seemed academic to people in the ghetto. What reason would white people living out on the lake have to break into a grocery store anyway? The jails were filled with black folks who also had a way of getting themselves killed.

The only thing different about Jimmy was that for once someone was suggesting that a wrong had been done. The amount of money they were asking for was a poor approximation of the violence the police had brought against the black community. Yet if Olivia had not shed a tear over Jimmy, she was passionate about the money, and Sarah thought she had a right to be. There weren't many ways for a black family to strike back.

"Charlie's a realist. He's worried about raising your hopes."

Olivia brushed this aside. "Oh, I know that, honey. But you got to have hope, have faith, even if sometimes you aren't really sure you'll win."

"And you believe that?"

"I do. In my heart I know this time they'll listen, and do the right thing. Sometimes at night in my bed I hear Jimmy or Daddy telling me to keep on fighting, encouraging me, you know. And I will. You know that."

Sarah had never heard voices herself, but this didn't seem strange. She never heard from her own parents and they were alive. "What about your husband?" she asked, surprising herself because she hadn't consciously been thinking about it and had never met nor even seen the man on any of her visits.

Olivia's face took on a wily expression, as if they were sharing confidences. "T. O.'s not in this," she said. "He lives his own life, you know, lets me live mine." She raised her eyebrows. Sarah said nothing and Olivia edged closer, her teacup rattling in its saucer. "Thing is, T. O., well, he's not really around very much anymore, so he's not in this with me."

"You're divorced?" Pictures of a black man looking strangled by a tight collar sat on the end table. Sarah had assumed this was her husband.

"No need for that. No need at all. We just live our own lives."

Sarah waited but Olivia offered nothing more. There was no reason it should seem strange, since it was exactly the arrangement she had with Andy. Theirs was more curious since they continued to live in the same house. She put her hand on Olivia's. "I do understand," she said.

Olivia nodded. Sarah was tempted to ask about the ledger, about Hometown Properties. There was probably a simple explanation, something she wouldn't have thought of. But then Olivia rose to take the dishes into the kitchen, and Sarah decided again that it was none of her business.

Tommy left for San Diego feeling reassured about the situation in Milwaukee. On Bob's advice he checked into a flophouse near the station under a false name. Then he took a bus to Sea World and watched the dolphins jump over bars and kiss their trainers. All the kissing seemed odd, because the kids were really into it, puckering up like Friday night at the drive-in. Tommy wondered what a kiss meant to a dolphin, if it was a sign of affection or just something they did if you fed them. Dolphins were supposed to be smart as hell, but Tommy didn't know about making love to a fish.

All around him people were on vacation, middle-aged fat guys like Tommy, wearing funny hats to cover their bald spots, spending money on their children. It made Tommy regret that he and Lu hadn't stuck it out back then, maybe adopted if they couldn't have their own. Sadness washed over him in the bright sunshine, then some brat spilled a snow cone down his back and he figured maybe he was lucky.

Tommy was used to pushing bothersome thoughts out of his mind. He'd have a few drinks and suddenly it was Disneyland behind his forehead, all bright colors. He considered this a necessity for survival. All the shit that had gone down in his life, he'd go crazy if he thought too much. But the counselor up at Manty had told him was it was better just to feel whatever you were feeling instead of running away. So sitting in the brightly painted grandstand with families laughing and having fun all around him, Tommy tried it. He thought about the kids he never had and the wife he had loved but couldn't love enough. When he felt himself tearing up, he didn't move or try to hide the fact that he was crying like a baby in this amusement park where the whole idea was to have fun. But none of the people sitting around him said anything, and finally the feeling passed and Tommy realized he was hungry.

Before checking out of the hotel, Tommy called Joseph again, but the reporter seemed to want to get off the phone. At first Tommy was annoyed, but then he figured out it had nothing to do with him. Back in Los Angeles, the coast was clear. The landlady reported no new calls, so Tommy resumed his routine, going to the park to shoot the shit and checking for sales at the farmer's market. He even got lucky when he struck up a conversation over the cantaloupes with an old broad who said she used to be an actress. Afterward, she took him home and they got along pretty well until Tommy got up in the middle of the night to go home instead of staying for breakfast.

"You're just like all men," she said. She was crying, which Tommy thought made her look a lot older.

He started to protest, but he couldn't really see what was bad about it. For him, it was an improvement to be like everyone else. "Yeah?" he said.

"You're just afraid to commit," the woman said.

Since they had known each other for all of twelve hours, Tommy wasn't sure why *she* wanted to commit to anything. But he knew better than to say this. Anyway, she was right. The last thing he wanted was to get into anything permanent. "Sorry," he said. "See you at the market."

After that, he kept it simple. Out in the morning for a walk, the park in the afternoon, then a nap and dinner. He'd watch a little TV at night with the landlady or maybe go to a movie. Once in a while he'd make the trip into Hollywood and his agent would bullshit about what a great "property" he was, even though it made him uncomfortable to talk about himself as if he were real estate. One thing Tommy liked was the way everyone in Hollywood always seemed to be kissing you. Tami gave him a hug and mashed her tits against his chest whenever he came in. It was a cheap thrill, but what the hell. He figured it beat dolphins and was all the sex he was likely to get for a while. "Be patient," Tami said today. "It takes time for word to get around."

Tommy smiled benignly. "I've got all the time in the world," he said.

After seeing the agent, Tommy went to a deli to read the trades, which is what he'd heard Tami call the *Hollywood Reporter* and *Daily Variety*. He knew he wouldn't get anywhere if he couldn't speak the language, but it was hard to understand what they were talking about sometimes. Still, all the talk about boffo pics and overseas film sales made him feel optimistic. Someone was making a hell of a lot of money out here, even if it wasn't him.

Outside, he shifted his body to hide his half hard-on from Tami's embrace and was startled to see someone on his right shoulder. Instinctively, Tommy raised his hands, then he recognized the man and relaxed.

"You're not easy to reach," Dolan said. "It cost a lot to send me out here and you know how the mayor is about money."

Conditioned by a lifetime of taking orders, Tommy nodded and held out his hands, resigned to his fate. The district attorney laughed, his voice harsh in the empty street. "Put your hands down, for Christ's sake. I'm not going to cuff you and you're not under arrest. But we've got to talk."

Thirty

Charlie sat alone, listening to the courtroom fill. It was a private tradition, coming to court by himself and being quiet in the hours before he would have to stand before the judge and argue for his clients. His ritual was set and had been for years. Up at six for the bike before breakfast at Benji's. He'd read the papers then stop by his office for messages before walking the four blocks to Wisconsin Avenue if he was involved in a federal case, or all the way up Wells if he was due in county court. He always walked and made a point of speaking to no one except his secretary. Those who were close to him took this in stride. It was Charlie's way of becoming focused.

He supposed it was different for prosecutors because for them motivation was part of the package. Someone had come forward with a complaint. If you were for the defense, you had to consider exactly what or whom you were defending and, if it came to that, how far to go in a lost cause. Charlie's forte was an almost unshakable calm that communicated itself beyond the jury to the bench and ensured at least a respectful hearing. Everyone knew that if Charlie Simons was your lawyer you had a chance.

Yet, however it may have seemed to others, Charlie needed to find that distinctive calm deep inside for each new case. When he reached the courtroom, this transformation would already have occurred and any doubts would have been resolved because Charlie never took cases he couldn't believe in. But that didn't mean he was never ambivalent at the outset.

Experience had taught him that almost all clients lied, but this was not necessarily an indication of guilt. Some were scared and some didn't trust him, which of course was true of the Normans. It bothered him that he had been unable to get closer to them. We're the family, they seemed to say; you work for us. Which was true, but Charlie didn't think of himself as a hired gun. Still, he knew they were under no obligation either to like him or reinforce his sense of himself. As far as Charlie was concerned all the obligations were his.

He reviewed the issues. Though they were only beginning jury selection, it was important to keep the whole trial in focus. The amount of money they had asked for was going to hurt. It was the lead in every newspaper article, and finding jurors who hadn't heard or didn't care would be impossible. The only thing to do was forget it and hope the jury would too. But Charlie was disgusted with Isaacson and with himself for giving in.

The more important questions revolved around Rogan and the police. The jurors wouldn't have to decide Rogan's culpability because he had already pleaded guilty. But it was important for Charlie to pose the question of whether Rogan meant to shoot Jimmy Norman in order to anticipate and discredit the self-defense theory. Inevitably, there would be sympathy for the lonely cop doing a dirty job. Charlie's job was to convince the jury that what was really dangerous about being out at night was killer cops operating with the tacit consent of a corrupt hierarchy. This wouldn't be easy.

Making things even more difficult was that in a civil rights case it wouldn't be enough to prove Rogan's gross negligence. He had already admitted that. They must also prove it had been a racial killing, which was what made Tommy Paley important. He had been there and might be able to give some insight into Rogan's state of mind. So the questions would demand sophistication and patience from a jury that would likely have neither. Charlie would have to convince them of the importance of motive.

He needed to demonstrate that it mattered whether Rogan's act was intentional, especially in a race killing. He would have to make the jury decide if it was self-defense or merely an unfortunate accident, as the city would claim. This panel was going to have a lot of choices, which, in Charlie's opinion, was a disadvantage because there was a natural inclination to mitigate acts you didn't understand. To win, he would have to prove Norman's murder was an intentional race killing and nothing else. It was that simple. But to do that, he would have to call Rogan as an adverse witness, something he normally avoided. Let the other guy defend himself was the conventional wisdom; why give him a soapbox on your time? But the undeniable fact was they needed him, especially with a lush like Paley as their star witness.

Finally, there was the statute of limitations, which gave Dolan the basis for an appeal before they even started. What worried Charlie more, however, was proving the official conspiracy existed. Alberts had given him an open door to nail the city, but it would be hard to convince the jury because he had to do more than name names. Cops sticking together wouldn't necessarily strike jurors as being conspiratorial. What this case was really about was a group of police officials protecting a white cop in a racial murder because of their own prejudices. Cops hating blacks wasn't enough and who the police liked or didn't like wasn't relevant. Charlie had to prove first that there was a conspiracy and second that it existed solely because the city's highest police officials were racists. And while in his heart he knew this was true, convincing the jury would be another matter. The fact that the bigots in question were gone only made it more difficult. A lot of ordinary people would consider this speaking ill of the dead. The fact that they deserved it would be irrelevant.

He heard the others gathering now. Most lawyers met their clients at the office and accompanied them to court. It was a nice, human touch, but Charlie had delegated this and now he saw something in Olivia's eyes. Charlie tended to trust his instincts. He had found that when people were evasive it was usually because they had something to conceal. He didn't know what Olivia might be keeping from him, but he hoped it wouldn't affect the trial.

Marge Pancost came in and pulled a large file from her briefcase. "You've been busy," Charlie said. Marge smiled but said nothing. Charlie pushed the file toward Isaacson. "You want to start or should I?" he asked.

Isaacson hefted the folder as if it was a dumbbell. Bill knew his limitations. "Go ahead. I'll jump in when you get tired."

Charlie nodded and started leafing through the file. Marge had made a face sheet for every potential juror, listing age, race, occupation, marital status, residence, and number of children. Political or union affiliations were noted, and credit histories were included if the person had filed for bankruptcy or had a car repossessed. People with financial problems were supposed to be sympathetic on financial rewards, but it could be galling for an unemployed white factory worker to see blacks win a huge settlement from the city.

Charlie thought there were more lines in Alberts's face and remembered reading in the papers that the judge had been traveling the fast track recently. Alberts's personal life had been unexceptional until his wife died of cancer a year before. But this seemed to have released the judge from anonymity. He had accepted a new Buick from a local dealer on terms that were rumored to be favorable, to say the least. And he had been seen driving around the east side with an unidentified blond. Nothing wrong with that, but then his oldest son, who ran a bar on Farwell called Bobby's, had been named in a drug investigation. Alberts had always been an active judge, interrupting lawyers' arguments and getting involved with witnesses. But now he was taking speaking engagements in which he attacked the lax moral standards of the public schools. The latest was a campaign to get patrolmen stationed outside Riverside to arrest kids caught smoking during lunch hour.

Strictly speaking, none of this had anything to do with Alberts's caseload. Charlie didn't blame Alberts for busting loose after the death of his wife. Who could say what he'd do in a situation like that? But talk around the courthouse was that the judge wasn't playing with a full deck. Charlie wondered if Alberts's overburdened expression reflected this.

Now he called the attorneys forward. He nodded at Dolan and Charlie but ignored Isaacson, which made Charlie think the rumors about their mutual dislike were true. "Mr. Simons has filed a motion for individual, sequestered voir dire," the judge said. "What does city say to that?"

"We have no objection," Dolan said, which was surprising. Charlie had assumed the district attorney would object reflexively to anything they proposed. He wondered why Dolan would suddenly become reasonable.

"Granted, then," Alberts said. "I'm putting a limit of thirty minutes' questioning for each potential juror, however, and I want you both to stay strictly within that limit." He stared at Isaacson, as if he expected Bill to argue, but Isaacson was on his best behavior. Then Alberts glanced at Charlie and Dolan, to make sure everyone understood who was boss. "Now there is another motion," Alberts said looking at the court papers. "That racial prejudice be considered cause for striking. Mr. Simons, what about this?"

"Race might not be a valid reason for striking in another trial, Your Honor. But we intend to prove that Norman's murder was inspired by racial prejudice, that the conspiracy was racially based. If a person's responses during voir dire show he couldn't be fair in a race case, he should be excused."

Dolan cleared his throat. "Objection. It's not the court's business to define racism. Who can say if one's political beliefs would preclude fairness?"

"Racism isn't politics," Isaacson said angrily.

Dolan smiled slightly. "Whatever it is, this is a legal matter. We're introducing our own motion that race not be a reason to strike. But there's an alternative. Since the inception of common law, peremptory challenges have required no justification. If plaintiff feels strongly about this, he can disqualify anyone he considers a racist. But he shouldn't be allowed to strike for cause anyone who might happen to disagree with him."

Dolan spoke quietly, confidently, and in another setting Charlie would have agreed. Isaacson would call Republican Party membership prima facie evidence of racism. But in this context, it was hard to imagine racist ideology and fairness toward blacks co-existing.

Alberts removed his glasses and massaged the bridge of his nose. "You don't need to lecture me on English common law, Mr. Dolan," he said. "And philosophically, I agree with you. We can't hold jurors to an unreasonable standard of moral rectitude; nor can we insist that they satisfy some political litmus test. Their only obligation is to be impartial. Still, Mr. Simons is right: this is an unusual case where racial attitudes are concerned. I'm going to rule for city and agree that plaintiff can't strike for race. But on plaintiff's motion, I'm going to be very liberal in my interpretations. Now, let's get started."

The audience was sparse. A few reporters and family members were the only ones in attendance, except for the lawyers, the judge, and his bailiff, which wasn't surprising. Jury selection wasn't entertaining or newsworthy and it took time. The first person called was a tall man in work clothes named Eugene Johnson, with an expectant look on his face that made Charlie like him. Johnson actually seemed eager to serve on the jury, which was unusual. But Charlie ignored this as he began his questions. He had skimmed Johnson's face sheet and noticed that he lived in the suburbs, so he started there.

"Mr. Johnson," he began. "I see that you work for American Motors. Are you in the main plant on Capital Drive?"

Johnson nodded that he was.

"But you live in Germantown? That must be a long trip for you, especially during rush hour?"

"Takes me forty minute. More if the weather's bad."

Charlie pursed his lips. "And how long have you lived out in Germantown?" The "out" was calculated; he wanted to make it sound remote, though everyone knew it was a bedroom community contiguous to Milwaukee.

"Just a year," Johnson said, not seeing the point.

"Before that you lived in the city?" Charlie asked.

"All my life. I owned a home on Palmer Street."

"In the central city," Charlie said. "Could you tell me why you decided to leave, especially to move to a suburb so far from your work?"

The eagerness was gone now. Johnson's face was tight. "It was that my oldest daughter was starting high school."

Charlie hesitated, as if he was having trouble understanding. "Your daughter would have gone to North Division, isn't that right, Mr. Johnson?"

Johnson looked to Alberts for help, but the judge said nothing. Finally, he muttered, "That's right. I didn't want her to go to North."

Charlie looked at his notes. "But you graduated from North."

"Things were different then," Johnson said testily.

"Tell us how they were different," Charlie said, feeling sympathy for the man. He could see why Johnson didn't want his daughter to be one of a handful of whites at a black school. But it wasn't his job to be understanding.

Johnson ran a finger under his collar. "They've just changed a lot since then," he said. "The people have."

"When you say 'the people,' Mr. Johnson, don't you mean that there are more black students at North Division now? Wasn't the real reason you moved to get your daughter out of a predominantly black school?"

"What's wrong with that?" Johnson said.

"It's not my place to decide if there's anything wrong with it," Charlie said. "But isn't it true that if you found for a black family against the police department that it would be hard to go back and face your neighbors?"

Johnson nodded, beaten now. "That would be pretty hard to do."

Dolan objected that moving to the suburbs shouldn't disqualify a juror, but Alberts leaned over and said gently, "You're excused, Mr. Johnson."

Over the next two hours, they interviewed five people and qualified one, a housewife from Mequon without children who claimed she had no feelings about race. Charlie didn't believe her, but that wasn't a reason to strike.

The next man was a CPA named Norton, who wore a brown suit and a serious expression. Isaacson took the accountant and referred to a notepad. "Mr. Norton, this case involves racial matters. Would you start by telling us the last time you spoke to a black person?"

Norton seem taken aback. "I'm not sure," he said. "I guess it was last week. I talked to a telephone operator."

"Where was this, sir?"

"I was in my office," Norton said.

"You didn't actually speak to the telephone operator face to face?"

"Of course not," Norton said.

"I wonder, then, how you knew she was black?"

This stopped Norton. "I suppose it was her voice," he said slowly. "Her accent, I mean."

"Could you characterize that accent for the court, sir?"

"It was a southern accent," Norton replied.

Isaacson let this sink in. "Do you believe, Mr. Norton, that only blacks have southern accents?" Then, without waiting for Norton's answer, he said, "Obviously, this man couldn't be fair in a race case, Your Honor."

Alberts excused Norton. As they broke for lunch. Isaacson was plainly pleased. "How'd you like that?" he asked.

"Impressive," Charlie said. "Except I'm not convinced the guy was a racist. A lot of people would say the same thing about black voices. Norton might have been OK for us. I'd like to have some professionals on the jury."

Isaacson looked wounded, but he didn't reply. Instead, he gathered his papers and walked out of the room, calling after Olivia. Marge Pancost was still seated at the table. "Come on," Charlie said. "I'll take you to lunch."

The courthouse had originally been Milwaukee's main post office and was built around a large well where they had sorted the mail. They walked outside and stood on the stone steps. The lake was visible in the distance and Charlie smelled spring in the air. "We could go to the Pfister."

"I'm sick of hotel food. Is there anything near the lake?"

Charlie remember going to Pieces of Eight with his mother to watch the ducks in the late afternoon when she was dying. Chemotherapy had taken her hair and she seemed diminished, smaller and thinner than he remembered. But she hadn't let cancer drain all life out of her. Instead, she got on a plane and flew out to spend a month with them. He remembered her, elfin in a blue Mao cap, smiling as the mallards ducked each other.

"The museum," he said softly. "There isn't much time."

As they walked, Charlie thought of the pleasure his mother had taken in almost every aspect of life. But now she was gone, like Nate, whom she never knew, even if they both lived in Charlie's thoughts every day of his life. "What did you think of the morning?" he asked now, to clear his mind.

"This could take a while, especially if you let Bill do the questioning. Did you see Alberts's expression when he was letting Norton have it?"

"I didn't notice," Charlie said. "I guess I should have."

"He was pissed," Marge said. "He knew he had to excuse the guy, but he didn't like what Isaacson was doing."

"Probably I wasn't fair with Johnson either."

"Johnson did something, moved out of town because he was afraid of blacks. That could affect the kind of juror he'd be. Saying you can tell a black on the phone isn't the same. I'd be careful is all I'm saying."

They bought hot dogs at the snack bar, then walked through the galleries that had opened the year before. Designed by a famous New York architect, the museum was a striking building that had begun strictly as a war memorial. It jutted out into the lake and provided the southern boundary of the shore for people on the east side. But nobody had taken its collection seriously until a few large gifts had transformed it in the last few years.

"Not bad," Marge said now. "Especially the Impressionists. To tell the truth, I didn't expect much."

Charlie had gotten over feeling defensive about Milwaukee. The city was home now, odd as that would have seemed twenty years ago. "How did you have time to learn about art with all your other responsibilities?"

Marge looked at him. "What are you, a wise guy?"

Charlie laughed. "Most lawyers don't know anything about art, including me. Except I know what I like."

She smiled. "I went to Smith, and they have a nice little museum. All the scholarship girls had to do something, so I worked as a docent."

Charlie hadn't thought about her past, which was unusual. Donna complained that he interviewed everyone. "Are you from New England?"

She nodded. "Northampton. Sophia Smith set up a program at the college for underprivileged girls."

"Decent of her," Charlie said. "And you were underprivileged?" He had never heard anyone describe herself quite that way before.

"You are a wise guy," Marge said. "My father taught high school. That was close enough for Smith."

Charlie laughed, and they started back. He realized that he was more interested in Marge than he wanted to be, but feeling something and acting on it were different things. He set his mind on jury selection.

They interviewed fifteen people in the afternoon and qualified three. Alberts's patience was wearing thin, but Dolan convinced him to excuse a woman who believed it was impossible for a black person to get a fair trial in America. Charlie wouldn't have wasted a strike, but he was just as happy to see the woman go. Zealots irritated people, even if they were on your side. The woman's heart was probably in the right place, but she annoyed him too.

Now Charlie was questioning a housewife named Ida Szymanski. Remembering what Marge had said about Isaacson, he tried to be gentle.

"Mrs. Szymanski, could you tell me what the Civil Rights Act means to you?"

Ida was a small woman with a pinched face and wore a kerchief over short brown hair. She looked as if she had just come from a cleaning job and seemed confused by the question. "You've heard of it, haven't you?"

"On the news, I think," she said.

Obviously, civil rights was not a popular topic in Menomonee Falls, but that could be good. "Well, then," Charlie said. "What does it mean to you?" He smiled again, hoping to encourage the woman.

Mrs. Szymanski looked doubtful. "Everybody's equal?" she said, as if it were a test, which in a way it was.

Charlie nodded. "And do you believe that?"

"The Lord makes us that way," Ida Szymanski said.

"That's what the Constitution says too," Charlie added, pulling them back into the secular arena. "But do you think everyone makes out equally?"

Mrs. Szymanski had brightened momentarily, but now Charlie's question made her anxious. She started kneading her fingers as if they were braids of dough.

Judge Alberts came to her rescue. "Get to the point, Mr. Simons."

"I'm sorry, Your Honor. Mrs. Szymanski, do you think there are more black criminals than white?"

"It seems like it," Mrs. Szymanski said, "but I don't really know."

"Well, what reason could there be for that? Do you think blacks have less respect for the law than whites?"

For the first time, Ida Szymanski seemed neither intimidated nor confused. She seemed truly engaged by Charlie's question, as if the subject really interested her. "A lot of my friends do think that," she said. "But I grew up on the north side, and my best friend was a Negro girl. I got to know her family, and they were fine people and belonged to a good church. So I don't really know about criminals, but I don't believe Negroes are any worse than we are. There were plenty of white boys down there who got in trouble too."

Ida Szymanski took a deep breath as if her answer had required enormous energy. Charlie paused briefly. This could be an unexpected break, if he could get Ida past Dolan. "Mrs. Szymanski," he said gently, "could you be fair and impartial in a trial involving a black person?"

She nodded vigorously. "Yes, I could," she said.

"Then I have only one more question," Charlie said. "Do you think the police are ever wrong in the way they perform their jobs?"

"They're human. Everyone makes mistakes."

Except you, Charlie thought. But all he said was, "Thank you. Plaintiff has no objection, Your Honor."

With Alberts pushing, Charlie and Dolan finished questioning by noon the next day and ended with a jury consisting of equal numbers of men and women and only one professional, an unemployed teacher from Racine. There were no blacks, which made a kind of sense since prospective jurors were drawn from voting lists and black registration had never been high.

"Cheer up," Marge said as they were leaving. "At least Dolan didn't fight over the racial bias disqualifications."

"I wouldn't fight either if I were in his shoes," Charlie said. "He's got an all-white working-class jury from outside the city. Now we'll go out and see 'Support Your Local Police' stickers on their cars."

"I already checked," Marge said. "That's what you're paying me for, remember?"

"Sure," Charlie said, but something about this made him nervous. Then it occurred to him that he hadn't seen Sarah Hedig in court, which was strange. Unless she was holed up with Bob Joseph or had given up on the book. But that seemed unlikely, just like everything else.

Charlie felt like he was trying to make his way through a fog, which created the illusion that he was off balance, even though he could plainly see that he was walking a straight line. He wondered idly if he had a brain tumor, but who had time for doctors and what good would an examination do anyway? This would pass and he would go on, just like before. It was natural to be nervous. But even in the midst of his own reassurances, the disequilibrium returned and he had to steady himself on a banister. When, he wondered, would things begin making sense again?

Thirty-one

Sarah had skipped jury selection because she felt a need to step back temporarily from her life. She awoke early, slipped on a sweatshirt, and went outside. A wet wind was blowing off the lake and the streets were empty. She decided to walk north, enjoying her solitude and the mild morning.

As she walked, Sarah told herself, *Je ne regret rien*. She did not regret anything. It was necessary for her to pull away from Andy. What bothered her more was that she wasn't excited about her new life. She always looked forward to seeing Bob, but she thought a grand passion should be something more. At times they were passionate, of course, but more often it was just comfortable, which didn't seem to justify destroying her marriage.

As she made the turn out of the park onto Lake Drive, Sarah picked up the pace. She remembered long walks with Andy when they were young and full of enthusiasm. He would pound the air with his fists, and his excitement was so exhilarating that Sarah often became sexually aroused. She'd come home wet from their walks and they would make love. That was the way she wanted to feel about Bob. A marriage might become uneventful after twenty years, but the idea of a relationship starting out that way was disappointing.

Which was unfair to Bob. Probably she shouldn't expect a man to provide the spark in her life, but whatever political sense feminism made, it would never give you anything to come home to. Sarah wanted to write, and more than that, she wanted to *be* a writer. But she also knew that she would always need a man. She just wasn't sure Bob was the right one.

Andy had gone by the time Sarah returned, so she sat at the kitchen table and leafed through notes from her interview with Olivia. On one page she had scribbled, "Hometown Properties—check." Now she thought she simply should have asked Olivia about it, though there was nothing innately suspicious about a ledger. But Sarah found it surprising that Olivia had that kind of financial sense. It wasn't the way she presented herself. Of course, it was possible that it wasn't Olivia's writing, but who else could it be? She had said that her husband wasn't around anymore. And if the ledger was for household records, then what was Hometown Properties?

Sarah had only a rudimentary idea of how to conduct an investigation. Hometown wasn't listed under Realtors in the yellow pages. So she called Bob. "How would I find out what a company does?" she asked.

"What it does?" He sounded sleepy.

"I mean who owns it and where its offices are."

"That's different from what it does," he said. "Companies that do business with the state are registered." He was slowly coming alive. "If the company is privately held, they don't have to provide much information, unless you get their tax returns somehow. Even then it's hard."

"Why?"

"What is this, Twenty Questions? By the way, good morning."

"I'm sorry," Sarah said. "I have a reason for asking."

He didn't ask her reason, which Sarah appreciated. "Unless someone wants to be found, it's just real easy to hide," Bob said patiently. "Company X is owned by Company Y, which merged with Company Z, which is registered in the Bahamas. What company are we talking about anyway?"

Sarah hesitated, unsure whether to tell him. What if this turned out to be nothing? But she couldn't just ask questions. "Hometown Properties."

"Never heard of them," Bob said. "I'm not exactly a real estate expert, though. I could check the morgue. There might be something there."

"That would be nice," Sarah said. She felt a mixture of curiosity and dread because now she had started something, even if it was only between the two of them. Still, she admired competence in men, and the way Bob had calmly taken her lead made her feel supported. Maybe she loved him after all.

"Am I ever going to see you again?" Bob asked.

"Probably. What are you doing for dinner?"

"Nothing important. If there's anything in the files, I'll bring it."

The surge of December had brought in enough volunteers to allow Jimmy to provide captains for every precinct in the city and organize phone banks. But the last time Andy had visited the office, fewer people recognized him. Jimmy said they weren't getting new volunteers and that the old ones were losing enthusiasm. "You can't really blame them when the candidate's in hibernation," Jimmy snapped. Andy couldn't argue with that.

Sitting in his study looking at the lake, he wondered if he had made a mistake. Of course, whatever he did or didn't do, circumstances beyond his control would influence the campaign in important ways. But as much as he wanted to hold himself aloof and maintain distance from the campaign, it bothered him that they had lost momentum. It made him uncomfortable to admit that in addition to having a desire to govern, he wanted to beat Emil Mueller. But it was the truth. Maybe it was time to get honest with himself.

Andy dialed headquarters. When Jimmy answered, he asked, "When does the Norman trial begin?"

"Next week. Why?"

"I need everything you have on that. Then I want to call a press conference. I'm going to make a statement."

There was silence on the other end of the line. Finally, Jimmy said, "You'd better see a doctor. I'm thinking brain tumor, but what do I know?"

Sarah and Bob met in a German restaurant at six. The advantage of her new understanding with Andy was there was nothing to hide. Most people assumed Andy had deserted Sarah for a younger woman. Andy had been gracious enough to allow this to become accepted as truth with the result that their friends considered Sarah fortunate to have found a man, even if he happened to be a newspaper reporter with thinning hair and baggy pants.

Now Bob passed a file across the table. "This actually turned out to be pretty interesting," he said.

Sarah opened the folder and started reading. Most of the clips were from a series in the *Times* on slum properties. Hometown was underlined in blue whenever it was mentioned. One article said the company owned fifty inner-city buildings, and another told of a protest to focus attention on a building whose tenants had gone without heat throughout January. A picture of Marcus Jackson standing in front of Dairyland Savings ran adjacent to the text.

"What's Marcus doing in front of the bank? They don't own the apartment house, do they?"

Bob peered at the yellowed article. "Probably as close as they could get. No one wants to be identified as a slumlord. The owner's not going to come forward voluntarily and say he's sorry."

"What about the city?"

Bob shrugged. "Jackson probably started there. The housing authority may have sent out inspectors or even issued repair orders. But as long as the owner's paying his taxes, they'll basically leave him alone."

Sarah didn't understand. "What does the bank have to do with it?"

Bob checked a note. "Hometown Properties is what's called a land trust," he said. "The bank is probably the trustee, which would explain what Jackson is doing there. Or was. This clip's two years old."

"What good would it do for Marcus to go to the bank?"

"Probably no good at all." Bob looked at the paper. "If anything's changed, I haven't heard about it. Oh, they might have replaced a few windows and patched up the heating system to get the water running, but I'll bet it's business as usual down there. I can check if you want."

Sarah was trying to organize this new information in her mind. "So no one except this bank really knows anything about Hometown Properties?"

Bob nodded. "That's right. And that's more than you can usually find out in situations like this. It would be interesting to know how Marcus figured it out. Often a trust is only identified by a number, or even a letter."

"And that's legal?" Olivia's involvement in Hometown was beginning to seem less innocent. Sarah still felt guilty, but Olivia's secret was becoming burdensome. She wanted to tell Bob what she knew.

"Damned right. Under Wisconsin law, businesses don't have to reveal much about their corporate structure. The legislature figured that would encourage corporations to move here and, who knows, they may be right."

Sarah drank some wine. The dark window reflected the room behind her, which was filling up with an affluent evening crowd. She was growing increasingly curious, though Sarah had no reason to doubt Olivia. What could she have to do with slumlords and dummy corporations?

"Any chance you'll tell me what this is about, Sarah?" Bob's expression was friendly, but his jaw was set. Sarah thought he was entitled to an explanation after all her questions. Yet she was aware that in addition to being her lover, he was a reporter. The news that Olivia Norman Brown was part of a large land trust would be a major story made bigger by the trial, even if the two things had nothing to do with each other. And Sarah didn't actually know that Olivia was involved. A ledger on a desk proved nothing.

Besides, she wanted to be fair. The simple fact that Marcus Jackson was protesting wasn't enough to make her condemn Olivia. Marcus protested a lot of things and, as Bob said, land trusts were legal. Yet even assuming that all landlords had trouble with tenants, where would Olivia have gotten the money to buy fifty buildings? And if she had that much money, why sue the city? Despite Sarah's empathy for the other women, the fact that for Olivia justice and money were always intertwined bothered her.

"I feel as if I'm having dinner alone," Bob said now.

"I'm sorry," Sarah said. "There's a lot I don't understand, but I might know who owns Hometown."

Bob sat back, impressed. "The paper had three guys on that for a month," he said quietly.

Sarah smiled. So he had been holding something back too. "Were you one of them?"

Bob shook his head. "Not my beat. But it was a big story."

Andy had always said everything was political and now she understood. Jimmy Norman was shot down, and twenty years later his slumlord sister's lawsuit to avenge his death had become a political issue that might elect a new mayor, who, coincidentally, was her biographer's estranged husband. Sarah wondered if everything really was connected or if it just seemed that way because Milwaukee was a small town trying to act like a city.

She reached for Bob's hand. "I'm sorry to be mysterious. If I tell anyone, I'll tell you." She looked into his intelligent blue eyes and felt foolish.

"It's OK. I'm used to people holding out on me."

Sarah laughed. "I'd never do that."

Bob smiled. "Then let's get out of here," he said.

Thirty-two

The *60 Minutes* segment featuring the Norman case aired the Sunday before the trial was to begin. Charlie watched it in Marge Pancost's hotel room, where they had been working. "Just in case there was someone who didn't know about the case, it's taken care of now," he said afterward.

"I wouldn't worry," Marge said. "If Dolan was serious about pre-trial publicity, he would have said so already." Her burgundy sweat suit gave her the authority of the fit. Health didn't lie, Charlie thought.

The segment took only five minutes, but there was time to interview Olivia Brown and Tommy Paley and limn the case's history. They mentioned Charlie in passing and showed a file photo of Isaacson with his hand tucked in his jacket pocket, as if he were imitating someone famous. The police had refused to cooperate, and so had Rogan. There was a short Q&A with Bob Joseph about breaking the story, but Olivia was clearly the star of the show right up to the close, which was a freeze-frame in which she mouthed, "Justice."

Marge shut off the television. Files and notes covered the blanket, making Charlie feel overwhelmed by all the crap he had managed to accumulate without getting a handle on the case. Paper often gave him the illusion of control, but now he didn't have a clue. "Cheer up," Marge said. "At least we've got a decent judge."

She was trying to be supportive, but her cheerleading was annoying. "I'm just tired," Charlie said. "I get suicidal before trials." He started stuffing papers in his briefcase. When he looked up, Marge was smiling slightly.

"Why is everything always so intense with you?"

The question caught him by surprise because he seldom thought of himself as being one way or another, never thought it had anything to do with volition. Things and people just were whatever they were. Morality was only a means of justifying one's own behavior. He didn't honestly think he was better than anyone else because he did what he did. It just interested him more than defending corporate big shots or writing wills and contracts. He assigned no particular value to intensity, but the truth was he didn't mind being the way he was, didn't think it was a bad thing. If you weren't intense about life, what would you care about? "Just lucky, I guess," he said. "See you in court."

60 Minutes hadn't covered the mayoral race, and Andy Hedig's campaign re-entry was not as dramatic as a national television appearance, but it upset Emil Mueller more. "TV's one night!" the mayor exploded when Fischer told him Hedig had surfaced at an Elk's club luncheon. "No matter how popular the goddamned show is, half the people are doing something else or don't give a shit. Why didn't he stay on vacation, for Christ's sake?"

Fisher was sympathetic. The hardest thing about running against Hedig was that he was unpredictable. They had known about his neighborhood centers and grass roots organizing, but this on-again, off-again activity was hard on everyone. Hedig would be all over the television for a week, and then he'd disappear mysteriously. It was like guerrilla warfare. And the electorate had changed. In past campaigns, people had been afraid to oppose the mayor, but now registration was up in the ghetto and the south side neighborhoods where the Poles had given way to Chicanos.

Mueller couldn't mobilize enough volunteers for a grass roots campaign, but he didn't have to. The mayor's name brought in enough money to buy TV time through election day. But the way Hedig was generating attention, Fischer figured he'd be on the tube every night too. And while the mayor was right about *60 Minutes* being transient, the program had served to underscore the importance of the Norman case. It would be hard to claim it was a nuisance suit after it had been featured on national television.

Yet Fischer didn't say any of this to Mueller. Part of his job was to encourage his boss. "Maybe he'll drop back again," he said hopefully.

Mueller nodded. "Sure, maybe my sainted mother will rise from the grave and write some new recipe cards, but I doubt it. The worst thing is no one really gives a shit about civil rights, but give them a reason to believe in a cover-up and I'll be on my ass faster than you can say Kosciusko."

Fisher knew this was true. Wisconsin voters were sensitive about corruption in high places. He remembered an administrative assistant in a senator's office who was fired for calling his dying mother on the state WATS line. Which didn't help anything. In fact, after watching Hedig's press conference, Fisher considered advising his boss to take some time off. Looking fit and rested, Hedig handled the press easily when they pushed him about his absence. After listening to his call for full disclosure, a reporter from a radio station asked why Hedig had waited so long to comment about the Norman case.

"That's funny," Hedig said. "My wife asked the same question." When the knowing laughter died down, he added, "Seriously, I thought it was inappropriate to comment. There could have been a pre-trial settlement."

Mueller admired the way Hedig implied that the city might want to cut a deal. And he wasn't wrong in this. The truth was Mueller wished Dolan could have pulled it off, but there was no deal to make. He couldn't just hand millions of dollars to the Normans, and his own people were stonewalling him. Tanner told the mayor he'd been home watching television with his wife when Norman was shot, and Dolan had learned nothing new from Tommy Paley. "Maybe the goddamned kid committed suicide," Mueller muttered to Fischer.

But the worst thing was their new polls showed Hedig had regained the momentum and was now within ten points. Mueller could lie low and hope to coast in or go all out and take the chance that they'd make more mistakes. But Emil Mueller didn't back down. If the fucker wanted to fight, then they'd fight. "I want you to put me on every talk show, every voters' forum you can find," he told Fischer. "I don't want to eat a meal alone between now and election day. If I go to the john, I want a registered voter there to hold my dick. I'm tired of this bullshit. I'm not a statesman; I'm a guy from the north side, and I'm going to kick Andy Hedig's ass."

Bob had not pressed Sarah for information about Hometown Properties both because he sensed it would not help and because it really had nothing to do with him. But he couldn't see why Hometown should matter to Sarah. Of course, there might be things he didn't know. While their relationship was now public, there were ways in which they were more private than before. But this didn't stop Bob from turning their conversation over in his mind. As he interviewed farmers about the market for their hogs, he thought about Sarah. She had never asked for his help before, which made her request significant, but what really piqued Bob's curiosity was the nature of the request.

Against his better judgment, Bob placed a call to Marcus Jackson and asked what came of the Hometown protest. The reverend sounded weary. "Jack shit," he said. "Off the record, of course. They got the furnace going long enough for the inspector to pass on it, but that building's as bad as ever, maybe worse. And that's not even talking about all the other apartments they own. I could take you on a tour. You want to do a piece about it?"

Bob told Marcus he wasn't cityside anymore. "Maybe later," he said.

"No problem," Jackson said. "Haven't seen you around."

"I'm covering the 4-H these days. Anything you want to know about hog futures, I'm your man."

"Tired of black folks?" Jackson asked. "Or was it Mrs. Hedig? I heard about you two. Andy's an old friend, but I never did think he paid enough attention to that girl. Still, I hate to have two friends going at each other."

"Life's a bitch," Bob said. But he had learned that whatever Sarah's concern was about Hometown it didn't involve Marcus Jackson.

Back at the office he filed the hogs story and went for coffee. When he returned to his desk, he leafed through the phone book until he found a number. "Dairyland State Bank," a cheerful voice said. Bob asked for the trust department and a new voice came on. "Arnold Melcher speaking." Bob identified himself as a reporter and Melcher's voice changed immediately, taking on a crisp, formal tone. "Could you tell me your number so I can verify your employment, Mr. Joseph?"

Bob wondered if they got many calls about Hometown or if this was just a procedure they had developed to harass the press. He gave Melcher the switchboard and hung up. He had made a copy of the clip file. Now he took a map of the city and, using the articles, plotted the locations of the Hometown holdings listed. Starting with the Center Street tenement, they described a rough circle of the inner city with the westernmost located at 17th and Locust, and a building on Capital Drive being the farthest north. Downtown formed a natural southern boundary, and there were a couple of buildings in the ruined blocks of lower Third Street to the east.

There was nothing especially sinister in this. Someone had to own those blocks, and plenty of people had gotten caught holding questionable buildings when neighborhoods were red-lined by real estate agents offering ten cents on the dollar. What was unusual was that Hometown seemed to have gone after these properties after the riots, instead of being stuck with them. And the buildings that they owned seemed barely habitable.

It was possible, of course, that the company was a remnant of "black capitalism," which had turned out to be a national joke. When someone turned off the federal faucet, the black capitalists found another hustle, leaving behind those people who had sunk their life savings into their businesses and were left with huge loans and no way to repay them. But they would have been out in the street protesting along with Jackson. No, Bob thought, someone knew exactly what he wanted to do here. Buy low and squeeze all the profit you could out of the buildings for as long as possible. Hometown had the look of a very profitable little operation. Or maybe not so little. All he had was a list of buildings published in the paper. There could be many more.

The phone rang. "Mr. Joseph, this is Arnold Melcher at Dairyland. Sorry to check on you, but it's policy." Someone must have told Melcher to cooperate because his voice had become syrupy in the interval between calls.

"Can't be too careful," Bob said. He liked to keep his distance, but Melcher had information he wanted, even if he wasn't sure why he wanted it.

"I'm afraid I can't tell you very much about the Hometown," Melcher said. "It's one of our older trusts. And a very solid account, I'll say that."

"How old would that be?" Bob asked.

"I'm afraid I couldn't say," Melcher said.

Why bring it up then, asshole? "But they're still active? According to the newspapers, they own almost fifty buildings in the inner city."

"I just can't say. But I assume that information came from somewhere. You'd know better than I whether your reporters are accurate."

Bob had seen reporters' notebooks and wouldn't vouch for them. He had to verify this himself. "Probably you could give me a list of Hometown's holdings or its officers?"

"I really wish I could help, but I can't." Melcher's voice approached real regret now. "We do have our rules."

Bob looked at the rough map of the inner city he had drawn. Hometown's buildings were in red. "Fine. I just have one more question for you. Is Hometown still diversified or are they focused on real estate now?"

"I don't think the trust's holdings have changed much recently," Melcher said, glad to be able to answer something. "Their character, I mean."

An interesting choice of words. Character, indeed. "So they're still investing in a number of different areas?"

But Melcher had caught on. "I'm afraid that's as much as I can say, Mr. Joseph. I'm really very busy."

Bob sat staring into space, then at his map, then into space again. What he had learned didn't amount to much, even if it was more than the banker wanted him to know. Hometown Trust was a major owner of slum properties, but that wasn't all. They were still in business and apparently acquiring things, though he didn't know what. He rubbed his eyes and leafed through the clips again. This time something new caught his eye, a face in a photograph, someone he recognized. On a whim he dialed another number.

"Rocket Car Wash, Taking Off," a voice said so fast it took a moment to register. This time Bob didn't identify himself as a reporter but as an investment analyst specializing in minority business opportunities. "Say what?" the voice said.

"Let me speak to the manager," Bob replied.

He felt vaguely guilty as he waited. This had nothing to do with any story he could remotely be working on. In time, a woman who said she handled the books told him they weren't looking for investors.

Bob said, "Could you tell me the name of your corporate parent? For our files." The question didn't make a lot of sense, even to him. A corporate parent for a car wash? Still, you never knew unless you asked.

But the question set off an alarm. "Who is this anyway?"

Bob hung up and called the bank again. "Yes, Mr. Joseph," Melcher said wearily. "What is it now?"

"I'm just trying to verify some information," Bob said. "I know you can't tell me what Hometown owns or who its officers are, but could you tell me if they've sold a particular property in the past year?"

Melcher sighed as if the weight of the world was on his shoulders. "I suppose there's no harm in that, as long as you don't quote me."

Bob assured him that this was only background information. He read five properties listed in the news articles then added "Rocket Car Wash."

Melcher said he'd check. As he waited, Bob was aware of a tightening sensation in the middle of his chest that he hadn't felt since he started covering the suburbs. Then Melcher was back. "None of those properties have been sold," he said in a bored voice. "Is that all now?"

Bob thanked him and sat back in his chair. The window in front of him was dark blue. He had spent most of the afternoon on a story that didn't officially exist. But that was the nature of the job. You followed a lead until you hit a wall, then you started another and another, and eventually you might end up with something. But what he had learned was troubling.

Either T. O. Brown's car wash was owned by a slumlord trust or Brown was the slumlord. Which might implicate Olivia Brown. Bob wasn't sure what to do with this, but he knew some people who would be interested.

Despite Marge Pancost's encouragement, the fact was that things weren't going well. Charlie's study was a welter of news clippings, notebooks, and reminders he had written himself to do things that were now forgotten. Reconstructing a twenty-year-old crime would never be easy, but considering the nature of the crime, Charlie had expected to do better with the black community. According to newspaper accounts, there were 150 people on the street within fifteen minutes of Jimmy Norman's death, but they all seemed to have disappeared—even the man whose car Paley had commandeered. And Olivia had been of little help. The ministers, with the exception of Marcus Jackson, were gone and so were most of the press. Bob Joseph had told Charlie what he remembered, but he hadn't been at the scene.

Using reverse directories and old telephone books, Charlie had been able to identify everyone living on Wright Street the night of the murder. He had written letters to everyone he could identify, but so far had heard from no one. Which left him on the night before the trial with a strategy built around supposition, rumor, and Tommy Paley.

If you worked long and hard enough, something usually broke. Anyway, there was nothing else to do at this point, and sleep was out of the question. He was going over his notes in a desultory way when the phone rang. Donna had gone to bed hours before. No one called at two in the morning except wrong numbers and death threats. "This is Charles Simons," he said, hoping the noise hadn't awakened his wife.

"Mr. Simons?" It seemed redundant to repeat his name, so Charlie waited. The voice was ponderous and, it seemed, afraid. "My name is Warren Fenster," the man said, as if this would explain everything.

The name was familiar, though Charlie couldn't place it. He free-associated. Fenster was German for window, but he was in no mood for guessing games. It was late. "Refresh my memory," Charlie said.

The man cleared his throat. "We've never actually met, but I got your letter and then I heard them mention you on the television the other night."

"About the Norman case?" Charlie tried to help the man along.

"The one about the colored boy, the one who was killed."

Charlie looked at his watch again. 2:10. He wished Fenster would come to the point, unless there was no point, which was equally possible. "I'm one of the attorneys for the Norman family. How can I help you?"

"Well, the thing is, I heard you wanted to talk to me," Fenster stammered. "I wanted to say something before, but it seemed no one cared."

Charlie didn't remember Fenster, but something was beginning to tug at him. He should know this guy. He knew everyone, had spoken to everyone. So who was Fenster? "I don't mean to be rude," he said now, "but what exactly should you have told us about the Norman case?"

There was an intake of breath, as if Fenster were shocked or surprised. "I thought you knew," he said. "I mean, well, I was there. I saw it."

"Saw what?" Charlie said, alert now, reaching for a pad of paper. "Tell me exactly what you saw."

"The murder. I saw them shoot that boy down out my window."

Suddenly, it came clear and Charlie cursed his stupidity. Fenster was the white guy in his pajamas and, more important, a witness, a fucking witness. One who wasn't a drunk or an ex-con. A real person a jury might actually listen to. Fenster had come across the street to talk to Rogan and Paley, and he had tried to testify at the coroner's inquest. Lathrop destroyed him and the guy had faded away. But he had tried, give him credit for that. His name had come up early on, but they couldn't find him at his old address and assumed he had died. Charlie had written Fenster and enclosed his phone number, but he hadn't followed up otherwise and now he was embarrassed at his ineptitude. It made him wonder what else he might have missed. "Jesus," he said. "I'm sorry, Mr. Fenster. You're absolutely right. We have been looking for you, sir."

"Some of my friends called to tell me you'd been around asking for me," Fenster said. "But I moved out to Sheboygan fifteen years ago, and to tell the truth I wasn't in a hurry to get back into all that."

There was the obvious question. "Why are you calling me now?"

"When I saw it on the TV I just had to," Fenster said. "I'm an old man. I want to do the right thing before I die."

Charlie figured this was part of the truth. Probably Fenster thought he'd get on *60 Minutes* himself, but he wasn't about to question the man's motives. It was the first positive result of the pre-trial publicity.

"Mr. Fenster," he said, flipping through his file. "You just said you saw Rogan kill Jimmy Norman, but according to my notes that isn't what you told the coroner." He found the paper and read. "This says you told them you saw the boy on the ground but you couldn't testify as to how he got there."

"I was scared," Fenster said, his voice tremulous. "You can understand that. The times were different. I was getting phone calls at night."

"What kinds of calls?"

"They'd come late, like this, people saying I was a nigger lover and they'd kill me if I testified. The thing is, I saw more than I said. I was at my window and the boy ran by with the one cop after him, and then I heard a shot and the boy went down and the other cop came running up. I went outside, just like I said, but they said go away, that they had things under control."

Charlie felt a pulse in his forehead and was aware that he was sweating in the cold house. He pulled his robe tightly around him. "Did you see a knife, Mr. Fenster? Did the boy threaten the officer?"

Fenster coughed into the phone, but when the man spoke his voice was stronger, even angry. "There was never no goddamned knife, Mr. Simons. Everyone knew that, even back then."

Charlie sat quietly for a moment, thankful to the miracle of television for bringing this man his way. "Everyone, Mr. Fenster?"

"Why, sure," Fenster said. "Not that they'd admit it. It's just that no one was going to do anything because of how things were."

Even assuming Fenster was exaggerating, Charlie knew he would be a valuable addition to their case. Unless there was a criminal record or mental illness he knew nothing about, he had a reliable white witness to corroborate Tommy Paley's story. "Mr. Fenster, I'm going to give you an address and if you could, I'd like you to come in tomorrow morning. I'll be in court, but I want my associate to interview you."

"You going to want me to be a witness?" Fenster sounded wary. ·

"Yes, sir, we certainly will. And thank you for calling."

Then Charlie sat in his bathrobe looking out into the winter night wondering what he had done to deserve this. It was 2:30. His alarm would go off in less than four hours, but he didn't feel the least bit tired. Tommy Paley might be all the things they said he was, but goddamnit, he had been telling the truth. Charlie realized now what he hadn't admitted to himself before, that deep down he hadn't been entirely sure. It was so easy to be put off by personalities, especially a personality like Tommy Paley's, that sometimes you lost sight of the important things. A person could be a scumbag and still tell the truth. But none of that mattered now. It didn't matter that Fenster hadn't appeared until the eleventh hour. Olivia's attitude didn't matter, and Isaacson didn't matter. What mattered was that they had a witness. They were going to make this work; they were going to win. That was what was important.

One thing stuck in Charlie's mind. The old man had said everyone knew there was no knife, and he had repeated it when questioned. The police may have been racists and the racial climate different, but something still bothered him. Why hadn't the Normans pushed harder? The money the city offered was nothing, so why accept the settlement when every black minister in town was ready to march on MacArthur Square? It didn't make sense.

Unless there were still things Charlie didn't know about, things that might make a difference. His doubts about Paley had been satisfied, but Fenster's call raised other questions. As he climbed into bed, Charlie had a premonition that there would be more surprises before this was over.

Thirty-three

Andy had promised he would work harder to make up for lost time. "Just schedule me," he told Jimmy. "I'll get everything in." And he had, moving easily from meeting halls to banquets and plant gates. Furthermore, he felt more at ease with people on the streets, even finding their problems interesting rather than troubling. Yet Andy's new level of commitment had not enabled them to pick up ground. No matter how early they arrived at a campaign stop, Emil Mueller always seemed to have preceded them. It was ridiculous to think a man nearly twice his age would have more energy than Andy did, but the mayor was running hard and their supply of volunteers had dwindled when they might have expected it to increase. It was all Jimmy could do to keep the office staff.

Most disturbing, however, was the mayor's effectiveness. Mueller had not been active in recent campaigns and had instead sent surrogates to represent him. That was all over now. Mueller had the ability to talk comfortably with anyone, and for the first time in twenty years he was doing plant gates in the morning and greeting the second shift when they came on in the afternoon. He seemed to be giving speeches constantly, repeating his message of prosperity. A vote for Hedig, the mayor claimed, would be stepping into a frightening unknown. "It's a big chance to take," he would say, knowing his audience had no fondness for risk taking. "If it ain't broke, don't fix it," he told the Sertoma Club, and they gave him a standing ovation.

He seldom mentioned Andy by name and never failed to allude to his youth. "My opponent is too young to remember what this great city was like before Emil Mueller," he would say with a coy smile. "Let's hope enough of you do to give this young fellow a history lesson. The voters of Milwaukee are too wise to trust their pensions to a man who's never met a payroll."

In Milwaukee, this played well, and while Andy didn't enjoy being represented as a callow youth, he had to admire Mueller's strategy. The polls were flat and had been for two weeks. Without the Normans, Andy knew he would be out of the race. But the trial was scheduled to begin this week.

The waitress had refilled Bob's cup twice by the time Sarah threaded her way toward him through the crowded cafe. As she approached, he was struck again by her jet-black hair and angular figure. It seemed amazing that anything had happened between them, much less this, whatever this was. She leaned forward and kissed him. "Sorry I'm late," she said.

After the waitress took Sarah's order, they sat facing each other. Outside, morning traffic streamed past on Farwell, heading downtown and seeming significant. There was a pleasant hum in the restaurant, which made Bob regret his decision. "I've been thinking," he said.

"Oh yes?" Sarah said. She leaned forward, smiling and expectant. "I like it when you're thoughtful."

"About us, I mean." It was important to stay on the subject or he might lose his train of thought, lose the sense of what he was doing, the sense that it made sense. Which wasn't easy with Sarah looking the way she did. "I've been thinking about us," he repeated, then felt stupid. "Jesus."

Sarah's elbows touched his, and, as usual, he felt the electricity. "What have you been thinking about us?" she asked, mocking him gently.

The truth was everything about her distracted him, not just her hair and body but her elbows, her eyes, her perfume, her knowing smile. It made him less sure. "We never see each other anymore," he said miserably. "I have to make a fucking appointment if I want to have dinner with you."

Sarah's expression betrayed annoyance, but then she smiled again. "Well, we're both busy."

"It's not that," Bob said. "We've always been busy, but I saw you more before you told Andy what was going on."

"I know." Sarah slumped in her chair as if the conversation weighed her down. "In a way it was easier then. Now there are all these assumptions."

"Assumptions?" Bob had been so deep in real estate that his first thought was that she wanted a loan.

"Sure. We both assume I'm going to leave Andy and then we'll live together and probably get married. And we assume he'll be OK because he'll get some young chickie, and besides he's going to be mayor anyway. Right?"

Bob breathed deeply. This wasn't what he had expected, but at least they were talking. And she was right, basically. That was the way he figured things would work out. "You don't seem very happy about that."

She nodded. "I'm not. But what about you, Bobby? You said you'd been thinking. Are you happy? Is it just me?"

He reached for her hand, aware of her. "Of course not," he said. "I want you more. I probably want more than there is."

"Maybe what you really want is less," Sarah said. "You gave up your career and what have you got? A middle-aged lover who's usually not around and isn't much fun when she is."

Giving up his career was an exaggeration, even if that was the way he usually thought about it. But love wasn't enough either. Or perhaps it was just that the kind of passion that had moved them in first place couldn't last forever, couldn't sustain them or make up for all the things they would lose. Something had to supplement it. For a while the suburbs had been amusing and new, but he needed more. "I don't think about it that way," he said.

"Maybe not, but it's the truth." Sarah said. Then, insistently, "Isn't it?"

Bob stretched and looked around the restaurant, but there was no escape. "No, it's not the truth that you're a middle-aged lover and not much fun. That isn't it. The truth is I'm dying in the suburbs covering rodeos, and I want to get back into the middle of things. I keep thinking being with you should be enough, but it's just not. I shouldn't have to choose between you and my job, but that's the way our lives are, and choosing makes me judge you in a way I wouldn't otherwise. It makes me more demanding and dependent than I want to be. Life isn't simple. I can't help it that we didn't meet twenty years ago, and maybe it wouldn't have made any difference if we had. I miss going downtown to work and I don't like what missing it is doing to me."

She stroked his hand. "I don't blame you," she said quietly. "I just don't know what to do, because the funny thing is I really love you and I don't love Andy anymore. Whatever else might be wrong, I don't think that's going to change. I can't even remember how it felt not to be in love with you. I can't go back now; I'm out here for good. That might seem strange, but it's true."

It didn't seem strange at all. It was the way he felt. But without either of them saying so directly, something had been settled. They sat while the waitress brought coffee and the traffic continued to go by. This wasn't working, and it wasn't going to work even if they were in love, so they had to stop because they didn't want to end up hating each other. Bob wanted to believe it was temporary, that they would start up again sometime, but there were no guarantees. His sentimentality brought him back to reality. To change the subject, he said, "I found out who's behind Hometown Properties."

"I thought you would," Sarah said.

"Is that why you asked me? So I'd start digging and get interested and then this would happen?"

"I'm not that deep," Sarah said. "But I knew something was there. And I guess I knew telling you was a risk."

"For who?"

She shrugged. "I don't even really know. Are you on the story?"

"What story?" Bob asked. "Olivia Brown owns or is part of a group that has fifty slum buildings. That's interesting, but it's not really a story. It does make me wonder why she's suing the city for a hundred million, though, since she's worth millions already. I'd like to know where she got the money to start Hometown. Beyond all that, she's making all these moral judgments about the cops and the mayor, but meanwhile, people in those buildings have to sleep with their feet in the oven. How do you put all that together?"

"Maybe you should ask Marcus Jackson."

"It's not my job to keep Marc current," Bob said. "I'm asking you."

But Sarah didn't answer directly. "So you're not going anywhere with all this," she said hopefully.

"Not exactly," Bob said, shifting in his chair. "What I said was there's no story. But I won't protect Olivia Brown."

"What do you think will happen?"

Sarah's questions made Bob uncomfortable because he did think something would happen. People usually made mistakes when large amounts of money were involved. "I don't know, but I'm going to hang around and see."

"Writing about Hometown could ruin Charlie's case."

Bob shook his head. "That doesn't make any difference at all. Look, you asked me who owned the company. You gave me that. I even think there's a good chance you did it because it bothered you that the grieving sister is making money off poor people. Olivia's playing a dangerous game, and so far she's doing all right. My editor agrees with you, though, so I can't do anything yet. I'll say this: one person who should know is Charlie Simons."

"Are you going to tell him?"

Bob hadn't gotten that far, but he was more concerned about the lawyer than he was about Olivia. "That's not my job, either. First, I've got to get out of Menomonee Falls. If I can't do that, I won't be covering anything."

Sarah leaned forward. "I love you like this—mad and passionate."

"Yeah," Bob said. "Irresistible, that's me." He paid the bill and they stood outside, holding hands under the awning. It surprised Bob that he and Sarah were peaceful with each other, even affectionate. Something important had happened and it wasn't over. It was more like a sabbatical. He had tried to do the right thing, but it wasn't the right thing for him.

Sarah kissed him again. "I've got to go," she said.

In the moment before she walked away, he felt a powerful tug. Then he let her go. "See you in court," he said.

Color of Law

Thirty-four

The trial opened on a gray Monday and Alberts's dour expression matched the weather. A hundred people had pushed into his courtroom, and the judge seemed to consider this a personal intrusion. Seated high on the bench with the bailiff, court stenographer, and all the attorneys spread out below him, Alberts's distaste for the situation seemed palpable.

Before everyone had sat down, the district attorney asked for a change of venue owing to excessive publicity. But this was the wrong morning to trifle with the judge. "As far as I know, *60 Minutes* is a nationally televised program," Alberts said dryly. "Jurors would be as likely to have seen it in Green Bay as here in Milwaukee. Motion denied."

Alberts looked at Charlie. "Plaintiff will proceed," he said.

Charlie didn't believe in elaborate opening statements. The close was more important because you summarized your argument then and tried to leave the jury with a dramatic conclusion to the case. At the beginning, people were still trying to figure out where to sit and most of what you said went right by them. He liked to keep it simple.

"What this case is about is official misconduct," he began. "Most of us simply assume that the people authorized to run important city offices are honest. We assume that they work hard and treat everyone fairly. What we will show in the next few days will challenge this assumption, and for that reason it will be difficult for some of you to accept. In the testimony that follows you will hear witnesses say that the highest officers of the Milwaukee police department did not act fairly, that they in fact condoned racist attitudes among their officers, and that finally, tragically, this resulted in the death of an innocent boy. To make matters worse, these high officials then conspired to cover up the true circumstances of Jimmy Norman's death, and this cover-up prevented the true facts of this killing to be known to the general public.

"Now, John Rogan has already pleaded guilty to a reduced charge in this death and is serving his sentence in a federal penitentiary. He is not on trial here. What we will ask you to decide is whether the responsibility for Jimmy Norman's death ends in John Rogan's plea or if the officials who helped conceal this crime should also be held responsible. In presenting our case, we ask from you what the police department did not allow Jimmy Norman: open minds and open hearts. We ask that you consider what we are about to show you without bias and make your decision based on the facts." Charlie looked seriously at the jurors and returned to his seat.

Dolan responded by saying that the police department was among the best in the nation and that Charlie's claims were wild and unfounded. He cited Cap Norman's settlement and said the trial was frivolous and a waste of everybody's time. He asked for the jury's forbearance and then sat down. Charlie didn't blame Dolan; he would have done the same thing. It was in the city's interest to make light of their claims. Though everybody knew there had been a conspiracy, proving it on legal grounds would be hard. What was going to hurt the city would be the appearance of official wrong-doing. Since the police were supposed to be above reproach, the appearance of any corruption might be enough to throw the jury in their favor and force Mueller to make a good settlement offer. Then Charlie would have to convince Olivia to come off the hundred million dollars and accept it. But he could worry about that later.

Alberts read the names of six jurors who would be alternates and excused them. Then Charlie held up a file. "Plaintiffs introduce this certified copy of the guilty plea and conviction in Circuit Court of John Rogan in the 1959 killing of Jimmy Norman. I want this marked as received in evidence, Your Honor." He handed the file to the bailiff. "Plaintiffs call as their first witness, adversely, defendant Clarence Martin." It was important to identify Martin as a hostile witness because it allowed Charlie to ask leading questions. It also put the jury on notice.

There was a rumble as Martin entered. The press row was full, and people waited in the hall for seats to open. The Norman family was out in force, and Sarah Hedig sat just behind Olivia. Bob Joseph was present too.

Martin was sworn and Charlie approached. The former chief had flown up from his winter home in Florida, but hadn't changed his clothes, except for a red and white striped tie to complement his pale blue leisure suit. Tough and antagonistic, he knew what to expect from Charlie and was on guard.

"Mr. Martin," Charlie began, "on the night of February 8, 1959, you were Chief of Police in the city of Milwaukee?"

Martin's mouth curled, as if he was going to say something sarcastic, but all that came out was, "Yes."

"At that time, were Deputy Inspector Halloran, Chief of Detectives Tanner, and Detective Moran under your supervision?"

"They worked for me," Martin said. He seemed bored, as if he had a tee time and wanted this to be over.

"And Patrolmen Rogan and Paley, were they as well?"

"I couldn't know every bikeman in the city."

"Of course not," Charlie said. "But they were in the department. Now, Mr. Martin, was there anything unusual about February 8, 1959?"

"Sure," Martin said. "Two of my officers, the guys you just said, shot the Norman kid. Ain't that why we're here?"

The crowd chuckled at the chief's feisty attitude, but Charlie ignored the joke. "Both of them?" he asked.

Martin sighed as if Charlie were an idiot. "Rogan fired the gun."

"Could you tell us how you learned that Officer Rogan had shot Jimmy Norman?" Although Charlie couldn't say Rogan had murdered Jimmy, it was important to make clear that this was not just an accident. He had planted the idea that Rogan had been allowed to cop a plea, but killing wasn't going to be good enough. The jury had to be thinking murder from the beginning.

"The officer on duty called me at home," Martin said.

Charlie looked at his notes, though he had memorized them. "So you weren't directly involved in questioning the officers that evening?"

"Like I said, I was at home. Ask my wife."

There was more laughter at this, which seemed to buoy up the chief. He smiled and sat straighter in his chair.

Charlie waited a moment. Then he asked, "Would you say that this murder was a significant event, Mr. Martin?"

Martin looked puzzled, as if he hadn't understood the question. He looked at the judge, but Alberts's expression gave away nothing. "Objection," Dolan said now, seeing Martin was in trouble. "Counsel is asking the witness to draw conclusions about events on a night twenty-one years ago."

"It seems like a fair question to me," Alberts said.

Charlie turned back to Martin, who looked as if he had no idea what "significant meant." "I guess so," he said.

"A death is a significant event in your opinion?"

"I just said so," Martin said petulantly.

"Especially one involving police officers?"

Dolan objected again. "Counsel is badgering the witness," he said.

The judge seemed to agree. "Make your point, Mr. Simons."

Charlie nodded. "Yes, Your Honor." He walked to the plaintiff's table and picked up a book. "This is a copy of the Milwaukee Police Department Rules and Regulations, which we'd like to be identified as Plaintiff's exhibit 1." He looked at Martin. "Are you familiar with this, sir?"

"Sure," Martin said. "I wrote half of it."

"Then you can tell us if they were in force on the evening of February 8, 1959?"

Martin shrugged. "I guess they must have been."

Dolan objected. "Relevance," he said. "It's obvious that the rules and regulations were in effect. What of it?"

Alberts looked at Charlie. The trial had just started and already the judge seemed irritated. "I plan to show the relevance of the book to Chief Martin's conduct that evening," Charlie said.

Alberts hesitated a moment, as if he was thinking this over. He looked over at Dolan, then back at Charlie. "I'm going to allow this," he said, "but I expect you to get on with your argument, Mr. Simons."

Charlie repeated his question and Martin said, "They were in force."

Now Charlie handed Martin the manual and faced the jury. "Chief," Charlie said, emphasizing Martin's title, "please read aloud for the record number 8 of these rules and regulations, which you helped to write. Just the first sentence, please."

Charlie expected Dolan to object, but the district attorney was silent. They had caught him by surprise. Martin squinted as if he needed glasses, but then he read haltingly: "At the conclusion of each shift, the Deputy Inspector shall report any significant events to the Chief of Police. A full and complete report shall be required." Martin looked at Charlie.

"You testified that the duty officer called you at home to report Jimmy Norman's murder. Would you call that a full and complete report?"

"I thought it was OK," Martin said sullenly.

"Did you read the police reports later on?"

"I think so," Martin said. "I don't really remember."

"But according to these rules, you should have had a full and complete report from your deputy. My question is, did this happen?"

"No," Martin said.

"Then these rules and regulations were violated?" Charlie held up the book for the jury to see. It was a little theatrical, but what the hell.

"Objection," Dolan said. "Conclusion."

Alberts sustained this, but it didn't matter. It was obvious to everyone in the room that Martin hadn't had his eye on the ball. Anything could have happened downtown that night and he wouldn't have known. Charlie could have tried to determine what Martin did know and when he knew it, but the fact was two cops had killed a black kid and the chief of police hadn't cared enough to drive down to headquarters and find out what was going on.

"Chief," Charlie said, "there have been reports that there was a conspiracy to cover up the truth about this murder. Were you aware of this?"

Dolan was up again. "Foundation," he called out. "He's asking the witness to testify about something of which he has no direct knowledge."

It would have been easier to question Chief Martin if the district attorney weren't interrupting constantly, but Dolan's defensiveness created an impression of guilt, so Charlie welcomed it. He rephrased his question. "Were you part of a conspiracy to cover up the truth about this murder, Chief Martin?"

Charlie knew it was a mistake to ask a hostile witness a question when you didn't know the answer, but he was fishing. "No," Martin said.

Stupid, Charlie thought. What the hell was the guy going to say? He tried to recover. "Well, then, do you know if Chief Tanner or former District Attorney Lathrop were involved in a cover-up conspiracy?"

Predictably, this brought forth an objection. "Foundation," Dolan said. "Witness is not competent to testify as to the actions of his superiors."

"I only asked if he knew if they were involved," Charlie said, "not what they actually did."

"It comes to the same thing," Dolan said.

"Sustained," Alberts said, but Charlie detected the hint of a smile on the judge's face. They could strike his question from the record, but everyone knew it was impossible to order a juror to disregard what he had seen or heard. And Chief Martin, who seemed about to slide out of his chair, had the look of a guilty man. What was more important was the fact that Charlie had managed to bring Tanner and Lathrop into the case, even if only tangentially.

"Just a few more questions," Charlie said. He handed Martin copies of the *Times* articles. "Have you read these reports?" he asked.

Dolan couldn't object, since Charlie's question did not relate to the substance of the articles but only to Martin's having read them. The chief's eyes were small and mean. "It's all lies," he said, his voice low and angry.

"What, Chief? What's all lies?"

"Everything," Martin said. He seemed to reel in his chair, holding onto the rail of the witness box so tightly that his knuckles were white.

Charlie gave the jury time to take note of the chief's demeanor. Then he continued. "In the original reports in the *Times* of February 10 and 11, 1959, it was stated that a full and complete report was submitted to you concerning the events of February 8. You have testified that you received no such report. Which account is true, Chief Martin?"

"Lies," Martin said, out of control now. "It's all lies. Those sonsabitches don't give a rat's ass for the truth when a cop's involved."

Dolan rose from his chair, but there was nothing he could do to rein in the witness. Martin was chewing his tongue and spittle rimmed the side of his mouth. His small red eyes glowed with hatred and his tie was unraveled. Charlie let Martin's answer sit between them. The jury could decide who was most likely to be lying. They might agree with Martin about the press in general, but it would be hard not to think this witness was guilty of something. Finally, Charlie said, "Thank you, Chief Martin."

Dolan passed on cross-examination. The damage had been done. The only sensible thing from their point of view was to get Martin out of the room and hope the jury would forget him by the trial's end. Charlie had asked Isaacson to handle the next section, which involved witnesses who filled out their case but were not likely to be seriously challenged by the district attorney: a man who had served on the coroner's jury in 1959, a ballistics expert, and one of the cops originally summoned to the crime scene. Each was important, but none was major or controversial. Isaacson had to do something.

As Charlie watched Bill work, however, he was again aware of the difference between an experienced trial lawyer and a politician with a law degree. Isaacson's questions lacked design; too often he made speeches rather than pursuing specific points. Charlie preferred to stand well back of the box and pretend the witness was alone in the room, but Isaacson was all over his witnesses, and this was distracting. He roamed the big room, playing to the jurors while the witness sat, ignored, like an orphan. Finally, Dolan objected, more out of impatience than anything else, Charlie thought.

"Restrain yourself, Mr. Isaacson," the judge said, but Isaacson did them no real harm, and when he was through Alberts dismissed them for lunch.

Charlie had looked forward to eating alone, but as he made his way out, Bob Joseph called his name.

"I thought you were off the story," Charlie said.

"Things have changed," Bob said self-consciously.

Charlie didn't see Sarah, but she would be with Olivia. "Want to have lunch?" he asked. Joseph seemed to have something on his mind.

"I've got to file," Bob said, but he didn't move. "There's something I need to talk to you about."

Charlie was stuffing papers into his briefcase. "I'm listening."

"Not here. Could we have a drink later?"

Charlie looked up, but Joseph didn't appear distressed. Maybe it wasn't personal. "Sure," he said.

Bob nodded. "I'll find you this afternoon," he said.

Charlie had been too involved in preparing for the trial to think much about Bob and Sarah and Andy. Joseph had always interested him, but because of the way their lives had developed the two men had never become friends. It was often like that: Charlie would meet someone, feel a connection, and then nothing would happen because he was too busy or his wife didn't like the other man's. Then for years in idle moments he would wonder why he had so few real friends without either knowing how to do anything about it or caring very much. Intimacy was not his gift, but now he was curious at Joseph's insistence that they meet. What did they have to talk about?

Of course the other man was a reporter covering a trial, but he had acted more urgent than that. It was a mystery, but Charlie would find out soon enough, and he only had an hour to eat.

Thirty-five

Leaving the courthouse, Bob practically ran into Marcus Jackson, who was standing just outside the double doors. Below, a tight circle of Guardians led by Father Moretti chanted over and over, "Black Power! Think about it!" It wasn't very exciting, but the kids had some style in their berets and leather jackets. Except for a couple of cops and a television crew, however, the steps were empty, making the marchers seem more pathetic than menacing, their voices nearly drowned out by the traffic.

"Hiding out?" Bob asked, nodding at the priest.

Jackson smiled. "Just keeping my eyes open. You never know when cops'll go crazy around black kids."

Marcus was dressed in a gray pinstripe with a burgundy pocket square. "Were you at the trial?" Bob asked.

"In and out. You're the one ain't supposed to be here."

"I'm back on the story," Bob said simply. He was tempted to tell Jackson about Hometown, just to get his reaction. After all, in a way, Marcus was responsible. But then the kids started chanting again, and, despite his practiced cynicism, it made Bob sad. For himself and the years that had rushed past when he wasn't paying attention, but mostly for the kids protesting the murder of a boy none of them had known. This was what it had all come down to, the marches and the voter-registration drives, the violence and hope and passion of the sixties. Some kids and a publicity-mad priest trying to make the evening news on a cold day in Milwaukee.

"Anything I can do?" Jackson asked, misunderstanding.

Bob felt a sudden warmth for Jackson. "I was just thinking about Selma and King and Rap and Stokely, you know, the movement, how optimistic we were. Now it's all gone except for a bunch of lawyers in there cleaning up."

"Some of us are still here," Jackson said quietly. "But you looked like something else was bothering you, Bobby."

Bob wanted to be honest, but he hadn't figured out where his real obligation lay. Sarah had confided in him, even though they both knew he would use it if he could. "I'm OK, Marc. Maybe later."

Bob decided not to interview the priest. Thanks to Chief Martin, he already had his story. After leaving Sarah, he had gone to Klein's office. "What are you standing here for?" Mike had asked after he told him what had happened. "Get your ass over to the courthouse." Then he smiled. "Give yourself a day or two to get back into it. I've already got a guy there."

"OK," Bob said. "But there's something else."

Mike Klein listened attentively as Bob told him about Hometown, interrupting only to ask an occasional question. When Bob finished Mike said, "You're something, you know that? Even when you're not supposed to be working you get more than anyone else. That's a hell of a story."

"But what can we do with it?"

"I'll tell you what you do," Klein said. "Nothing. We've got a big race trial starting today and you come in here saying the plaintiff's a slumlord? Come on. We can't break a story like that. Not now."

"That wasn't exactly going to be my lead," Bob said. "But we'd go with a story about Chief Tanner, wouldn't we? We'd run with that?"

"Goddamned right," Klein said. "So you think there's a double standard around here? You're absolutely right. But think about it. If we print a story about Olivia Brown, any concern about the cover-up will disappear. This is a historic moment, Bobby. I've never seen a case like this before and I don't expect to live long enough to see one again. One time. We let those assholes off the hook and they're gone forever. I don't think that's right, do you?"

"I thought we were supposed to report the news, not make judgments." Bob said.

This amused Mike Klein. "How long have you been in the business? We make judgments every day and you damned well know it—or you should. Every time I send a reporter out to cover something, or decide not to send one, I'm making a judgment, saying this is worth our notice and that's not.

Same thing when I decide how many people I'm going to assign to cover city hall or the Safety Building. I make a judgment when I tell you how many inches I'll use on the election story and where I'll slot your piece when it's done. Because I know if I bury a story on page 30 not as many people are going to see it, whereas if I give it a big headline people who look at nothing else will see that article. You think we've got thirty reporters in the sports department because it takes that many to write down the baseball scores? Or four in Madison because nothing important ever happens around the state capitol? Don't be naive. Something in the governor's office might get by us, but I'll tell you this, Bobby: We're not going to get beat by the other paper on anything about the Packers, the Brewers, or the Bucks. Judgments, my ass."

"So this is just more of the same?" Bob said.

Mike Klein's lower lip rolled stubbornly around his teeth, making him look like a terrier. "Bet your ass. I'll make a judgment on this and I'd do it every day of my life. I'm going to hold off on a story about a black woman being a slumlord because I think what's at stake in that trial is more important."

"What is at stake, Mike?"

Klein shrugged. The indignation drained slowly out of him. "Maybe not so much compared to world wars or famine in the Sahel. But I've lived in this town for thirty years, and I know about the racists and anti-Semites because I've lived with them. I know about restricted neighborhoods and private clubs. I know plenty of people in Milwaukee who'd feel vindicated if they knew about this, but I don't want to give them that satisfaction. I don't want anything we do to take away from the fact that two cops murdered that boy and then the police department tried to cover it up. I want the people of this city to take a long look at the police, because when they're looking at Paley and Rogan and Tanner, they're really looking at themselves. I don't think it's good or honorable that Olivia Brown owns slum housing, but, really, what difference is it going to make if we expose it? Tell me, is that rationalization or good judgment?"

Put that way, Bob couldn't disagree. He was going to put in something about the people's right to know, but he wasn't sure he really believed it. That was the kind of chestnut reporters pulled out when there was something they wanted to write about. Then the people had a right to know. Usually the people didn't give a shit if they knew or not.

But Mike was still wound up. "And it isn't only that. Say what you want about Milwaukee being the most segregated city in the country, there are decent people here too. I'd like to give this jury the chance to speak for them, to say the cops were wrong. And as far as the money goes, considering what she's gone through, I don't blame Olivia for making her pile any way she can."

Bob left the office dissatisfied, but the important thing was that he was back. Whether he agreed or not, there wasn't really anything to write about Hometown yet, so it didn't matter. But this didn't stop him from feeling guilty. He should have told Jackson, no matter what Klein said.

Tommy was in the witness room when they brought Rogan in. He was in manacles, which seemed excessive, and waited patiently while the marshal unlocked him. The fact was John looked like shit. He had lost weight in jail, and his cheap suit hung on him like a rag. The silver-tipped cowboy boots were the only reminder of Rogan's former arrogance. John was handcuffed to a marshal, even though it was pretty obvious that he wasn't going anywhere. Rogan barely had the strength to sit down. Tommy felt self-conscious, sitting there in his California clothes, but he held up his hand in greeting anyway. "How's it going?" he asked, immediately feeling stupid.

Rogan smiled ironically. "Not as good as you. I saw you on *60 Minutes.* Liked your make-up."

Tommy flushed. They had made him up to look like a ten-dollar whore. "I thought you'd be on too."

Rogan lit a cigarette with his free hand. "They asked me, but why make money for those assholes?" He looked Tommy over with undisguised amusement. "Jesus, Tom, you're dressed like a goddamned pimp."

In spite of himself, Tommy laughed, then Rogan did, and finally even the marshal joined in. "Everyone dresses like this out there," Tommy said. Then he added, "California."

Rogan looked interested. "No shit? You out in El Lay?"

Tommy nodded modestly. "West Los Angeles," he said, downplaying it. Location would probably mean nothing to John, but he wanted to be friendly. He was surprised and pleased by Rogan's apparent lack of bitterness and continuing interest in Tommy. It was more than he had gotten from anyone else and, not for the first time, he was struck by the irony of the situation: his only friend was a man he had sent to prison.

"So you're going to be in the movies—our story, I mean?" It was obvious that Rogan wasn't displeased.

Tommy thought of Tami's dingy office with the posters of Shamu next door. Rogan was so hopeful that he hated to disappoint him. "They say it takes a owhile," he said. "So I'm hanging in. Tell the truth, I haven't been able to find anyone out there who gives much of a shit."

"Is that so," Rogan said sympathetically. He crossed his booted feet and took a slow drag on his cigarette. "Well, at least you got the clothes, then. Hey, they flew us out here first class. Figured I was so dangerous the marshal needed more room to keep me under control. I don't guess they planned on him drinking all that champagne, though. My Aunt Mary could have escaped. Thing is, I really wanted to come. You get that—first class?"

The marshal ignored them, staring straight ahead, still enjoying the buzz from the flight. "Where were you coming from?" Tommy asked.

"I can't even tell you," Rogan said. "Big secret. See, you could maybe tell a reporter, and then he might tell the Black Panthers, and they'd get word out to all the spooks in jail, and they'd kill me. So it's hush-hush. I've been moved so often since they sent me up that I damned near don't know where I am myself half the time. Now they got me in the hole, for my own protection." He smiled grimly. "Tell the truth, after a few months talking to yourself, getting raped doesn't sound so bad. One hole's the same as another, right, Partner? So I guess that's about where I'm at. That's just about it."

Tommy wanted to say something encouraging, but John had pretty well summed it up, and it was hard to find a bright side. Still, he admired the other man's stoic acceptance of his punishment. Tommy knew he wouldn't have handled it as well. He would have hated John if their positions were reversed. But there was an easy feeling between them, speaking of familiarity and friendship. Then the bailiff stuck his head in and called Rogan's name.

"I'll see you, John," Tommy said, offering his hand.

Rogan grasped it, his eyes watery. "I doubt it," Rogan said. "I seriously doubt that, Partner. So you just take care of yourself."

Charlie had put Rogan on his witness list because he needed him, and he knew he couldn't count on Dolan. While most jurors considered a defendant's reluctance to testify to be a sign of guilt, that wasn't important in this case. Everyone knew Rogan was guilty. There wouldn't be much for Dolan to gain by putting him on the stand. But Charlie wanted his testimony because he might implicate others by giving details about the conspiracy.

Looking at him now, however, Charlie was not optimistic. The witness didn't seem angry or hostile, but he'd clearly suffered, and Charlie didn't know what effect that would have on the jury. What they knew about John Rogan from previous testimony was twenty years old: that he had been a bad cop who liked to hurt people and did it frequently. Even the other officers were uneasy around him. But no one had anything fresh because Rogan had never said anything on the record. There was no confession, just the guilty plea, and putting aside the lame alibi he and Paley had concocted the night of the murder, Rogan had never really said why he shot Jimmy. If it had been a mistake, Rogan could have said so at the time and saved everyone a lot of trouble. And if he killed the boy on purpose, why chase him so far before doing so? It remained a mystery, but Rogan's motives were irrelevant here. The case Charlie was going to try wasn't about that. For those purposes it didn't matter if Rogan were a contract killer for the Aryan Brotherhood.

Except that it mattered to Charlie. It affected the way he would approach this case, but Rogan wasn't going to care about helping him with that. And even if he did talk, it would be easy for Dolan to impugn his credibility. Yet there was really no other connection between the murder and the department. Rogan's testimony might not help, but without it they had no chance.

Charlie's hope was that Rogan had some lingering resentment about the way he had been treated. You didn't have to be excessively egalitarian to realize that he'd been hung out to dry by higher-ups in the department. But if this grated on Rogan it wasn't apparent. Everything about the witness seemed to say, "I'm here because I have to be, but I don't care. I don't care about you or the Norman kid, and I don't care about the city. I don't give a shit. Now, can I go?" It made him seem oddly self-effacing, which was not the way Charlie wanted the defendant to look in a conspiracy trial.

Charlie had tried to get Rogan to talk about the cover-up when they deposed him, but he hadn't gotten very far. So he had decided to make his questions more focused. As he was about to begin, however, he heard movement behind him and turned to see the Norman family taking their seats.

"Plaintiff," Judge Alberts said suddenly, his voice strained. "I want your clients in court on time. We all operate on the same clock. Is that clear?"

Charlie couldn't believe Alberts would make an issue of Olivia's being a few minutes late. "What the fuck's the matter with him?" Isaacson whispered. Charlie shrugged. It was a bad sign. They had assumed Alberts would be on their side; now it looked like he wasn't even going to be neutral.

"Beats the shit out of me," he muttered under his breath. To the bench, he said, "Yes, Your Honor."

Rogan smiled and his arrogance made Charlie mad. "Mr. Rogan, I want to go back to the report you filed the night you shot and killed Jimmy

Norman. Originally, you said you were six feet away from the victim when you shot, but later you changed your testimony and said you were much closer than that. My question is, did anyone influence you to change that testimony?"

"I don't recall," Rogan said. "It's twenty years now."

"That is a long time," Charlie said, "but I'm sure you remember that night very well."

"Objection," Dolan said. "Argumentative."

"Did Chief Tanner ask you to change your story?" Charlie asked.

"I don't remember," Rogan said.

"Did you talk to Tanner about it?"

"Ever?" Rogan asked, his eyes cold and insouciant.

Of course, Asshole. "Yes," Charlie said. "Ever. Did you ever discuss this case with Chief Tanner?"

"I don't remember," Rogan repeated.

Charlie knew he couldn't let this get to him. He had to use the witness. Dolan objected again. "He's badgering the witness, Judge" he said. "He already said he doesn't remember."

"Get to the point, Mr. Simons," the judge said.

"Mr. Rogan, do you believe this is a race case?"

Rogan looked at him as if he didn't understand. At last he said, "You're the lawyer."

The judge instructed Rogan to answer. "I guess it is," Rogan said.

"Thank you," Charlie said. "Since this is a race case, could you tell the court if you have anything against blacks?"

"I don't like them," Rogan said. "But I only killed one in my life, and that was an accident."

"A very unfortunate accident," Charlie said. "Do you regret it?"

"Objection," Dolan said. "The witness is not on trial."

"Goes to motive," Charlie said. "Of the departmental conspiracy."

Alberts shook his head. "Witness will answer," he said.

"I don't think about it every day."

"That wasn't my question. Do you have remorse for what you did?"

Rogan shrugged. This wasn't what he wanted to talk about. "It ruined my life," he said. "So, sure, I regret it."

A great humanitarian, Charlie thought. "Let me ask you, Mr. Rogan, when you came back to the Safety Building that night did you have the feeling you were being ostracized by the other officers?"

"Objection," Dolan said. "Conclusion."

"Sit down," Alberts said quietly. "He's asking how the witness felt."

"I didn't get that word," Rogan said. He seemed subdued now, almost thoughtful.

"Ostracize. Did the others set you apart, make you feel you were wrong, or did you feel general approval?"

"Neither," Rogan said. "They put me and Tommy off by ourselves right away, and no one said nothing to us except for the chief and the D.A."

"And did you feel they approved of what you had done?"

"I wouldn't say that. It put them in a spot."

"You mean that it put the whole department on the spot, that they represented the police in general?"

Rogan nodded. "That's how I felt. That's why they canned me."

This was better than Charlie had hoped. Rogan was making his case, but he didn't want an alliance with the witness. "Isn't it true, Mr. Rogan, that you were cited for nine instances of police brutality before that night?"

"I didn't count," Rogan said sullenly.

"Your Honor, I wish to enter a copy of Mr. Rogan's service record as Plaintiff's exhibit 2." Charlie retrieved the file from the table and handed it to the bailiff. Then he turned back to the witness. "Mr. Rogan," he said, "weren't eight of those citations for incidents involving blacks?"

Rogan was alert. A nerve in his face jumped as Charlie looked steadily at him. "I guess they were," he said at last.

"Thank you," Charlie said. "Now, you've stated that Jimmy Norman's death was accidental. Does that mean you didn't intend to kill him because he was black?"

"No, I already said so," Rogan whined.

"Even though Thomas Paley has reported you told him you 'wanted to get some niggers,' and your police file is filled with brutality complaints?"

Rogan just looked at Charlie. Then he turned to the judge. "I didn't understand the question," he said.

"Neither did I," Alberts said. "Mr. Simons?"

Charlie felt like walking away. "Mr. Rogan, did anyone in the department at any time express disapproval over what you had done?"

"Well, like I said, they kicked me off the force," Rogan said.

"That was later. But on that night or in the days immediately following, did anyone, Chief Martin or Chief Inspector Halloran, for example, ever say or even imply that you had done something wrong?"

"No," Rogan said simply.

Charlie stepped back, giving the jury a chance to consider this. "Did any of these men endeavor to help you to understand the dynamics of race, why blacks and whites have so much trouble getting along together?"

"No."

"Did they make any effort to rehabilitate you or perhaps offer to help you obtain psychological counseling?"

"There was a jailhouse shrink, but no one ever told me to see him."

"Do you have any idea why they didn't suggest this?"

Rogan shrugged. "I guess they figured I was pretty much like everyone else."

"What do you think about that?"

Rogan shrugged. "I can see it," he said. "I was pretty normal. I always got along, in sports, in the service. I had friends, you know, the usual."

"I see." Charlie almost felt sympathy for Rogan, but he pressed on. "Tell me more about your racial attitudes. Compared to other policemen, Chief Martin, for example, would you say your feelings about blacks were similar?"

Dolan objected. "Calls for conclusion. It's obvious that the witness is in no position to make judgments about Chief Martin's racial attitudes. Mr. Martin has testified that he didn't even know Mr. Rogan."

This could be true, but Charlie could tell he had the jury. Because fairness and common sense had come into play. In any group with shared attitudes on race, there were moderates and extremists. It was reasonable to assume that Rogan would have known if he was out on the fringe or if others shared his views. The judge was obviously enjoying the interplay. "I'm going to let it go, Mr. Dolan. As long as it doesn't go on much longer."

"I'm almost finished, Judge." Charlie didn't want to lose momentum. "Mr. Rogan, in your opinion, did Detective Moran like black people?"

"I doubt it," Rogan said.

"How about Chief Inspector Halloran?"

"I never heard him say so."

"Was there any high official in the police department of the city of Milwaukee who in your opinion was sympathetic to blacks, Mr. Rogan?"

Dolan was on his feet objecting, but the judge ignored him. "I never knew anyone who said so," Rogan said.

"I see," Charlie said, drawing out the word. "So after you came to these men who were your superiors and admitted that you had unintentionally killed an unarmed black teenager and further stated that you had made a mistake in doing so, no one in the police department hierarchy expressed any overt disapproval, shock, or dismay? No one said you had done anything wrong?"

"Not that I remember," Rogan said.

"In fact, didn't they schedule meetings for you with the District Attorney so that you could concoct the best possible defense for your actions?"

Charlie expected Dolan to object to this, but he was unexpectedly silent. "Cops hang together," Rogan said.

"Exactly," Charlie said. "And you all hung together to cover up the nature of this crime, didn't you, Mr. Rogan."

Now Dolan did object, but Charlie said, "I'm finished, Your Honor."

In his cross-examination Dolan drew a vivid picture of the cold winter night and the dangers of police work. He elicited from Rogan the fact that he had won a sharpshooter's citation, something that didn't fit with the rest of the patrolman's career. Charlie sat quietly, studying the jurors' reactions. He noticed a woman in the second row whose lips moved in unison with the district attorney's and who was close to tears by the end of his cross. Charlie couldn't remember much about her, but she was going to be a problem.

When Alberts recessed, Charlie called his office and learned that Fenster had come in as promised. They planned to call the old man after Paley and finish with Magnusen, but while he had been reasonably successful with Rogan, Charlie didn't feel very hopeful. On his way out he ran into Joseph.

"Waiting for me?" he asked.

"Actually I was. Have you got a minute?"

"I've got an hour," Charlie said. "What's up?"

Joseph looked around. The floor of the empty corridor shone with wax, and the brass handrails gleamed. It was a very public place. "Not here."

They drove to a bar on Water Street, and when they were settled in a back booth, Charlie said, "So what is it, Bobby? What's so secret that we can't talk about it on the street? Or did you just want private time with me?"

Joseph took a sip of beer. "Sorry," he said. "I didn't mean to act like an asshole." He traced a line on the waxed tablecloth. "I broke it off with Sarah. It wasn't working out, and I couldn't stand covering 4-H for the zones."

Charlie nodded, but he was disappointed. He was tired and didn't feel like playing Ann Landers in a dump like this. "I figured something had happened when I saw you in court," he said. Bob seemed preoccupied, as if he hadn't heard a word Charlie had said. "I'm sorry," he added.

Bob nodded. "It's OK. It's not like we're enemies; there just wasn't enough there, you know. No glue."

Charlie knew all about glue. His whole life was bound up in arrangements that were both limiting and rewarding. "So you're back on the Norman story?"

"I am, but what I've got to tell you has got to stay between us."

Charlie's interest picked up. The lonely-hearts stuff had been a way to make contact, not the point of the meeting. But he had learned not to promise confidentiality lightly; concealment was an important part of his life, and he couldn't afford to be generous with it. It was ironic, though, because normally he was the one asking for discretion. "It's about the trial?"

"It could be," Joseph said vaguely.

An interesting choice of words, as if the information's relevance was conditional. In other hands it might not matter; in his, it could.

"I can't promise I won't use it. Maybe you shouldn't tell me." It was a gamble, but he couldn't afford to hamstring himself. The other man would have to need to tell him badly enough to take a chance.

Bob hadn't expected this response and it troubled him, though he liked Charlie. This secret was like a hot coal being passed from hand to hand. It occurred to him that maybe he should break the chain and keep quiet. No maybe about it—he knew he should. He felt disloyal to Mike Klein, who had told him to sit on the information, to bury it. But Mike was wrong. And even if he couldn't write a story, this shouldn't be covered up, any more than the murder should have been. This shit had to stop somewhere. There weren't good and bad conspiracies. How could it be wrong for the cops but all right for Olivia? The whole goddamned thing was wrong. People always wanted to make lying complicated, but this was simple. Bob took a deep breath. "OK," he said. "It's about your client. Olivia Brown."

Charlie had learned through experience that people spoke more openly if he said very little, so he listened attentively, not even interrupting to ask questions. Every so often he'd nod or make a note on a cocktail napkin. When Bob was finished, Charlie asked, "How do you know it's Olivia?"

"We don't, not really. It's a guess, but it's a good one. Sarah saw the ledger on Olivia's desk in her living room, and Hometown owns her husband's car wash. Then there's this." He passed a copy of the newspaper photograph across the table. The print was grainy, but Olivia was clearly recognizable.

"She could have been part of the protest," Charlie said.

"Why protest against the company that owns her husband's business?"

"It happens," Charlie said, but he didn't believe it. One of the problems they had with Olivia was that she had no history with the movement. Even Marc Jackson thought she was an opportunist. "Anyway, this is all circumstantial. Where would Olivia get the money to buy all these buildings?"

"If I knew that, I'd be writing the story. Look," Bob said, "I agree with you. None of this really proves anything, and my editor told me to forget about it. He says the important thing is nailing the cops for conspiring to cover up Jimmy Norman's death. He's right, but the fact is this bothers me. You're an honest guy, Charlie, but tell the truth. Doesn't it make you a little uncomfortable to know that while Olivia is suing the city for millions of dollars, her bagman is out collecting rents on fifty buildings that violate code?"

Charlie had trouble imagining Olivia as a real estate magnate. She seemed unsophisticated about money, though she clearly wanted as much as she could get. But he couldn't answer Bob's questions. Olivia had never told Charlie about the ledger, and he had never met her husband. What really troubled him, though, was the growing realization that he had no idea who his client was. "Sure," he said at last. "It bothers me."

Bob had given up his right to confidentiality, but he was curious. "What are you going to do?" he asked.

"I'm going to talk to Olivia," Charlie said.

The weather changed again. Warm wet winds carried a promise of spring that Andy knew from experience to be false. In another week they'd have a blizzard followed by freezing temperatures. Then another thaw, then more snow, until June. Spring would last a week before the heat wave they called summer set in. Still, there was no reason not to enjoy the mild weather while it lasted. After a dinner at the VFW post, Andy decided to walk home.

There was no longer time to run in the morning, but despite his schedule Andy wasn't tired. He slept four hours a night, and as the last weeks of the campaign approached their polls showed him within five points of the mayor. This engendered frenzy among the staff and volunteers were coming back. He could still as easily lose as win, but Andy felt more self-assured.

Sarah was holding a cup of tea when he walked in. She was smiling. "You look pleased with yourself," she said.

"I just walked back from the Cudworth post. Not bad for a man my age." He took off his coat and sat next to her. "Something wrong?"

"I'm fine. Actually, it's surprising how good I feel considering Bob and I just broke up."

She sounded like a high school sophomore, but Andy took in the news without saying anything. He wanted to be sure how he felt. Yet he didn't feel anything beyond mild surprise. Without consciously thinking about it, he had expected Sarah to have him served and then to remarry after a period of time. Now that he had learned the truth was something different than this, however, it mattered less than he would have expected, and he experienced this as a loss. "I'm sorry," he said. "I know that meant a lot to you."

His words sounded detached even to him in the quiet room, but it was the best he could do. The question was, what did he expect now—of himself, of her? Andy felt as if Sarah's announcement represented a new obligation, but to do what? The right thing, whatever that was. The fact was he neither needed nor wanted more obligations. Sarah didn't seem to mind. "I guess it did. I mean, sure, it must have. Look at all the trouble it caused."

"I wouldn't worry about that," Andy said, but he didn't really mean it. She *had* caused him a great deal of trouble—why pretend otherwise? Still, his main feeling was irritation. Sarah's confession annoyed him because he had been feeling so good about things. He had adjusted to their life, found new things to care about, and was no longer attuned to the slightest variation in her mood. He found her slowed-down speech and intimations of great significance depressing. She really had no right to impose her tragedies on him. "I'm sorry," he said again. Then he yawned.

"I'm OK," Sarah said again. "What I really want to know is, does this make a difference? Between us, I mean."

Andy looked at his wife for a long time. He saw her not only as she was now, a middle-aged woman, but as she had been when they met. He wanted to feel more than he did, wanted passion to grow out of the sense of vindication he was entitled to. He wanted to take Sarah in his arms and tell her that, miraculously, they had come through a terrible storm and somehow emerged whole on the other side, their love intact. He wanted the music to swell and the titles to come up.

Except that he didn't feel any of this. Turning your back on thirty years should hurt more, he thought, if it meant anything to begin with. But beyond a kind of numbness, there was nothing. What had gone was gone for good. Andy reached for his wife's hand and was surprised at how large and coarse it seemed. He had imagined Sarah as having delicate hands with long graceful fingers. He had thought she should play the piano. "No," he said softly. "It doesn't. Not for me."

Sarah shuddered, though Andy couldn't tell why. Could it really matter what he said when just the day before, the week before, she had been desperately in love with Bob Joseph? Or perhaps he represented safety and security in the known as opposed to what lay outside the front door. But then whenever it was, or might have been, was gone. Her eyes were clear. "Let's get everything done then," she said. "Lawyers, all that. And I'm going to move into my studio for good."

"You can wait two weeks. The election?" They weren't being unfriendly now, just businesslike. But the transition was remarkable. How quickly you moved from intimacy to this.

Sarah nodded, but as Andy stood to leave he realized he was still holding her hand. On an impulse, he bent deeply at the waist like an old-time gallant and kissed it tenderly. When he straightened, there were tears in Sarah's eyes, but neither of them said anything. And in the morning, when Andy awoke, she was gone.

Thirty-six

Charlie had finished his workout and breakfast by eight o'clock. Court was adjourned for the weekend, but he needed time to think. He drove west on North Avenue and before long found himself in Hillside, the housing project where Marcus Jackson had his office. The project was a succession of red brick buildings meandering along several burned-out blocks and bisected by a concrete park. Bordered on the east by a highway with a chain-link overpass, it looked like an armed camp. Despite the grimness of the place, however, the streets were alive with women in colored turbans and children in bright clothes who looked at Charlie with undisguised curiosity, as if they had never seen a white person before. He saw no men. It was an unusual place to take a walk, but Charlie found himself parking the car. Then he strolled the perimeter of the playground before taking a seat on a park bench in view of the teeter-totter. The conversation with Bob had hit him harder than he would have expected, though he wasn't terribly surprised. Clients generally lied to their attorneys, and Olivia had been holding back from the beginning. It seemed a little odd that she'd be so consumed with the amount they were going for, but he had thought she was right not to trust white people.

What bothered him went deeper than that, though, to his own motives. For however sophisticated or cynical he could appear to others, Charlie had a rather uncomplicated view of things that hadn't changed since the eighth grade, when he had seen two white men beat a black senseless in front of his father's store. He became a lawyer because he wanted to fight injustice. It was that simple. He believed in good and evil and never took on a case that he knew to be tainted. Yet if he was honest, he knew he had let his ego get in the way of good judgment in dealing with Olivia. He had wanted to be Olivia's White Hope, and she had let him delude himself.

Still, the fact that the dilemma was of his own making didn't resolve anything. Was a cover-up by white policemen wrong but that by a black slumlord acceptable? Not to him, but he didn't know what to do about it, except turn the case over to Isaacson, which would be tantamount to handing it to Dolan. Olivia hadn't broken any laws. She could be indicted for nothing except betraying Charlie's trust. By this point in a trial, he expected to know his own mind, and yet he didn't. He rose and walked toward the building.

Inside, the secretary told Charlie that Marc hadn't come in yet. He could wait. Charlie didn't know what he was waiting for exactly, but he had time, so he walked into the empty lounge. A connecting door stood open, and when he looked in, Charlie saw a small white woman sitting at a table surrounded by children's watercolors. The woman smiled at Charlie. She had large gray eyes and a long face, and there was something terribly attractive about her.

"I'm sorry," Charlie said. "I'm waiting for Marcus."

She bobbed her head. "You could wait a long time. But come on in and look around." She had a soft, southern accent, but her rough tweed skirt and paint-spattered hands clashed with Charlie's memories of Nashville.

"You sound like you're from somewhere else," he said. It was amazing to him how many white southerners Jackson seemed to find. Former Peace Corps volunteers or conscientious objectors were always around.

"Kentucky," the woman said. "But that was a long time ago. I guess I'm really a Yankee now."

She said this with regret, and Charlie felt as if he should sympathize, until she smiled again. He turned over a few of the children's drawings, which seemed to be full of rainbows and machine guns. One had written "God is love" with bullets piercing the ornate letters. Charlie noticed the woman watching and wondered if she expected him to comment.

"I know you," she said. "You're the lawyer for the Normans. I saw your picture in the paper."

"Charlie Simons," he said, offering his hand. "I should have introduced myself before."

The woman took it in hers, which were as dry and fine as paper and cross-hatched with small blue veins. An aristocrat, Charlie thought. "I'm Louise Bryan," she said. "Are you going to win?"

The question was so direct that Charlie wasn't sure how to answer. He started to offer a bromide but stopped himself because she really wanted to know. "It's a tough case. Tougher than I thought it would be. I'm going to try."

"You remind me of my boy," Louise said. "He was always the smallest one in any game he'd play, but he wanted to win more than anyone else, so usually he did." Her voice sounded wistful, which made Charlie wonder if her son was dead.

"Does he live in Milwaukee, your son, I mean?"

Louise shook her head no. "I told him he should get out of Wisconsin and start somewhere else, which was good advice, I guess. But now I miss him. He's a legal aid lawyer in Springfield, Massachusetts."

"We are alike then." Charlie wished his mother had been as proud.

"That's a good thing you're doing," Louise Bryan said. "It was awful how they killed that boy and worse that no one did anything about it. Of course, he wasn't the only one, but getting them for one is better than nothing."

Charlie nodded. Now he felt that he would let this woman down if they lost. But what was it to her if one or a hundred black kids were killed? Then he felt ashamed of himself because Louise Bryan made nothing of herself, or the sacrifice she might have made in being here teaching art. "What happens to these kids?" he asked, gesturing toward the drawings.

Louise shrugged, though not from lack of interest. "I see them until third or fourth grade. Then the boys start disappearing. After that, I'll see them on the street for another year or so. Then they just go away."

Charlie didn't need to ask where they went. The same places Jimmy Norman had gone, most of them. What Louise said was almost elegiac in its simplicity. Everyone was the same at the beginning, alive, curious, filled with excitement about the world. But as these kids got older, they just faded into camps, or jails, or worse. "Doesn't that discourage you?" he asked.

"I never like to lose good artists," Louise said. "But no, not really. Of course I don't have to do this and you don't have to do what you're doing. So why do we? I can't speak for you, but I don't come down here because I'm a slave to my conscience. Some people find it hard to understand, but the truth is I really like teaching the children and I try not to think about what happens later. At least they have this much art in their lives. And it's a lot more interesting than staying over on the east side and going to openings on Downer Avenue. There's more excitement here, don't you think?"

Charlie fought the impulse to smile. Louise seemed to feel sorry for people who didn't spend their lives in housing projects, who had to make do with white wine and designer clothes. "Your son is lucky," he said.

"Tell him. Maybe he'd come home once in a while. They had a new baby and I had to fly out there just to see her."

"Maybe I'll visit instead, for coffee?" Charlie said hopefully.

Louise squinted skeptically, but then he saw that wonderful smile. Without prompting, she put her arms around his neck and pulled him close. It was a simple gesture, but it brought Charlie close to tears. Emotion always surprised him, and now he was grateful, standing there in the dusty basement in the arms of a strange woman. "I'd like that," Louise said. "Anytime you want."

Charlie saw it was time. Jackson hadn't appeared yet but it didn't matter. "Well, good-bye," he said.

"You get those cops," Louise replied, waving him out.

Olivia arrived late as usual, wearing a red turban and a black fur coat. With her height and bearing, it was easy to imagine that she was related to African royalty. But today she seemed ill at ease. She sat on the edge of the couch, a line of smoky thigh showing where the coat broke on her legs.

"What do you want to talk about?" Olivia asked.

Charlie was surprised that she'd be confrontational, unless she knew what he had learned. But how could she? No use being paranoid. "Olivia, as your lawyer, I've got to ask you questions you don't like. I have to ask so that I can do a better job for you. Do you understand that?"

Charlie realized how patronizing this sounded, but Olivia was used to being condescended to by white people. She thought it gave her an advantage. "What do you want to know?"

"Have you ever heard of Hometown Properties?" Charlie asked. There, let it out right away, no guile. Sometimes a shock produced the truth.

Olivia didn't look surprised. "She tell you that?" she asked. Neither indicated directly that Olivia was referring to Sarah Hedig, but they both knew. "Huh," Olivia said. "So what if I do?"

Do what? Charlie wondered, but rather than pursue this, he asked another direct question. "Do you own Hometown, Olivia?" Why baby her when she had been withholding evidence?

"Maybe," Olivia said. She seemed diffident, as if Charlie's question were relative; she might, then again, she might not.

"I think you do," Charlie said. "I think you are Hometown Properties. What puzzles me is how you've been able to hide this for so long— from me, the newspapers, even from Marcus Jackson. How did you do that?"

"Maybe this nigger's smarter than you think." But Charlie was determined not to let things go that way, even if he had underestimated her.

"Look," he said. "I don't really care how many buildings you own. I can't say I admire what you're doing, but it's none of my business, unless it affects the trial. If that happens, then it is definitely my business."

Something made Olivia sit up straighter in her chair, maybe his mentioning the trial. "Where did you get the money?" he asked. "And how did you get the idea to form a land trust? Who told you about all that?"

"Why you want to know?"

"Olivia, you're a poor woman with a large family. You come to me and say you want to sue the city. You say you want justice, which turns out to mean a lot of money, which is OK, which is fine. So we sue for a hundred million dollars, and, I'll be honest with you, that's more money than I've ever asked for in court. It's a fucking lot of money, Olivia. Now I find out you're already a millionaire. So I think I've got a right to ask where the money came from. You already told me you never cashed the city's settlement check, but that didn't amount to much anyway. So how did you buy fifty buildings?"

It was growing dark outside. The only light came from Charlie's desk lamp, which spread a warm circle in the room. Olivia's face was obscured in shadow. The secretaries had gone home, and they were alone.

"You're my lawyer, so you can't tell nobody, right?"

Charlie wondered whether the ghetto diction was part of her act, as it seemed to come and go. "It's a protected relationship," he said.

Olivia nodded, reassuring herself. "When Jimmy died, the man give me something," she said.

Charlie didn't know if she meant a particular man or the white establishment generally. "He gave you something?"

Olivia nodded. "Gave me an envelope with some money in it, told me to keep quiet. I didn't even look at how much at first—I was scared. But I knew it was more money than I'd ever seen. So I put the envelope in a jar down cellar and left it there. Never looked at it and never told no one."

"Was it a settlement?" Charlie needed to know.

Olivia shook her head. "Wasn't no settlement. I never agreed to nothing," she said proudly.

Charlie let this new knowledge settle over him; it was what he'd known all along but hadn't wanted to admit. Because otherwise none of it made sense. Someone had to have been paid, somewhere, sometime. And it started here; if the family was satisfied, there could be no protest, and Olivia was the family. It was what he hadn't understood about the case, but really it was the same old thing, the same old corruption, the same old evil.

"So they bribed you," he said. Because it was simple finally. You could make it more complicated, but in the end it was a bribe, impure and simple. While he had been concentrating on the cover-up, he hadn't asked the obvious question: Why had Olivia gone away and then resurfaced twenty years later? The police had packed the coroner's jury and bribed the family. They camouflaged it with Cap Norman's phony settlement while slipping Olivia the real money. Charlie had to hand it to them. They had been smart in approaching Olivia. If they got her, the brothers would be no problem.

Olivia sat still, her face betraying no emotion. Charlie expected her to deny it, but all she said was, "Call it a bribe, but it was all I was gonna get."

Charlie thought of the black ministers preparing to march back in 1959, which was a brave thing in those days. And of the newspapers that started slow but ended up saying the right things. He thought of his own naive belief in the legal system. But he couldn't say Olivia was wrong. She was just out for herself. "I called it a bribe because that's what it was," he said. "They offered you money and in return you kept quiet. Who gave it to you, Olivia?"

She looked at him again, as if for reassurance. Her eyes were moist, and for reasons he didn't understand, Charlie felt a sudden strong sexual attraction to her. He wanted to take her on his office rug and bury his face between her gray legs. The feeling was so strong that his hands began to quiver and as if she sensed this, Olivia crossed her legs and smiled slightly. "The chief," she said.

Charlie thought of the fat, perspiring retiree. "Martin?"

"That man wouldn't even talk to me. The other one."

"Tanner?" Charlie said, incredulous. Amazing, and yet it made perfect sense. Tanner would have been Martin's bagman, removed from the direct line of command but in touch with everyone. There would have been no reason for anyone to suspect him.

Olivia nodded. "We knew each other," she said.

Charlie looked at the woman, astonished, for while he might have thought of the bribe, he had never suspected this. "You were lovers?"

Olivia didn't respond directly. This wasn't her language. "We knew each other," she repeated. "He gave me the money so we'd have something, for Jimmy being killed, you know."

Olivia seemed to consider Tanner's bribe to be in the nature of a humanitarian gift. As she said, she wasn't going to get anything else. It was completely understandable, depending on your assumptions. Sometime after the initial confrontation, Tanner would have been dispatched to see if anything could be worked out. The D.A. wouldn't have wanted to know, but it would have been implicit in his instructions. Resolve this any way you can. Tanner could even have acted on his own, could have sensed something from Olivia's manner. And so Tanner had done his job and it only cost the city a few thousand dollars. Then they got rid of the two cops, and everything would have been fine if Paley hadn't had an attack of conscience.

Charlie wondered what Tanner thought of his girlfriend's suing the city for millions after all this time, but he doubted the chief was concerned. While Charlie now had proof of the cover-up, he couldn't say anything, because anything he said would implicate his client and ruin the case. It was clever.

"How could you do it?" he asked. "Didn't you care?"

Now anger replaced Olivia's soft sexuality. "Do what? Take the money? 'Bribe' is an easy word for you. Easy for you to make fun because I want money for my baby brother. But tell me this: if money's not important, then how come white people have it all? Why is that, Mr. Lawyer? I never had anything, so I bought an apartment and used the rent to take care of my family. My brothers were so hurt up they never got right. Two of them are still out to the hospital. I used the money to help them. That's just life for black folks."

"Don't forget you helped yourself, Olivia."

She stood up. "Damned right, and I'm glad I did. But you said yourself, ain't nothing you can do. So you go back to court and convince that jury to get us our justice. That way I can help my people some more."

Then Olivia turned and walked out of the office, her footsteps echoing down the hall until finally the slamming outer door silenced them and Charlie was left alone in the darkened room.

Thirty-seven

On Sunday mornings, Bob felt invisible. It was a hole in the week that reminded him of the holes in his life, places where people should have been. It was as if he belonged nowhere. He knew he had lived in Milwaukee too long. He couldn't walk down the street without remembering something he would have preferred to forget. The papers were always writing about roots, but Bob's were more like tourniquets.

Occasionally, he fantasized about moving someplace else. He would even browse the ads in *Editor and Publisher*, trying to imagine what it would be like to live in Arizona or Hawaii, where he wouldn't know anyone. But except for his short stay in New York, he had never gone anywhere. His family hadn't taken vacations, and when he was married they couldn't afford one. Now he had some money, but no one to take along. Like it or not, he was probably stuck with Milwaukee and it with him.

But who had to travel? Downer Avenue seemed as broad as the Champs-Elysées this morning and just as austere in the late winter sunlight. Few cars were moving, and except for the crowd entering the Episcopal church, there weren't many people either. Bob watched his reflection walk by the empty shops and wondered idly where it was going.

He turned in at the Coffee Trader and reflected that it was nice to have a restaurant in the neighborhood where you could get dried cashews and white wine even if you never ate such things yourself. But lately the ambiance had begun to pall on him. When nice Catholic girls from the south side

started to fake British accents and wear black nail polish, it was time to find
another hangout.

Someone waved, and Bob recognized Andy Hedig sitting alone. He
looked around, as if Andy might be gesturing to someone else, but he was
the only one in the vestibule, so he walked over. A paperback copy of *War
and Peace* lay open on the table and might have been put there for show if
the pages hadn't been falling out of it. Most politicians confined their reading to pornographic novels and the newspapers. Andy was wearing a corduroy jacket and looked remarkably relaxed for a man in the middle of a
campaign.

"Catching up on your reading?" Bob asked.

Andy smiled, embarrassed. His teeth were gapped, and there were small
fine lines around his eyes. "It's better than position papers. Anyway, Tolstoy
teaches you humility, and a politician can always use more of that. Sit down?"

Bob took the chair and a waitress brought coffee. They took their time
buttering rolls, then Andy said, "I'm glad you came by. I wanted to call, but
it seemed awkward."

It was awkward all right. Bob couldn't figure the guy out. He had been
sleeping with his wife for months, and now Hedig wanted to talk. Still, Bob
couldn't help liking Andy, with his books and wrinkled forehead. If things
had been different, they would have been friends. Andy smiled self-consciously. "Of course we both know about you and Sarah," he said.

"Of course," Bob said, then, not wanting to be a wise-ass, he added,
"That's over."

Andy nodded. "I'm not so sure you're right about that."

Bob didn't want to seem too interested, but the hairs on the back of his
neck began to tingle. "What do you mean?"

Andy shrugged. "It's none of my business, but I've known Sarah a long
time. She doesn't like to give up on things. I don't think she really knows
what she wants yet."

Andy sounded like a marriage counselor, but it was generous of him to
say this. He didn't have to make the gesture, or any gesture, toward his
wife's lover, and most men wouldn't have. But there was no point in Bob's
getting his hopes up. If Sarah wanted to go on together, all she had to do
was tell him so. As much as he hated the suburbs, she could have kept him
there for life by saying she wanted him, and she hadn't. "Maybe," he
admitted.

"We're getting divorced," Andy said. "Sarah's filing the day after the
election. I thought you'd like to know."

Bob was surprised. He had thought Sarah would go back to Andy out of insecurity. And while he appreciated Andy's telling him, it was confusing. He wondered where he stood. All around them people were eating, the heavy Sunday *Times* spilling from their tables onto the floor. His picture and byline were everywhere, yet no one recognized him. Still, it seemed inappropriate to be sharing confidences with Andy. He drank his coffee and changed the subject. "How's the campaign going?"

Andy spread his hands in a gesture of resignation. "You probably know better than I do. Everybody talks about strategy as if we know what we're doing, but by the end it's the blind leading the blind. I go where they tell me and shake every hand I see. To tell the truth, I don't think it makes any difference. Someone told me Roosevelt beat Al Smith the first time because a majority of the voters thought he was Teddy running for reelection."

Bob laughed. Hedig had changed. He was more relaxed now, more open. "That's a good story," he said. "But it probably wouldn't work for you."

Andy nodded. "But we're doing all right. I'm a little surprised, frankly, considering the mayor's popularity."

"Sounds like you're getting soft on your opponent."

Andy smiled at the double entendre. "Not exactly. It's like two fighters beating each other's brains out for fifteen rounds and then hugging. I think Mueller's getting to like me a little better, though. He walked over to shake hands after our last debate."

"Is that why you're here drinking coffee on a Sunday instead of standing outside a church on the north side?"

"Don't tell my campaign manager."

"Your secret's safe with me," Bob said. "Seriously, though, what's going to happen?"

"Seriously, as in off-the-record and I didn't really say this?" Taking Bob's silence for assent, Andy said quietly, "I think I've got a good chance." He spoke softly as if he couldn't quite believe it. "Mueller's been hurt badly by the Norman trial. I think they made a serious mistake by not trying to settle earlier. Now, it doesn't really matter who wins. Voters will figure where there's smoke there's fire. And he's old and he's been in for a long time. In some cultures, that would be an advantage, but not here, not even in Milwaukee, which, when you look at it, is kind of like another culture compared to New York or San Francisco."

Bob noticed that Andy didn't use the royal "we" the way most politicians did, nor did he speak of himself in the third person. He was a modest man, though most people wouldn't see it through the clothes and the house. "What would you do?" Bob asked.

"If I won, you mean? My mother used to say that the trouble with applying for something is that you might get it, but I think I'd really enjoy being mayor. I've got some ideas and a file cabinet full of position papers, but the truth is I have no idea what I'd do. I guess I'd hire the best people I could and then we'd see."

This was about as honest as candidates ever got. But it wasn't Hedig's fault. Voters expected politicians to sound as if they had the answers to everything. If a candidate admitted he didn't know something, the word would go out that he was indecisive. There was security in believing that someone somewhere knew what the hell was going on, even if it wasn't true. The fact was politicians were no different than anyone else. No matter how much they talked about their experience and legislative records, most weren't prepared to do the jobs they were elected to do. They learned what they needed to know while doing them, which was as good a system as any, as least the good ones did.

"Maybe you'll get a chance to find out," Bob said.

"Let's hope so. I'm glad we had a chance to talk." Then Andy gathered his things and left Bob alone at the table. Except he no longer felt alone. People moved noisily around him, and Bob had a sense of possibility that had been lacking for too long. The owner of the restaurant was trying to make a comparison with Ghirardelli Square in his advertisements. Bob had never been to San Francisco, but now he imagined he was having breakfast there. Fans turned languorously on the ceiling moving the heavy air, and it reminded him of Sarah.

Suddenly, he was tired of being single. Since Margie left, he had gotten used to coming home to an empty house and making dinner with only the evening news for company. He had become accustomed to sleeping alone and waking up in an empty room. Even the minor-league deprivation of solitary weekends and canned cranberry sauce in cafeterias on Christmas Day had become acceptable.

There were no children and his parents were dead. So he no longer had a family, and most of his friends were married or had moved on. It had happened gradually, this isolation, and he had always believed it would be temporary. Something—*someone,* let's be honest—would come along to end it, and so he had waited, figuring this was how things happened, that it was like ordering pizza or getting your television repaired.

Even when he moved into his parents' house, his inheritance, and had

begun the endless pattern of mowing and raking, of spackling and paint-
ing, of sanding and varnishing walls and floors that would only need to be
painted and sanded again, he had assumed it wouldn't last. For it was obvious that the house was too much for a single man. He was just getting it into
shape. Sooner or later he would move, but it had been twelve years and
slowly, gradually, the house had fallen into disrepair, mirroring its owner.
His hair was turning gray and there was loose skin under his jaw, and still
there was no end in sight.

It tired him to think about it, exhausted him in fact. He wanted to ask
Sarah to have him back. If he wasn't exciting enough, he'd try to revitalize
himself. Because out of all the loneliness and longing and ambivalence about
his job, he had finally made a decision. She was what he wanted, actually
what he needed. He didn't know why a Sunday morning chat with her
husband was what it had taken to convince him, but that's the way it
had worked out. Now all he needed to do was persuade her to want him
too.

After talking to Olivia, Charlie called Donna and said he was going out of
town overnight. Then he drove north with no clear destination, passing
through quiet towns with orderly main streets and neatly laid-out neighborhoods, not noticing where he was until he arrived in Sister Bay at ten
o'clock.

Door County was a tourist mecca in the summer, filled with people
escaping from Chicago and Milwaukee, but at this time of year there was
only one motel open and no restaurant. Charlie bought tuna fish, milk, and
bread and ate dinner on his bed. He spent the next day walking in Peninsula
State Park. At night he drove to Sturgeon Bay and ate whitefish in a restaurant with a polka band. If people thought there was anything odd about a
stranger in a business suit visiting Door Country in mid-March, they were
too polite to say so.

Charlie's conversation with Olivia had had a powerful effect, though
not one he could have predicted. He would have expected to feel outrage.
She had withheld evidence as he was preparing to go to trial, evidence that
could not only prejudice the jury but could even result in criminal charges.
Charlie knew he had a right to be angry, but he wasn't. He didn't even want
to quit the case. Left out was closer, but mostly he felt like a fraud. Olivia
had toyed with him, and when he tried to confront her, she just walked out.
What right did he have to represent a woman who was clearly tougher and
more intelligent than he was?

Olivia had used what she had—her body—to make a deal, and it was a good one, a stake in life. Then she turned this into a fortune. In a way, it was the American Dream. If things were different, they would be writing her up in the women's magazines as the model female CEO. And while Charlie thought this ought to bother him, the fact was it didn't. He wondered at his lack of moral indignation. Because caring was what Charlie was all about, what his career was based on. It was what he gave his clients, what made him a good lawyer. If he didn't object to Olivia's behavior, didn't care about graft and corruption, what was he anyway? One of them? His client was suing the city, and they had bought her, even if she wouldn't stay bought. It was confusing.

But money wasn't. Money was very real, which was why people sued other people for it. You couldn't gauge love or compassion or even guilt except in concrete terms. You were this guilty in years in prison or in dollars you had to pay. Yet money had always made Charlie uncomfortable. Donna said he was phobic on the subject, but Charlie thought he was realistic. In almost any situation, people liked to reassure themselves by saying that it wasn't the money, whatever the "it" might refer to. Money was never the acknowledged reason things happened. There were always other explanations. The trouble with this was that in Charlie's experience, it was never true. It was always the money. Money had kept Olivia quiet after her brother was killed, and the possibility of more money brought her into his office to reopen the case. It wasn't that Olivia didn't care about Jimmy, but Charlie hadn't seen a tear since they met. She would probably say she couldn't afford to cry.

Money was what it was all about. Justice, if it should happen to occur, was only a by-product. And if Charlie had trouble accepting this, it shouldn't have to trouble anyone else. Alone in the woods, however, Charlie knew that what had really upset him was the fact that he was deluding himself. For years, he had labored under the conceit that he understood himself, knew what was really important. So now he was going into the biggest trial of his life, defending a slumlord who had taken hush money, and he wanted desperately to do it. This wasn't Charlie Simons. No one who knew him would say it was.

And if Charlie didn't exactly blame Olivia—the truth was he didn't know what he thought about her—he wasn't at ease suing the city under these circumstances. Olivia's taking a bribe didn't make what the police had done right, but it changed the way Charlie felt about Rogan and Paley. They were assholes and probably should never have been cops in the first place.

But it was harder to condemn them now. Compared to Tanner and Martin, with their offices and vacation homes, Rogan and Paley seemed like dupes with bad teeth and blue-collar accents.

Charlie wondered if he had taken the case for the wrong reasons, because he wanted the police department to be worse than it was, more evil, and therefore needed to see corruption where there was really nothing wrong. But there was plenty wrong here. The whole thing smelled, and he felt stupid for taking so long to see it. He imagined Dolan and his team laughing at his bumbling attempts to build a case.

But why should that be so important? It was sheer vanity to think his stupidity mattered. What really counted was even more basic, though he seemed to have forgotten it. A boy had been shot, not an especially good boy, not an honor student or a Merit Scholar. But a boy nonetheless. A boy who hadn't had a chance to live out his life and make the same mistakes everyone else made. And he had been murdered by public servants who had then been allowed to walk away. The city had tried to conceal this. That was wrong and should be punished. So what it came down to was really very simple: the guilty should be punished. It didn't matter what Charlie thought of Olivia or she of him. It didn't matter if Tanner and the others thought he was a Boy Scout. It didn't matter what kind of person Jimmy Norman had been. None of that counted. All that mattered was persuading this jury made up of ordinary, scared people that the police had done something wrong. This new realization was enough to allow Charlie to get back in his car and go home.

The phone rang at two in the morning. Charlie heard laughter and a voice made hoarse by drinking and smoking. "So you found out about my little girlfriend," Tanner said. "Too bad you can't do fuckall about it."

"I don't need to. I've got enough," Charlie said, knowing he shouldn't be talking. But Tanner intrigued him. He wouldn't be doing this if he weren't fascinated by evil.

"Maybe I'll just tell that reporter everything."

"I wish you would," Charlie said. "You can't say anything about Olivia without implicating yourself, and then you'd make my case, save me some work."

The laughter was gone now. "Maybe you should just think about this: your witnesses are scared shitless and your client doesn't trust you. You don't watch it, you might get some of that police brutality you talk about."

"Tough guy," Charlie said. "Hitting on women and old men. You're just not that bad, Tanner. I'm going to get your ass any way I can." It was true. He wasn't scared, sitting on the edge of his bed. But after he hung up, he couldn't get his hands to stop shaking for fifteen minutes, and then he was wide awake, thinking, but not about Tanner or even Olivia.

He remembered walking with his father back in Hartford. It was cold, and he couldn't have been more than four or five. Men like his father didn't wear casual clothes. No down jackets or blue jeans, even on Saturday, because it would mean they were working class. Even on his day off, his father wore a tie. Charlie remembered his red ears and the misted lenses of his steel-framed glasses, remembered the slight hesitation as his father reached in his pocket for a dime for the Salvation Army and the respectful way the pharmacist greeted him. Then the long walk home in the cold until finally it was too much and his father lifted him in his strong arms and carried him. Then, aloft in his father's arms forty years later, Charlie slept.

Thirty-eight

A larger crowd gathered when the trial resumed on Tuesday, but Charlie doubted it would last. Trials had a half-life of a week. If they dragged on beyond that, people got tired and followed the proceedings on TV or in the paper. As he made his way through the clutch of people at the entrance, he saw Dolan waving at him. "What's up?" Charlie asked.

"I've been authorized to offer a settlement."

Charlie was surprised but not astonished. Their case wasn't as strong as he would have liked, but every day the trial went on it embarrassed the mayor. With the election two weeks off, Mueller wanted it to go away, but his lawyer looked miserable. "I thought you were going to kick my ass," Charlie said smiling.

"I would, but this wasn't my idea," Dolan said. "Two million, no admission of guilt, and it's over. What do you say?"

Despite his ambivalence about Olivia, Charlie hated to be cut off, to be cheated of a verdict. Win or lose, he wanted to follow it through. "I'll have to talk to my client," he said.

"Talk fast," Dolan said. "Court's in ten minutes."

Charlie took the family to a meeting room. "It's not a hundred million, but it's fair," he said. "With this jury, we might end up with nothing. I advise you to accept."

The brothers nodded their heads as if they agreed, but Olivia looked around the room as he spoke. Charlie knew she had talked to Tanner, but what could he have said? Settle or we talk to the papers? It would benefit no one if the story got out. The brothers remained silent, waiting for Olivia. "What does Mr. Isaacson think?" she asked.

The trial seemed to have shrunk Isaacson, who now deferred to Charlie in all things. Bill ran his fingers through his long hair. "I think Mr. Simons is right," he said. "It's not all we hoped for, but it's reasonable."

Respect drained from Olivia's face, and Charlie felt sympathy for her. The offer might be fair, but it was a fraction of what Isaacson had encouraged her to go for and now he was telling her to take it and go away. Her smart Jew lawyer was giving up and Olivia was plainly disappointed. "Don't seem fair to me," she said. "And I don't care if it is. Jimmy and Daddy died over this, and we got a courtroom full of people out there waiting. The city wants us to give that up, they got to be willing to pay more than this."

Charlie could see where she was going. "If you want to go on, Olivia, we will," he said. "It's up to you. But the district attorney didn't want to settle. He's acting on orders direct from the mayor. This is probably as good an offer as we'll get. I mean, this is it."

"Uh-huh," Olivia said. "And it ain't good enough." Now the brothers nodded, though they didn't seem enthusiastic. Olivia stood to end the meeting. "You'll just have to beat them, Mr. Lawyer." Then she surprised Charlie by smiling broadly. "And I know you can."

Charlie couldn't help laughing at Olivia's turnabout. He was on an enormous merry-go-round with no idea where it would stop, but the ride was exhilarating. "I'm glad to have your support, Mrs. Brown," he said. "Let's go in there and kill them."

Charlie and Isaacson had agreed to save Fenster and Tommy and lead with Magnusen because he was the stronger witness. In a way, it was a wash. They could lead with Tommy and finish strong, but the way things were going, Charlie thought they'd lose the jury if they didn't do something impressive. He wanted to feel confident going into his closing argument. He hadn't been getting much help and it was just the family; he couldn't understand why Andy Hedig wasn't more aggressive. If he were running for mayor, he 'd be putting out press releases every day. Even the media seemed to be holding back. He smiled at the irony. Here he was, in a crowded courtroom, surrounded by reporters, and he felt ignored.

The witness was sworn in and Charlie approached. Magnusen was wearing a brown suit and green tie and looked alert. "Mr. Magnusen," Charlie began. "You are presently employed by the Federal Bureau of Investigation, aren't you?"

Magnusen nodded. "I've worked for the Bureau for eighteen years," he said.

"Before that you were on the Milwaukee police force?"

"First I was a patrolman, then a detective." You could see Magnusen was still proud of his promotion.

"Were you present on the night Jimmy Norman was killed?"

"I was first on the scene. First plainclothes, I mean. I came with Detective Moran."

"Detective Moran is deceased," Charlie said for the benefit of the jury. "Would you describe briefly the scene when you arrived and what happened immediately afterward?"

Magnusen produced a small notebook. "We arrived at 9:12 P.M.," he read. "Mr. Norman was down, and a crowd had begun to gather with people coming out of the tavern across the street. Moran and I each took one of the patrolmen. I got Rogan."

"Was it your impression that Officer Rogan was nervous?"

"No," Magnusen said. "That surprised me. He was cool as a cucumber. He showed me where he was when he shot, and I put a block of ice there and wrote my report."

"There was disagreement about this later, wasn't there?"

Magnusen nodded. "He said that in all the commotion, he'd pointed out the wrong spot and that he was really a lot closer, which is what the ballistics report said."

"But you testified that in your opinion Rogan wasn't nervous."

Magnusen nodded. "There wasn't any commotion either. Just a few guys standing around. Later, more people showed up."

"Are you saying then that Officer Rogan was lying?"

Dolan objected almost before Charlie could finish the question. "Conclusion," he said irritably. "How can one man know another's state of mind?"

"We're not talking about his state of mind," Charlie said. "I asked Mr. Magnusen his opinion as to whether or not Rogan was lying."

"Go on," Alberts said.

"Sure he was lying," Magnusen said, and seemed glad to say it. "How can you make a mistake like that? He had to know how far away he was when he fired. He almost blew the kid's head off he was so close. He was just trying to cover himself, make it look like he couldn't have stopped him any other way."

Dolan objected to this. "Your Honor, I ask that this last statement be stricken from the record and that the jury be asked to disregard. It's an improper opinion."

Alberts scratched his ear. "You're probably right," he said. "But this has been a long trial with a lot of testimony, so I'm going to let it stay. Denied. Go on, Mr. Simons."

Technically the judge was wrong, and everyone knew it. Alberts had been letting too much in all along. Dolan had a right to be pissed. But Charlie was grateful for any breaks. "So you think it was unnecessary for Officer Rogan to shoot the victim?" he continued.

"Not if he was as close as they said he was, six feet or whatever it was."

"The ballistics experts said Officer Rogan's gun was only inches away when he fired," Charlie said. "Your testimony is that if he was that close there was no necessity to fire, that he could have stopped Jimmy Norman some other way?"

"Of course," Magnusen said simply, as if Charlie were slow.

"Is it your opinion that Officer Rogan was encouraged to change his story by someone else in the department, Mr. Magnusen?"

Dolan objected before Magnusen could answer, and this time Alberts sustained.

"Let me put it this way," Charlie said. "Were you personally disturbed by the response of the department and the district attorney to Jimmy Norman's murder?"

"I was disgusted. It's stayed with me for twenty years. That's why I quit."

"Do you think the response of police department officials was motivated in any way by race, Mr. Magnusen?"

Dolan objected again. "He's asking the witness to speculate on matters he has no personal knowledge of," the district attorney said.

Charlie turned to the judge. "This goes to the heart of our case. How can I demonstrate a conspiracy to cover up the truth about the murder if I can't show motivation?"

Alberts thought this over. "I'll allow it. The witness may have some special knowledge of the workings of the department at that time."

Magnusen spoke slowly, as if to a child. "Sure, it was racial," he said. "Everybody knew that. It was a racist department."

Dolan objected, but Alberts sat him back down immediately.

"Why was it racist?" Charlie said. "I mean, in what way?"

Magnusen shrugged. "There were no black officers to speak of, and it was openly talked about, 'nigger this, nigger that.' It was very casual—no one made much of it, but no one had to. It was common knowledge, like I said."

"That may be true," Charlie said, "but the district attorney is right. You can't really testify about the opinions of others. So just to clarify, these observations are opinions you have based on your personal experiences as a police officer, is that right, Mr. Magnusen?"

Magnusen agreed and Charlie went on. "Even if what you say is true about the department in general, most officers never shot any blacks. Most did their jobs regardless of their feelings about race, wouldn't you agree?"

"Sure. There were a lot of good cops on the force."

"So Officer Rogan's racism was of a more virulent sort than usual, and this led him to value human life less than others did. Jimmy Norman's death was the result of his racism, but the conspiracy to cover the murder up was also motivated by racism, according to your testimony. In other words, Chief Martin and the district attorney wouldn't have acted as they did had the victim been white, wouldn't have tolerated Rogan's behavior. Is that correct?"

"That's my opinion," Magnusen said.

"Fine. What we want here is your opinion. Now, let me ask you this. In your work with the FBI, have you seen other police departments attempt to cover up crimes?"

Magnusen nodded. "Probably fifteen or twenty over the years. It happens a lot."

"How would you compare the Milwaukee investigation with these other cases?"

"It was the worst," Magnusen said. This produced a rumble in back, and Charlie waited a moment until it subsided.

"What made it so bad?" he asked.

"What you said before. It was racial. Everyone knew Rogan was a bad cop. Everyone knew it, but no one did anything."

"Was that unusual? As you said, racism was common in the department in 1959. Things were different then."

Magnusen nodded. "Sure, that's right. Plenty of guys didn't like blacks, but Rogan was different. You'd hear stories about him in the locker room, and he had a file a mile long. When the chief and the D.A. got behind him, it wasn't like backing up any other cop, which you'd expect. They were saying this killer was OK. It made me sick to my stomach."

"Were you encouraged to tell this to the coroner's jury?"

Magnusen smiled grimly. "It was the opposite. They kept trying to get me to rewrite my report so it would agree with Rogan. But I stuck to what I said the first night."

Charlie waited a moment for this to register with the jury. Then he said, "Mr. Magnusen, you have testified that you were so disillusioned by the official cover-up of Jimmy Norman's murder that you left the police force. Can you tell us now, in your opinion, just who was involved in this race-based conspiracy?"

"I think it went all the way up," Magnusen said.

"All the way up," Charlie repeated. "I'd like you to be very specific about what you mean. Are you including, for example, the deputy inspector and the chief of police?"

Magnusen nodded. "Sure, they were in it," he said.

"And in your opinion, was the district attorney a part of this cover-up conspiracy?"

"They were all working on it," Magnusen said. "I'd go in and they'd be in the office, and it was pretty obvious what they were talking about."

"But you never heard them discussing this openly?"

"No," Magnusen said. "It was just kind of understood."

"You mean you understood this to be the case?"

"Me and half the guys in the station house."

"But you're not speaking for them," Charlie said, anticipating Dolan's objection.

"Nobody can. Most of them are dead already," Magnusen said.

"What about the mayor? In your opinion, did it go that far?"

"All the way," Magnusen repeated. This caused an undercurrent of whispering, and Alberts used his gavel to quiet the room.

Charlie waited. Then he said, "That's all I have."

The district attorney hadn't said much when Charlie turned down his settlement offer, but the way he approached Magnusen, Charlie could see Dolan was angry. Probably he had argued with Mueller and only made the offer in the first place because he thought it would be accepted. Now he was embarrassed to have misjudged the situation. "Mr. Magnusen," he said sharply. "You testified that the reason you left the Milwaukee police force was that you were disgusted with the corruption in the department, isn't that so?"

Magnusen nodded his head.

"You further testified that this has bothered you for twenty years," Dolan continued. "Well, this is terrible. I'm certain that a man as conscientious as you are would suffer for it. I wonder, did you express that concern by joining in the civil rights movement in any way?"

"No," Magnusen said. "I was a federal agent."

"Of course," Dolan said. "But as a private citizen you might have made a donation, say, to the Urban League or the NAACP Legal Rights Fund? Perhaps the Southern Christian Leadership Conference or the United Negro College Fund?"

Magnusen shook his head no.

"Were you perhaps active in counseling troubled black youths?"

"What would I have counseled them about?" Magnusen asked.

Dolan ignored this. "Did you join the Big Brothers, help out with the Boy Scouts, the Boys and Girls Clubs?"

Magnusen continued shaking his head. "I didn't join anything like that."

"Ah," Dolan said. "Not a joiner. Well, did you do anything else, anything at all I might not have mentioned, to express your support for black people and your outrage at their suffering, or did you just feel bad?"

This was a rhetorical question. Dolan was just trying to undermine Magnusen's testimony. Charlie felt for Magnusen, but there was nothing he could do. Dolan was like a matador, positioning the bull then inserting his swords while he pirouetted around.

"The thing that puzzles me," Dolan said now, "is why you didn't say anything when it might have done some good. Why you waited those twenty years to speak up?"

"I tried," Magnusen said.

"Really?" Dolan said. "That's interesting because there is no record in department files of your having tried to do anything to reverse this supposed miscarriage of justice. No letters or reports. Nothing. Just like your record of support for black people."

"What could I do?" Magnusen protested. "It was their word against mine."

"I see," Dolan said. "So instead of trying to improve what you say you saw as a racist institution, you just walked away?"

"Not really," Magnusen said.

"And now," Dolan said, gaining momentum, "twenty years later, you tell us how much all of this has been bothering you. It's easy to say, isn't it, Mr. Magnusen? And isn't it also easy to slander men who served the city faithfully and didn't quit just because things didn't go their way? Men, I might add, who are dead and thus unable to contradict your testimony?"

"It's not easy," Magnusen said quietly. But Dolan had made his point and made it well. What kind of outrage did you put on ice for such a long time?

"You also testified that you've seen twenty police cover-ups in your time with the FBI, Mr. Magnusen."

David Milofsky

"About that many," Magnusen said.

"Too many to count?" Dolan said. "It seems you're a man who is drawn to corruption without ever being involved yourself. But tell me, have you ever intervened in any of these cases, spoken out, exposed the corruption you've seen? It must be tempting."

"It isn't like that. I'm a field agent."

"Exactly," Dolan said. "Just as you weren't in that dark street facing Jimmy Norman, so you weren't involved in any of these other alleged cover-ups. Your specialty seems to be coming in afterward, maybe even twenty years later, and then pointing your finger."

Magnusen was stunned. His mouth opened and closed like a fish, but he said nothing because there was nothing he could say. Dolan hadn't asked a question. He was just beating Magnusen up and there wasn't a thing Charlie could do to stop it.

"One more question, Mr. Magnusen," Dolan said. "I'm sure that an officer of such personal integrity and character would be recognized by his superiors. In your long career with the FBI, have you received any awards or commendations, any citations for bravery or distinguished service?"

Magnusen's reply was inaudible.

"I'm sorry," Dolan said. "I couldn't hear that and neither could the jury."

"No," Magnusen said.

Dolan hesitated for effect. Then, "I thought not. Thank you, Mr. Magnusen."

"He *should* thank him," Isaacson whispered. "He just kicked the hell out of our star witness."

Charlie had not been able to depose Fenster, but it didn't matter because what he had said on the phone was all he had to say. Still, that was valuable enough, assuming Dolan didn't find a way to demolish him too. When the old man came into the courtroom, however, Charlie's heart sank. Fenster was at least seventy, and his suit hung on him like a tent. He wore steel glasses and a set expression that made Charlie wonder if the man's jaw was wired shut. Fenster parted his hair in the middle, and a harsh horizontal line bisected his forehead, so Charlie decided to start with personal details in an attempt to humanize him.

"Mr. Fenster, even in 1959, it was somewhat unusual for a white family like yours to be living in the central city."

"I'd lived there for years. Owned my home. I couldn't afford to move."

"But you did get along with your neighbors there?"

"Didn't know them," Fenster said. "I used to have friends, but they'd moved by that time. I moved myself a few years later."

Charlie nodded. "Well, then, let's talk about the night of February 8, the night Jimmy Norman was killed. Could you tell the court exactly what you saw that night?"

Fenster leaned forward and looked directly at the jury. "I saw everything," he said. "From beginning to end."

"That's very good," Charlie said, a cold feeling beginning to spread in his stomach. "But could you be more specific about exactly what it was that you saw?"

Fenster sat back and squared his shoulders. Charlie noticed that his Adam's apple was prominent and red. "I don't know why I noticed, to tell the truth," he began. "It was a cold night, and there was nothing to see in the street, so I don't know why I was looking out the window, except I'd heard a car out there."

"Was that unusual? For cars to run up and down the street?"

"Not *unusual* maybe, but there was some shouting too. Anyway, I looked out and there was this police officer chasing a black boy. First they were just running down the street, and then the boy went up the walk of the house across the street from us."

"Mr. Fenster, do you have any idea why Jimmy Norman would have run up to that house? Had you seen him before? Did he have friends in the neighborhood?"

"I'd never laid eyes on him, and I know because later on I got a good look. I don't know why he ran, except he was trying to get away from that cop."

"All right. What happened next?"

"The one cop ran up after him, and then there was an explosion and the boy was down on the ground."

"Where was the other police officer all this time?"

"I didn't see him right away. He was in back, I guess. Anyway, I went over there with my boy, and he told us to go away."

"Who told you?"

"The second one did. I never said a word to the first one, didn't want to talk to him."

Charlie waited a moment. Then he said, "Mr. Fenster, did you at any time see Jimmy Norman make a menacing gesture or come at the first officer with a knife?"

Fenster shook his head no. "There wasn't no knife," he said. "Until later. When we came back from calling the station, they had put one in his hand."

"How do you know they did that?"

"Where'd it come from otherwise?" Fenster asked with inescapable logic.

Charlie waited again. He was pleased and surprised by Fenster's certainty and wanted the jury to notice it. "Thank you," he said finally. "No further questions, Your Honor."

After Dolan's cross of Magnusen, Charlie expected the worst, but Fenster seemed almost to rise in his seat to meet the district attorney, and his voice was strong as he answered Dolan's questions. "Mr. Fenster, I notice you're wearing glasses. With your vision, how can you be so sure there was no knife in Jimmy Norman's hand that night?"

"Didn't wear glasses then," Fenster said. "I don't even need them all the time now." The audience tittered and Fenster allowed himself a small smile. "Anyway, I was talking about when I walked across the street. Don't need 20/20 to see ten feet away."

Dolan nodded. Then he said, "I must say, Mr. Fenster, after reviewing your testimony in 1959 to the coroner's jury, I'm surprised by some of the things you've said today. You're aware of the inconsistencies?"

"I didn't tell the truth then," Fenster said baldly. "Not all of it."

"Then why should anyone believe you now?" Dolan asked.

"I'm not scared anymore. I was younger then, had a wife and family, a job. They could threaten me. But what can you do to me now, kill me? I'm going to die soon anyway."

Dolan backed off from this, but Fenster had managed to turn a negative comment around. There was no good way for Dolan to deny that threats had been made. "And why have you come forward at this time?" Dolan asked, pushing his only advantage. "Publicity?"

"I wouldn't have known about it if I didn't read the papers," Fenster said. "And I hope a lot more people read about what I'm saying because it's the truth. But that ain't why. I'm a sick man and I want to have a clear conscience when I go."

Fenster looked anything but sick, and Charlie felt some sympathy for Dolan. What had worked with Magnusen had fallen flat in his cross-examination of Fenster, but who could have predicted that? It was what made the law interesting. Dolan stood silent for a moment as if he were trying to think of some new way to shake Fenster's story, but nothing good was going to come from letting the old man continue to declare his willingness to die. Finally, he turned to the judge and said, "I have nothing more at this time."

"Back from the dead," Isaacson said as Alberts dismissed them for lunch. Charlie tried to thank Fenster, but he was surrounded by reporters and Charlie decided to let him have his day. As the old man had said, he didn't have much time left.

Tommy had never been a gazelle, light on his feet, graceful, or a good dancer. Even when he played basketball, he was no twinkle toes. The coach would look down the bench and say, "Go in and mix it up, Paley." And Tommy would. Six feet wasn't big anymore, but it was OK in those days, especially since he had the good shoulders on him. Tommy had always gotten respect from the other team, clogging things up inside while the other guys moved around, doing most of the shooting.

The only thing clogged up now was his sinuses, and they had been ever since he got off the plane. He had been freezing his ass too. You'd think it wouldn't bother him since he had grown up in Milwaukee, but Tommy couldn't stay warm. Anyway, he told himself, it was different now; before he could handle it, but he could handle lots of things then. Walking toward the courthouse, sliding on the slick pavement as the snow soaked through his cheap Italian shoes, he felt depressed. His whole life was one big fall waiting to happen.

But he still liked hanging around the courthouse, bullshitting the reporters covering the trial and talking to the lawyers. He'd miss it when it was over, though he wasn't exactly the star of the show. He wasn't even part of the lawsuit, and the Normans wouldn't give him the time of day. Not that Tommy expected them to thank him exactly—he knew he didn't deserve any medals for ratting out Rogan—but they wouldn't be here without him and that was a fact.

Tommy knew he wasn't like Magnusen, whom the press wrote up as the fair-haired boy, or even Rogan, who wouldn't talk to anyone. The Garbo of Wisconsin. But Tommy had something they didn't: Tommy was the only one who'd both been there when the kid was shot and was willing to talk about it. You had to figure that should count for something.

He walked up the courthouse steps and went to the second floor, where the lawyer was waiting. They had already gone over his testimony, so he didn't see why they were meeting again, but it wasn't his call. "So," he said, "today's the big day."

Simons wasn't smiling, but that was nothing new. Tommy didn't know why he couldn't buy some decent clothes. Lawyers had all the goddamned money, but this guy looked like his uncle Joe, who worked as a mortuary assistant down at Turner's and got his clothes off the stiffs. Tommy knew the trial was serious, but what would it cost Simons to crack a smile every month or so? They were on the same side, after all. Yet the lawyer always treated him like shit. Tommy liked the reporter better. Joseph was a regular guy who'd have a drink with you and shoot the shit a little. Simons always acted as if something smelled funny and the something was Tommy.

The lawyer had a blank legal pad in front of him and about a dozen pencils. "We've covered most of your testimony," he said. "I just had a few more questions."

Tommy was savvy enough to know that you didn't arrange last-minute meetings if everything was going according to plan. What were they going to discover now? "Magnusen fuck up?" he asked.

Charlie ignored this, but he moved in a way that let Tommy know he had hit something. This pleased him, though Magnusen had never done anything to him. It was just the self-righteous way he'd acted when they set up the tap on Rogan. You didn't mind seeing a guy like that fall on his face. "I want to go over the cover-up again," Charlie said. "Just to see if there's anything you might have forgotten."

"Forgotten?" Tommy had told the story so often, he could practically recite his testimony by heart. What was there to forget? The trouble was the opposite: he *couldn't* forget it. But there was no point in trying to explain that to this guy.

"We don't want any surprises when you get inside," Charlie said.

Tommy didn't like the implication that he'd been holding out. They'd have no fucking case without him. But he wasn't going to duke it out with Simons. "Go ahead," he said.

"OK. Moran and Magnusen were first on the scene. They took statements from you and Rogan, and then you went downtown. After that, the trouble started. You and Rogan had different versions of the murder and so did Magnusen. You say you tried to tell Moran the truth, but he didn't want to hear it. Am I right, so far?"

Tommy had an ancient superstition about speaking against the dead. Moran was a guy from the neighborhood. Tommy had known his mother and father, his cousins, the whole family. Besides, the detective had been OK with him, nothing that special, but OK, which was more than you could say for the others. He didn't like making it seem like Moran was dirty, but there wasn't much to do about that. "That's it."

"All right," Charlie continued. "So then you go in to see the chief and Tanner's there. They tell you to get your stories straight and, make a long story short, you do. Lathrop gets you off with the coroner's grand jury and everything's quiet for twenty years until you come forward with your statement. What I'm wondering is, did it ever occur to you that things went a little too smoothly back then?"

Tommy felt uncomfortable because he didn't know what the lawyer was getting at. It hadn't been so smooth for him, with Lu moving out and then getting bounced from the force. For that matter, the next twenty years weren't that quiet. The time he was in the joint wasn't smooth for damned sure. That was why he was here. But this guy was so cool and tough that Tommy knew he didn't care about how he'd been feeling, that that wasn't what he wanted to know. "Maybe so," he said carefully. "I didn't think about it that way."

"Were you surprised that the Normans went away so quickly and that none of those protest marches came off?" Charlie paused, not wanting to put words in Paley's mouth.

Tommy had mainly felt relief that it was over, but looking back, he could see the lawyer's point. He had expected two thousand screaming niggers to descend on them, but nothing happened, nothing at all. "Like I said, I didn't think about it," he said. "But now that you're asking, it does seem that way. You have to remember back then they didn't have these Guardians and all that shit." All week, Tommy had had to fight his way through crowds of chanting protestors to get to the trial. He was always worried someone would recognize him, but to these kids he was just an old white fart.

"Given what you know now, can you think of any reason things should have gone so smoothly then?" Simons went on.

The guy was really pushing this. It was like Twenty Questions; Tommy didn't know what he was supposed to say, but he wanted to give the right answer. Then, suddenly it was crystal clear, even if it had never occurred to him in 1959. "The fix was in?" he said, a touch of wonder in his voice.

It was so goddamned simple. Why hadn't he thought of it before? They had pressured them all to work on their stories, get them right. He remembered Moran saying they were going to get the jurors drunk at lunch. But no one had said a thing about money changing hands, and now Tommy felt cheated. He hadn't even been important enough to buy.

Simons didn't agree or disagree. "OK, now concentrate," he said. "Did any of those guys say anything to you about paying off? Did you see anyone being given a bribe?"

Tommy felt like an asshole, more stupid than wrong. "No," he said with real regret.

"To your knowledge," Charlie said, "did Chief Tanner or any elected official offer money to anyone connected with the case in order to make him change his story?"

Tommy shook his head. "They didn't have to," he said. "They just scared us into it." His clothes felt even flimsier now, and he worried that they'd fall off and leave him exposed in the courthouse. There seemed to be a draft somewhere in the room.

Simons closed his folder. Tommy could see he hadn't given him what he wanted. "Let's go on inside," Simons said.

After Dolan's dissection of Magnusen in the morning, Charlie figured the afternoon would be anticlimactic. Most of what Paley had to say was common knowledge and everyone knew he was a liar and a drunk. The only reason they were using him was that, except for Fenster, he was the only one who had actually been there. And cops, even bad cops, had credibility with juries. If Magnusen had been great, they might have tried to do without Paley. As it was, they had no choice. To make matters worse, he looked like hell in his lime-green sport coat and wrinkled shirt. Charlie didn't know what Dolan could say to make Paley look any more unreliable than he did. Maybe he'd just let the jury look at the sonofabitch for fifteen minutes.

It was depressing to think this was all they had left, but Charlie would just have to do what he could. He wondered if Olivia had any regrets now about turning down the city's offer. "Mr. Paley," he began, "I'm going to ask you some questions about the night of Jimmy Norman's death. First of all, did you know Officer Rogan well before that night?"

"Not really," Tommy said. "I'd see him around, you know. We played basketball against each other in high school."

"Did you know him well enough to understand his attitudes toward black people?"

"He didn't like them," Tommy said.

"How did you know that? Did he tell you?"

"He didn't have to—it was obvious. He called them jigs, spades, jungle bunnies, things like that."

There was some movement in the courtroom. Things had changed enough in twenty years that people were now uncomfortable with what had once been common parlance, at least in informal conversation. Anticipating Dolan's cross, Charlie asked, "Did you ever use words like this yourself?"

Tommy shifted in his chair. "Everyone did back then. I'm not proud of it, though."

Charlie ignored this. "If everyone used racist terms, if in fact the whole police department was racist . . ."

"Objection," Dolan said. "Conclusion is based on hearsay. Witness can't speak for the whole police department."

Alberts sustained. Charlie bowed his head for a moment. Then he continued. "In your opinion, Mr. Paley, what made Officer Rogan different from the others?"

"John was a tough guy," Tommy said. "He carried this special gun, it was a .357 Magnum, which wasn't so unusual, but it had a custom stock with stones on it for everyone he had shot. But it wasn't just that; like I said I knew about him from before. You weren't exactly scared of him, but John Rogan was known as one tough sonofabitch."

Dolan objected and Charlie raised his hand in resignation. "I want to ask you now specifically about the night of February 8, 1959. On that night did John Rogan say anything to you about blacks?"

Tommy nodded. "He said he was going to go check the houses on the block and see if he could get some niggers."

Charlie waited a moment for effect. "There were no blacks on the street at this time?"

"It was cold as hell," Tommy said. "You'd have to be crazy to be out on a night like that, but we were." The audience tittered, which buoyed Tommy up.

Charlie ignored the comedy. "And no one was committing a crime or disturbing the peace in any way?"

"Like I said, the street was deserted."

"There were two taverns in the vicinity," Charlie said. "Taverns in which considering the neighborhood, one might assume there would be black people. But Officer Rogan was not talking about going there. Your testimony is that he wanted to go into those houses instead. Now, when he said he was going to 'get' some blacks, what did that mean to you?"

Tommy looked bewildered, as if there was something beyond the obvious that Charlie wanted. "I didn't know, I mean, not really. He could have just been talking. John was a big talker all the time, you know. I told him I wouldn't go with him, though."

"He asked you to go with him?" Dolan would ask anyway, so Charlie might as well get it in first.

"I thought that's why he was telling me," Tommy replied.

Charlie nodded. "All right. Mr. Paley, we realize many people, including yourself, didn't like black people in 1959. But did you consider Officer Rogan's suggestion that you go and search for blacks to be unusual?"

"Sure, I did," Tommy said. "Most coppers wouldn't go looking for a fight."

"And that's exactly what Officer Rogan was doing, wasn't he? He wanted to go and look for people with the specific intention of doing them harm because they were black, isn't that correct?"

"Yes, sir. At least until Norman came along."

Charlie nodded grimly. "Exactly. Into this situation came Jimmy Norman, who admittedly was driving without a valid license, but otherwise was doing nothing wrong except for the defective taillight on his vehicle. Let me ask you, Mr. Paley, do you think Officer Rogan would have pursued a white driver as vigorously as he did Jimmy Norman?"

"Objection," Dolan called out. "Conclusion. Witness can't know how Rogan might have acted in a different situation."

Alberts thought this over. Then he said, "I assume Mr. Simons is trying to make a point with this. Go ahead."

"I doubt it," Tommy said. "But I don't really know."

"Well, then do you know of situations in which police officers did not pursue autos with defective taillights?"

"On a cold night like that, you'd usually forget it. The wind'll freeze your balls off if you go chasing a car on a cycle at twenty below."

"Thank you for the colorful detail, Mr. Paley. Now could you tell us if Jimmy Norman did anything to inflame the situation? Did he resist Officer Rogan, for example?"

"Not that I recall," Tommy said. "I wasn't right there, though. I was back a ways."

Charlie walked away, leaving Tommy sitting alone in the wooden witness's chair facing the room. "So, in your opinion, the only reason that Jimmy Norman was stopped, chased, and finally shot is that he was black. Is that correct, Mr. Paley?"

Tommy wouldn't have put it that way if he had a choice. He believed Rogan hadn't meant to shoot the kid, but he remembered how calm John had been and the smoke hanging in the cold night air and the smell of cordite. And how he had thought that to Rogan, Norman was just some nigger kid who had gotten himself dead, but basically so what. "That's about it," Tommy said. "That's how it looked to me."

"No more questions at this time," Charlie said and retreated to the plaintiff's table.

Dolan made a lot of Tommy's alcoholism being the reason for his discharge from the force. He went over his prison record, but he couldn't shake his testimony about Rogan, and, watching, Charlie thought Tommy displayed a kind of dignity in the midst of squalor. He cut an odd picture sitting in the witness chair in his bargain-store blazer, but somehow he managed to maintain a sense of himself and even rose to humor when Dolan said, "And now you're living in Hollywood, trying to make money out of this sordid episode."

Tommy smiled. "That's right. If you hear of anyone who's interested, I'd appreciate you giving him my number."

As they were leaving, Isaacson said, "Paley surprised me. I heard he was a real loser, but he did pretty well."

Charlie was thinking ahead, to Dolan's defense and closing arguments. "This case is full of losers," he said, mostly to himself. "Some just lose bigger than the rest."

Thirty-nine

Bob was used to having secrets. It was part of the business, knowing things and hoarding information. Reporters had gone to jail for the privilege, but on a more prosaic level it was simply a necessary element of the job. You accumulated facts haphazardly, often over a period of years, not knowing exactly how they would fit into a story, and sometimes they never did. He always laughed when a judge asked for a reporter's notes because most journalists carried their files in a pocket, and those were the organized ones. Many relied on their memories, which was as good a system as any.

Despite this habit, Bob was having trouble filing away Hometown Properties. It continued to work at him, and he didn't think it was because he had been ordered not to write about it; at least it wasn't only that. It bothered Bob that Olivia Brown was becoming a liberal icon while he sat on information. It wasn't up to him to decide these things, but he thought about it whenever he saw Olivia's serene dark eyes looking out at him from the newspaper. Which was why he went to Marcus Jackson's office that Saturday morning.

"A pleasure, Bobby," Marc said. "Slow news day?"

"Saturday always is. That's why you have your marches then. But actually I wanted to talk. Something's been on my mind and it sort of involves you."

Jackson had a large, kind face with tired eyes. Often he used banter to cover up his sadness with the way his life had gone, but now he gestured toward his office. "Come on in."

Framed pictures lined the walls of the room, pictures of Jackson and Martin Luther King, Jr., Jackson and Bobby Kennedy, Jackson and H. Rap Brown, and there in the corner, Jackson and a much younger Andy Hedig. Other than the photographs, the room was as spare as a priest's cell. Marcus settled himself behind his desk and looked expectantly at Bob. "What's on your mind? It's been a while since I've done any pastoral counseling."

For a moment, Bob didn't understand. Then he was embarrassed. "This isn't about Sarah," he said. He had been so absorbed in the trial that he'd practically forgotten about her, but naturally Marc had assumed that was why he had come.

Jackson looked confused, perhaps even annoyed. "Well, you're upset about something."

"I've been sitting on a story," Bob said.

Jackson shifted in his chair and crossed his legs. "What kind of story?"

"I'm not sure, but it started with you, actually something you were involved in a while ago. The Hometown trust protest?"

Jackson nodded and shrugged his large shoulders, to release the tension. He was almost imperceptibly more alert, though his eyes were still sleepy. "I remember. But I didn't see you there; you weren't working on that, were you?"

Bob shook his head. "No, I came across the clips a few weeks ago, when I was looking for something else."

"You don't want to tell me what that was, do you?"

Which was the point when you came down to it. Just as Sarah had come to him because she was uncomfortable holding onto what she suspected, so now Bob had come to Marcus Jackson. They were each trying to shift the load. "Can we keep this between ourselves?" Bob asked, feeling foolish. But he had promised Mike Klein. Telling Charlie Simons about it was one thing, but Jackson would hold a press conference, which Bob would have to cover. In effect he would have created his own story.

Marcus smiled, his teeth straight and white. "You're making me very curious, Bobby." He sat quietly for a moment, thinking. Then, "OK, sure, everything we say here is deep background. I will go to jail rather than reveal my source."

Marc was joking, but Bob knew he would keep his word. More important, he wanted to tell Jackson and he thought he should. Marc listened intently and made notes, but otherwise he didn't say anything. When Bob finished Marc shook his head. "I should have known," he said. "Makes me feel stupid. I mean, I should have figured something was funny when she

came in here asking about a lawyer. I knew about Jimmy getting shot, but it
was really before my time. I was just coming on here. I didn't know Olivia,
not really, so why come to me for advice?"

"She wasn't active down here, wasn't involved?"

Marcus laughed. "I think Olivia Norman Brown spent the last twenty
years shopping on Capitol Drive. Thing is, I didn't trust her, not at all. That
first day I remember I felt like I had got caught up in something, but I kept
making excuses for her and now I feel like a fool." He shook his head.
"What are you going to do?"

Bob moved in his chair. "Nothing. Mike Klein says there's no story. He
doesn't want to distract people with the trial going on. He says the press
would focus all the attention on Olivia's buildings and forget about the
cops."

"Smart man," Marcus said. "I agree with him too. Does that surprise
you?"

"A little," Bob said. Actually, he was relieved. He had done his duty and
no harm had come of it.

"You figured maybe I'd go picket the trial, and you'd be in the clear
because you didn't do it, right?"

"No. I asked you to keep this confidential, remember?"

"True enough. What, then? Expiation of guilt?" His voice was gentle
with an edge.

"Closer. The truth is it just pisses me off to see her on the tube every
night talking about justice."

"And is Olivia the first hypocrite you've dealt with, Bobby? What if she
was white? What would you be doing then?"

Bob felt anger rising. "If she was white we wouldn't hesitate a minute.
We'd have her ass all over the front page and pictures of her children too.
I'd get her son beat up in the schoolyard, and we'd do our best to get her
husband fired. Then we'd go down to the press club and buy drinks all
around and we'd feel good about it. We'd feel great. We're only cutting
Olivia a deal because she *is* black, which is what it always come down to
with you in the end, doesn't it, Marcus? Black and white."

"Damned right and you know it or you wouldn't be here on a Saturday
morning. We're friends, Bobby. I don't forget that. Friends look out for
each other. But you wouldn't be talking to me if you didn't think I had
some support. You're hoping I'll maybe do something you can't do or, if
not, give you permission to lay off. Whichever it is, my authority comes
from the color of my skin and I accept that. So go in peace and don't

worry about this anymore. It's OK with the niggers if Olivia Brown gets
her piece of the pie."

Bob couldn't help smiling, so Marcus did too. "How about you?" he
asked. "Is it all right with Marcus Jackson?"

Marc's smile became a grimace. "I don't like the woman," he said.
"God knows, I tried, but I just don't. I don't trust her either. But, yeah, it's
OK with me. I just want Charlie to win that damned case."

Bob stood to leave. He felt awkward now. "Maybe pastoral counseling
was what I needed after all," he said.

"I wouldn't be a bit surprised," Jackson said. "Half the people who
come in to see me have no idea what they're looking for." He laughed and
Bob could hear his bass voice echoing through the empty building as he
walked out to the street.

Tommy hated being back in Milwaukee. Thinking about it ahead of time,
when he was out in Los Angeles, it had seemed OK. Frightening but exciting too. Even when Dolan leaned on him, Tommy had reassured himself
that there was nothing they could do because he had already said what he
had to say. The one he feared was Rogan, who was in jail and had enough
to worry about just staying alive. But otherwise it had seemed all right. He
would come to town not like a celebrity maybe, but as someone anyway. He imagined being interviewed by reporters, jostling with the lawyers in court, and having his picture taken at Ratszch's with important
people.

It hadn't turned out that way, not even close. Since Simons had no
money, Tommy was staying at a retirement hotel on Kilbourne with halls
wide enough to accommodate walkers and wheelchairs. The stale smell of
flowers was always in the air, to cover the piss they'd be smelling otherwise.
And since he was on a per diem, fancy restaurants were out of the question.
If he went out at all, it was to the drugstore cafe at the Knickerbocker,
whose clientele seemed to consist exclusively of middle-aged women in
toreador pants and guys with more time on their hands than money. The
whole scene was so depressing that usually Tommy stayed in his room and
made beef stew on the hot plate in the corner while he watched old movies
on channel 18.

Still, it was funny how you could get your hopes up, so when this lady
next door knocked one night and said he had a call on the hall phone,
Tommy stopped and slicked his hair in the bureau mirror as if whoever
was calling was going to be able to see him. When he got to the phone, he

was breathing heavily, but the voice caught him by surprise. "You always were a shitty cop, Paley. It's good to see some things never change."

Tommy's heart beat in his throat, but he was curiously flattered. "Who is this?" he asked, though he knew.

"Never mind. Just remember whose town you're in."

"I already testified," Tommy said.

"You're up again this week." Which was true. Dolan had called him for the defense. "Why don't you tell the truth for once?"

"You mean perjure myself?"

"Call it what you want. Use your fucking brain for a change, know what I mean?"

Tommy's heart was beating so hard he was amazed it wasn't audible. "You can't scare me," he said hopefully.

"I can do anything I want, asshole. Remember that." Then there was a dial tone.

Tommy stood, holding the receiver in his hand until he noticed a small woman standing behind him. He wondered if she had heard the conversation, because she was looking at him funny. Then he noticed the receiver shaking in his hand. "Are you waiting for the phone?" he asked, putting it back.

The woman had gray hair and was wearing a pink pillbox hat that she probably bought to imitate Jackie Kennedy twenty years ago. She was just on the edge between possible and old. "You go ahead," she said. "I can wait."

Tommy thanked her and dialed. When Joseph came on, he said, "Tanner just called. He told me to watch out."

"How do you know? Did he identify himself?"

"I recognized his voice; you don't forget that. But he didn't care. He said he could do anything he wanted to me."

"Stay where you are," Bob said. "I'll be down in fifteen minutes."

Tommy looked terrible. He was still wearing the pastel jacket, but now the creases in the arms were lined with dirt and his stomach stretched the buttons on his open shirt. Bob could see why Simons hadn't been enthusiastic about him as a witness, but he couldn't help liking the guy. Tommy embraced him in the doorway, causing two matrons who were standing there to look. "You've been in California too long," Bob said.

"Thanks for coming." Tommy's hands were still shaking. "I could use a drink."

"Here?" Bob looked around the lobby. A pinochle game seemed to be getting started in the lounge.

Tommy made a face. "Let's go to the Knickerbocker."

On the way, Tommy talked and Bob listened. He was pretty sure Tanner was harmless, but for the chief the stakes were high. And while Bob wouldn't have considered Tanner a potential murderer, calling opposition witnesses was a pretty desperate move. Beyond anything else, it seemed incredibly stupid. Assuming the caller *was* Tanner, but Bob believed Tommy when he said he recognized the voice.

"What did Dolan say to you out there in L.A.?"

"He just told me how much the city had done for me, what I owed them, that kind of shit."

Bob cocked an eyebrow. "You serious?"

Tommy shrugged. "Is the Pope Catholic?"

"There must have been more to it," Bob said. There was always more to everything in his experience, and you always had to dig for it. Tommy screwed up his face, as if he was deep in thought.

"I was at my agent's," he said. "I came out and Dolan was just standing there, waiting. Like he was in the neighborhood." Tommy laughed at his own joke, embarrassed by the memory. "I did this incredibly stupid thing. I stuck out my hands, like he was going to cuff me, you know, arrest me."

It didn't seem so stupid to Bob. Tommy felt guilty about Jimmy Norman and disloyal to his partner. Guilt was what this guy was about. He probably thought he deserved to go to prison. "For what?" he said. "It's out of his jurisdiction."

"I know," Tommy said. "I felt like a real asshole. Anyway, we had coffee and he asked me a lot of questions and that was it. I never heard from him again."

"What kind of questions? What did he want to know?"

Tommy puffed his cheeks and drank some beer. "Mostly about when Rogan popped the kid and what happened after. You know, what did they tell us and who did we talk to."

Bob had no sense of whether Dolan was ambitious or an ally of Mueller's, but he thought he was OK. Probably, he was just doing his job. "What did you tell him?"

"What I told everyone, about Lathrop and Moran telling us to change our stories and how we did it."

"Did Dolan try to move you away from that?"

Tommy looked confused. "From what?"

"Did he ask if you were sure things happened that way?"

Tommy shrugged. "He was OK. Except, now that I think of it, he asked about Tanner and the mayor. A couple of times."

"Asked what?"

"You know, did they talk to me. I told him I never knew those guys. I was shit under their feet. Tell the truth, I think Dolan was really trying to find out for himself."

That made sense. Whatever Tanner knew about the cover-up, there would be no point in telling Dolan. Better to keep him in the dark. "So why's Tanner bothering you now?"

"Damned if I know," Tommy said. "I think the guy just likes to kick ass. But it ain't going to work with me."

Bob kept thinking everything would become clear at some point and he'd understand. But the longer the trial went on, the more confusing it became. He knew there was a cover-up and he knew Tanner was involved, but he couldn't write about it because no one had given him chapter and verse. Besides, Mike Klein didn't want him to jeopardize Olivia Brown's case. And maybe Mike was right. God only knew.

Yet here was Tommy Paley, not a guy who mattered very much in the big picture, not in the least admirable, maybe not even very good. But scared—Jesus, he was scared—despite his bravado. You could see it in his bloodshot eyes and his dirty fingernails. Here was Tommy, deficient as he was, whose whole adult life had been dominated by this case and who, unlike Olivia Brown, had neither press attention nor a string of apartment houses to provide for his old age. Tommy deserved consideration, but there was nothing Bob could do, except sit with him in this run-down bar on a cold night and hope that sooner or later the liquor would do its job. It didn't seem like much.

"Drink up," he said. "I've got the next round."

Forty

Sarah awoke early, though it had nothing to do with Andy or the creaking of the old house anymore. It was the silence that disturbed her now, the almost uncanny sense in the darkness, that she was nowhere, as if the absence of place were something you could inhabit. She turned on her light and saw the bed, the walls, the table with her papers on it, the book she had been reading. The clock read 4:28. All of which was reassuring, but now she was awake. She couldn't go out before dawn, so Sarah made tea and sat watching the sun rise as she thought about what she would say to Olivia.

She tried out phrases in her head, practicing: "Olivia, it has come to my attention that . . ." Too much like a bureaucrat. How had it come to her attention anyway? Because she was snooping among Olivia's private papers. "Olivia, in good conscience I can't go on with the book, knowing what I know." Pompous, plus it would be hypocritical to cite her conscience considering what she had done. What was good conscience anyway? Guilty conscience was more like it.

"Olivia, in fairness to both of us . . ." But was fairness really the issue? Fairness might count in the trial, but what bothered Sarah was that Olivia hadn't been honest with her. Yet she hadn't really lied; she just failed to mention the fact that she was a slumlord. Which was a pretty large omission, though Sarah hadn't been completely honest either. She hadn't given Olivia a chance to explain, and now Sarah's feelings were hurt because Olivia hadn't confided in her. Biographer or not, Olivia still thought of Sarah as a white woman with a big house on the lake. What bothered Sarah was the fact that this was true.

Yet when she was actually sitting in Olivia's unused living room with the tea cozy on the pot and cups in their hands, Sarah didn't know how to begin. She was surprised and relieved when Olivia said, "You know about Hometown, don't you?"

This would have been the appropriate time to talk about what in fairness she was due, but Sarah didn't say that. She just nodded, embarrassed, and looked into her cup.

Olivia shifted in her chair. Usually she dressed for these interviews, but today she wore slacks and a sweater. "My lawyer asked me about it," she said. "Wanted to know why I didn't tell him. If I'd told him, he wouldn't be my lawyer is why. Just like now you ain't going to write my book."

Olivia looked indignant, but Sarah didn't respond to the implied question. She still couldn't get over the fact that Olivia considered it to be her book. She treated illiteracy as a mere inconvenience. "Who are you mad at? Charlie or me?"

Olivia shook her head. "Ain't mad. What good does that do? But I ain't sorry either. I did what needed to be done. That's all."

Sarah wasn't sure what she meant exactly, but it wasn't what interested her. "How did you do it?" she asked. "How did you start Hometown and keep it a secret for so long? Did you have some business training or know someone in real estate?"

Olivia smiled broadly. "Training? Honey, I ain't had training in nothing except staying alive, and that's on-the-job training. It just happened, little by little. When I got some money, it was just enough to make a down payment, so I would. I thought about sharing it, but you know, those boys would have just wasted it all. So I bought this one building cheap, and it should have been cheap because it was about falling down." Olivia shook her head at the memory.

"At first, I was a good little landlord, running over whenever a light bulb burned out or a toilet overflowed. Then after a while, I got enough ahead to buy another building down the block from the first one, then a third one, and it all got to be too much, so I hired a super to look after things, only it turned out he was mainly interested in looking after the ladies."

"So this was, what, twenty years ago? And about that time my husband comes and says he's got a chance to buy this car wash, only he doesn't have the money. So I said I'd try to get a second on the buildings to buy the car

wash, and this lawyer—same one we had back when Daddy sued the city—
said we should start a corporation, and he fixed up all the papers with the
bank. I didn't know much about trusts, but when the buildings started going down and I didn't really want people to know who owned them, it
worked out fine. It went on like that for years. We'd get a little ahead and I'd
call the bank and they'd buy us a building, and after the lawyer died there
was no one left who knew how it all started. Even when the newspaper did
those stories a few years ago, no one found out. Until you came along."

Olivia's voice was even, as if none of this had anything to do with her.
And it really was remarkable, Sarah thought, that she had parlayed the bribe
money into a small empire that would be increased further by whatever
Olivia got out of the trial. Sarah knew she should be shocked, but the fact
was she was impressed and a little envious. She was also proud that Bob
had discovered all of this, but she felt out of her depth here, an imposter.
"It's kind of amazing, Olivia," she said. "It really is."

Olivia nodded, pleased. "You going to tell?" she asked.

The question made Sarah laugh out loud. "Tell who?" she said. "I already told Bob Joseph and the *Times* won't touch the story. Bob must have
told Charlie, and he's still your lawyer, so that takes him out. Who would I
tell, Olivia?"

"There're still some black folks who'd be pretty mad."

"Marcus Jackson?" Sarah said.

Olivia nodded. "That one, oh, he'd be real mad. He's the one that sent
me to the lawyer in the first place, and he was protesting in front of my
buildings before that."

"I won't tell Marcus, but you're right, I can't write your book now
either. To tell the truth, Hometown's the most interesting thing I've learned
about you." Olivia looked down and Sarah wondered if she had hurt her
feelings. "Not that the other things weren't interesting," she said. "About
your father being a minister in Arkansas and everything."

"Oh, I don't care about that," Olivia said. "I'm just going to miss this."
She gestured at the tea service and Sarah understood. Olivia was lonely.
There were few women who had done what she had, black or white, but
the book had given them a premise for friendship, for sharing their stories.
She would miss Olivia too. When she was a young mother, Sarah had had
girlfriends, but they all seemed to have jobs now.

"We could still do this," she suggested. "I mean have tea and talk. We'll
just forget about the book. I'd rather work on my novel anyway. I was just
doing this to feel useful."

"That's what we'll do then," Olivia said. "We'll be friends."

There was something touching about the way she pronounced the word that made Sarah think this was important. It was crucial to achieve justice in court, but something significant had happened in this quiet room. Two women had taken a chance and become friends. She took Olivia's hand in hers and squeezed it tightly.

Andy was standing in the receiving line outside Shining Mount Baptist Church as his wife and Olivia Brown talked. He had been shaking hands and talking to parishioners for fifteen minutes when he noticed Marcus Jackson. Though Marc was a minister, it struck Andy as odd because Jackson had no pulpit and seldom visited community churches. As the stream of parishioners slowed, Marc made his way to Andy's side.

"It must be close if you're working the churches this late in the campaign."

"Can't take anyone for granted," Andy said. "Especially our good friends in the central city. I'm surprised to hear you talking this way, Reverend. Actually, though, I took some time off a few months ago and now Jimmy's scheduling me wherever he can as punishment."

Marcus glanced at the dilapidated church and shook his head in amusement. "The Lord works in strange ways. But what about it—are you really going to win?"

Though Marcus was joking, he wanted to know. But Andy wouldn't jinx himself by predicting victory. "Supposedly, we're even," he said. "But even isn't even if you're the incumbent. You've got to knock the champion out. Anyway, I don't see hordes of supporters anywhere. It's close."

Marcus looked at the empty street. The church doors were shut now. "It's a hell of a time to expect hordes, Andy. Probably ten below with this wind."

"Figure of speech," Andy said, blowing on his hands. "But speaking of the weather, what brings you out?"

Marcus dropped his bantering tone now. "Got time for a walk down the block?"

Andy blew on his hands again. It was too cold, but he knew Marcus wouldn't be here if it weren't important. "Sure," he said. "What's on your mind?"

They walked toward Ninth Street. The houses were small and rundown, with broken screen doors flapping in the wind. Andy remembered being in one of them for a coffee and joking about going into the kitchen for a snack. Everyone got very quiet, and he found out why when he discovered the refrigerator was empty except for a few quarters of butter. Andy had Jimmy send over a hundred dollars' worth of food, but it didn't make up for embarrassing his hostess. Now he imagined shivering children and empty refrigerators behind every door. When they crossed Ninth, Marc said, "I had a visitor the other day. You remember Mr. Joseph, don't you, Andy?"

"Very well," Andy said. "A representative of the Fourth Estate. What did he have to say for himself?"

"We didn't discuss *that,*" Marcus said. "Mr. Joseph wanted me to know about a story he wasn't going to write. That struck me as kind of odd, but I thought it might interest you."

As far as Andy was concerned, concealment was an essential part of Bob Joseph's character. It didn't surprise him to learn that the reporter was holding something back. He did wonder why he'd be going to Marcus with it. "So he wanted a response quote from you on this non-story?"

Marcus smiled thinly. "No, he just wanted me to know about it; I think it made him feel better to tell me." His voice was harsh and angry in the cold air.

Andy nodded. "And now you're going to tell me? Will that make *you* feel better?"

Marcus looked at him quizzically. Andy had been joking, but now he realized something and he didn't know why he had never thought of it before. Though their friendship served both of them, it didn't go very deep, and the reason was that they wanted it that way. They were political allies but not intimates. Andy didn't know if Marc had financial or marital problems; he knew nothing about his children, his parents, or his health. There was genuine feeling and loyalty between them, but it only went so far. And now he had come close to insulting Marc by joking about something important to him. "Is that it?" Andy asked.

For a moment, the other man looked vulnerable, then it passed. "I just wanted to tell you what Joseph told me," Marc said. "I can't do anything with it; maybe you can." Politics as usual, Andy thought. Back to business; Marc had covered up.

In the car going downtown, Andy thought about what Marcus Jackson had said. Everyone had reasons for protecting Olivia Brown: Mike Klein was concerned about the effect the news about Hometown would have on the trial; Charlie Simons was too, but for him there was the additional frustration of having proof of the conspiracy without being able to use it. Bob

Joseph was protecting Sarah, and Marcus Jackson knew that exposing Olivia would cause a backlash in the black community. No one wanted to hear bad news about a sister, especially from a black man. But Andy had nothing to lose and no one to protect. If he held a press conference, the papers would have to go with the story, no matter what Mike Klein thought. It would destroy Mueller, yet something held Andy back, something that he understood only vaguely but that seemed important.

It wasn't that he didn't want to win the election; he wanted to win it with a desperation he would have thought impossible a month before. Certainly he had little sympathy for Mueller and Tanner, and he didn't care about Olivia, whom he had always considered an opportunist. None of that mattered to him. What bothered Andy was that the news had come to him providentially, delivered by a friend after church, like an answered prayer. Andy had never trusted prayer.

Throughout the campaign he had been depicted as a wealthy east side liberal who drank white wine on his way to the club to play squash. Now the story would be that he had won only because of the scandal Tanner had created in Mueller's administration. Jimmy would be furious if he knew, but Andy thought he would rather lose than win that way. So just like all the rest, Andy Hedig decided in the end to keep Olivia's secret. But there was a difference: Unlike the others, it was no burden for Andy. There was no one he wanted to tell, and for him, there was no guilt. This was where the story stopped.

Forty-one

It was raining when Charlie awoke. Late winter rain didn't depress him, but it made the trip into the city longer and the courtroom smelled of wool all morning, which caused a good deal of sneezing and coughing.

Dolan was resplendent in his blue suit and red tie, but while the district attorney was businesslike, he seemed unenthusiastic as he began his defense. Charlie had expected more. The man seemed enervated, even depressed, as if he had been dragged into the case against his will, which might have been the truth.

There was nothing to be gained for the defense by calling Paley again, but Dolan wanted the jury to know about Tommy's expulsion from the force and his criminal record. By the end of Dolan's questioning, Tommy looked so miserable that Charlie didn't know if he could survive the cross. He started gently.

"Mr. Paley, before February 8, 1959, had you received any sanctions at all from the police department? Any complaints? Had you been written up for anything?"

"No, sir," Tommy said.

"Like many Milwaukeeans, you drank socially, but had you ever been identified by a social worker or counselor as an alcoholic or received treatment for that condition?"

Tommy shook his head no.

"So, in contrast to John Rogan, whose file was filled with complaints and was known among other officers as a troublemaker, you were nearly a model officer?"

Dolan objected, but the judge wanted the jury to hear this testimony. Tommy was sitting up straighter now. He looked around the courtroom to see what the press was making of this, if anything.

"Mr. Paley, as the district attorney has pointed out, after the Norman murder you were dismissed from the police force and subsequently incarcerated for petty theft. Did you ever think that this awful murder and the cover-up that followed might have contributed to your alcohol dependency?"

Dolan was up immediately. "Foundation," he said. "Witness isn't competent to answer. He's not a doctor or a psychologist."

"Rephrase your question, Mr. Simons," Alberts said.

"Mr. Paley, were you despondent and guilt-ridden after the shooting?"

"Damned right," Tommy said. "I couldn't think about anything else, couldn't sleep. My wife left me because of it. I lost everything—"

"Thank you," Charlie said, cutting him off. "And did this despondency cause you to drink more heavily than you had before?"

Tommy nodded. "But it was the worst after I got kicked off the force. I was living alone and working as a rent-a-cop. There wasn't that much to do, so I got drunk a lot."

"But you weren't diagnosed as an alcoholic before your dismissal?"

Dolan objected, but Alberts allowed the question. "I was drinking," Tommy said. "I got to be honest about that. But I always made it to work."

"Did it ever occur to you that your dismissal from the force wasn't really due to alcoholism, but was in fact revenge?"

Dolan started to object, but Alberts told him to sit down. "I always thought that's exactly what it was," Tommy said. "Lots of guys drank more than I did, but really they just wanted me and John out. We were embarrassing them."

"In fact," Charlie said, addressing the jury, "what we see here is the record of the destruction of a promising career and very nearly a man's life because the police department was more concerned about its image than about helping its officers."

"That's no question, it's a speech," Dolan said. But Charlie was finished. "No more questions," he said.

Tanner was Dolan's star witness, a man of such authority that most people in the city assumed the mayor took orders from him. And why not?

While Mueller had to run for reelection every four years, Tanner's reign as chief of police would continue uninterrupted no matter who sat in city hall. Seldom in the news, Tanner's power was nevertheless legendary. He ran his department with no interference from anyone, and Charlie thought the jurors reacted visibly when Tanner walked in, dressed in a gray flannel suit. The chief looked more like an important businessman than a police official. Charlie was impressed too. It was the reason he hadn't called Tanner himself, despite the weaknesses in the chief's deposition.

Tanner wore a patient expression as Dolan led him through his testimony, communicating tolerance for what he clearly considered a waste of valuable time. He didn't remember meeting either Rogan or Paley prior to the Norman murder, but it would have been unusual for him to socialize with patrolmen. He had never heard of instructors in the Academy teaching recruits to carry throwaways. He knew nothing about a cover-up and Chief Martin had never discussed one with him. Together, Tanner and Dolan commiserated over the fact that a couple of unworthy officers could tarnish the reputation of a department known nationally for its even-handed administration of the law. It was quite a performance, Charlie thought, as Dolan turned the witness over to him.

Tanner hadn't brought his logbook to court, but he responded so easily when asked where he had been the night of the murder that Charlie realized his only chance was to surprise him by asking something Dolan hadn't anticipated. "Chief," he said, "was there a meeting to discuss the Norman murder on February 9, 1959, in the morning?"

Tanner looked down, as if trying to remember. "I went off duty after the night shift," he said, irrelevantly.

"That wasn't my question," Charlie said. "Was there a meeting that morning, the morning after the murder, and were you present at that meeting?"

Tanner nodded.

"Could you tell us who else was there?"

Tanner's voice, which had been strong and self-assured, was softer now. "Deputy Inspector Halloran, Detective Moran, Chief Martin, and Rogan and Paley," he said.

"A moment ago you testified that you didn't discuss the case with Chief Martin. I assume you meant you didn't talk about it with him individually, because you did participate in this meeting that was called to discuss the Norman murder."

Tanner said that this was what he had meant.

"Well, then," Charlie said, "could you tell us what you talked about at this meeting?"

"Besides what happened the night before?" Tanner had begun perspiring and dabbed his forehead with a pocket square.

"Officer Paley testified that the district attorney was upset that the officers' reports were at variance with one another. Was this one of the points you covered that morning?"

"We might have," Tanner said.

"Don't you remember?" Charlie asked, his voice insistent.

"I suppose we did," Tanner said.

"I suppose you did too," Charlie said. The audience laughed, which helped. Anything he could do to bring Tanner down to his level would be to their benefit. "And what did you tell the officers to do about these differences in their reports?"

"I didn't tell them anything," Tanner said. "I was only the night captain of detectives. I was just there."

The value of the jury's seeing Tanner reduced to a whining child was nearly as valuable as his testimony, but Charlie pushed on. "Of course you were there. And the reason you were there is that you were part of the leadership of the police department and the Norman murder was becoming a public relations problem. Now, let me ask you, Chief, did you or anyone at this morning meeting ask Officer Paley or Officer Rogan to change his report, to remove the inconsistencies?"

"I don't remember," Tanner said.

"You don't remember?" Charlie said incredulously. "You remember when this meeting was, who was present, and what was discussed, but you can't remember whether anyone asked the officers involved to change their reports? Mr. Magnusen and Mr. Paley both remember quite clearly how they were pressured, and the record shows that Officer Rogan changed his story at least three times. To your knowledge, did anyone help him with this? That is, did anyone instruct him as to what he should say?"

"I don't know." Tanner sounded foolish because everyone knew this was exactly how it must have happened.

"Nevertheless," Charlie continued, "there was this meeting with high-level officials, after which, miraculously, the officers' reports conformed more closely to each other."

"I wouldn't exactly call it a miracle," Tanner said, trying to regain some of his authority.

"Oh, I didn't mean that literally," Charlie said. "But what would you call it, Chief? Inspiration? Coercion?"

Tanner retreated again. "I don't know," he said dully.

"I see," Charlie said. "Well, tell me, did you at this time have contact with any member of the Norman family?"

"Contact?" Tanner's posture changed again. He was leaning forward, as if he were going to charge into Charlie.

"Yes. Did you talk to them, offer condolences for their loss, anything of that nature?"

"No," Tanner's reply was gruff and dismissive.

"Well, they were all down there at the Safety Building the night Jimmy Norman was murdered, weren't they?"

"I don't know who's in his family. They might have been."

"Oh, no, they *were,*" Charlie said. "It was reported in the papers. There were even pictures. But you had no contact? Remember that you're under oath, Chief."

"There was nothing that I recall," Tanner said.

"How about later on, just before the meeting of the coroner's grand jury, say?" Charlie was fishing, but he had nothing to lose and Tanner was shaky. Whatever the chief said would compromise him. If he didn't meet with the family, he was heartless; if he did, he was admitting that he knew more than he had been letting on.

"I don't think so," Tanner said.

"I wish you'd try to remember," Charlie said, and people laughed again. "This is pretty important. Perhaps you met with Cap Norman to discuss the settlement offer?"

"That wasn't my job," Tanner said.

"Of course not," Charlie said. "You've already told us that. But how about other members of the family? Olivia Norman Brown, for example. Did you meet with her?"

Tanner looked past Charlie. He could have been making eye contact with either Olivia or Dolan. Charlie remembered the hoarse voice on the phone talking about "my little girlfriend," and he had a strong desire just to nail Tanner, to expose the sonofabitch for what he was in front of everyone, no matter what it cost them. "No," Tanner said now.

"You didn't meet with Mrs. Brown during this period?"

"I said I didn't," Tanner said. It was a direct lie, but Charlie couldn't prove it without exposing his client, which would get him disbarred. It would almost be worth it.

"Well, since you didn't know Mrs. Brown, you couldn't have offered money to keep her quiet, could you?"

Tanner started to rise in his seat but thought better of it as Dolan objected and Alberts gaveled them down. Charlie hadn't expected Tanner to answer, but the look of pure hatred on his face was plain to see, as was his guilt. "No more questions," Charlie said.

The chief took his time leaving, and Charlie knew he was trying to regain his bearing, but dignity is one of those things that once gone is forever lost. Tanner just looked old and mean as he brushed past the plaintiff's table. Though Charlie hadn't established the chief's complicity in a plot to suppress the truth about the murder, he had put him in a room with people who had been accused of doing that, and the jury was impressed. And while Tanner hadn't said he knew Olivia, he hadn't denied it either.

Dolan's apathy had completely disappeared now. His face was red and his hair looked as if he had been giving himself a scalp massage. He shot a look at Charlie, then said, "Your Honor, defense calls Olivia Norman Brown."

There was noise in the courtroom at this, but no one left. Olivia's eyes were wide. "Can he do that?" she whispered.

"Sure he can," Charlie said. He couldn't reassure her because he didn't know what was going on. In a criminal case Dolan wouldn't be allowed to call Charlie's client, but this was a civil suit, so he could make no objection, especially since Dolan had taken the precaution of naming Olivia among his potential witnesses. He had listed the whole family, including the two brothers who were in the state mental hospital. It was common to list anyone remotely connected with a case so you wouldn't have to ask permission later. Still, even if Olivia wasn't exactly a surprise witness, Dolan had surprised Charlie. When they hadn't deposed her, Charlie assumed they had ruled Olivia out, and he would probably have been right about this if Tanner had done better. So it was Charlie's fault for beating up on the chief. Dolan had to try to recover the momentum, and considering Olivia's anxiety, Charlie thought that wouldn't be hard. "It'll be all right," he said. But he wasn't at all sure.

The bailiff swore Olivia in, and she sat facing the district attorney. Though she still held her head erect, she seemed smaller and was visibly scared. This wasn't the way it was supposed to go. She had sued thinking she had the advantage and that they'd be rich, and now she was facing another angry white man asking questions she didn't want to answer.

"Mrs. Brown," Dolan began, "could I ask you why you initiated this lawsuit against the city of Milwaukee?"

"For justice," Olivia said quickly. And Charlie was suddenly proud of her. Olivia would go down fighting.

"Justice," Dolan repeated ironically. "Which in this case translates roughly to a hundred million dollars."

Olivia looked at Charlie, but there was nothing he could do. That was about it. "There's no need to answer, Mrs. Brown," Dolan said. "It's a matter of public record."

"I know how much we're asking for," Olivia said stiffly.

"I'm sure you do," Dolan said. "Down to the penny. Justice is very expensive these days, isn't it?"

Charlie wasn't sure whether or not this was a veiled reference to Tanner's bribe, but Olivia handled it smoothly. "Is that a question?" she asked. "Because if it is, I'll tell you how expensive justice is. It cost my baby brother his life and my daddy's too."

Dolan took a step back and nodded slightly, as if conceding the point. "We all regret that, Mrs. Brown. But tell me, isn't it true that your father, Aesculapius Norman, accepted a settlement offer from the city?"

"Never cashed the check," Olivia said.

"Perhaps not, but that's beside the point. He, or his attorney, accepted the settlement as just. That's also a matter of public record. And isn't it also true that two of your brothers, Albert Norman and Randy Norman, have been residents of the county psychiatric facility for a number of years and that other members of your family have received various kinds of public assistance from the city of Milwaukee?"

"Relevance," Charlie said, rising. "What has this got to do with the conspiracy to cover up Jimmy Norman's murder?"

"I'm getting to that," Dolan said.

"Get to it faster," Alberts put in.

"They wouldn't have needed that if Jimmy hadn't been killed," Olivia said now. "Those boys were never the same after that; neither was Daddy."

"Really?" Dolan said. He retreated to the defense table and picked up a file. "According to the city's records, Mrs. Brown, both Albert and Randy displayed antisocial tendencies before Jimmy was shot. Both dropped out of high school, and neither has a service nor a work record. My point is, your family has received literally hundreds of thousands of dollars in public funds already. What's more, your father agreed to a good-faith settlement of his case before he died. It seems to me that the city has already been more than fair. Do you really think you have a right to ask for more?"

It was a good argument, especially the business about Cap Norman's accepting the settlement. It had bothered the judge in pre-trial arguments, but the jury hadn't heard it before. And the whole family's being on welfare wasn't going to help. Charlie admired Dolan's resilience. The way they kept going back and forth, he thought it might come down to whoever spoke last, in which case he could give up right now.

"Just a few more questions, Mrs. Brown," Dolan said. "You say you initiated legal action for justice, in the form of a hundred million dollars. Did someone else suggest that?"

"Suggest what?"

"Suggest that you sue."

"It was my idea," Olivia said, and she seemed sure about it. "When I read in the papers about that cop."

"You mean Mr. Paley?"

Olivia nodded. "That one," she said.

"So, Mr. Paley's crisis of conscience stimulated a desire for"—Dolan hesitated here for effect—"justice. And no one else suggested that in the current climate you might be able to get, shall we say, somewhat more for justice than the thousands your family had already collected from the city?"

"No," Olivia said stubbornly.

"Not the Reverend Marcus Jackson, for example?"

Olivia shook her head.

"But you went to see Mr. Jackson, didn't you? Wasn't the very first person you chose to consult a black activist?"

Charlie knew Marc would be pleased to be described this way, and it amused him. "He got me my lawyer," Olivia said.

"Exactly," Dolan said. "An important function to serve. And are you paying Mr. Simons a fee?"

Charlie objected and Alberts sustained, but Dolan was rolling. "I'm still troubled by the hundred million dollars. Of course, we know that no amount of money would bring back Jimmy, but we can always try, can't we? How did you arrive at this figure, Mrs. Brown? I mean, why not two hundred million?"

Olivia mumbled something.

"Speak up, Mrs. Brown," Alberts said.

"My lawyer," Olivia said now. There were tears in her eyes, tears Charlie thought of humiliation rather than grief.

"Mr. Simons suggested the hundred-million-dollar figure?" Dolan said. He clasped his hands together and waited.

Olivia shook her head. "The other one."

"Ah, Mr. Isaacson, then," Dolan said, as if at last everything made sense. He waited a moment and then returned to his seat. "No more questions, Your Honor," he said.

Charlie felt enormous sympathy for Olivia, despite his anger at her for deceiving him. He should have prepared her for this and hadn't, but how could he have known?

Olivia looked terrible, leaning forward in the witness chair, her eyes huge and afraid. Whatever arrogance she'd had was gone; Charlie's job was to restore her sense of herself.

"Mrs. Brown, how long have you been married?"

The question was so unexpected that Olivia sat upright. "Twenty-eight years," she said.

"Twenty-eight years is a long time, especially nowadays. How long have you lived in Milwaukee?"

"I came here in 1949," Olivia said. "I knew there was nothing for black folks in Arkansas."

The idea of Milwaukee as a land of opportunity seemed pathetic in view of what had happened subsequently, but there were factories here and people could work and improve themselves by going to school. There was a large black community. Apparently, it was better than Arkansas, or it had seemed that way then.

"So you came here as a young woman?" He didn't know where he was going. They were just talking in front of an audience.

"Nineteen years old," Olivia said.

"And I believe you found a job very quickly."

"First I worked as a waitress, then out to the county."

"The county hospital. And after that you married and started bringing the rest of your family here, isn't that right?"

Olivia nodded. "They all came here sooner or later, except Daddy. He just couldn't stand to leave that Arkansas." She shook her head at the memory.

"And when your large family arrived, you and your husband helped them out, even though you were young yourself and hadn't much money?"

"We did what we could." Charlie liked the way she bowed her head in modesty, because it was all a play, even a morality play, and it was important to play your part well.

"Which is all anyone can do," Charlie said, helping Olivia along. "In fact, some of your siblings lived with you for a time, including your brother Jimmy, isn't that so?"

"Jimmy was living with us the day he died," she said.

Charlie stepped back, as if this were a shock. "How much older were you than your brother?" he asked.

"He was fifteen years younger than I was."

"You were nearly old enough to be his mother," Charlie said, knowing there were many mothers within a mile of the courthouse who hadn't yet reached their fifteenth birthdays.

She nodded. "That's what he called me, Mama. Sometimes Sisterma, but usually Mama."

Charlie turned to face the jury, his back to Olivia now, and studied their faces. "So despite the hardships of your own life in a city that must still have seemed strange and foreign, you brought your family here because you thought things would be better for them. And you took your little brother Jimmy into your home and had him live with you. Let me ask you, Mrs. Brown, in all honesty, was Jimmy a troubled boy?"

Olivia hesitated, then to Charlie's surprise she dabbed her eyes with a handkerchief. "Oh, my," she said, "I think that boy was born in trouble. We couldn't keep him in school, and he lost his job, and the police was always after him."

"Without meaning to be callous, then," Charlie said, "why did you bother? Jimmy was your brother, it's true, but you had your own life and a husband who needed you. Many sisters might have washed their hands of a brother like Jimmy. Why didn't you?"

Olivia's voice dropped and she stammered, "Why? Because he was my baby brother, my flesh and blood is why. Our mama had died and our daddy was away. Who else did he have in the world except me?"

Her voice was a groan and Charlie waited. "Family is important," he said. "If that wasn't so, you wouldn't have arranged for yours to join you here in Milwaukee. And despite Mr. Dolan's attempts to indicate otherwise, you took as much care of your family as you could before asking for help. But I want to go back to Jimmy. Is there any reason other than family responsibility that you took him into your home?"

He didn't even know why he had asked this, wasn't sure what he wanted to know, but he could see immediately that it was the right question. He had hit on something unexpected within Olivia, something new. A slow, sweet smile spread over her face. "Yes," she said quietly. "It was more than that I had to do it, more than feeling I should. When I would come home after standing up all day, Jimmy would have a pan of warm water and a mustard plaster ready for me, and he'd wash my feet so gently that the pain would go right away.

"Then he'd tell me jokes and stories he'd heard off the radio to make me laugh. And he'd sing to me. His voice was high, like a girl's, and I just felt so lucky to have a little brother to love me like that. On Christmas, he'd make chains of popcorn and cranberries, working the needle and string through so carefully, and I still remember how funny that looked, those popcorns so white, and him as dark as he was. At midnight we'd go to church and come back to open presents. As poor as we were, Jimmy always had something for everyone, and it was always the right thing exactly. He was just so thoughtful and so sweet."

She stopped talking and looked directly at Charlie and then past him at the members of the jury. Her eyes were glistening, but she hadn't used the handkerchief again, as if these were tears she was entitled to and wiping them from her eyes would represent a compromise of some sort. The room was hushed as Charlie stood quietly by, moved by what Olivia had said, pleased that he had drawn this from her. It was more than he had expected, more than he had known before that moment. For the first time since the case had begun, he liked his client. He smiled at Olivia, then nodded at the jury. "No more questions," he said.

Forty-two

The meeting convened at 4:30. Seated around the large desk were Dolan, Fischer, and Tanner. The mayor scowled at each of them, then held up the afternoon paper. The headline read: CHIEF DENIES BRIBE TRY.

"I suppose you gentlemen have seen this?" he said.

The story carried Bob Joseph's byline and summarized Tanner's testimony. While it didn't say Tanner had tried to bribe the Normans, the suggestion was there for all to see. The papers had been more circumspect before this, but now suddenly they had become aggressive. If the trial hadn't been a big story before, it was now, and Mueller had spent the afternoon denying he knew anything about bribery. Which explained the meeting and his mood.

"It's not really as bad as it looks," Dolan said hesitantly.

Mueller looked at him with interest. Then he pointed with his pencil. "You know, Mr. Dolan, you've been saying that to me in one way or another for months. First you said the judge might dismiss the case or it would be over fast and we wouldn't have to worry about its effect on the election. Well, Alberts didn't dismiss and he took his time setting a court date, but you said that didn't matter because no one was paying attention anyway. When we got a standing-room crowd at the courthouse, you said the Normans would accept a settlement. When our offer was rejected, you said that was all right because we'd beat them anyway. Now the paper's saying my chief of police bribed the plaintiff and, according to you, things aren't as bad as they look."

The mayor got up and walked to the window. Outside, the sky was turning dark blue and Water Street was filling with people on their way home from work. He shook his head. "I blame myself. I should have known better and I didn't. I wanted to believe you and so I did. But I'll tell you this right now, Mr. Dolan: however much you might know about the law, you're a horse's ass when it comes to politics. This couldn't be any worse than it looks. And if you don't know that, then you're not as smart as I thought you were."

Mueller's voice rose as he spoke, and the other men seemed to recede into the backs of their chairs. "All right," the mayor continued. "We are approaching the end of the campaign, and Mr. Hedig is winning. It's close, but he's winning. Call a spade a spade. And do you know why he's winning? It's not because of his record, because the voters don't know very much about that. And it's not because of his character, because it's common knowledge that Mr. Hedig's wife is fucking the *Times*'s star reporter and the voters of this city don't respect a man who can't hold onto his wife. It's not because of Mr. Hedig's good looks or his Ivy League education, because the people of Milwaukee think Yale is a padlock. No, Mr. Hedig is winning because we're letting him win, and that's the only reason.

"I said I blame myself and I do. I didn't take enough interest in the trial, which was stupid. I've been mayor for a long time and I've made my share of enemies, including the editorial board of our most important newspaper. I don't expect any favors from the *Times,* but I'm thinking about the next week or ten days. What I want to know is, why can't we make a deal?"

It had become darker since Mueller began talking, but no one moved to turn on a light. The tension in the room bound them together. "I don't know," Dolan said. "I really thought they'd just take the money when we offered it to them. I think Simons advised them to do that."

"Then what happened?" Mueller's voice was soft now, but with an edge.

"I think this woman really means it when she says she wants justice. I think she wants the jury to hammer us."

The mayor took a deep breath. "My original feeling was that settling would make us look bad. We'd be admitting guilt." Now his voice became urgent. "But I haven't done a goddamned thing and I'm put in the position of defending people I don't even know while Tanner's denying he bribed Mrs. Brown. I haven't practiced law for a long time, but this is beginning to smell funny to me. I want to know what you're planning to do, Mr. Dolan."

Dolan spread his hands in a gesture of resignation. "We could make another offer with more money this time. But that wouldn't make us look any better, and I doubt that they'd take it anyway."

The mayor nodded. "What are our chances of winning the case?"

"It's hard to read a jury," Dolan said carefully. "Simons has done a good job of planting suspicion in their minds. Even if they don't know exactly what happened, they think something did. On the other hand, people are generally sympathetic toward the police, so that's still in our favor."

"You didn't answer my question," the mayor said. "Can we win?" His voice was rasping and insistent.

"I doubt it," Dolan said quietly. "And it could be bad. I'm sure the jury will award the family something. I have no idea how much, but in a way that doesn't matter."

Mueller looked at Fischer and something passed between the two men. "So at least we know the worst, which might also be the best we can hope for. We've been talking about this and there are two considerations: what's going to help us win the election and what's the right thing to do. Sometimes they're the same in politics; usually, they aren't."

Fischer took his cue. "It's hard to turn the momentum around in the last week of a campaign, but to even have a chance, we have to do something dramatic."

Mueller didn't really seem to be listening. He turned now to Tanner. "You denied giving this woman a bribe," he said. "Denied it under oath. But I don't believe you and no one else does either. Simons wouldn't just ask that question out of the blue. I don't even blame you. Maybe you were just following orders to get the thing out of the way. Doesn't matter now, and I don't want to know. You're through. I want your resignation before you leave the building today."

Tanner had been only half listening because he wasn't involved in the campaign. "You can't fire me," he said, but his voice was more plaintive than angry.

"Like hell, I can't," Mueller said. "But look at it this way: if Andy Hedig gets elected, you're gone anyway. What difference does it make if it happens a week earlier?" He looked at Dolan. "Double the settlement offer and put a deadline on it. From what you said, there's still a chance we can buy our way out of this. Do it now, this afternoon." He looked around the room. "Anything else?"

The district attorney was amazed. Like everyone else, he had assumed Tanner was beyond sanctions, but Mueller was right. He could fire any department head. "I'll call Charlie Simons as soon as I leave here," he said.

Fischer was pleased, both because it was their only chance to shake things up and because it had been his idea. "I can get a press release out by five," he said.

Mueller said, "This meeting is over."

Word traveled quickly and soon Tanner's resignation was common knowledge in the city. Andy held a press conference in which he praised Mueller's integrity. It was the only way to play it, but Jimmy was disgusted. "If he had so much integrity, why didn't he get rid of the sonofabitch a long time ago?" he said. "And if he really didn't know what was going on before, he's the only person over the age of twelve who didn't. Integrity, my skinny ass."

Bob Joseph spent the evening in Mike Klein's office. In addition to Bob, Mike had called in the metro editor and the editorial board. "OK," he said. "It's late and we've got to decide what to do with this. We already lost the jump on the resignation. It's going to be on the news tonight and in the morning papers. By the time we get to it, we'll be dealing with a pretty cold corpse. Obviously we've got to do something else. Pete?"

The editorial-page editor cleared his throat. "We've already endorsed Hedig," he said, "so there's no point in congratulating ourselves for what a good decision that was. We can talk about justice or send the mayor a delayed valentine, but that bastard wouldn't have fired Tanner unless he felt he had no choice."

Klein grunted in agreement. "George?" he said.

"It's a big story," the metro editor said. "New developments, all that. Tanner's been in a long time, and there've been rumors about corruption in the department but never anything solid before. Maybe we'll do a history of the case for the three people in town who haven't been following the trial, then a bio of Tanner. Something about who's next."

"How about the bribe?" Bob put in.

"He denies it. What can we do, a story on how much he denies paying out? Anyway, we don't really know who got paid."

Klein looked at Joseph. "How about you, Bobby?"

"I want to run with it," Bob said. "We don't have to name people, but I've never liked sitting on what we have, and I sure don't want Tanner to look like an innocent scapegoat."

The other two editors suddenly looked interested. "Is there something here we don't know about, Mike?" George asked.

Klein clasped his hands in front of him. "Bob turned up something a while ago and I didn't think it made a story, but maybe I was wrong then and maybe I'm wrong now." The other men listened as he told them about Olivia Brown and Hometown.

When he was through, the metro editor said, "All that's very interesting, but what it comes down to is Tanner's resigning and Olivia Norman Brown owns some ghetto property. I guess we could run some kind of news analysis, but the whole thing seems a lot like gossip to me."

"It's a lot more than that," Bob said. "Olivia Brown used the bribe money to buy those buildings."

"Sure," George said. "And we've got that from a source we can't identify. I mean this isn't exactly Watergate. We haven't got canceled checks, a paper trail. Without that, you can't put someone's name in the paper and say they were on the take."

Bob started to protest, then felt his anger ebb. He was losing his grit, his arrogance, and his presumption, but he didn't feel like arguing about it half the night and losing. The important thing was that Tanner was out. And it didn't really matter how or why it had happened. "I'll do the thumb-sucker," he said.

"Good," Mike said. "But I want you at the courthouse bright and early. The rumor is that they're going to try again to settle. If it happens by noon we can make the first edition."

Tommy Paley heard the news wedged into a corner of the bar at Glorioso's. When he saw them flash Mueller's mug on the tube, he said, "Tony, turn that up a little, will you?"

Few of his patrons were interested in current affairs, but Tony obligingly turned up the volume. Tommy had only a vague recollection of the anchorman. His name was Brett, he thought, or maybe Brent. Not a Milwaukee guy, not a Milwaukee name. A bowl of blond hair sat on Brett's head, and he wore a serious expression as he read the news of the chief's resignation off the TelePrompTer.

Tommy sat back, surprised by emotion. This was what it came down to finally, from Rogan plugging the kid, the cover-up, and twenty years in the boonies after being kicked off the force. From years of working odd jobs and doing time for bad checks that should have been good, because at bottom Tommy was all right, a stand-up guy who didn't fuck people. If none of this had happened he wouldn't be sitting alone in a cheap suit drinking in a Brady Street nightclub at ten o'clock at night. If it had never happened, he might still have a wife and maybe even some kids. But he had lost everything: his self-respect, his job, his family—all gone, and why?

Because of assholes like Tanner, who thought other people's lives were their property.

Tommy didn't especially like the Normans, and while that priest up in Green Bay had gotten to something inside him, this wasn't really about guilt either. He'd felt bad about Jimmy, but the D.A. was right. If he'd felt that terrible, he wouldn't have taken twenty years to come forward. But that didn't change the feeling of satisfaction he had now. Without knowing exactly how or why, he had done something good. What's more, in his own way he had stuck it to Tanner and all the other assholes on top.

Tommy wasn't big on moralizing about how coppers treated niggers. It made him uncomfortable because he knew he wasn't any hero when he was on the force. But you didn't have to be Martin Luther King, Jr., to know Tanner was part of the cover-up, even if he was going to be the only one to get the ax. There would be a lot of deep thinking going on downtown tonight, and that was good. Tommy felt a warming sensation spread through his gut and chest, and for once he knew it wasn't heartburn.

He signaled the bartender and held up his glass. "Do it again," he said. "And I want to buy you one too."

"I can't drink on duty," Tony said.

"I'm buying anyway. This is a big night for me."

Tony slapped his towel on the bar sink and poured himself a brandy. "What are we celebrating?" he asked.

"Life," Tommy said. "Life itself. What a fucking ride it is."

Forty-three

It didn't take Olivia long to make up her mind. "We've got them now," Isaacson said. "All we've got to do is close the door." But Charlie didn't really agree. If money was the primary consideration, and for Olivia it had always been important, this would be the best time to deal. With the election coming up, the mayor was vulnerable. But the jury wasn't running for anything and might side with the police regardless of Tanner's resignation. Even if they won, they could still lose financially because the jury might award less money than the city was offering now. Charlie wanted to continue, but there were risks involved.

"Then why go on?" Isaacson asked him. "If you push Olivia, she'll listen to you."

"Because it's important to really win," Charlie said. "If you accept their offer, there's always going to be the question of whether we could have gotten it from the jury. The money could be less or more. Frankly, I don't give a shit. I just want everyone to know what the police did. That's what's important."

"You make this sound more like a crusade than a case."

Charlie didn't know what to say to that. But now he understood how relatively unimportant the principles of the case really were to Isaacson. He had assumed Bill would be invested in it because of his liberal reputation, but he didn't seem to feel that way at all. "Goddamned right it's a crusade," Charlie said. "Right now, it's everything."

The courtroom was full, and Alberts wore an expression of strained tolerance as he took his seat. The judge had been a disappointment to Charlie. He hadn't been especially harsh or unfair, just unmoved by what was happening in front of him. Without Alberts ever saying anything, Charlie had gone into the case assuming it would be a high point in his legal career. Yet the judge had been inattentive, irritable, and in a hurry to reach conclusions. Things seemed to be working out, but that didn't change the fact that Alberts had done a lousy job. They would have been better off with a conservative who ran a better courtroom.

"Mr. Simons," Albert said now, "are you ready?"

Charlie had learned from experience that the best approach was to simply talk to the jury during closing arguments, not harangue the other side or defend what you had done. It was a time to summarize the points you had tried to make, to frame your argument for the last time. He was wearing what Donna called his sincere suit, a gray worsted, with a dark red tie. Now he tucked it inside his jacket and took a position just to the right of the jury foreman.

"The hardest thing in any trial," he began, "would appear to be the simplest. What is it all about? Why are we here for the plaintiffs and what is it we are asking you to decide? Simple, or so it would seem. Yet the simple truth turns out to be very difficult to discover, in part because we lawyers do our best to make you see only our own points of view. In the process, what is simple becomes complicated.

"The facts are usually a good place to begin, but the facts in this case are not in dispute. The district attorney and I agree that Jimmy Norman was killed by John Rogan on the night of February 8, 1959, and that his death was not justifiable because of armed resistance as was originally ruled. This is why Officer Rogan is currently an inmate in a federal prison. There is no disagreement about this. There has been a good deal of testimony devoted to the examination of Officer Rogan's motivation and character, but there is no question about what he did. This is not a murder mystery.

"There are some other things, however, about which the district attorney and I do not agree. He believes this is a case that should never have been tried. He says it is a rehashing of something that has been decided and is essentially frivolous and vexatious, a waste of everyone's time. While he is willing to concede that John Rogan should not have shot Jimmy Norman, the district attorney wants you to believe that this was an isolated incident and not one for which the city or the police department should be held responsible."

At this point, Charlie paused and walked to the defense table. He picked up a file and opened it. Then he turned to face the jury. "I want to read a passage from section 1983 of the U.S. Civil Rights Statutes." He looked up and made eye contact with the foreman. "'Every person who, under color of any statute, ordinance, regulation, custom, or usage of any State or Territory or the District of Columbia, subjects, or causes to be subjected, any citizen of the United States . . . thereof to the deprivation of any rights, privileges, or immunities secured by the Constitution and laws, shall be liable to the party injured in an action at law.'"

Charlie replaced the file deliberately. "I want you to notice the use of the word 'color' here," he said, "because it has a special meaning in this context. According to the legal tradition of English common law, color means a pretext, or a semblance of something concocted for the sole purpose of cloaking the truth in order to give a show of justice to something that is intrinsically unjustifiable. It means to give the appearance of reason to something that is not reasonable, to lend the impression of fairness to something that is manifestly unfair, to make the false seem plausible, and to make evil seem good. What is especially diabolical about all this is that the practitioners of this sort of falsehood specifically use what we all trust as being good, the law, as the agent for their injustices. That is what is meant by the phrase 'under color of law.'

"Jimmy Norman was killed under color of law. The officers and detectives involved were persuaded to change their stories under color of law. The coroner's jury handed down a verdict of justifiable homicide under color of law. Then Officers Rogan and Paley were made scapegoats for the police department and pretexts were found for their dismissal under color of law. Finally, the whole sorry episode was covered up in a criminal conspiracy by the city hierarchy under color of law. Why weren't we told the truth in 1959? They would have you believe that other things were more important. Things such as public confidence in the police and law and order. In other words, they lied under color of official excuses. But is confidence in a corrupt bureaucracy truly more crucial than the truth? I don't think so.

"It is tragically ironic that were it not for the color of his skin, Jimmy Norman would be alive and we wouldn't be talking about color of law. But Jimmy was killed by a racist who, according to the testimony of his partner, specifically sought out black people for the purpose of brutalizing them.

"Despite what the district attorney would have you believe, John Rogan was not an anomaly, a bad apple in an otherwise upright department. This man was trained to kill by racists in the Police Academy who anticipated just this sort of situation and instructed him in the details of covering up the crimes they assumed he would commit. Even these instructors, however, were only a manifestation of the strain of racism that ran through the whole department. This is why it became the mission of that department to conceal the nature of Rogan's crime, to try to shift the blame to an innocent boy. In a sense it would be reassuring to believe John Rogan was indeed a rogue cop, acting out of his own private madness. Unfortunately, the truth is much more disturbing than that.

"Jimmy Norman was killed by people who believe black lives to be worth less than white lives. John Rogan pulled the trigger, but he wasn't alone in being responsible for this murder. That is the simple, ugly truth. It would be comforting to be able to tell you that such racism is a thing of the past in our enlightened society, but that would not be true.

"Which is why this case is so important. Your verdict can send the message that official violence is no longer acceptable in Milwaukee. We have the opportunity to make our actions as a society fit the magnificent language of our statutes. Finally, I find it appropriate that members of the community will make the final judgment in this case, not me or the district attorney or Judge Alberts. As representatives of our city, it is your duty to render a fair and honest verdict."

Charlie was sweating. He took a deep breath before continuing. "Because this is a civil rights case, you must agree that the acts committed here were of a racial nature, that discrimination occurred, and that this discrimination was due to the victim's race. Our suit is based on the conviction not only that Jimmy Norman was deprived of his civil rights because of the manner of his death, but that the entire Norman family was also injured because they have been deprived of the companionship of their brother and that they have been further injured because of a racial conspiracy that deprived them of a full and complete knowledge of the circumstances of their brother's death.

"Had Chief Martin or District Attorney Lathrop come forward in 1959 and said, 'A terrible mistake has been made and your brother is dead, but the murderer will be punished,' then things would have been substantially different. As it was, the opposite occurred. The official position was that Jimmy Norman forced Officer Rogan to shoot him because he menaced the officer with a knife. This seems absurd now, but it took the courageous actions of Thomas Paley to correct this travesty. As a reward for his honesty, Mr. Paley has been the victim of character assassination and veiled threats. Far from being the recipient of large film contracts, as the defense has implied, he is nearly destitute. But it is typical of the police department that honesty is considered cowardly while dishonesty is praised."

Charlie paused to let this sink in. "We need your help. We have called our witnesses and made our arguments, but now it is up to you. The Norman family needs your help in order to put this tragic incident behind them and begin to heal. But most of all, Milwaukee needs your help. Our city has been known for years as being among the most segregated in America. We need to change this, and your decision can be the catalyst. I am confident we can count on you."

Charlie stood facing the jurors, hands clasped before him, then nodded his head slightly. "Thank you," he said.

Dolan's rebuttal was ironic, almost mocking, which, considering Charlie's speech, was probably the right thing to do. His best chance was to sow doubt. "Mr. Simons wants you to believe he is a simple man. And he is convincing. What's more, he's right in saying that color is a vitally important principle in civil rights cases. But Mr. Simons is anything but simple. He is a distinguished graduate of one of our finest law schools, a brilliant trial lawyer, and a perceptive student of the law. It is hard not to like Mr. Simons. I like him myself, but this is not germane to the case. For despite Mr. Simons's charm and rhetorical brilliance, what is important is the law, what is important is order, what is important is reason and objectivity. Much more important than sympathy for the plaintiffs, who have undoubtedly suffered.

"The truth is that there was no conspiracy and no bribes. Though they would like you to believe otherwise, the Norman family of their own free will accepted a settlement for damages resulting from their brother's unfortunate death. These are the crucial facts for you to remember as you make your decision today.

"The suffering of the Norman family is not relevant. We agree that they suffered. The question is whether it is right to hold the city of Milwaukee and the individual defendants liable for that suffering. Plaintiff has not shown that there was a conspiracy, because he can't show what does not exist. Whether Mr. Simons likes it or not, the law in this city is color-blind. What is necessary for you to make your decision is neither passion nor sympathy, but fairness. In fairness, I am confident you will rule for the defense."

Alberts's instructions took longer than the closing statements. The questions the jury had to consider fell into three categories: the stop, chase, and apprehension of Jimmy Norman; the shooting and killing of Norman;

and the conspiratorial cover-up after the shooting. Alberts told the jury to disregard testimony that had been stricken from the record and not to give special weight to the testimony of police officers or officials. As he spoke, Alberts's voice because softer, with a distinct rasp. Charlie wondered idly if he would make it to the end.

Then the jury was led out by a marshal who would take them to a hotel and watch over them until they were through. It was a kind of genteel imprisonment. The hotel would be adequate but not luxurious. Their meals would be brought to them, and they would be deprived of newspapers or television. Charlie didn't envy them.

As the room emptied, Charlie gathered his things into piles. "How long do you think they'll be?" Isaacson asked.

Charlie was affected by his close and didn't want to talk. "Two days, maybe three."

Isaacson patted him on the shoulder. "You were good, Charlie," he said. "Not just the close, all the way through. Sorry I wasn't more help." Then he turned and left.

It *was* good, Charlie thought, if not the best that could have been done, at least the best he could do. He had surprised himself with his intensity and depth of conviction. It was too easy to become cynical and accept things that should never be acceptable. He had managed to summarize their argument in a way that represented both his real feelings and the issues in the case. Passion was like a precious mineral and he had always used it sparingly, probably because it was so painful to be passionate in defeat. Today he was passionate not because it was the right strategy but because he couldn't help it. That was what surprised him. He had been out of control and it felt right.

The room was empty now. The ornate judge's chair, witness stand, and jury box standing in contrast to the spare, functional furnishings of the court. As the emotion of the day drained from him, Charlie felt terribly alone. It was frightening to acknowledge even to himself how badly he wanted to win.

Forty-four

The jury was out for two days, and it was raining when the call came from the courthouse. For Charlie, it was time that didn't really exist, just an empty envelope between events that mattered. The idea of getting involved in something else was impossible, though his desk was piled high with unopened mail. And while he knew it did no good, Charlie couldn't help anticipating the worst. So he spent the time considering all the things he might have done differently had he been smarter or more imaginative or more energetic.

The papers carried exhaustive accounts of the trial and conducted a daily opinion poll, which, surprisingly, was running in their favor. Though Tanner had dropped from sight, it was generally agreed that Mueller had had no choice but to fire him. Still, the mayor had antagonized some traditional supporters by doing so. Little was said about Olivia Brown and nothing about Hometown, for which Charlie credited Mike Klein.

He ran into Andy Hedig one morning at Benjy's and sat at his table. "Looks like I got you elected," he said. "Does that entitle me to a job?"

"Name it," Andy said, but when the waitress came to take his order, Charlie wasn't hungry. He shook Andy's hand and left. He needed to keep moving, doing something, even when there was nothing to do.

The courtroom was full by the time Charlie arrived, and as the jury filed in, he knew he had been right to expect the worst. The jurors gave nothing away, but a woman Charlie had noticed earlier, whom he had feared was against them, looked proud, even defiant.

"Have you reached a verdict?" the judge asked.

The foreman stood. "We're deadlocked, Your Honor. We feel it would serve no purpose to continue to deliberate."

There was an explosion of air, the sound of two hundred people sighing. Charlie shook his head in disbelief. It was the one thing he hadn't anticipated. He had imagined they would rule against him, had imagined his own humiliation, and had even allowed himself the fleeting hope of victory. He had thought the verdict might be mixed; that they might win but receive an inadequate settlement . But he had never conceived of this. How could they listen to two weeks of testimony and decide nothing? He dropped his forehead onto his hands and felt a vein throb. Then the judge cleared his throat to indicate that this wasn't over.

Alberts was wearing the half-glasses and had the aspect of a priest or a scholar. "This is a very important trial," he said. "All trials are important, of course, but this concerns a very old case and important charges of official malfeasance. It has taken a very long time and has cost the taxpayers an extraordinary amount of money. When you say you are deadlocked, I understand how frustrating that is, but I am not yet satisfied that all that could be done has been done to reach a verdict. Therefore, I must ask you to try again even if it seems hopeless. I want you to continue to search for a way to reach a decision."

Charlie was amazed. Alberts wasn't going to let them go home. He wanted a decision, one way or the other, and Charlie sensed it was for his own reasons. If they decided to retry the case, Alberts wouldn't be the judge of record. Despite his listlessness, it was obvious now that in his own way he cared as much as the rest of them. And because he cared, this jury wasn't going anywhere. He had phrased it as a request, as if they had a choice, but everyone understood that it was an order.

The foreman was taken aback. Clearly he hadn't considered this possibility. Charlie thought he saw the grim smile on the woman juror's face waver slightly. "All right," the foreman said without enthusiasm, "we'll go back and talk some more."

Charlie slept for the first time in three days. The jury's inaction had in some way validated him; now he felt satisfied that he had done all he could. Had he been incompetent, they would have ruled against him, but that hadn't happened. He and Dolan had fought to a standstill, which, considering the public's sympathy for the police, was a victory. It wasn't enough, but it allowed him to sleep.

He awoke refreshed, biked, ate, and was at his desk by eight-thirty. He read the papers and signed letters. Then almost without knowing why, he put on his coat and walked into the outer office. His secretary was just replacing the phone. "That was Judge Alberts's office."

"I know," Charlie said. "They've got a verdict."

The courtroom was full again. Charlie had the illusion that no one had gone home because it seemed they were all in the same seats, creating the effect of a tableau. As the jury filed in, however, he noticed a difference. The defiant woman looked gray and drawn, her shoulders stooped, as if the other jurors had been beating her all night. Charlie felt a flutter in his chest and put his hand to his heart, as if he were reciting the pledge of allegiance.

This time, the foreman said they had reached a verdict. Alberts nodded and began reading from the papers in front of him. "This verdict must be rendered in three parts," he said. "Part A is concerned with the stop, chase, and attempted apprehension of Jimmy Norman. You must answer separately to each of them. The first question is: Did the defendant, John Rogan, violate the constitutional rights of Jimmy Norman in stopping, chasing, and/or attempting to apprehend him on February 8, 1959?"

"No," the foreman said emphatically. There was noise in the court-room but Alberts gaveled it down.

"Regardless," Alberts continued, "what sum would fairly and reason-ably compensate Jimmy Norman's estate for his pain, suffering, fright, emotional trauma, and deprivation of constitutional rights?"

"Thirty thousand dollars," the foreman said, and there were loud mur-murs. If Norman's constitutional rights weren't violated, why was the estate entitled to compensation?

"Did the defendant act in such a way in stopping, chasing, and attempt-ing to apprehend Jimmy Norman as to make appropriate an award for punitive damages?" Alberts asked.

"No," the foreman said.

Despite the reaction in the courtroom, Charlie wasn't particularly sur-prised. Even he had developed some sympathy for Rogan. He was a racist, but not the mad dog Dolan wanted him to be. The other sections of the verdict would be more revealing.

"The next questions deal with the shooting and killing of Jimmy Norman," Alberts said. "The first is, did John Rogan violate the constitutional rights of Jimmy Norman in shooting and killing him on February 8, 1959?"

The foreman answered in a firm voice. "Yes," he said.

"All right," one of the Norman brothers said, and there was some clapping in the room.

Alberts used his gavel again. "The next question has four subsections. The first is, what sum of money will fairly and reasonably compensate the estate for the loss of Jimmy Norman's life and the enjoyment thereof?"

"One hundred thousand dollars," the foreman said to a murmur of approval.

"What sum will fairly and reasonably compensate the Aesculapius Norman estate for loss of society and companionship?"

"Seventy-five thousand dollars," the foreman said.

"What sum for funeral expenses?"

"Six hundred and seventy dollars," the foreman read.

"And what sum for the eleven brothers and one sister of Jimmy Norman for loss of society and companionship?"

"One hundred thousand dollars."

Which was not much when you divided it up, but the constitutional principle was important. Jimmy Norman's rights had been violated, the defendants were going to have to pay damages, and this had been stated publicly in a court of law.

"Continuing on," Alberts said. "Did the defendant, John Rogan, so violate Jimmy Norman's constitutional rights as to make appropriate an award of punitive damages?"

The foreman nodded. "Yes, Your Honor," he said.

"What amount do you deem appropriate?"

"Twenty-five thousand dollars," the foreman said, which was nothing, except that it meant that even if Rogan had received only a slap on the wrist, the jury had ruled in the Normans' favor on the question of constitutional rights. Everyone knew that as far as Rogan was concerned, you might as well say twenty-five *million* dollars because the man was in jail and had no money anyway.

"The final section of the verdict concerns the conspiratorial cover-up of the killing of Jimmy Norman," Alberts said. While he didn't comment directly, his voice seemed to grow in timbre as he read. "This court finds as a matter of law that John Rogan and Thomas Paley did agree and conspire to cover up the true facts of the shooting," he said. "That is not in dispute. The question here involves the following named defendants, that is, Clarence Martin and Eugene Lathrop, or any or all of the following named alleged non-defendant co-conspirators, that is, whether George Tanner, Howard Moran, or William Magnusen participated also in the conspiracy to cover up the true facts of the killing. Answer for each in turn: Clarence Martin?"

"Yes," the foreman said.

"Eugene Lathrop?"

"Yes."

"George Tanner?"

"Yes."

"Howard Moran?"

"Yes."

"William Magnusen?"

"Yes," the jury foreman said quietly. And this was the only thing Charlie regretted. Magnusen was being thrown in with the others because of Dolan's skillful cross and it wasn't right because Magnusen had been a good cop who left the department because of what happened. The jury was punishing him for being disloyal to the uniform, which was irrational, but there was nothing to be done about that.

"The next question is whether Jimmy Norman's race was an operative factor in this conspiracy," Alberts said.

"Yes," the foreman said, and echoing cries of "Yes!" came from the crowd.

The judge continued reading relentlessly, almost oblivious to what was happening in the room, as the foreman's affirmations continued to be echoed.

"Did the city of Milwaukee, that is, the Milwaukee Police Department, have a policy, practice, or custom on February 8, 1959, of advising its police officers to plant throwaway knives on victims of police shootings, and, if so, was this a factor in the cover-up?"

"Yes," the foreman said, and cheers erupted, giving rise to an impromptu parade through the aisles. For once, Alberts didn't use his gavel. The judge looked bemused and let the demonstration go on for a few minutes, before quietly asking the bailiff to restore order.

"The next question has two subsections," he said. "What amount will fairly compensate first the estate of Aesculapius Norman for the deprivation of due process of law?"

"Seventy-five thousand dollars," the foreman said.

"And what amount will fairly compensate the eleven brothers and one sister of Jimmy Norman for this deprivation?"

"Two hundred and seventy thousand dollars," the foreman said, but his answer was drowned in whistles and shouts.

Alberts waited again. Then he said, "What amount will fairly and reasonably compensate the estate of Aesculapius Norman for the deprivation of racial equality?"

"One hundred and fifty thousand dollars," the foreman said.

"What amount then will fairly and reasonably compensate the brothers and one sister?"

"Three hundred thousand dollars."

The amounts had become meaningless. Charlie didn't know whether it was more or less than Dolan had offered and he didn't care. They were winning all the important points. He glanced at the recalcitrant juror and felt a twinge of sympathy for the woman. A day before it had seemed she would be able to stop this. Now, she looked miserable.

But Alberts wasn't finished. "Did any one or more of John Rogan, Thomas Paley, Clarence Martin, Eugene Lathrop, Howard Moran, George Tanner, or William Magnusen so participate in the conspiracy to cover up the true facts of the shooting as to make appropriate an award of punitive damages?"

"Yes."

"What amount is appropriate as to John Rogan?"

"Twenty-five thousand dollars."

"Eugene Lathrop?"

"Three hundred and fifty thousand dollars."

"Clarence Martin?"

"One hundred and fifty thousand dollars."

"Howard Moran?"

"Seventy-five thousand dollars."

"George Tanner?"

"One hundred thousand dollars."

The biggest cheer was saved for last. Tanner was the villain, at least for the people in the courtroom. In some parts of the city he would be considered a scapegoat, but not here. It was over and they had won, and that was all that was important now.

Alberts thanked the jury and then excused them. Charlie was grateful too, though he still didn't understand how after being deadlocked they could have come to agreement on a complicated verdict in such a short time. The only explanation was that it had been five against one all along. Once they broke the woman's resolve, the other issues fell into place easily. The fact that they had gone easy on Rogan and included Magnusen among the defendants probably represented a compromise, but the majority hadn't given much away.

Alberts thanked Charlie and Isaacson and Dolan, and court was adjourned. Charlie thought he might have said something to the Normans, might have expressed sympathy for their long wait for justice, but except for chastening them for being late, Alberts had not seemed to notice them at all during the trial and didn't now.

Charlie shook hands with each of the brothers. Then Olivia drew him to her. With her arms clasped tightly around his neck and her lips on his ear, she whispered, "Thank you."

Outside, it was pandemonium. The hall was clogged with spectators, reporters, and camera crews recording the scene. A small lectern had been set up, and the television stations had attached microphones to it. Instinctively, Charlie started to go around. Isaacson could speak for their side. But someone caught his arm, "Could we have a statement, Mr. Simons?"

Charlie leaned on the lectern. The tension of the last few days was concentrated in his shoulders, and for a moment he felt faint. "This is a historic occasion he said. "You probably know this is the most important civil rights case in our state's history." He stopped, not knowing what else to say. That seemed to be enough, but they expected more. "I'm proud to have been a part of it," he said simply.

"Mr. Simons," someone called. "Was this a case of right winning out over wrong?"

Trust the press to capture the complexity of things. The question was so simplistic that it seemed unfair to everyone, even Tanner. Charlie shrugged. "I wouldn't put it that way," he said. "What you saw in there was the legal system working about as well as it can work. I think that's important. It took a long time—too long—but the law finally won out."

"Mr. Simons?" Charlie thought there was something inappropriate about all this, or maybe he was just afraid of embarrassing himself by saying something stupid. The questioner was a young woman he didn't recognize. He couldn't remember having seen her in the courtroom. Now she looked quickly at her notes. "Whom did you admire in the trial?"

The question was unconventional enough to interest him. He had been asked about official corruption, bribes, and police brutality, but no one had asked if there was anyone who had behaved admirably, who had done what he was supposed to do. He smiled at the young woman. "I admire the jury," he said. "Few people appreciate how hard their job is. No one is trained to be a juror. They took time off from their jobs and families and came in and listened to testimony that was often confusing. Then they made a very difficult decision involving people's lives. Obviously, I agree with their verdict, but even if I didn't, I would admire the jury for taking this seriously and carrying on until the job was done."

He paused briefly. "I also admire Bill Magnusen and Tommy Paley. It's hard for a cop to testify against other cops, and they did because they thought it was the right thing to do." He hesitated, thinking there should be others he considered exemplary, but names wouldn't come. "Thanks," he said finally and forced his way through the crowd, leaving the microphones to Isaacson and the Normans.

Forty-five

Andy was nearing the end of his book, one so long and complex that he realized now he had never really expected to reach the conclusion. But the Norman trial had made the campaign's last week anticlimactic, so on the morning of the election, instead of standing in some schoolyard passing out palm cards, Andy was turning the last pages of *War and Peace*.

Andy's sympathies lay with the deposed general of the Russian army. Having defeated Napoleon, Kutuzov was ungraciously retired by the tsar, who wanted younger generals to consolidate the peace.

> Kutuzov had no notion of what was meant by the balance of power, or Napoleon. He could not understand all that. For the representative of the Russian people after the enemy had been annihilated and Russia liberated and raised to a summit of her glory, there was nothing left for a Russian as a Russian to do. Nothing remained for the representative of the national war but to die. And Kutuzov died.

Though the comparison was far-fetched, the passage made Andy think of Mueller. Having controlled the city for twenty years, he had become almost invisible since Tanner's resignation, and Andy, like the tsar's young generals, was moving smoothly to take over city hall. Rather than being feared or hated, Mueller was now viewed with pity or contempt, depending on your political views, but most often he was simply disregarded. He just didn't matter anymore.

This made Andy feel mildly guilty, but why blame himself for the mayor's downfall? "Chance created the situation," Tolstoy had written. "Genius made use of it." Andy knew there was more to it than this, but the phrase had a ring to it. He had worked in politics for twenty years in order to be ready when his chance came. And if it hadn't come he might have waited another twenty. There were no guarantees. He wouldn't describe himself as a genius, but Milwaukee could have done worse. Modesty didn't become politicians; no one ever believed you anyway. His chance had come and Andy had taken advantage. That might be less than genius; it was certainly more than mere opportunism.

The sun was up now, and the tree trunks across the street in the park were black against the new snow. Andy recalled long walks with Sarah in the mornings and remembered that he was picking her up shortly. Their last official appearance as husband and wife would be at Maryland Avenue School, where photographers would take their pictures after they voted. The lawyers had worked out most of the details of the divorce, but for today, Sarah would still be his supportive wife. She would have added "long-suffering," but Andy didn't think he had made her suffer very much. The thought of their marriage ending so quietly made him grateful, and sad.

As Andy replaced the book, he thought of all that had happened since he started it and wondered idly whether things would have been different if he were a faster reader. Tolstoy, as usual, had the answer: "All the strange discrepancies, which we find incomprehensible today, between the events as they happened and the official records arise solely because the historians writing their histories have described the noble sentiments and fine speeches of various generals, instead of giving us a history of the facts."

Given the facts, things happened inevitably as they must. Jimmy Norman had been murdered out of historical necessity, given the fact that he was a young black man alone on a dark street in 1959 with two white policemen in the vicinity. The cover-up had occurred for the same reason. Tommy Paley's confession, Sarah's affair with Bob Joseph, and Olivia Brown's successful petition in federal court were also simple facts, as was Tanner's downfall, and now, if things developed as they should, Andy's election as mayor. All of these things had happened and altered lives in profound ways, but what drove everyone to distraction was the illusion that it could have been otherwise.

Andy took a deep breath as peace descended. He wondered if he should stay in the house. It was too big for one person, probably it was too big for two. But he would decide that later. He looked around the study, his gaze lingering on the matched sets of books he had purchased in New Haven. At the framed pictures of Kennedy, Roosevelt, Churchill, and Martin Luther King, Jr., carefully arranged in a row behind his desk. It was a young man's collection and no longer either appropriate or very inspiring. In his new office in city hall, he would have a plain table and a Hopper lighthouse on the wall. He had enough to think about without Churchill and Roosevelt getting involved. He shook his head at his own thoughts and went down to the car.

Bob was in the city room working on his election story. People would be voting until seven, but he had a noon deadline. Everyone knew Hedig was going to win, so it hardly mattered. There wouldn't be much of a story no matter when he filed. "Write it anyway," Mike Klein had told him. "Sometimes it's good to write when there's nothing to write about."

So Bob walked over to watch the mayor and his wife vote in the basement of a church, and he was surprised at the changes he saw in Mueller. He seemed smaller now, slighter and less intimidating in his tweed overcoat. But mainly he seemed relaxed, as if the foreknowledge of his defeat came as a relief. His young wife clutched his arm, and Bob imagined that they would go off together for a vacation when this was over.

Mueller came out of the booth and approached Bob, hand outstretched. "Good to see you," he said, and Bob suddenly realized they were alone. No other reporters had come out. Mueller was already old news.

Because there was nothing else to say, Bob asked the mayor how he was feeling.

Mueller smiled broadly. "I feel fine," he said. "The campaign's over and I'm damned glad. You tell Mike Klein I said so too." Then he patted Bob's shoulder and walked out.

Back in the office, Bob called Marcus Jackson. They hadn't talked since the morning Bob had gone to his office to discuss Olivia Brown. "Pretty quiet down here," Marc said. "We're getting out the vote, though. I've got my boys going door to door, giving folks rides and whatever else they need."

No white candidate had seriously attempted to organize the ghetto before Hedig. Mueller hadn't needed or wanted the black vote. So Jackson and his friends were working hard, even if it wasn't crucial. They would produce the largest black turnout in the city's history and the new mayor would be grateful.

"Has the Norman trial had an effect over there?" Bob asked and immediately felt stupid.

Marcus didn't laugh. "In general or on the vote?"

"On the vote," Bob said.

"I think everyone down here already knew how he was going to vote," Jackson said. "You quoting me?"

"I don't know yet," Bob said. "Why?"

"I was going to try to think of something impressive to say, like that Andy Hedig brought the ghetto back to life, or that this community has a heartbeat again. Something like that." Bob heard Jackson's husky laugh and knew he was being mocked, but in a way he had it coming.

"Do you believe that?"

"I don't know," Marcus said. "I might. Anyway, you can quote me."

"How about you?" Bob asked. "Forget the community. How do you feel now that it's over?"

"I feel good," Marcus said. "Like I knew that I would." Then the bluff manner was gone and he spoke without affectation. "For once in my life, I think a black family got some justice for itself. And it's about time. Don't get me wrong. I'd like it a lot better if it hadn't taken twenty years, but you've got to start somewhere. It was almost worth the wait to watch those fat cops sitting in that courtroom and then see their mouths fall open when the jury came in with that verdict. To see them take it because they had no choice and then realize that this shit's going to stop now. That was sweet. It's more important than who gets elected today, even if it happens to be Mr. Hedig, who's my friend and a good man."

"Maybe I'll quote you on that," Bob said.

"Hell, yes," Marcus said. "You want me to repeat it for you slow?"

"It's OK," Bob said. "I think I got it the first time."

"Then I'm in a hurry," Marcus said. "Got to go buy me some votes. See you at the victory party tonight."

It was still only ten o'clock, so Bob called the election commission to get an idea of the turnout, but there was no reason it shouldn't be high. The sun was shining and the Hedig phone bank had been in gear for two days to get out the vote. Shortly before eleven, Bob filed and left the building.

Sarah had been staring out the window since Andy dropped her off. She had intended to write, but the lake distracted her. She had always said she needed the view to write, but perhaps a bunker would be a better idea. Just four blank walls in a basement. White noise on the speakers. The thought made her smile.

Now she rose and stretched. She had expected to feel something when she and Andy went to vote. Sadness, guilt, perhaps even pride that her husband was going to be mayor of a major American city. But beyond a mild nostalgia, she didn't really feel anything. It was just over, that life, and she had few regrets. She wasn't sorry she had married Andy and wasn't sorry they were divorcing. She thought she *should* feel something more, but the fact was that she didn't.

Sarah thought a walk would clear her head, but when she opened the door, Bob was leaning against a tree. "What are you doing out here?" she asked.

"I've been waiting casually for you to come out," he said. "Another two hours and I probably would have gone home, but actually I'm glad you came out. A squad car's gone by twice. I figure the next time they might chase me."

"Why didn't you just come up?"

"I didn't want to invade your space," Bob said.

Sarah took his arm and they started north on Prospect, crossing over when they got to the bridge leading down to the lake. Considering that it was March, there was a good deal of activity at the McKinley Marina. A couple of kids ran after their dogs. Old people from the Jewish home walked haltingly, holding each other erect. There were even a couple of tanning fanatics in swimsuits surrounded by aluminum reflectors.

"Looks like Andy's going to win," Bob said.

Sarah nodded. "I'm glad, and I even think he'll be a good mayor."

Bradford Beach came into view, then the old water-treatment plant, and Bob struggled with his thoughts. It was so hard to just say it. Even with all the time they'd had together and the things that they had already said. That was before Sarah moved out, before she had told him to go away, before the trial, before the election. It was easier then; the words seemed to weigh less.

Just past the Gun Club, the walk sloped uphill toward Kenwood, and as if by prior agreement, they stopped. Not knowing how else to ask, Bob, said, "What are we doing, Sarah?"

She liked the fact that he said "we." Whatever was going to happen now would happen to both of them. It wasn't up to her alone, wasn't a decision she had to make and then wonder if it was right. "I love you," she said.

His face was red and pinched; his eyes were swollen. "Move in with me then."

Sarah was going to say something clever, as she usually did in emotional situations, but she stopped herself. That was over too, making light of things that mattered. He looked so anxious, so cold. She noticed now that he was wearing only a corduroy sport coat, no scarf or gloves. But he wasn't thinking about that. "Please," he added.

She felt buoyant in the brilliant sunshine with the white caps hitting the shore in the distance. It took so little to be happy that she didn't know why most people were miserable all the time. "Yes," she said. Not "Yes, I will," or "Yes, darling," or "Yes, that's what I've been waiting for you to say." Just "Yes." But this seemed to be enough.

Bob shivered violently, as if he were shaking loose of something. Then he held her to him. "Thank God," he said.

And Sarah, unable to help herself, said, "Or someone." Then they walked slowly back the way they had come.